1

LONDON, APRIL 1917

Sally Harper turned to speak to her husband Ben and saw that he'd fallen asleep again in his chair. His newspaper lay beside him – the headlines declaring that America had entered the war – and the cup of tea she'd poured for him ten minutes earlier, untouched by his side. Despite several warnings to Germany from the USA, its submarines had carried on attacking neutral ships carrying cargo bound for Britain. The American President had therefore signed the declaration of war. The news had delighted Ben, who considered that his country ought to have joined long before this so that they could throw the weight of the United States behind her allies in a common desire to bring peace and stability. He considered himself British these days and thought the way an Englishman would that the Americans had dragged their feet.

Sally had no idea where her husband had been for the past couple of weeks but had immediately seen how tired he was on his return home late the previous evening. He was sleeping soundly and though she ought to be leaving for work soon, there was no reason why Ben shouldn't snooze in his chair if he wished.

He worked long hours in his job for the British War Office. She had hoped to have time to talk about what they needed to do for the best at Harpers, the prestigious store he and his sister Jenni owned in Oxford Street. Jenni had her own ideas, but Sally was their chief buyer and for once she wasn't in agreement with her sister-in-law. Normally, they got on really well and were the best of friends, but just lately Sally had found that she didn't agree with some of the things Jenni wanted to do in the store.

Her unease was partly due to the fact that Jenni seemed grumpy and distracted, which was probably down to problems in her own life rather than disagreements between them. Jenni now lived in her own apartment and had an entirely independent life after work. She was trying to negotiate a divorce from her husband, who was a General in the American Army, and Sally believed that it was proving difficult for her, though Jenni didn't speak of it much. The problem at the store was simply that Jenni believed they should just fill the shelves of Harpers' departments with whatever they could get, regardless of quality, including substandard goods, but Sally was wary of lowering standards too much. Yes, Jenni was right to say it was expected when there was a war on. People had to accept less than they'd been able to insist on in normal times and would be grateful for whatever they could get. While Sally agreed to a certain extent, she still felt they had to be careful. However, she was just the buyer and she needed Ben's backup if she wanted to fight her corner. Jenni was part owner so therefore her opinion carried a lot of weight and if she insisted, Sally must, of course, give way. It would help if she knew what Ben felt about it.

He'd carried on with his war work throughout these past months, leaving Sally to run the store with the help of the manager, Mr Stockbridge, and various supervisors, though Jenni was a big help now she was living in London. It was her stubborn refusal to return to America that had widened the rift between her and her husband, and her feelings for Mr Andrew Alexander, a brilliant surgeon, that had made her ask for a divorce. Something her husband seemed reluctant to grant.

Jenni's problem with her husband was perhaps the underlying cause of her recent moods, but the problem with Harpers was ongoing. As the war bit ever deeper, and Britain was more and more reliant on home-produced goods, it was becoming harder to find enough decent stock to fill their departments. Of late, one or two of their regular suppliers had let them down, supplying either poor-quality materials that Sally had had to return or sending only partial orders. Sally wasn't sure which annoyed her the most. Jenni said she was too fussy and that they needed to keep their shelves stocked even if some goods were not as good as they were accustomed to selling.

'We're in the middle of a war,' Jenni was fond of reminding her. 'If a customer complains, remind them of that fact, Sally. It's not your fault the Government has ordered manufacturers to cut down on production of certain goods – or that we can't get enough imported goods these days.'

'No, it's the Kaiser's and our Government,' Sally had replied the last time Jenni had brought it up. 'Why they had to start fighting and ruin everything, I do not know…'

Jenni had simply laughed at her frustration. 'That's men all over! It's centuries since your last civil war, not so very long since ours back home in America – and that's even worse, when you fight your own people. Shortages are annoying, Sally but it isn't like you to let it get you down?'

'I know—' Sally had sighed deeply. 'I think it is just Ben being away so much of the time – and Jenny has been a bit fractious recently. It must be because she misses Ben. She is far more aware of the fact that he isn't home now than when she was just a baby.'

Their lovely little daughter was now a lively toddler of three years and into all sorts of mischief. Named after her aunt, she was everyone's little darling. Sally was no longer able to take her to work and settle her in a cot in her office, because she wanted to be into everything. Pearl, her nurse, still came in a few days a week, but also worked three days at the hospital, where the wards were overflowing with injured men sent home from the war. Mrs Hills, Sally's housekeeper, was very good with little Jenny, but whenever she could, Sally tried to work from home. However, that was not always feasible and sometimes she did take the little girl into the office. Jenny loved it because all the staff fussed over and she was thoroughly spoiled, not least by her adoring aunt and namesake.

'She's an absolute imp but adorable,' Jenni had replied, because she loved her niece and was always indulging her with little gifts and treats of all kinds. 'If Ben being away is getting you down, you should tell him, Sally. I'm sure if he knew, he could cut down on these trips. I mean, have you any idea what he does when he is away?'

'None at all...' Sally had frowned. 'He says the official title for his job is logistics controller – whatever that is.'

'It means he's buying and moving stuff on behalf of the Armed Forces, as you well know,' Jenni had replied with a frown. 'But why can't he do that from an office in London?'

'He says that he needs to prod officious store managers into sending what is needed for the troops,' Sally had said and made a wry face. 'Ben says that if he simply puts a chit in for them to send ammunition to a certain location, it might take weeks for it to be actually sent. By going himself and overseeing the packing and transportation, choosing the men escorting it himself, he gets results in a tenth of the time...'

Jenni had nodded her agreement. 'Yes, I can see how that

would work. We like to get on with things back home, Sally. You English tend to take your time – and the amount of red tape is maddening.'

'Yes, Ben is forever complaining about that...' Sally had laughed. 'You two are so alike in so many ways. Did you know that?'

'We're both Americans,' Jenni had shrugged and then smiled. 'And we did have the same father. I suppose we may think alike in many ways...'

'You do...'

Jenni had just laughed, clearly pleased to be compared to her brother.

Now, on this sunny morning, Sally's thoughts were interrupted as Ben opened his eyes and smiled at her. 'You look pensive,' he said and yawned. 'Something wrong, sweetheart?'

'In a way... but it needn't concern you, Ben...'

He held out his hands to her, indicating she should sit on his lap. 'Come and tell me what is wrong, Sally.'

'Oh, just a little niggle concerning Harpers. It's the quality of some of the stock these days... it isn't what we're used to, Ben.'

'Ah...' He nodded but looked resigned. 'I know just what you mean. I made a stink about some boots that were delivered to an Army depot while I was there. The leather was not up to standard and they will probably fall to pieces after a couple of weeks of marching. I sent them back, but the quartermaster was furious. He said he'd been on to the suppliers every day for months to get them and what was he going to do now...'

'What did you say?' Sally was interested.

'I went to see the factory myself and inspected what they were doing. We sorted out the problem between us and we've been promised replacements for next month.'

'How did you manage that?'

'Part bribery, part threats,' Ben said. 'It is a game we play all the time, Sally. They will pass off faulty goods if they can, but if you put your foot down hard, they normally come through. I threatened to take the contract away from them unless they pulled their socks up sharpish.'

'Could you do that?'

'Yes.' Ben's mouth set hard. 'I've done it before now. Men need decent boots to march in, Sally – just as they need to get their ammunition when they require it and to be sure that the rations they receive are enough to keep them fighting fit.'

Sally nodded and smiled at him. She supposed she'd always known that what he was doing was important work, but she'd never seen it in terms of men's lives before, but now she understood more of what he had to do. 'No wonder you look worn out when you get home sometimes.'

'It isn't always easy,' Ben said with a smile. 'It involves a lot of driving from one end of the country to the other and hundreds of forms to fill in – and that's when everything goes to plan. When it doesn't, I have to spend ages trying to find the right person and that is sometimes more difficult than it sounds.'

'And then I worry you with my trivial complaints...'

Ben pulled her on to his lap and kissed her. 'Nothing you do or say is trivial to me, my love. Is anything else worrying you?'

'What happens if I can't find enough of the right stock to fill our shelves? Harpers is a big store, Ben, and our stockroom is getting emptier by the week – soon we shan't have any reserves.'

'Remember what you did to raise money for the wounded?' Ben asked. 'You bought seconds cheaply and sold them for very little, giving a contribution to the fund for wounded men. Do something similar again... take the poor-quality goods but at a lower price and make a thing of civilians sacrificing for the sake of our men over there...'

Sally nodded, looking at him with respect. It was more or less what Jenni was saying. 'Yes, that could work. Those boots you rejected for the Army for instance—'

'Would probably last civilians for a few months – bought cheaply enough they would be fine.' He grinned at her. 'I think a certain factory manager would be delighted to sell them to you very cheaply, Sally...'

'Good. I'll get on to it in the morning,' she said, smiling and feeling much better than she had in a while. 'Yes, I can just see the signs we'll put up – and for each pair of substandard boots we sell, we'll give something to the wounded fund again...'

* * *

Naturally, since she'd suggested it first, Jenni thought it was a good idea and the pair of them sat down and started to make lists of firms to contact. When they explained that donations would be made to the wounded men from any substandard goods bought cheaply, most of the factory managers wanted to join in. Almost all of them had small runs of goods that had faults in them and were glad to offload them for the price of the materials.

As one of the tableware manufacturing managers said, 'Sometimes it is a small hitch in a machine. We're running with half our experienced staff away in the Army and the new girls don't always notice until someone picks up the fault. It can be expensive and if we have an outlet it will help.'

'Well, we have shelves to fill and we feel small faults are acceptable while there is a war on,' Sally told him. 'We all have to pull together, Mr Simmons, and help each other.'

'Yes, well, we'll be glad to send you samples of the seconds, Mrs Harper. We normally have an end-of-season sale, moving faulty goods cheaply to market stall men, but if we can sell to you more often it will give us a better cash flow.'

Sally agreed, feeling pleased. The blue and white china they sold was good quality and she knew the seconds would simply have small faults in the firing or the transfer pattern that they would not like to try to sell as perfect. Anything of that nature would have large signs on in Harpers store, telling customers exactly what they were buying.

When she'd tried it with knitwear the previous year, Sally had had queues in the shop and most customers had been delighted with what they'd bought. She would have a prominent notice-board explaining that it was to help out with shortages due to the war and that donations to the fund for wounded soldiers would be made.

Rachel Bailey, the supervisor in the bag, hat and jewellery department, and a close friend, was a little bit dubious about the scheme and warned Sally to be careful. 'People tend to have short memories, Mrs Harper,' she'd said when they were discussing it. 'When the war is over, the china will still have that flaw and they will remember where it came from. You don't want customers thinking Harpers sells seconds all the time.'

'That is a valid point,' Sally agreed. 'I'm going to make sure that everyone understands why we've taken this step and I want staff to explain it when they sell seconds – and to impress on their customer what the price of the perfect stock will be.'

'Yes, well, I'd prefer not to have seconds in my department, Mrs Harper.'

Sally nodded her understanding. 'Your department is one of the luckier ones. Hats have never been rationed and the raw materials for most are home-produced, which means we have a regular supply from local milliners and our leather bags are the same. Scarves and gloves are still available, though some of the very best leathers are scarce, because they come from overseas. We can still buy English-produced jewellery too, so there is no problem there.'

'Yes,' Rachel agreed. 'But if I were you, I'd limit the number of substandard products you buy elsewhere or Harpers may acquire the wrong kind of reputation.'

Sally thought over her friend's advice. Rachel had quite a bit of retail experience and she knew her customers well. It might be sensible to have these sales of seconds just now and then...

Jenni was scornful when she told her she was limiting the amount of substandard stock and intending to have it in just one or two departments at a time. 'But why? Back home a lot of the stores do it all the time – they have what they call basement sales and everyone knows that they are not top quality.'

'People are different here,' Sally said. 'It is a good idea, Jenni. I haven't changed my mind completely, but we do need to be careful – or it might come back and bite us.'

Sally made a tour of the shop, spending some time in each department. She investigated the stock for each one and discovered that in both the men's and women's clothing departments there were several rails of stock pushed to the back of their stockrooms. These things were from several seasons previously and had been moved out to make room for new stock each year.

She decided to bring all the surplus out to a special sale rail in the departments and told them to sell it as seen for fifty per cent of the original price. It was not faulty, though a couple of female items had lipstick marks on them and they were sold at even less money. They would not make a fortune from selling these items, but it would be better than buying in seconds and they took up some space, making the rails look full again.

As it turned out, the sale rails proved more popular over the first few days of the clothing sale than the substandard goods and so Rachel was proved to have the right idea. However, some things like the china with tiny little faults and the ex-Army boots sold out very quickly.

Asked what she thought, Beth Burrows looked reflective. Beth had worked in Harpers in the bag and jewellery department with Sally, leaving the previous year when she'd had her first child. She lived in her father-in-law's house but missed her friends and often called in at the store to talk to them. Fred Burrows was in charge of the stores and responsible for checking everything that came in and delivering it to the right departments.

'I don't mind using china that has a tiny flaw no one notices,' she said, 'but if there was a mark on a bag I liked or a snag in my best scarf, I'd hate it. Women are fussy like that... Maggie hated selling those scarves with a fault last time, though a lot of women were glad of them...'

'Yes, I agree,' Sally smiled at her. 'Have you heard from Jack recently?'

'No...' Fear touched Beth's face, because her husband's long sea journeys always made her anxious. The merchant ships Jack worked on brought vital supplies to Britain, from raw materials needed for manufacturing to food. 'Though now they are sending convoys to protect the ships we aren't losing as many...' A hundred merchant ships had been lost to enemy U-boats the previous month, but the last convoy from Gibraltar had reached home without loss. It was still a dangerous life, as everyone understood, and Beth could only truly relax when Jack was home.

Sally nodded but changed the subject immediately, because it clearly distressed her friend. 'Have you heard from Maggie this month?' she asked. 'It is more than two months since I had a letter from her, even though I sent her something a few weeks ago.'

'That isn't like our Maggie,' Beth said. 'She was quiet for months after Tim was killed, but her letters usually come regularly. I had one just over a week ago. Perhaps yours is in the post, Sally.'

Their friend and one-time fellow worker at Harpers, Maggie Gibbs, was still serving in a field hospital near the French border with Belgium. She'd been out there for ages now but wouldn't return to England even for a short leave. Her letters said that she had good friends there and stayed at a farm for short breaks.

Some of the nurses have been to Paris for a few days,

Maggie had written in one of her letters to Sally.

I have been asked if I'd like to go. One of the officers takes the girls to the station and they go by train. He meets them when they return and they bring back things for their friends. There are shortages over here, but Paris is Paris and they all buy perfumes and clothes...

Sally had smiled over that.

Maggie had told her about some of the seamstresses that made clothes for the big firms who were so expensive.

I think you might employ some of these little firms to make beautiful clothes for Harpers after the war, Sally. I spoke to one of them when she visited the farm and she told me she is hoping to start up independently when all this bother is over. I'll get her details from my friend Marie and when we're all settled again, you can contact her if you wish.

Sally sighed as she remembered her friend's letter. Maggie

was so much better than she had been for a long time after the man she'd hoped to marry had died. Maggie obviously still thought about Harpers and planned to return when the war was over. Unless she got married, of course. Sally sometimes wondered if there was another man in Maggie's life, because her letters sounded so much more cheerful. Sally hadn't said anything, but perhaps it was too soon after Maggie's fiancé's death to be certain how she felt. Maggie had loved Tim Burrows so very much. He'd been a pilot and his plane had gone down over the sea. She'd thrown herself into her nursing, giving herself no rest or chance to recover from her grief, preferring to work and help others.

Dismissing the troubling thoughts, Sally looked at Beth who was expecting her second child. Her first, a boy, was just over a year old and she'd fallen quickly for her second. Time seemed to fly and Beth was happily settled as a mother, though Sally knew she still half-wished she was working at Harpers. 'So, are you looking forward to the birth?'

'Yes and no.' Beth looked at her and frowned. 'I've booked into hospital, because I can't expect Fred to run up and down stairs after me for two weeks. I'm not looking forward to that, but I'll be glad when the baby is here, of course.'

'Couldn't you have hired a nurse or someone to help you?'

'I might – but most of them are too busy to live in these days. We lost a good half of our nurses to the military hospitals.'

Sally nodded. 'Yes – before the war there were plenty of young girls willing to come in and help out in the store for a few weeks when someone was having a baby, but now they're all working in the factories or for the VADs.' Sally silently cursed the war. Damn it for taking away Beth's husband when she needed him, and Ben to a lesser extent – and damn it for making life harder at Harpers.

'I'd better get home,' Beth said. 'I'll see you at the weekend, Sally.' She gathered her bits and pieces and they gave each other a quick hug.

'Yes, I'll look forward to it.'

After Beth had gone, Sally sat for a moment reflecting on the way life had turned out – not quite as she, Beth or Maggie had expected when they'd first met prior to being interviewed for a job at Harpers.

Bringing her mind back to the present with a sigh, Sally stared at her stock lists until she felt like throwing them at the wall. Whatever she did, they were not to her satisfaction. Maybe she should close down a part of Harpers' vast space and make each department smaller. Yet Ben had paid good money to expand their premises and she would hate to take such a step. Whatever she did, she couldn't make them grow to their pre-war status. It was, purchase the substandard goods and do the promotions that would keep trade ticking over, or see the shelves with empty spaces.

She picked up a new catalogue showing items for the home made from wood; there was a good range of things, like bread boards, ashtrays, ornaments and book ends. The wording suggested they were using home-grown materials and also recycling recovered timber from derelict buildings. Perhaps she should try a few – at least they would fill some empty shelving.

Sally reflected that her competitors must be suffering the same problems, including Selfridges just down the road. Perhaps Harry Selfridge had held a larger stock before the war.

Sally sighed and decided to give up and go home to Pearl and see how Jenny was faring. Her almost four-year-old daughter was running all over the place at the moment. She would take her to the park rather than sitting here worrying over something she couldn't solve.

2

Maggie Gibbs wiped the sweat from her forehead. It was sweltering hot in the tent that housed the most seriously injured men; her head ached and she was feeling drained after a long day. Any moment now she would be off duty and could seek her bed in the small hut she shared with two other nurses now that her friend Sadie Meadows was living at the farm with Marie. What she wanted most was a cool drink and some sleep.

'Nurse Gibbs – can you help me please?'

Sister Hawkstone's voice seemed to come from a long way off, but Maggie moved to obey her. Her head had started to thump now, just as if someone was banging a large drum inside it and the senior nurse's face was slightly hazy.

'What is the matter with you, nurse?' the sharp voice demanded. 'I asked you to assist me five minutes ago. I haven't got the patience for time-wasters! We have injured men needing attention!'

Maggie tried to apologise, but the words just wouldn't come. Her tongue seemed glued to the roof of her mouth and she made a gasping sound and then collapsed in a heap at the feet of the irate nursing sister. Everything had gone black around her and she never heard the exasperated shouting that followed her collapse. Nor was she aware of another nurse, Sister Mayhew, giving Sister Hawkstone an equally sharp set-down.

'Can you not see this young woman is exhausted and ill?' Sister Mayhew asked in a withering tone that made even Sister Hawkstone cringe. 'She is neither lazy nor stupid but one of the best nurses I have worked with and she hasn't taken a break since she got out here.'

'Then she ought to have done. Fainting on duty just causes more trouble.'

'She is ill,' Sister Mayhew said. 'If you were a caring person you would have seen that and sent her off duty hours ago.'

'I needed her here...'

'Are there no others available or are you determined to kill this particular nurse?' the cutting reply stunned the angry Sister Hawkstone for a moment. 'Maggie Gibbs has worked tirelessly for this service and you've taken advantage of her dedication. You should be ashamed. If we didn't need every nurse we have here, I should seek your dismissal for unfair treatment of a young girl.'

'I didn't realise she was actually ill—' the unfortunate sister spluttered, well aware that Sister Mayhew was being promoted to Matron for the hospital and would shortly be in charge of not only this but two other field hospitals, so highly was she thought of in the service. A word from her could blight or even finish Sister Hawkstone's career. 'I apologise for not noticing – but we were busy—'

'We're all busy but we have to take time to look out for our staff as well as the patients,' Sister Mayhew replied evenly. 'I shall excuse it this time – but if you neglect another young nurse you will be suspended...'

Suitably chastened, Sister Hawkstone retired from the lists.

She even went so far as to ask one of the other nursing sisters that evening how Nurse Maggie Gibbs was doing and was told she had a fever caught from nursing the soldiers and was seriously ill.

'I'm afraid that if she recovers – and at the moment that is touch-and-go – she will be sent home immediately. She will no longer be able to nurse men at the Front, because of the risk. Should she pull through, her lungs may be affected and another bout of a similar disease would most certainly kill her. We can only hope that she will recover enough to live another kind of life at home – she certainly deserves to after all the wonderful work she has done out here. Sister Mayhew – sorry, I mean Matron Mayhew now – is recommending her for a medal of honour for the way she has dedicated her life to these men – and, of course, she risked her life going up to the front line to bring back seriously injured men when they lost several of their medical men in a raid and was instrumental in saving lives...'

'I didn't realise she was such a heroine...' Sister Hawkstone said in a spiteful tone and received a look of disgust in return from the nurse who walked off abruptly. She flushed hotly, realising her bad temper had earned her an unpleasant reputation and the very next day visited Maggie, taking her a bar of chocolate someone had sent her.

'That is kind of you, sister,' the nurse bathing Maggie's forehead said. 'She is too ill to know, but when they ship her out of here, I'll make sure that it is in her things with a note to say who gave it to her.'

'Oh, don't bother about the note...' Sister Hawkstone walked quickly away. Seeing the girl lying there so close to death had brought home to her what she'd done by her careless demands far more than anything Matron Mayhew could say or do and she felt it keenly. It was not her fault the girl had picked up the fever – any of the nurses could catch any number of things in the course of their work – but had she noticed sooner they might have caught it before it got so bad. She turned back after a few steps and asked, 'When are they sending her home?'

'There is a transport coming at the end of the week,' the young nurse said. 'They think she will do better back home – and they say the risk is equal either way. If she is left here, she takes a nurse from other duties and may die in any case. It is hoped that a change of climate and good hospital conditions will improve her chances.'

'Yes, I'm sure that's best for her – and Matron will let her people know?'

'Yes, of course...' the nurse looked at her in surprise. As she told her friends later, 'You could've knocked me down with a feather. Old fire and brimstone Hawkstone asking a thing like that...'

'Guilty conscience,' one of the nurses said. 'She should have noticed Nurse Gibbs was ill and sent her to the doctor. I hate being sent to her ward. She is a first-class bitch...'

There was a murmur of agreement from the others. Sister Hawkstone was not the most popular of the senior nurses.

Matron Mayhew was missed on the wards as she now had to move between three field hospitals and had far more paperwork to do than before. However, she was always likely to turn up on the wards and watch you, though if she criticised a nurse, it was always fair. It was the reason everyone liked her. They knew that if they had to report to Matron they would be treated with kindness and understanding but any misdemeanour would be firmly reprimanded and the appropriate punishment would follow, even dismissal if a nurse flouted the rules too much.

'Maggie Gibbs is lucky they're shipping her home,' one of the nurses named Mira claimed. 'My six months is up next month and I can't wait to get on a ship back to England.'

Some of the others looked at her oddly, but she ignored them.

'Maggie won't see it like that,' Nurse Rita said with a note of authority. 'I've been sharing accommodation with her for three months and she intended to stay out here until it's over.'

'Will it ever be over?' a couple of voices asked.

'Maggie said things are getting better,' Rita said firmly. 'She says we're winning, though it might not seem like it yet...'

'Well, where does she get her information from?' a voice asked. 'I've seen nothing that makes me think it will be over any time soon...'

Rita shrugged. 'Maggie said a friend told her that he thinks another year or so will see us out...'

'If she was planning to stay out another year, she's mad,' Mira replied.

'She might be,' Rita said, 'but it was what she wanted...'

* * *

Maggie was not aware of the debate or varying emotions her collapse had stirred amongst her colleagues. Matron came to see her into the hospital transport taking her to the coast, where she was to be put aboard a ship heading for England. Brave doctors and sailors were risking their lives by coming so close to the coast to pick up the sick men, because while they were stationary, they were sitting targets for the enemy planes and bombardment from hostile ships.

'You're being taken home to a good hospital, Maggie dear,' Matron Mayhew told her, gently holding her hand. 'Your friends came to visit – Marie and Sadie. They brought you some letters, which you will find in your things when you're well enough to read them.'

Maggie tried to whisper her thanks. She hadn't been aware of friends visiting and wished she'd been able to thank them and say goodbye, but she was still hardly able to follow what Matron was telling her and, in the ambulance, her fever took over again and she barely knew it when she was carried on board the ship.

The ship's doctor saw how pitiful her condition was and gave her something to make her sleep, which she did throughout a gale mid-channel and woke only when she was being transferred to a hospital bed by porters dressed in white coats.

'Where am I?' she whispered and a pristine nurse bustled up to her.

'You are in a military hospital, young woman. Your fever is highly contagious and we need to isolate you until you're over the worst.'

'Am I in France?'

'No, you're in Wiltshire, England,' the nurse replied. 'You are very lucky to be alive, young lady – especially after the journey you've had. You can thank Doctor Simpson when you're well again. He bravely came all the way out there to fetch you and the badly wounded men home.'

Maggie fell back against the pillows, exhausted. She had no more energy to ask anything, even though she tried to protest that she wanted to return to work because she was needed. Sister Hawkstone would be furious with her for causing all this trouble...

* * *

It was more than a week later that Maggie woke to see a doctor standing by her bed and recognised him as such. He smiled down at her. 'Well, Miss Gibbs – so you've decided to come back to us at last, have you?'

'I didn't know I'd been anywhere...' she said and he laughed.

'That serves me right,' he said good-naturedly. 'You've been very ill and wandering in and out of consciousness since they brought you to us just over a week ago. I'm glad to tell you that you've beaten the fever and will now make a full recovery.'

'Thank you, sir.'

'Doctor Simpson. I took advantage of a temporary lull in the fighting and brought you back from France in my transport. We fetched two hundred and fifty wounded men home and one very brave young woman.' He laughed. 'You are something of a hero, Nurse Gibbs.'

'The men are the heroes, not me.' She sat up as best she could, grimacing at her own weakness. 'How soon can I go back to my work?' Maggie asked and then coughed.

The doctor frowned and a nurse bustled up, giving her a glass of water to sip and rubbing her back for a moment until the coughing subsided.

'I believe you will work again once you are fit enough,' he told her. 'The fever you had kills many men supposedly stronger than you, Miss Gibbs – but we shan't be sending you back out there.'

'Why not? Did I do something wrong?' She sat back against the pillows.

'No, indeed you did not. I understand you're being recommended for a medal of some sort. However, your lungs have undoubtedly been affected by the fever you took from your patients and that means you would not live through another such illness. We only just managed to save you this time and so you will not be returning. Some light private nursing when you're really well again, or another job – but no more of the strenuous work you've been doing – for over two years, so they tell me...'

'Was it that long?' Maggie asked and closed her eyes.

She slipped away into sleep and when she woke again, she discovered that Beth and Sally were sitting by her bed and looking at her anxiously. What were they doing here? Beth looked as if she might be pregnant.

'What's wrong?' she asked. 'Is someone ill?'

'You've been very ill,' Beth said, while Sally reached for her hand and held it gently, saying, 'We've all been worried about you, love. They wouldn't let us visit for the first week... We came down on the train and we'll stay overnight in a hotel – it was a long way, Maggie, and that means we can't visit as often as we'd like.'

'I'm better now,' Maggie said and tried to sit up again. She discovered she was too weak and flopped back against the pillows. 'I thought I was...'

'You will be,' Sally said and smiled at her encouragingly. 'Doctor Simpson told us you'll need to convalesce for some weeks or months and then you can come home to us.'

'I can't wait for that to happen,' Beth said. 'We brought you flowers and fruit, Maggie dearest. Is there anything else you need?'

Maggie shook her head. At the moment she was too weary to think of anything she might ever need.

'Beth and I came together today,' Sally said, 'but after this we're going to take it in turns to visit. It's a pity you're not nearer London so that we could visit all the time. However, if you need anything just tell the nurse – Nurse Shelly – and she will let us know and we'll bring it for you, or send it through the post if we can't get down.'

'I'm such a nuisance—' Maggie said and when her friends shook their heads, chorusing 'No,' she sighed: 'I feel it.'

'We love you and we're proud of you,' Beth told her, stroking the back of her hand. 'Anything we can do, you only have to ask...'

'We shall be ringing every day, so don't forget to tell Nurse Shelly if you need anything.'

'Everyone is so kind...' Maggie said and closed her eyes.

She drifted into a restless sleep, punctuated by memories of France and the terrible injuries she'd seen and others, even worse, of Tim Burrows clinging to a life raft until he was picked up, his eyes open and staring. Her lost love, dead for hours and yet not swallowed by the sea. His death had broken her heart, giving her no reason to live but for her work. She might have found some happiness if her friend Mick O'Sullivan had been there, but he'd been sent to another war zone and she'd lost touch with him, leaving her nothing but the grinding ache of grief. She tossed restlessly in her sleep, calling out to Tim and then to Mick from the depths of her despair.

When she opened her eyes again, it was night and her friends had gone.

A nurse came up to her.

'My friends were here...' she said, not quite sure if she'd imagined their visit.

'So they were and for quite a long time. Sister let them stay longer because of the journey they'd had to get here,' she agreed. 'I'm Nurse Shelly and you're looking a little better, Miss Gibbs. Do you think you could fancy anything?'

'Could I have a cup of cocoa please?'

Nurse Shelly's face lit up in a delighted grin. 'Bless you, my darlin', you can have anything you like when I'm on duty. You nursed my brother Sam out there. He told me you were an angel and it was you who saved his life – told me he would have died if you hadn't watched over him. So, you ask for anything you need.'

Maggie smiled. 'I remember Sam, Shelly. He was so brave. He lost both his legs, but he didn't just give up like some of the others. He fought for his life and I nursed him. We sent him home in a wheelchair.'

'And now he's back doing what he always wanted, painting –

he's a true artist is our Sam and he has more paintings of Nurse Gibbs than I could count.'

'Oh...' Maggie looked at her in surprise. 'I'm so glad he is getting on well.' With Nurse Shelly's help, she eased herself up against the pillows. 'Do you know, I think I feel a little better...'

3

Sally was busy going through her list of suppliers that late spring morning when the door of her office opened and Beth peeped round. She looked a bit uncertain, so Sally smiled and waved her in, getting up to kiss her cheek.

'How are you feeling, love?' she asked, because it was now mid-May and Beth's second pregnancy was into its fifth month and she looked a bit tired. 'Come and sit down.'

'I'm fine really,' Beth told her with a rueful smile. 'Little Jack has been into everything this morning. He can crawl faster than I can walk these days and he keeps us both on our toes.'

'I'm sure he does,' Sally agreed. 'Jenny was having tantrums when I left her with Pearl and Mrs Hills. I think she has been utterly spoiled and demands her own way whenever she's thwarted. She will be four at the end of June and is getting quite the little madam.'

'She has loving parents, a doting aunt and two devoted nurses in Mrs Hills and Pearl,' Beth said reasonably. 'It would be a wonder if she wasn't spoiled, Sally.'

'I know. I'm guilty too.' Sally sighed. 'But where is young Jackie?' Sally asked, looking round as if expecting Beth's small son to suddenly appear.

'I left him with Fred in the basement. He told me to, because he has a young assistant he is training and intends to spend the morning showing him the ropes.'

'Yes,' Sally nodded. 'Fred wasn't too happy when his last assistant went off to join the Army. They keep on doing it and so I found him a fifteen-year-old boy, just left school but strong and willing. At least he can't volunteer for a few years.'

'Yes, Fred likes young Joshua. Says he's good material and he's banking on the war being over by the time he's old enough to join up.'

'We're all hoping that,' Sally said. 'What does Fred think? He knows as much about the war as anyone I know. Does he think the end is in sight yet?'

'No, not really – but he says he thinks we are just beginning to turn the tide.' Beth sighed. 'With General Pershing making plans for a landing in France, the Americans will soon be stuck into the fighting and that is bound to make a difference. I just wish it was all over and we could go back to how we were before it started...' She shivered and shook her head. 'So many men have been killed, Sally... Do you think things will ever be the same?'

Sally frowned. 'I think they will have to give women the vote after the war, Beth. A lot of women have shown they can hold down a man's job – and quite a few are out there at the Front, giving their lives to save the men from dying alone and in agony. Surely the Government can't ignore that?'

'I wouldn't put it past them – but the Women's Movement won't stand for it. We'll make things happen, you wait and see...'

Sally nodded. She knew Beth was taking more interest in the Women's Movement these days since she'd had to give up working for Harpers, to care for her family. Beth had joined several groups run by the Women's Movement and was more militant than she'd been before the war. Sally still felt women should be given more say and a chance to do higher-paid work, but she wasn't really concerned in the Suffrage Movement as she was too wrapped up in Harpers and her family.

'I rang the hospital,' she said to change the subject because she didn't really want to get into the rights and wrongs of women's suffrage. 'Maggie is sitting up eating and drinking again. She would like some fresh nightwear and she'll need clothes soon. I think she only has a few things she brought back from France. I dare say she hardly ever changed out of uniform. I thought I'd take her some clothes down on Sunday. Does she have anything at yours you think she might like?'

'A couple of dresses and a nice skirt and jacket...' Beth frowned. 'Shall we buy her a couple of new outfits from Harpers?'

'Yes, I was planning on a nice dress and a couple of skirts and twinsets or a blouse but wondered if there is anything, in particular, she would really like from what she left behind...'

Beth nodded. 'I'll pay my share of whatever they cost, Sally, and I think she might have a best blouse she didn't take out with her.'

'I know she bought a couple of things from a seamstress in Paris,' Sally mused. 'One of her nurses went there for a break and told her about the workshops who had opened their doors for her. She might have got there herself for a few days if she hadn't been taken ill. One of her letters said she might go with some of the other nurses.'

'I think it got cancelled because they had a huge influx of wounded,' Beth told her, frowning. 'Maggie let the others go and stayed on to help – she just told them to bring her a few bits back.'

'Yes – and I think her friend Marie knows someone who owns

or works in one of the seamstress shops in Paris. Maggie was quite enthusiastic about getting some of their things after the war for Harpers, but then she seemed to forget and her letters got briefer...'

'Yes, I noticed that the last few months before she was ill,' Beth agreed. 'I don't know if she just didn't have time or whether she was too tired to bother with letters. The last three I received were just thank you notes really.'

'Perhaps she wasn't allowed to write more,' Sally suggested. 'Ben says that a lot of the men only send official postcards, just to let their family know they're still alive – but Maggie was writing letters until a few months back. I wonder what happened...'

'Well, perhaps she will tell us.' Beth stood up, pressing a hand to her back. 'I'd better go and see if Fred is fed up with my young monster.' She smiled because they both knew that Fred doted on his grandson and had even offered to give up work and help Beth look after him. Beth had refused his generous offer, but she'd told Sally that when both her children were old enough for school, she might let Fred retire to care for them so that she could return to Harpers. Fred had a lady friend who visited for tea sometimes on a Sunday, but as far as Beth could tell he wasn't interested in marriage, content to have his daughter-in-law and grandson as company.

Sally and Beth walked down to the basement together and discovered that Fred was nursing his beloved grandson, who was fast asleep, on his lap, while his young assistant was carefully unpacking a crate of glassware.

'That will need dusting,' Fred was telling the lad as they entered. 'Be careful you don't chip one of them glasses – or I'll have your guts for garters, me lad.'

'Yes, sir,' Joshua said respectfully and carefully set the last of the glassware on the wooden counter. He fetched a clean linen cloth and began to wipe the glass free of clinging straw and dust from its packing, his cheeks pink and clearly aware of three pairs of eyes watching him.

'How are you getting on, Joshua?' Sally asked kindly. She often broke Harpers' rules about using only surnames and the boy blushed crimson as he replied, 'I'm all right, Mrs Harper, thank you.'

'Good. We like our staff to be happy.' She smiled at Fred. 'I don't think I need to ask you, Mr Burrows?'

'I'm happy as a sandboy, Mrs Harper,' Fred said, because he never presumed to use her name, even though he often welcomed Sally to his home when she called on Beth. 'This young rascal has tired himself out. Take him home and put him to bed, Beth love.'

'Yes, I shall,' she replied. 'Thank you for having him, Dad.'

'That's my pleasure,' Fred told her. He glanced at Joshua, who had finished his task and was standing watching. 'Right, we'll take those up to the glass and china department – and then you can help me unpack the rest of the deliveries.'

Sally escorted Beth to the door of Harpers, waved her off as she walked towards the bus stop and then strolled back through the shop. On the ground floor, she stopped to watch as the assistant took charge of the new delivery of glass, exclaiming in pleasure to get such lovely things in. Their shelves had been close to empty for the past month, but Sally had managed to find a small glassworks who were able to supply her with tumblers and water jugs in a tinted glass and she'd bought as much stock as they could let her have. Customers were starved of nice things and she knew the glass would soon sell.

Experiencing an odd sensation at the nape of her neck, Sally turned her head. She had the feeling that someone was staring at her hard, but as she scanned the floor, the ten or so customers shopping were all looking elsewhere. She shook her head, trying to rid herself of the feeling that she was being watched. It was ridiculous, but she'd had the feeling several times when she was out recently – in the park playing with her daughter, even here in the store... No, she was imagining things. She must be. Why would anyone want to follow her? No one had approached her or even spoken to her on the occasions she'd felt this slightly creepy sensation. Surely it was just an overactive imagination...

* * *

Back in her office, Sally told her assistant Ruth that she didn't want to see anyone unless it was Ben or a very important business contact. She telephoned Mrs Hills and asked if everything was all right.

'Yes, it's fine, Mrs Harper,' her efficient housekeeper said. 'Young miss is having her rest now. Pearl has been playing with her all morning and now she's sleeping. I'll be here until four-thirty as usual.'

'I'll be home by four,' Sally told her. 'Thank you for all you do.'

'You're more than welcome, Mrs Harper.'

Replacing the receiver, Sally returned to her sales lists. She knew the store was ticking over, but even with the occasional boost of a campaign to sell slightly faulty goods, they weren't anywhere near as busy as they had been prior to the hostilities. She completely understood; there were a mixture of reasons – less stock was only one of them. People were feeling the hardship and those who could, made do with what they had; money was short in many households – and many women were widows with small incomes, struggling to survive without husbands. Even those with husbands still out there fighting struggled to make ends meet. Only the wealthier families still had the money to buy luxuries regularly. However, the new line of glassware was pretty and cheap so that should do well and the beautifully crafted wooden range she'd bought was selling out almost as soon as it came in.

She sighed and then glanced up as the office door opened and Jenni walked in. 'Any luck?' she asked, because her sister-in-law had been on a trip up north to try and find new sources of supply.

'Yes, some,' Jenni said and threw off her coat. 'It's two coats warmer here in London.'

'Did Andrew Alexander put you on to that hat maker?'

'Yes, he did. She's a nice lady and she makes most of the hats herself – bespoke quite often. They are beautiful, Sally. I asked her if she could supply us with a regular order and she gave me three of her favourite styles, which she said she could supply on a monthly basis – up to sixty a month...'

'That could mean twenty of each design – in various colours?'

'Yes. She is quite open to suggestions.'

'Good, but what of the men's clothing and the ladies' knitwear?'

'The men's clothing was mostly work shirts and cords.' Jenni pulled a face. 'Not really suitable for Harpers. I know I usually say buy anything if it is cheap, but I wouldn't bother. The ladies' knitwear is more hopeful. The manager was an older man and he said he would give me some samples to bring back but he can only supply a dozen of each of five lines on a monthly basis as he has a full order book, though he would like to sell to Harpers and says he will try to up his output to help us.'

'With a little arm-twisting from you,' Sally said and smiled at her. 'Did you see Andrew while you were up north?'

'He spared time to have dinner with me last night, but he was called back to the clinic before we got to desert.' She shrugged.

Andrew Alexander was a brilliant surgeon and his time was never his own. Jenni hadn't said much about it, though Sally knew she was more than a little attracted to the northerner. She thought there was something between them but wasn't sure how far it had progressed. However, Jenni was still married and as she received little communication from her estranged husband in America, it didn't look as if there was much chance of romance for Jenni.

'I'm sorry, love,' Sally said. 'You were hoping for more time together while you were up there.'

'Apparently, I chose a bad time,' Jenni shrugged again. 'What difference does it make, Sally? I'm trapped in a marriage I can't get out of – and I can't see us living together without marriage, can you? Andrew wouldn't do it—'

'You mean you would?' Sally looked at her and nodded. 'Yes, you might if there was no choice. I think I'd feel the same.'

'It may have to come to it – if Andrew cares enough. He says things, but we never have time to really talk it through.'

Sally looked at her sympathetically. 'Look, there's nothing I really need to do here. Why don't we buy something nice for tea and take it home? Jenny should be awake soon and she'll cheer you up.'

'Yes, she always does,' Jenni agreed and smiled. 'I shouldn't care – I'm not even sure I want to get married again...'

'Then tell Andrew how you feel,' Sally said. 'You could have a relationship without living together and causing a scandal, couldn't you?'

'If he wanted to,' Jenni looked at her and then laughed. 'You're wicked, Sally Harper – I don't know if you're a good influence or a bad one.'

'Good, because I love you and want you to be happy,' Sally replied, stood and embraced her. 'Come on, I'll treat us to some cream cakes and we'll go home and spoil Jenny.'

4

Rachel Bailey was busy checking her stock when Sally Harper walked in the following morning. She made a note of where she'd got to and closed and locked the cabinet before turning to smile at her employer's wife. They were good friends, but Rachel observed the rules whenever on the shop floor and addressed her as Mrs Harper.

'I was just checking those new gold bracelets we had in yesterday, Mrs Harper. I think they will prove very popular. We've sold two of them this morning.' She looked thoughtful. 'Men seem to be investing in gold jewellery for their wives more these days. I'm not sure if it's because they feel gold is always good currency and one never knows these days...'

'Or perhaps the war has made them more aware of their loved ones.'

'It could be a bit of both, but sales are rising for jewellery again.'

'Oh good,' Sally Harper said and looked pleased. 'I wasn't sure whether gold would sell as well at this time of year, though I know we sold several of those lovely gate bracelets last Christmas.'

'Yes, we did,' Rachel replied. 'One of my customers bought a gold bracelet and a chain with a locket for his wife and a gold bangle for his daughter. He said they will always be able to sell them in hard times.'

'Well, I suppose that is true enough,' Sally replied but frowned. 'If the currency was no longer worth anything, gold or jewels is a form of ready money, I suppose...' She made a wry face. 'I think I'd rather my husband bought me something as a gift because he thought I would like it, not because it was an investment.'

'It takes all sorts,' Rachel said. 'William is fond of investments. Since he was shipped home wounded, he's seems even more conscious of making sure I'm comfortable if anything should happen to him. He bought some Government bonds the other day in my name – he thinks they will pay handsomely one day.' Her husband, who had been a politician before the war but joined the Army at the start, had been put on light duties now but told that his fighting days were over. He'd been placed in an office, dealing with loads of paperwork, which he disliked but accepted as inevitable, at least until he was given a discharge from the services.

'Not as a birthday gift?' Sally asked.

'Oh no – he bought me a lovely new coat with a fur collar for my last birthday,' Rachel said and laughed. 'Point taken – but how are things with you and the family?'

'About the same – Ben is away again; Jenny is full of mischief and Jenni...' Sally shrugged. 'I'm not really sure. How *is* William, Rachel?'

'He is away on Army business again,' Rachel said. 'He isn't fighting, for which I am very grateful, but as far as I've been told

William is at a training centre helping with new recruits but spends half his time dealing with administration rather than hands on stuff.'

'Ah...' Sally sighed. 'Yet more young men to be sent off to the Front, I suppose. I wonder how many of them will come back to their families, but at least the Americans are in the war now. It won't be that long before they're fighting. I'm not sure how we could have gone on if they hadn't come in...'

'It doesn't bear thinking about,' Rachel said and shuddered. Trench warfare was particularly nasty, because the men were under constant bombardment and suffered from all kinds of horrors, including what was called 'trench feet', a condition caused by constantly having wet, cold feet, worse in the winter, but the trenches were almost always wet. Every time it rained, the ground became soggier and, even when the sun shone, it didn't seem to dry the water completely; the men could also awake to find a dead comrade lying beside them, sometimes being gnawed by rats. It was, her husband had told her, the soldier's worst nightmare. 'I was reading that report in *The Times* only yesterday about the conditions out there getting worse.'

'Yes, it is terrible. I can't wait for it to be over, Rachel, but Ben says nothing will come of the various attempts at peacemaking.' Sally glanced across at the counter to where Marion Jackson was serving, 'She has come on very well, don't you think? I wondered whether it was fair expecting her to do two jobs, but she seems to be thriving on it.' Marion, a young woman recently married, was one of the staff they'd recruited after Beth and Maggie had left Harpers. She'd started out as a counter assistant, but because of her flair for design, she was now assisting the window-dressing team to come up with new ideas as well.

'The window dressing only takes an hour or two of her time most days and I believe she finds the extra money very useful.'

Rachel nodded to herself. 'Her husband is serving overseas, I understand. He was in France before his last leave, but I believe he was posted elsewhere, though she isn't sure where because she hasn't heard for six months...'

'That must be such a worry,' Sally replied with a frown. 'She would most likely have been notified had anything happened to him but not to hear is awful – as you understand only too well.'

Rachel agreed. When her husband had been on active service, his letters had been infrequent, sometimes not arriving for months and then all together, but Marion Jackson had not had even one letter in six months and Rachel had seen the worried look in her eyes when she wasn't serving customers. Rachel felt for her, but so many other wives were in the same boat and many letters went astray, never to be delivered.

'So, everything is all fine here?' Sally enquired, interrupting Rachel's thoughts. She hastily brought them back to business.

'Yes. We're doing a nice steady trade and all the stock we've received has been perfect.'

'That is what I like to hear.' Sally beamed at her. 'I'll leave you to it then, Rachel. I would offer my sympathy to Marion Jackson, but it wouldn't help her. I'll just say a silent prayer for her that her husband turns up sooner rather than later.'

'I think it's all any of us can do until we have peace again.'

Sally agreed and left the department with a nod to the young girls working at the various counters. Becky Stockbridge had recently been promoted to a senior saleswoman in the clothing department and Rachel had another junior in her place. She was sorry to lose the girl who had become very reliable, which was why she'd had to agree to the promotion rather than asking to keep her. Becky deserved it and the new junior was doing very well. Shirley Jones was on the scarves and Marion oversaw the hats, which always looked superb, especially some from a new designer from the north, which had arrived only that morning and were already attracting attention, not least from Rachel who had seen a lovely midnight-blue velvet creation she very much admired.

Marion Jackson completed the sale of three hats, including one of the new designs, and then came up to Rachel. 'Would you like me to take my break now, Mrs Bailey? Only, I've been asked to attend a meeting about the new ideas for the windows in half an hour.'

'You'd better get off then – how long do you expect the meeting to continue?'

'It is usually an hour and ten minutes.' Marion laughed as she saw the look in Rachel's eyes. 'Yes, I know – but the meetings are *officially* an hour long – a representative from each department attends for one hour and then we return to our departments...'

Rachel nodded because this was the new arrangement until Mr Marco returned from the Army, when he would once again take over the window displays.

'It's only that someone always stops me and asks a question that takes several minutes to answer...'

'Ah, yes, I see,' Rachel said and smiled at her. 'Most of the displays are down to you these days, I understand?'

'With help from Mrs Harper and the heads of departments.' Marion Jackson wrinkled her smooth brow. 'I don't think it works quite as well as when Mr Marco was in charge, but it's the only way to do it for the moment. I shall be happier when he returns to Harpers.' Rachel nodded her agreement because Mr Marco was a popular member of staff and brilliant at his job. He was a personal friend of Ben Harper and had come with him from America when the store first opened. Of mixed parentage, he had been born in England but worked in America until returning to take up his job at Harpers.

'I think the windows look very nice. However, we must pray Mr Marco does return for his sake,' Rachel said. 'I know he sent a card to Mrs Harper last Christmas sending his good wishes to everyone – but I don't think anyone has heard from him since.'

'Perhaps he just can't write at the moment,' Marion suggested. 'I think it is the same for a lot of our men, Mrs Bailey.'

'Yes...' Rachel looked at her intently. 'Have you heard from Corporal Jackson?' Marion's husband had been promoted and she was very proud of it so had told her colleagues at work.

'Not for months, but my sister-in-law hasn't heard from her husband either—' Marion looked sad. 'We both worry, but we support each other – it's all we can do.'

'Yes, I know.' Rachel gave her a reassuring smile. 'Believe and pray I think are the best things to keep in mind.' She nodded briskly. 'You get off and I'll expect you when I see you.'

Marion Jackson flashed her a grateful smile and left.

Rachel called Shirley Jones to her and told her to take over Marion Jackson's counter, while the junior took over hers.

While Marion was gone, Rachel kept the other two girls at the counters but allowed them both to take their break together when her senior saleswoman returned.

'I think we can manage the department on our own for a while, Mrs Jackson,' she said. 'Did your meeting go well?'

'Yes, quite well,' Marion said. 'Mrs Harper was full of ideas and Miss Jenni Harper had some too. She is a big help with all kinds of things – but I still think the windows lack the flair they had when Mr Marco was here.'

'You do very well, all of you, but Mr Marco is very talented. We must just hope the war is over soon and he comes safely back to Harpers.'

* * *

Marion was thoughtful as she caught her bus home that evening, her mind still on the meeting for the window displays and the slight sense of annoyance she always felt after them. The ideas everyone put forward always sounded good but never seemed to work out just as they ought when it came to it and Marion knew that was to do with them missing Mr Marco's flair. He always knew how to make things come to life and truly sparkle and they needed him back at Harpers to return that sense of excitement to the displays.

Mrs Harper was always congratulating Marion on doing a good job for them, but a good job and a fabulous window that took your breath away were two different things in Marion's opinion. She sighed and shook her head. It wasn't for her to say anything; she was just doing her job as best she could and no doubt Mrs Harper was aware of the shortfall but had to accept that they could not do better for the moment. Perhaps it was as Mrs Harper claimed; they just didn't have the extra-special things in stock they'd often had in the past.

It was the fault of this war, Marion thought, feeling a little resentful. It affected everything these days, what they could eat, what they could buy, how often they saw their husbands. She hated it that Reggie's letters had been delayed or lost in the post. Both she and her sister-in-law Sarah were waiting desperately for letters from their husbands. Sarah hadn't had a letter from Dan for months either.

Pushing open their front gate, Marion walked round to the back kitchen and then caught the smell of one of Sarah's delicious casseroles cooking. Since Sarah had come to live with them for the duration of the war, Marion often came home to find a lovely meal waiting for her. It cheered her up immediately and she entered the spotlessly clean room to find her sister Kathy laying the table. Kathy and Sarah were chattering while Milly, her little sister, was doing a puzzle on a tray that Sarah had bought her recently and Dickon, her youngest brother, was already home from his work on the Docks and had just taken off his coat and was washing his hands at the sink. Dickon would be old enough to join the Army later that year, but she expected he would stay in his protected job, because his work was deemed necessary. The sights and sounds of home lifted her spirits even before her eyes went to the mantlepiece and she saw the letter.

'It came this morning,' Sarah said smiling as she saw Marion rush to pick up the envelope. 'I'm sure it is from Reggie.'

'Yes, it is,' Marion breathed as she tore it open and then she lit up from inside as she read the first few lines. 'He is well – just a slight scratch, he says – but they've sent him home to rest and recover. He's in hospital in Plymouth for a week or so and then he'll be home for at least a month...'

'That is wonderful,' Sarah said and came to embrace her. 'I'm so happy for you, Marion.'

'Have you had a letter too?'

Sarah shook her head.

'I'm sorry...' Marion's excitement was tempered a little by Sarah's disappointment. She knew how worrying it was when no letters came.

'I'll get one soon,' Sarah told her and smiled. 'He's fine, Marion. I know Dan is fine – it's just the wretched post, that's all.'

'Yes, I know,' Marion said. She kissed Reggie's letter and put it in her pocket. He was coming home soon and that was wonderful. She would pop round later and tell his mother, but for the moment she wanted to hug the news to herself. 'Dinner smells good?'

'Chicken and mushroom casserole,' Sarah said. 'The butcher only had boiling chickens so I thought I'd make it tasty by adding things we all like...' She frowned. 'There's nothing I can do to make your sandwiches better, Marion. They call this bread they're selling "war bread" and it tastes awful. I'd make some myself, but they've even asked us to cut down on the flour we use in pastry.'

'They'll have us all eating potato flour,' Kathy said. 'Our teacher was saying it is disgusting.'

'Well, that is all right in soups and stews to add bulk,' Sarah observed. 'But goodness knows what they've put in the bread...'

'Dan is lucky to have such a good cook for his wife,' Marion said. 'You're an artist in so many ways, Sarah – both your sewing and your cooking. You ought to be on our window display team. You have the sort of flair that Mr Marco has.'

'You and your Mr Marco,' Sarah said and laughed. 'Yes, I wouldn't mind helping you out, Marion dearest, and if you want to show me some ideas of yours, I'll help you tweak them with pleasure – but I have enough to do with our little Pamela and the cooking and my sewing orders, without working at Harpers. I told you I'm making all Mabel Clarke's wedding clothes...'

'Yes, I know how busy you are,' Marion said. 'Do you think this war will ever be over? I keep hoping they will all come home soon!'

'It will end one day, but who knows when,' Sarah said. 'Come and sit down – have your dinner and stop worrying, love. You'll make those windows look nice. You always do.'

'Nice, yes – fantastic, no,' Marion replied. 'The only person I know that can do that is Mr Marco – and I've no idea where he is now...'

5

Sally played with her daughter before putting her to bed. For a while she'd wondered if Jenny was a little slow learning to walk and talk, but Ben said she was just lazy and spoiled.

'Why should she bother to run after things when everyone is so ready to fetch things for her?' he'd said. 'And why bother with learning words when she can just point at what she wants.'

Sally was inclined to think he might be right. Jenny could run and play when she wanted and she was intelligent but she was inclined to be lazy and that was probably down to her being waited on hand and foot. Perhaps she needed a motive to make her do things, like this evening when Sally had played games with her.

Was that the problem – she wasn't always here and Jenny was left to amuse herself in her playpen while Mrs Hills worked? Immediately, she felt guilty about neglecting her beautiful daughter, but when she spoke of it to Beth later that evening she laughed.

'You worry too much and you expect too much,' she'd told

her. 'Children develop at their own rate and Jenny is absolutely fine. Ben is right. You've all spoiled her and now she expects it.'

'Yes, you're probably right,' Sally replied and hugged her. 'Thanks for coming over, Beth. It's in the evenings I miss Ben the most.'

'I feel the same,' Beth said. 'Fred took his friend Vera to the pictures as a treat. She does a lot of little things for us, so he thought she deserved it – but when he isn't there the house feels empty and I keep thinking about Jack. I start to worry and I miss him...'

'Yes, I know,' Sally agreed and looked at her with sympathy. 'When do you expect the baby, love? September, is it?'

'Yes, the end of September, I think.' She moaned and put a hand to her back. 'I'm getting a lot of backache now.'

'It won't be much longer. We're nearly at the end of June now, Beth.'

'Yes...' Beth sighed. 'Fred takes a week's holiday in July. I think he intends to have a few day trips to the sea.'

'Not going with him?'

'He asked me if I fancied a trip to Clacton for a few days in a hotel on the seafront, but I told him it would be too much trouble at the moment with Jackie teething and me like this—' Beth sighed. 'I suggested he take Vera, but he said he didn't think that was a good idea.'

'He's not courting then?'

'It's strictly friendship; she comes to tea and he takes her to the pictures, but that's about it. It's a pity really. I'd like to think he might marry again. If Jack and I wanted to move, it would leave him on his own and I don't think I could do that.'

'No, it wouldn't seem fair,' Sally said and smiled at her. 'Fred is very fond of you and his grandson.'

'He was so upset when that bomb went off in Upper North

Street School for infants and killed eighteen children the other day,' Beth said. 'Over a hundred and sixty were killed in all – they say the enemy planes dropped a hundred bombs – but it was those kiddies that upset Fred.'

'I think it did everyone,' Sally agreed. 'My secretary was in tears over it and Mr Stockbridge was really upset, as was Rachel.' She looked sad. 'I worry over Jenny if she doesn't say as much as I think she should – but those children will never have a chance to grow up.'

'I know—' Beth looked sad. 'I was thinking about Maggie, wondering how she is now, Sally. It is just too far for me to go down at the moment. I can't manage the journey with Jackie and if I leave him overnight it isn't fair on Fred. I know Vera is willing to help, but it is a bit much for her.'

'I wish they would transfer her to somewhere nearer London,' Sally agreed. 'We could go and see her more. I keep writing to her, but it isn't the same, and I wonder if she feels we're neglecting her.'

'I hope not,' Beth said. 'I wonder about all the others too – the young men who are serving in the trenches and Mr Marco.'

'Yes, I think about him a lot,' Sally agreed. 'He is so good with the windows and everyone likes him. I pray he comes back safely to us.'

'Has Ben had a letter recently?' Beth frowned as Sally shook her head. 'That seems a little strange. I mean, I think Marion Jackson's letters get delayed for weeks on end, but at least she gets them every now and then... I wonder why Mr Marco hasn't written to Ben...'

* * *

Marco watched Sadie playing with little Pierre and smiled. The child made life at the farm brighter and happier than he'd known for a long time – since Julien's death. His young lover had taken his own life after his father had shamed him for being different. It had broken Marco inside and he knew he would never feel that way again. But he had found a kind of content here in France on the farm with Sadie and Pierre. A child was the one thing Marco had envied his friend Ben Harper, but he'd been glad to see Ben happy in his marriage after some traumatic years, and their little girl was delightful.

Pierre was a ray of sunshine, too, and everyone loved him, including himself, Marco realised as he watched Sadie hand him a soft brioche roll. The child's pleasure as he chewed on it was evident and Marco felt a sudden desire to pick him up and hold him. Almost as if she'd read his thoughts, Sadie picked her son up and dumped him on Marco's lap.

'Will you look after him for a few moments, Marcel?' she asked, using the name he'd been given as cover for his work with the resistance here in France. He was officially Marie's cousin and, so far, it seemed to work well as no one had suspected anything else. 'I want to walk into the village and post a card home...'

'May I see it?'

Sadie handed him the card – a plain white one issued by the nursing detachment with an address in England. On the back she'd just written three lines. *Hope you're well. I'm fine. Love, Sadie.*

'Why don't you ask the hospital to send it with their mail?'

'Matron Mayhew is too busy to bother at the moment – and no one else would do it.' Sadie frowned. 'Why do you ask?'

'You do realise that it is unlikely your letters arrive safely. If they go in the military postbags, they have more chance. You haven't put a return address, which is sensible, but how can your family send a reply?'

'I don't want them to,' Sadie said and blushed. 'If they guessed I'd left the nursing detachment to have a baby they would disown me. I can't let them know where I am and I can't tell them about my little Pierre...'

Marco looked at her sadly. 'Are you sure they wouldn't accept it once they were over the shock?'

'My mother would turn her back on me and my father might kill me,' Sadie replied. 'He is a very proud man and he wouldn't have me in his house with a bastard child.'

'Then I am sorry for him,' Marco said and bounced Pierre on his knee. 'He is adorable, Sadie. Go to the village and enjoy your walk. Perhaps your card will get through.'

Sadie thanked him, giving him a brilliant smile. Marco smiled in return. It was wrong that she had been left in such a precarious position and he felt a stab of guilt. Her lover Pierre had died helping him to escape and that lay heavy on his conscience. Because of him, Sadie was exiled in France with no hope of a return to her family. Perhaps there was a way he could help her? Marco turned it over in his mind, trying to think of a solution, but the only one that came to mind was impossible – or was it?

A rueful smile touched his lips. He would have to think about this for a while...

* * *

Sadie enjoyed the walk, the sunshine and the fresh air. Sometimes it rained really hard but then the sun came out and it was lovely and fresh. She liked living in France with Marie, her son's great aunt, although there were times when she would have liked to go home. Living in the East End as a child, Sadie had been determined to escape and her way of doing that had been nursing. She'd met Maggie Gibbs during their rigorous training and she'd been truly happy for a while – if only she hadn't fallen for Pierre and been foolish enough to give herself to him.

She'd been intoxicated with romantic love, the warm scents of a summer night and a man she couldn't resist who had given her sweet white wine to drink as they lay on his blanket beneath the stars. She didn't regret that night of love – it was all she would ever have with Pierre – but falling for a baby had been unlucky. Now she was stuck here in France because the alternative was a life of drudgery back home. With no husband, she would find it impossible to get a good job or a decent house. Landlords didn't want to let property to a fallen woman like her – and she could never go home unless she was married.

Sadie wasn't sure she could marry just for the sake of it. She didn't want to go to bed with a man she didn't love – and it would be a long time before she could give her heart again. No, she was better off living with Marie and her friends at the farm.

Marie treated her like a daughter and Marcel – or Marco as his real name was – was the kindest and funniest man she'd ever met. Sadie knew his real name because Andre, one of Pierre's group, had once let it slip, but she'd known already that he was playing a dangerous game. Like the man she'd loved, he was a part of the French resistance force.

Marco was always teasing her and Marie and playing with Pierre. She'd sort of gathered from Maggie, who sometimes spoke of the Mr Marco she knew at Harpers, that he wasn't interested in women, at least, only as friends, and that suited Sadie. Maggie hadn't actually told Sadie that her Mr Marco and Marcel were one and the same, but she'd picked up on little things and worked it out. However, she had not passed her thoughts on to anyone else, not even Marie. Marcel or Marco, he was kind and always there for her and the child and she knew she was lucky.

Sadie smiled as she put her card into the little post box on the wall of the village's only shop. She wasn't sure how often mail was collected from the small sleepy village, and perhaps it would never get there, but at least she'd tried.

Shrugging, Sadie turned to walk home again. Life was quiet here with very little to do other than walk, eat, drink wine and work. She wondered how much longer Marco would be at the farm. One of these days, he would surely be recalled to England and then she would miss him.

6

It might be summer now, but it was still cold and damp lying in the ditch all night, the rain had been heavy for a couple of days and, on the battlefields, it churned to mud beneath thousands of feet. Marco stifled the longing for a warm bed and a hot meal. He had been watching the German patrol as it probed the border, and he knew they were an advance party for a division coming up behind and hoping to get round the British and French lines for a surprise attack. He waited another few minutes, until the column of men had passed him by, and then heard a shout as the patrol was intercepted by Andre's men. Shooting followed and Marco heard screams and yells and then cheering.

He rose wearily to his feet and walked back down the road to where the patriots were celebrating the easy kill. Marco nodded as Andre slapped him on the shoulder.

'We teach these Germans a lesson, no?'

'Yes,' Marco agreed, but he knew that the next night or the following one another patrol would take the place of those they'd slaughtered and wondered what they were truly achieving. Yes, the shooting would have alerted the Allied camps. He had no doubt they were peering into the darkness wondering what was going on and fully prepared for an attack, which was now unlikely to happen. The purpose of the German patrols was to find a way to surprise the British and Allied troops. Andre and several other partisan groups did their best to see that didn't happen, posting men in the fields and woods to report and alert the armed men roaming the border countryside.

What happened next came out of the blue. Several of the enemy soldiers were lying on the ground as Marco walked towards his friends, but one of them suddenly jumped up and fired at him. Even as the bullet penetrated his flesh, he heard several more shots but knew nothing more as he slumped to the ground and everything went black around him.

Marco was unconscious as the soldier was ruthlessly shot by several men, furious that he'd manged to kill their British agent. Andre had been protecting him, thinking him more valuable as a contact to the British Government than as a fighter. It was Marco who secured them guns, ammunition and money so that they could continue to wreak havoc on the enemy by blowing up lorries, trains and killing as many patrolling soldiers as they could. Without him, the group would have to fend for itself and the supply of ammunition would dwindle.

Marco wasn't aware of the curses or of someone feeling for his pulse or that he was hoisted, none too gently, as it was discovered he still lived, over Andre's shoulder and carried back to the farmhouse, where Marie soon had him on the hastily cleared kitchen table. The bullet was found to have buried itself in his side, glancing off his ribs and thus miraculously missing all his organs, as the doctor they called reported after digging it out.

They had no anaesthetic and Marco half woke and screamed

with pain, as the doctor probed for the bullet, but fell back unconscious as he was sewn up and his wound swabbed with alcohol. He moaned as he was carried up to Marie's bedroom but didn't wake.

'He will live?' Andre asked the doctor as he washed the blood from his hands at the deep stone sink.

'He should pull through. He's strong and he was lucky. A fraction lower and he would already be dead.'

Andre nodded and cursed. He looked at Marie as she came back to the large kitchen, which smelled of herbs and baking. 'You will take care of him?'

'Yes, of course,' Marie promised. 'Sadie is sitting with him now. She is a good nurse and she will know what to do when the fever comes.'

'Don't let him die. We need him,' Andre said and prepared to leave. 'He is important.'

Marie nodded but let him go without replying. Like Marco, she wondered what good the patrols did. They were harassing the enemy, she'd been told, and the British supplied the means for their explosives and their guns – but the war just went on. Sometimes, she despaired of it ever ending. Would life in France ever become normal again? Would she ever be able to cross the border to see friends and family?

She went upstairs and found Sadie looking at her patient anxiously.

'He should sleep – the doctor gave him a good dose of brandy and a sleeping powder,' Marie said.

'They should have taken him to one of the field hospitals where he could have had the proper drugs,' Sadie replied and frowned as she looked at the unconscious man in the bed. 'He could die after that mauling!'

'Andre didn't want to risk it,' Marie explained. 'He thinks

there may be other patrols out there – besides, the British wouldn't be too keen on a group of armed men asking for admission in the middle of the night.'

'I suppose,' Sadie said. 'That doctor – he was a butcher. Marcel will have a terrible scar...'

'I doubt he'll care if he recovers,' Marie replied. 'It was in deep, Sadie. He may get an infection—'

'We shan't let him die,' Sadie declared. 'He has been kind to me and to Pierre's son.'

'Ah yes, the little one,' Marie's smile softened at the mention of Sadie's child. 'How is my little Pierre?'

'Over his cough, I think,' Sadie said. Her son was robust and enjoyed his life on the farm, running half-naked in the French sunshine and enchanting all the workers. Maggie Gibbs had loved him too, when she'd found time to spend at the farm, but she'd worked too hard and fallen ill.

Sadie frowned as she thought of her friend. She had been shipped home to England and would be in a military hospital. Sadie hoped she was recovering. She missed Maggie and felt a bit lonely at times, even though Marie treated her as one of the family. Sadie's knowledge of the French language was slowly getting better, but she longed to speak English with her friends again – however, she wasn't ready to return to England yet. If she went, she would have to leave her child behind.

Marie would keep little Pierre if Sadie asked her and that meant she could return to nursing if she chose, but she'd discovered soon after his birth that she loved him too much to abandon him. Therefore, if she returned to England she must pose as a widow and hope to be believed and allowed to find work as a nurse. The one thing she couldn't do was to go home to her family...

'I will sit with Marcel for a while,' Marie told her. 'Rest, Sadie.

He will need much care from you in the next days – and for now
he sleeps.'

'Yes, that is true,' Sadie said and bent to touch her patient's
brow. He was warm but not hot. If he took a fever, she would need
to sit with him long hours, so for now she would take her friend's
advice and sleep.

* * *

Marco awoke to a sense of pain and blackness. Gradually, the
blackness receded and he saw the young women bending over
him, soothing his forehead with something that smelled delightful. He reached up and caught her wrist with a grip that was
surprisingly strong for a man who had lain in a fever for a week.

'That smells delightful, Sadie, but you need not continue. I'm
perfectly fine now,' he said and tried to rise but fell back as the
dizziness took him and he suddenly realised how much he hurt.
'Did the farm cart trample over me?'

'You were shot in the side. Luckily, it slid off a rib, avoiding
more serious harm and burying itself in muscle, so the doctor
said.' Sadie looked at him sympathetically. 'I imagine it hurts like
hell. I asked Matron Mayhew if she would give me some
painkilling medicine for you, but she was short of everything
again and couldn't help us.'

'Quite right,' Marco said. 'Those poor devils at the hospital
need it far more – I'll mend and I think I have you to thank for
nursing me?'

'You've had a nasty fever – the result of that butcher mangling
you,' Sadie said in a disapproving tone. 'He was a general practi-
tioner and no surgeon, but they didn't want to risk running into
another patrol and couldn't wait until morning, so you were oper-
ated on here.'

'Yes—' Marco closed his eyes against the feeling of weakness and pain. 'I suppose Andre and the others brought me back. I'm lucky to be alive...'

'He blames himself for not making sure that German soldier was dead,' Sadie told him. 'He has been here most days to ask how you are – he says you're too valuable to them to lose.'

Marco made a wry grimace. 'I'm useful at supplying information and getting supplies,' he admitted, 'but my ability to shoot the enemy is questionable. I can fire a gun but not as accurately as some of the others. I think that's why Andre tries to keep me out of the firing line.'

'Nonsense,' Sadie replied, showing she'd lost none of her nursing authority. 'If he protects you, it is because he needs your other skills – he told me you can see better in the dark and move more silently than most of the others and they use you to alert them to enemy patrols. You were sent out here to liaise and keep contact with the British not to fight, Marcel.'

A cynical smile touched his lips. 'So, if you know all this, why call me by that name?'

'Because Marcel is your name here,' she said and smiled at him. 'Marie believes that all her family and workers are loyal – but you never know who may be turned. Food is scarce in some places and if family are threatened, men and women will do what they have to, to protect them.'

'How wise she is for one so young.' Marco smiled up at her from the pillows.

'I was brought up in a big family in the East End,' Sadie told him and laughed. 'You had to scrap for whatever you wanted. There were six of us and though my parents were hardworking there was barely enough to go round, so as soon as you could, you started to earn a bit of money. I babysat for the newsagent's wife and I saved enough to leave home and get a job in an office as a junior. When the war came, I volunteered to be a nursing assistant and I wanted to be a nurse...'

'But then you met Pierre—' Marco's smile vanished. 'I'm sorry he died saving my life, Sadie. If I can do anything to help you...'

'Do you think I don't know you give Marie money for me and the child?' Sadie shook her head at him. 'You've been more than kind to me and I'm grateful.'

'But you're not truly happy, are you?' Marco looked at her keenly. 'Are you still grieving for Pierre?'

'Perhaps a little,' she said. 'I did love him – but we hardly knew each other and it seems such a long time ago. I suppose I was foolish...'

'Just in love,' Marco told her. 'The foolish ones are those back home who would condemn you for having a child out of wedlock.'

'Thank you,' she said and smiled. 'I feel the same. Where is the shame in bearing the child of a man you loved, even if he didn't get a chance to wed me? I know he would have, had I told him before...'

Marco reached for her hand and pressed it. 'If you were married, you might be able to return to work. I'm not sure if you could be a nurse, but there are some hospitals that might employ the widow of a war hero...'

'Yes,' Sadie nodded thoughtfully. 'I've wondered if I should go back to England after the war wearing a ring. I don't know if I'd need to produce a certificate...' She sighed. 'If my parents believed I was married, they would look after little Pierre while I worked and Matron Mayhew told me that she would take me on again...'

'You should marry, Sadie. It would make things easier for you – though, as I said, I do not consider you have done wrong.'

'I haven't met anyone else I like enough, let alone love – I think that's why I lost my head over Pierre...'

There was a short silence, then, 'You could marry me,' Marco said and she stared at him in shock. 'Let me explain before you say no, please. I should not expect to sleep in your bed and it would be a marriage in many ways but not that – as you may have guessed, I'm of what some folk think an unnatural persuasion... and in their eyes it makes me a bad person.'

'No! Don't say that—' Sadie exclaimed. 'I know you're different in some ways, but I like you as a person and you're not bad or wrong – just... different.'

'Yes,' he smiled as she tried to find another word that he wouldn't consider rude and couldn't. 'You're a lovely girl, Sadie, and I'm not surprised that Pierre loved you. He was foolish to give his life for mine when he had so much more to live for, but I should be proud to offer you my name, home, and support for your son as he grows up.'

'But why?' she asked in wonder. 'Why should you do so much for me? Or is it for Pierre – because you regret his death?'

'I do regret it,' Marco said, 'but living here at the farm with you and the boy, I have become fond of you both. I shall never have a son and I'd like to help bring up yours...'

Sadie nodded her understanding. He was very good with Pierre and would make a wonderful father but was unlikely to have his own child. 'I am grateful and honoured, Marco – will you let me think about it?'

'Yes, but don't take too long. They want me back in England and I'd like to get you settled there if you agree...'

'I'll give you my answer when you're up and about,' Sadie said, a hint of mischief in her eyes. 'It will give you an incentive to get better...'

Marco chuckled. He wouldn't be the first man of his sexual preferences to marry for reasons other than love and Sadie would give him something he'd never thought to have – a family of his own.

7

Sally read the letter from her old friend Mick O'Sullivan, who was with the Irish tunnellers overseas, with a frown. It had been sent some weeks back and asked if she knew how Maggie Gibbs was. Clearly, he was anxious because he hadn't heard from her in a while. The post from abroad was getting worse if Beth's complaints were anything to go by and Mick obviously felt something towards Maggie, the young woman he'd informed about the death of her fiancé. He asked if Sally had heard from her recently and hinted that he might be seeing her soon without saying it openly.

Sighing, she put the letter aside for answering later, though whether Mick would receive her reply, wherever he was, she had no idea. How she was to tell him that Maggie was seriously ill in hospital was a problem; however, she pushed it from her mind as Jenny came toddling towards her.

'Mum, mum, up...' she demanded imperiously. 'Mummy, lift Jenny up.' Up was her newest word and she added words infrequently. Ben was forever telling her that they spoiled Jenny, but he was as guilty as everyone else, because she was such an enchanting child.

Sally picked her up, kissed her, tickled her and then asked her if she wanted to go to the swings. It was a sunny summer day, though the wind still carried a chill, but Jenny liked to visit the open stretch of green where there was a children's play area, complete with a slide and a swing. On Sunday mornings it was always busy and there wasn't much chance of getting on the swing for a small girl, but today was a Monday and Sally had decided not to go to Harpers. She had no appointments with travelling salesmen and she would do what ordering was possible from home. Besides, Jenni was at the store and had an appointment of her own.

Sally tried to avoid clashing with her sister-in-law. They didn't always agree on what stock should be bought, but since Jenni was a part owner, Sally thought it best not to interfere in her departments. She'd taken over the buying for the men's department, the shoes and the glassware, leaving Sally with her jewellery, bags, scarves and gloves, as well as the stationery and ceramics. The chocolates, special cakes and flowers were standing orders, though the order could not always be met by suppliers these days and was nearly always incomplete. Toys were almost impossible to buy now, since so many of them had come from Germany or Europe. Sally wondered about closing those departments down for the duration, but hesitated because they were dear to Ben's heart. Everything else was shared between Sally and Jenni and mostly done from catalogues these days since firms had lost many of their salesmen to the war. Sally was quite pleased to be relieved of some of the responsibility. It had been a heavy burden at times these past years and she'd never been meant to carry it all, but some important staff had left to do their bit in the Army, giving her no option but to take over.

Sally bought a newspaper as she walked, holding tightly to Jenny's hand and just glancing at the headlines before tucking it into her bag. The Prime Minister, Lloyd George, had said, 'Peace will come through the German people not their rulers...'

Sally nodded her silent agreement. The ordinary German people did not want war any more than she or any of her friends did. It was power-hungry men looking for position and advantage that started wars in her opinion and she didn't care how they painted it. If the Government was sensible, it would go along with one of the peace plans that were being talked of in the paper. All ordinary folk wanted was for life to get back to normal, which would suit Sally Harper and Harpers Emporium just fine.

However, her thoughts were soon far from Harpers as she pushed her daughter high in the air on the swings, listening to her squeals of delight. Jenny wasn't too keen on the slide yet; it was a bit too high for her, so Sally stuck to the swings. After she'd had enough of them, they went to a little tea shop close by where they were well known. Sally had a pot of tea and a toasted teacake and Jenny had a small dish of ice cream, which she tucked into – apart from what she put on her frock and cardigan.

Sally cleaned her up and put her coat on after asking for and paying the bill. She took Jenny's hand as they left, walking home slowly and letting her daughter skip along happily at her side.

'Doggie...' Jenny cried suddenly and broke from Sally's grasp, running to the big dog and attempting to stroke it. The dog was startled and barked, but before it could make up its mind to snap, Sally had scooped her daughter up.

'I'm sorry,' she said as the man started to apologise. 'I didn't even know she knew the word dog...'

'They pick up all sorts of things,' the man told her with a smile. He was older, perhaps in his sixties. 'My daughter was always rushing up to dogs when she was small – she adored them. I hope Fido didn't upset her?'

'No, I don't think so,' Sally said because Jenny was still staring at the dog and didn't seemed bothered by its size. Fido had begun to wag his tail and graciously allowed Sally and then Jenny to stroke him. 'He's very gentle, isn't he?'

'He knows children. My daughter has three youngsters – is this one your only child?'

'Yes, she is,' Sally said and set her back on her feet while holding tightly to her hand. 'We hope for more one day – perhaps when the war is over.'

'The war,' the man scowled. 'It's a wicked waste of life. My son was killed at Ypres...'

'I'm so sorry,' Sally said. 'It is awful how many young men we're losing.'

'Yes.' His smile had disappeared. 'Well, I shan't take up more of your time.'

He walked off and Jenny started wailing. 'Want doggie, Mum, mum...' Jenny strained to follow the man and his dog.

'No, darling, the doggie belongs to someone else.'

She bent to pick up her daughter and then noticed a woman staring hard at her. Something clicked in Sally's mind. She was certain she'd seen the woman several times before – Yes! She was the person who Sally had thought had been watching her at Harpers and on other occasions too!

'Did you want something?' she asked, making a move towards her.

The woman turned and walked off hurriedly.

'Who are you?' Sally called after her.

The woman increased her pace, not looking over her shoulder once.

Had she frightened her – had she made a mistake? Sally felt

confused, a little embarrassed and concerned. If the woman was watching her, why hadn't she approached Sally?

A feeling of fear went through her. Was she one of those women that desperately wanted a child – was she after stealing Jenny?

No, thinking about the various times she'd felt someone was there, but couldn't see who it was, Sally was sure that she'd experienced it even when she was alone. Besides, she must be fifty or more and would not want the bother of a young child – and thinking about it, she looked tired and a little unwell. So, what *did* she want? Had she seen Sally in Harpers and thought she might give her money?

It was a mystery, but the more Sally thought about it, the more she was convinced that the woman had been following her for a while.

* * *

'What makes you think she is following you?' Beth asked when Sally took Jenny round to call on her a little later that afternoon. 'Perhaps she saw the incident with the dog and was curious. She may have thought Jenny was in danger from such a large animal...'

'It was some sort of sheepdog,' Sally told her. 'All Jenny can talk about is the doggie. I'm not sure whether to get her one...'

'You'd need to be sure it had a good temperament,' Beth said. 'I should wait for a while if I were you – she might not like it when she gets it.'

'Perhaps and dogs have to be taken for regular walks. We don't have a garden either in the flat.'

'Has Ben said any more about getting a house with a garden? We're lucky here. Fred's garden isn't the biggest, but it is nice and pleasant to sit in in the sun. Jackie can go wherever he likes and I know he is safe. If I take him to a green or playground, I have to watch all the time because he crawls faster than I can walk and he's taking a few steps now.'

'Gosh, he's doing well,' Sally said. 'Jenny was still crawling at a year old. It was a couple of months or more before she walked safely.'

'Maybe you just remember it that way – or perhaps you gave her whatever she wanted? Jackie is independent and he's going to get it for himself if he can.'

Sally nodded. 'Ben says we've spoiled Jenny. I think he is right. She knows words I haven't heard her say, but when she wants to, she comes right out with them.'

'Children are all different,' Beth replied, smiling as her son attempted to pull himself upright and fell back on his bottom. She picked him up and sat him on her lap, where he laughed and patted her face for a moment and then struggled to get down again. 'He is like his father – never sits still for long...'

Sally nodded thoughtfully. 'So, you think it was just a coincidence that the woman was staring at us.'

'You spoke to her and she went off,' Beth said. 'If she'd wanted money, that would've been the ideal time to ask and she doesn't sound like a child snatcher to me. Wealthy women who are childless might be obsessed with having one, but that woman sounds as if she was down on her luck – she wouldn't be thinking of grabbing a child. Well, not in my opinion.'

'I tend to agree,' Sally said. 'I suppose I'm worrying for nothing – but I know she has followed me more than once.'

'You're a successful woman,' Beth told her. 'Perhaps she just admires you.' She shook her head as if to dismiss the subject. 'I had a letter from Maggie – well, it came from a nurse, but Maggie told her what to say. She thinks they may be moving her to a convalescent home in the country. Apparently, it is one of those big country houses they've commandeered for the wounded. Maggie said she'd rather come home to Fred and me; she knows she's always welcome, because we've both told her and it was Tim's home, of course – but the doctors won't let her.'

'They know she'd be back to work tomorrow if she had her way,' Sally said. 'I told her she could have her old job back whenever she liked – but I'm not sure she was interested. She seems to have her mind and heart back in France...'

'She was out there a very long time,' Beth said. 'I suppose it seems more like home than England just now – and she still wants to help nurse the wounded.'

'Well, the doctors say she can't go out there again, because another fever like that one might kill her and they won't take the risk.'

'Perhaps they would let her go back to nursing here?'

'Yes, perhaps,' Sally agreed. 'I'm going down tomorrow.'

'They may have moved her already. You should check, Sally, or you could have a wasted journey.'

'Yes,' Sally agreed. 'It was easy to get to the military hospital by train. We shall have to catch buses or get a taxi if this convalescent home is way out in the country.'

'Yes, that's what I thought,' Beth said. 'I'm learning to drive, because Jack said it was sensible, but I couldn't drive a long way yet.'

'No, I wouldn't expect you to, Beth. I should learn myself, but I didn't much like it when I tried. I suppose I'm just lazy.' She laughed. 'Perhaps that's where Jenny gets it from. When Ben is home, he takes me wherever I want to go.'

Beth laughed. 'Perhaps you're a little bit spoiled, just like your daughter!'

Sally laughed but didn't answer.

When Ben rang that evening, Sally told him about the incident with the dog but didn't mention the mysterious woman following her.

'Any idea when you'll be home, love?' she asked as the line crackled. 'Where are you – or shouldn't I ask?'

'I'm in Scotland at the moment,' Ben said. 'I'll be home at the weekend – is there anything you'd like me to bring you? Not for the shop, for yourself?'

'I've got all I need, Ben – but if you see anyone who makes those lovely brooches with agates and other stones, you could bring some for Harpers. We always need something pretty for stock.'

'Will do, but I'll bring some whisky and some shortbread for you. Take care, darling. I love you.'

Sally smiled as he replaced the receiver. It would be nice having Ben home again and she hoped he would be around for a while. He'd said he would think about a dog for Jenny, but he'd been a bit vague over it, perhaps like Beth he thought it was too soon.

She reached for the telephone again. She would ring the military hospital and ask when Maggie was being transferred to a convalescent home.

8

Maggie was well wrapped in blankets and scarves for the journey. Although the county of Wiltshire was only eighty-seven miles from Devon as the crow flies, the car followed winding, twisting roads and it took almost four hours to reach their final destination, which was not far from Torbay. Two recovering soldiers were taken down at the same time and she sat in the front of the large car with the doctor and listened to their banter, smiling to herself as she heard their colourful language. The sound of injured men recovering and laughing was something she'd missed stuck in the hospital and she was glad to be moving on, though sorry they wouldn't just let her go home.

'I'll come down and see you one day,' Nurse Shelly had promised. 'It's where my brother convalesced and it's really nice.'

Highcliff House was set in large grounds at the end of a long drive through private grounds. Maggie had never been in such a house and thought it looked much too grand to shelter recovering soldiers. It must be at least two hundred years old and built in what she thought was the Tudor style, with two wings surrounding a courtyard at the back.

'Cor blimey!' one of the men sitting behind her said. 'Have we come to the bleedin' palace?'

'Mind yer language, Bert,' his mate told him. 'We've got a lady in the front seat...'

Maggie smiled but didn't say anything. She rather agreed with the sentiment, though she wouldn't have put it quite the same way.

In the shadows of the late afternoon, the house looked rather beautiful as they got closer and she could see the ivy growing up the old stone walls. A family must have lived here once, but now there were men standing about on the lawns or sitting in wheelchairs. Some were smoking cigars and in one case a pipe – something Matron Mayhew would not have allowed her patients to do and Maggie wondered what kind of a place she'd come to. Of course, the patients were supposedly recovering here, though some of them still looked quite ill to her practised eye, as the car halted outside the main entrance and then a man in a white coat was opening the car door. He asked them all their names, took charge of the men and left Maggie to the care of a shy-looking nurse who came forward to help her from the car into a wheelchair.

'I'm Nurse Mann – and I've been assigned to look after you for a few days.'

'I could walk,' Maggie protested, but the nurse shook her head. 'Sister would have me on a charge. You're here to rest, Nurse Gibbs. We want to look after you – we're all so proud of you. It's an honour to have such a heroine here with us.'

'Those men are the heroes,' Maggie told her but allowed herself to be wheeled inside and through a long corridor to the back of the house where there was a sunny annexe, built, she thought, in the last few years. 'Oh, this is lovely...'

'We have mostly male patients here,' Nurse Mann explained.

'This annexe was used as a day room, but we've turned it into a little suite for you – there's a toilet at the end and a bedroom, but also a sitting room so that you can be quiet when you wish. The men can be boisterous as they get better – restless too and wanting to be off home as soon as they feel fit, or back to the front line...'

'Yes, most of them want to get back out there and fight again,' Maggie said. 'They are so very brave, Nurse Mann.' She smiled at the young girl who was clearly a probationer. 'What is your first name? Mine is Maggie.'

'I'm Veronica, but Sister says I'm not to tell the patients—'

'Perhaps she thinks the men might become too familiar,' Maggie suggested. 'We used our first names out there, because the senior nurses thought it helped men who were dying or in terrible pain to be gentle and friendly. They do need a friendly smile when they haven't much hope of a future.'

Nurse Mann's face creased with sorrow. 'I wish I was there. I've only just passed my first exams and they sent me here. I asked to be sent out, but they said I was needed here...'

'We can't all go over there,' Maggie told her. 'You are needed here and perhaps your chance to nurse abroad will come. I think they are looking for qualified nurses now rather than volunteers. I got in at the start and learned on the wards. I've never taken any exams, but before I was ill, I was doing everything the nurses did.'

'Sister Andrews told me all about you. She says you've been awarded a medal—' She pressed her hand to her mouth. 'I wasn't supposed to say that—'

'Don't worry, Veronica. A friend of mine at the hospital told me I'd been put in for a medal of honour, but I don't deserve it. I just did my job...'

'Under fire a few times,' Veronica said and looked awed. 'It must have been so exciting...'

'No, not exciting, just worrying about your patients and doing what you were told,' Maggie said and smiled. 'Wait until you've experienced the dirt and the fleas and the smells and then you'll wish yourself back here again.'

'Yes, perhaps,' Veronica looked doubtful. 'You missed the official tea time, but I can get you a sandwich or a piece of cake and a cup of tea if you'd like?'

'Yes, please – a small piece of cake and a cup of tea. I'm not very hungry yet.'

'You soon will be here – it's the fresh air and the tranquillity. That's what the men say.'

Maggie nodded. 'Can the patients go where they like?'

'Yes, of course. The gardens are lovely and there is a lake – I like it there when I have a break. I'll take you when you feel up to it.'

'Tomorrow,' Maggie said. 'The journey was tiring. I'd like to explore tomorrow.'

'Yes, of course. I'll fetch your tea. Your things came earlier. I've unpacked them for you and if you want to rest, I'll help you into bed.'

'Just push me to the window so I can look out at the garden please,' Maggie said. She smiled as the young nurse obliged. 'That's just right, thank you. It's such a lovely view from here.'

'I'm glad you like it,' Veronica said. 'When they were wondering where to put you, I suggested it. The men have plenty of rooms to frequent and this wasn't often used – it is so peaceful here.'

'Yes, it is,' Maggie agreed.

When the young nurse had gone, she got up and walked a little unsteadily to gaze out of the window. It looked over a rose garden and then a lawn in the distance. Several men were sitting or standing about talking. And then she noticed a man in a basket chair wheeling himself out from under the rose arch. He waved at her imperiously, indicating what she saw was a glass door out to the garden. Walking unsteadily towards it, she found it opened wide enough to allow his chair through, into what she'd been told was *her* room.

'You're new here,' the young man said gruffly. 'Why aren't you in uniform?' His blue eyes were cold and hostile and Maggie knew that he resented what had happened to him.

She was saved from answering, however, by a booming voice from behind her. 'Now then, Captain Morgan, what are you doing here? You were told the annexe was no longer in use.'

The young officer – probably no more than twenty-four – shot a suspicious look at Maggie and then smiled sweetly at the senior nurse. 'I forgot,' he said. 'Are you cross with me, Sister Jane?'

'I am Sister Foster to you, Captain, as well you know. You're in Miss Gibbs' room – perhaps you would like to apologise and leave?'

The cold blue eyes fastened on Maggie. 'I apologise. I took you for a nurse—'

'I am – or I was,' Maggie said and smiled at him. He wasn't really so fierce – just frightened and angry at finding himself in a wheelchair.

'This is one of your angels from over there,' Sister Foster said and turned her formidable gaze on Maggie. 'You shouldn't be standing here. You should be in bed. Where is that wretched nurse?'

Right on cue, Veronica opened the door bearing a tray with a piece of Victoria sandwich and a pot of tea, but the smile on her face vanished as she saw Sister Foster glaring at her.

'Where have you been?' the senior nurse demanded. 'Put that tray down and take Captain Morgan through to the day room while I look after Miss Gibbs properly.'

The reprimand was clear and as Veronica scuttled to obey and wheeled the scowling Captain from the room into the main hospital, Sister Foster picked up the tray and ushered Maggie towards the bedroom.

'You may sit in the chair beside the bed to have your Victoria sandwich,' she said and placed the tray on a table that she wheeled to the chair.

Maggie obeyed. Sister Foster was a martinet and it was best not to argue. She had every intention of getting up once the bossy nurse had gone, but, when she'd eaten her cake and drunk her tea, Sister Foster indicated that she should get into the freshly made bed, and, after she'd gone, Maggie suddenly discovered she was very tired.

She closed her eyes and slept and the next thing she knew Nurse Veronica was in the room drawing back the curtains to let in the daylight.

'Is it morning?' Maggie asked, sitting up. She felt refreshed and so much better than she had since her return to England. 'I fell asleep—'

'I know – Sister Jenkins told me you slept all night. She looked in on you several times and said you were peaceful, so she just let you rest.'

'I think that's the best night I've had since I was ill,' Maggie told her, sitting back against the pillows. 'I feel wonderful.'

'Would you like breakfast now? You can have bacon, eggs and tomatoes – or just porridge and toast with honey if you wish.'

'I'd like the toast and honey,' Maggie said, 'though another day I might like the bacon. I feel utterly spoiled, lying here being waited on. I ought to be up helping all of you with the patients...'

'Sister Foster won't let you do that for ages yet,' Veronica said. 'You're our special guest and she's determined to look after you.'

'I'm sorry you were in trouble yesterday because you fetched me that tea...'

'Oh, I'm used to it,' Veronica told her with a rueful smile. 'Sister Jenkins is lovely, but most of the others are very strict. I suppose I deserve it. I do get a bit forgetful at times...'

'It's just getting used to the routine of the hospital,' Maggie told her with a smile. 'They threw us in at the deep end over there and I know I made lots of mistakes. Some of the senior nurses were awful to the new girls – but Sister Mayhew was wonderful. Her regime was strict, but she helped you rather than criticised all the time. I know she got me through a bad time. She is the Matron of three field hospitals now.'

'She sounds lovely,' Veronica said wistfully. 'I keep hoping they will send me to the Front once I've qualified...'

'If you wait for your full training, the war may be over,' Maggie said thoughtfully. 'A friend of mine told me he thinks things are going our way at last. He is an important man who knows quite a lot about the situation over there.'

'You know so many people...' Veronica sighed. 'Captain Morgan asked me so many questions about you. He wanted to know who you are and why you'd been given the annexe. It was always his favourite place, because not many of the men use it and he likes to be on his own.'

'I thought it might be something like that – he seemed so annoyed to find me here.'

'He thought of it as his room, I'm afraid,' Veronica told her and then gave a little giggle. 'I'd better fetch your breakfast or Sister Foster will have my guts for garters.'

Maggie laughed and the nurse went out. She was feeling so much better that she went into the little room, which had a toilet and a basin, and gave herself a strip wash, before going back to her bedroom to dress. It was sheer luxury to have a toilet and basin to herself! She'd had to book her turn to have a bath at the field hospital and the toilets often had queues outside, which could be difficult if you had a tummy upset, which so many of the girls had when they first got there and were not acclimatised to the food and conditions. The unwritten rule was that if someone was in dire need, you just waved them to the head of the queue and waited your turn. Maggie had known some of the nurses to squat down behind the accommodations huts if they just wanted to pass water.

When Veronica returned with her breakfast, she offered to give her a bed bath but looked pleased when Maggie told her she had already washed. 'You can have a bath twice a week, but we'll have to book your time, because otherwise you'll have the men banging at the door when you get in. A lot of them just leave it unlocked and the others just barge in!'

'What times do they like to bathe?'

'Mostly mornings, seven until ten, and evenings, eight until ten.'

'Then I'll have a bath in the morning about eleven, if that is all right?'

Veronica nodded. 'I'll take you there the first time and show you the ropes.'

'Where else can I go – or is most of it reserved for the men?'

'I think you should stay away from their day and games rooms,' Veronica said and made a wry face. 'The language can be pretty... well, fruity, my father would say. It doesn't shock me because I have four brothers.'

'Oh, lucky you,' Maggie said and laughed as she saw the nurse's look. 'Or not, as the case may be!'

'They bossed me around – I was little sister and they all tried to keep me safe, I suppose...' Her smile faded. 'They're all out there fighting at the Front and my father is worried to death over them. I keep thinking about if they're wounded...'

'If they are taken to a field hospital, they will get all the care you would give them yourself,' Maggie told her and pressed her hand sympathetically. 'Sometimes, we couldn't save their lives, but we did all we could to make their passing easier.'

'Yes, I know...' Veronica swallowed hard. 'Everyone has someone out there – but it would kill Dad if he lost them. My mother is very brave. She says she is proud of them and me, but we have to do whatever we think right.'

'She sounds wonderful,' Maggie said wistfully. 'My father was wonderful. I adored him. My mother...' She shook her head. 'She wasn't the same.'

'Oh, poor you,' Veronica said. 'I know I've been very lucky.' She smiled. 'I love this job. You meet such lovely people.' She had been moving round the room, tidying it as they talked but, now she looked at Maggie and nodded. 'Someone will come for the tray. I have to help Sister Foster for a while, but you can ring if you need me – oh, and you can go out into the garden, as you're dressed, but don't walk too far. I think you have some books to read, but we do have a library. It is just down the hall to your left. There are some newspapers and magazines as well.'

'Thank you – now get off, or you'll be in trouble.'

'Yes, I shall,' Nurse Veronica smiled and left Maggie to finish her breakfast.

It was a nice sunny day and she decided to venture into the rose garden a bit later, but first she would write some letters and then perhaps Nurse Veronica would post them.

9

It was Sunday morning and Marion was at home cooking lunch with her sister-in-law, Sarah, and her younger sister Kathy. Sarah had bought a nice plump roasting chicken as a treat for them all and they'd prepared the vegetables and Yorkshire pudding together before she took her son for a walk in his pushchair.

'I'll be back in time to help you set the table and serve,' she'd promised, but Kathy had told her she would do the table, because Sarah enjoyed her walks to the small green a few streets away where the council had recently set up a couple of benches and the young mothers would congregate with their children and the little ones could enjoy playing on the grass. There were no swings or slides there, but someone always had a ball or a hoop and the children made their own games.

Milly, Marion's youngest sister, had gone next door to Mrs Jackson, who Milly had adopted as her granny. It was convenient living next door to her husband's family, as they were always on hand to help out with Milly, who loved going there. When she came running into the kitchen, looking excited, Marion knew something nice had happened. She turned in anticipation and the next moment the tall figure of her husband came striding in the kitchen door.

'Reggie's here!' Milly announced; she'd obviously been warned not to say anything but was bursting to tell.

Marion crossed the room in hurried steps and was met in two strides to be swept up in her husband's arms and soundly kissed.

'You didn't let us know you were out of hospital,' Marion said breathlessly as he finally let her go. 'But I'm so glad you're here – how are you? Have you been next door?'

'Not yet. I wanted to see my wife.' He pulled her into his arms hungrily and she knew he was feeling fine. 'I miss you so much, love...'

'I bet I miss you more,' Marion said. She called to Kathy, who was pointedly keeping her head down and reading the book she'd borrowed from the library. 'Watch the dinner, Kathy love. I'm just going to show Reggie something upstairs.'

Taking Reggie's hand, she led him up the stairs, and once alone in the bedroom that was now theirs, she threw herself into his arms and they kissed passionately, before stripping their clothes off feverishly. Their loving was urgent, satisfying and wonderful – and noisy. Marion giggled as she cuddled up to him afterwards.

'I'm sure Milly wonders what on earth is happening,' she said and stroked the back of his neck. 'Oh, Reggie, it is so good to have you here. We've had hardly any time together since we married. How long have you got – your letter said several weeks?'

'Yes, it's true.' Reggie's smile lit up his face. 'I'm here for a month at least,' he said. 'I've done three tours of duty and they've sent me home for a rest – and training. I'm not sure what happens when that is over. I think I'll be here in England for three months at least, but I'll be away and visiting at weekends after my month's leave.'

'A whole month,' Marion sighed with pleasure. 'I've got two weeks holiday due – I'm going to ask if I can take it all now.'

'Yes, do that and we'll go away for a few days to the sea,' Reggie said, looking pleased. 'Your sister-in-law and my mother can manage here and it is time we had a decent holiday together.'

Marion leaned over and kissed him on the lips. 'This is the best present I've ever had,' she said. 'A whole month of having you here with me every night...'

'It's what I've dreamed of,' Reggie said and kissed her again. He lifted his head from the pillow. 'I can hear a child screaming. Sarah must be home and they will be wanting their lunch.'

'Yes,' Marion sighed. 'I suppose we'd better go down.'

'And I should visit Ma,' Reggie said and smiled.

'We've got plenty of time to be together now, Reggie.'

'We'll have two weeks at the sea somewhere and then we can stay in bed all morning if we want,' Reggie promised and pulled her from the bed.

Marion laughed. She'd never been for a proper holiday before; their honeymoon had been sweet but short and now the future glowed with promise. Reggie home for a whole month and a real holiday; it was almost too good to be true...

* * *

Mrs Bailey smiled and agreed to arrange Marion's leave from that Friday for two weeks. She said she understood how important and exciting it was for her to be given such a treat and told Marion that she would arrange cover for her.

'Mr Stockbridge will give me one of the girls from the ground floor as a temporary assistant,' she said. 'You deserve a treat if anyone does, Mrs Jackson. I am happy for you.'

Marion thanked her and took her station behind the hat counter. Life was so much better these days. It had started to improve when she got to know Reggie, but he'd had to join the Army; then Sarah had come along and it was because of her brother's wife that she could take this holiday alone with her husband.

'Of course, I'll look after the others,' she'd said when Marion told her of their plans. 'I know Reggie's mother would have Milly, but I can look after things here. Besides, Kathy is a wonderful help.'

'Yes, I know. She wants to leave school this summer and train to be a cook. I think she may as well, because it will be a good job for her – and she's been told about a job at a small hotel locally. It isn't much money for a start, but she will learn a craft that will always be of use to her.'

Sarah had nodded. 'She still says she will never marry. I've tried telling her she'll meet someone, but she won't listen.'

Marion nodded, feeling anxious as she thought about Kathy's reasons for saying she would never marry. At almost sixteen she was too young to make such a decision buy it was because of the way their father had treated Ma. Kathy had taken her death hard and that worried Marion. Would her younger sister's future happiness be forever blighted by their father's cruelty? Kathy insisted that she was going to learn to be a really first-class cook and it was all she wanted of life, but Marion knew she would miss out on so much if she never allowed herself to love or marry. She might lead a busy and fulfilling life for some time, but in the end, she would be lonely.

Seeing a customer approach, Marion thrust aside her personal concern for her sister.

The customer was young and wore that bewildered but happy look common to brides searching for their trousseau. If she was not mistaken, this young woman was about to choose a hat for her going-away outfit...

* * *

Rachel watched as Marion Jackson sold three beautiful hats to the young woman and carefully wrapped them. The bride-to-be was glowing with happiness but so was Marion. The pleasure of having her husband home and the prospect of her first real holiday at the sea had lit her up from inside.

Where had the excitement and joy gone from her own marriage? Rachel wondered why things had gone wrong between her and William these past few months. For a start, they'd seemed to be truly happy and Rachel had longed for him to come back from the war. When he'd returned injured, he'd seemed to be as loving as before, but, recently, she'd noticed a change. He seldom had much to say when she got home in the evenings and several times recently, he'd told her he was dining at his club with friends.

Rachel was aware that men of William's class did dine at their clubs sometimes. However, he'd broken with his family and had seemed to have no interest in them or his club until recently. It was unlike him and she was worried, because she'd never known him to be so reserved. Had she done something to anger him without realising?

Her thoughts were recalled to the present as Sally Harper entered the department and walked to greet her. 'Rachel, how are you?' her employer asked. 'I see this department is still busy...'

'We're fortunate that our stock hasn't been much affected by the shortages,' Rachel replied and smiled. 'Perhaps the Government knows the ladies need a new hat to keep them happy.'

'I think it's more a matter of what needs to be imported,' Sally told her. 'Hats are easily sourced and supplied here, most of the materials are home-made, of course. The silks and velvets we got from abroad are in short supply, but the English felts and straws seem quite adequate for now – I just wish we had more of the raw materials we need for other goods here. I've always bought as much made-in-England produce as I could, but some metals and hardwoods are in short supply and I miss the Venetian glass we used to stock.'

'Yes, it must be so difficult for you,' Rachel sympathised.

'Oh, I shouldn't moan,' Sally Harper said and smiled. 'I'm lucky. Ben isn't fighting and he's been home for a few days – and I have good friends and my lovely daughter.'

'Yes, you are lucky in those things,' Rachel agreed and something in her voice made Sally look at her and ask her if anything was wrong. 'Oh no,' she lied. 'I'm perfectly fine... Have you heard from Maggie recently? I wrote to her last week, but I haven't heard a word.'

Her question diverted Sally's curiosity. 'Perhaps you sent it to the hospital and she didn't get it before they moved her to the convalescent home. I had a letter just this morning. Maggie says she's getting up and spending some time in the rose gardens. She says it is lovely there and she feels *she* ought to be looking after the men, who are far more seriously ill than she is.'

'That sounds like our Maggie,' Rachel said and nodded. 'Yes, I did write to her at the hospital, but I thought she would've got it before she moved. Perhaps I'll write again to the convalescent home.'

'Yes – though there may be a letter waiting for you when you get home this evening.'

A customer headed for the counter then and Sally moved away to speak to Marion Jackson. She was smiling and agreeing with whatever Sally was saying and Rachel turned her attention to her customer, who was a gentleman she'd served before.

He smiled at her. 'I bought my wife a bag and a gold bracelet for her birthday here and she was delighted. I wondered if you could help me find a suitable present for our ninth wedding anniversary please...'

'Yes, of course,' Rachel replied smiling. 'What would you like to see?'

She was busy serving him for the next twenty minutes, after which he bought a gold locket and chain and departed looking pleased. Rachel tidied her counter and noted the sale in her stock book just as Marion Jackson came up to her.

'Mrs Harper asked me about the new window display. I told her what I'd thought of and also that I would be taking my holiday from Friday if it was possible, so she asked me to change the window on Thursday and explain my idea to the team this afternoon at three – when she will be holding a meeting.'

Rachel nodded. 'You'd best have your lunch now then so you'll be back in time to get ready for the meeting.'

'Thank you,' Marion said and went off clearly happy.

Rachel frowned to herself. She wished Mr Marco was still in charge of the window displays, because it took up more and more of Marion Jackson's time. Not that she begrudged the young woman the pleasure of helping with the window displays, but it made her short-handed on the department floor. Perhaps she would speak to Mr Stockbridge about getting an extra salesgirl on the floor. After all, they were one of the busier departments these days and it was foolish to risk losing sales because there was no one on a counter.

Rachel sent Shirley Jones to the hats counter and the new

junior to scarves. Her next customer was an older lady, who spent an hour looking at bags and jewellery and bought nothing. By the time Marion Jackson returned and the younger girls had gone to lunch, Rachel had forgotten the mood of sadness that had possessed her earlier. Perhaps she was just imagining it and she would try talking to William over dinner that evening.

10

Marco read the message he'd decoded again and frowned. London was recalling him. They were sending his replacement out and he was to organise the reception party to introduce the new agent to the group he'd set up and led for the past eighteen months or more. He felt a flicker of frustration. Why was he being recalled? He'd done everything his London contacts had asked, causing mayhem for the German patrols that tried to cross the border at the dead of night and get behind the Allied lines; they'd even managed to sabotage an enemy ammunition dump – so why order him back to England?

Marco looked up as Sadie entered the room. He smiled at her because she looked lovely with her young son struggling in her arms. She set little Pierre on his feet and he made a beeline for Marco.

'Pap ... pap...' he said and held out his arms.

Marco bent to pick the chubby little boy up and set him on his lap. He smelled delightfully of soap and a powder Sadie put on his skin and he chuckled as Marco lifted him. It still gave him pain in his side, but he gritted his teeth and ignored it as the little boy patted his face.

'You're getting heavy,' Marco told the little boy but swung him high in the air, holding him above his head for a few moments as he giggled with glee. 'What has Mummy been feeding you?' He put the child down and Pierre clung to his leg.

'Marie's bread and honey,' Sadie said and then frowned. 'Is something wrong? Marie said you were annoyed by the message that came through today?'

'You're not supposed to know about secret things like a message from London,' Marco told her, but he knew there were no secrets between Sadie and Marie. 'Not that it matters, because I was going to tell you – they have ordered me back to England and I'll be leaving next week when my replacement arrives.'

Sadie looked devastated. 'Why – why do you have to go back? We'll miss you, Pierre and I—'

'You could come with me,' Marco said. 'I know you don't want to marry me so I'll set you up in a decent home of your own.'

'I told you I didn't want that—' She hesitated, then, as he frowned, '—I'll live with you as my husband if you like... Pierre thinks you're his father. I don't know where he got the word from, but he calls you Papa or pap pap...'

'You want me to be your husband?' Marco grinned. 'You know I love Pierre and I can do the father bit. I'm not sure I can make you happy in bed...'

'It doesn't matter about that,' Sadie said and blushed. 'You told me the truth, Marco, but you also said we could live as husband and wife in other ways...'

'I thought you said no,' Marco remembered it quite clearly a few days after his initial offer. 'I don't want to make you unhappy...'

'I know I said no for a start, but I've thought it over, and I think it could work. I may be able do my nursing part-time, if I can find a clinic willing to take on a married nurse – my mother would look after Pierre for a few hours a day.'

'I told you, there's no need for you to work,' Marco frowned. 'I don't know why I'm being recalled. They may send me some-where else.'

'Yes, I know – but I do want to go home and this is the only way I have a chance of a decent life.' Her cheeks were hot. 'I'm sorry, Marco. You've been kind to me and that sounds as if I'm just using you – but you know I like you a lot...'

'Yes. I'm fond of you and the boy, Sadie. And I owe this to Pierre even if I didn't think you were a good person who deserved a better life. We'll have a civil marriage and if you ever meet someone you could love, I'll give you your freedom.'

'I don't deserve your kindness,' Sadie said. 'You didn't force Pierre to give his life to save yours. He had a choice and so do I – my son adores you and I'm comfortable with you. I said no at the start, because I thought it unfair to you. Why should you be saddled with me and a child you didn't father?'

'I thought it was something like that,' Marco said and smiled wryly. 'Don't bother about me, Sadie. If I can do something for you, it makes my life worthwhile.'

'Your life is worth a great deal. You've done so much out here – Marie and the others think the world of you...'

Marco shrugged, dismissing the praise. 'Then we'll be married and I'll take you back with me.'

* * *

The wedding ceremony was brief, but the reception was a big family party that was held under the trees in the orchard as a fierce July sun blazed overhead. Marie invited all her friends and also Marco's group.

'It is a farewell to you and my Sadie,' she told him, tears in her eyes. 'I shall miss you all – and the little one will leave a hole in my heart. Sadie will come back to see us once the war is over, she has promised – and you must too, Marcel. You are family...' She kissed both cheeks and he gave her a warm hug.

'You are family to me too,' Marco told her. Sometimes he felt as if he were her cousin Marcel. 'I'll come whenever I can, I promise – whether it's before the war ends or afterwards.'

Marie had fed them and the party had drunk the rich red local wine, many of them a little unsteady on their feet as they went off to bed later. Sadie and Marco shared a bedroom that night, but he slept on top of the covers and when Pierre woke and cried in the night, it was Marco who comforted him. Sadie watched him sleepily and thanked him.

In the morning, they left with Andre in the lorry he'd brought to take them to the rendezvous. As expected, the British sailors waiting to take them on board a small rowing boat baulked at the idea of a woman and child, but Marco insisted.

'She is the widow of a war hero and her life is in danger if she stays,' he told them. 'Give her and the child my cabin when we get to the ship and I'll stay on deck... it's either that or I stay here to protect her.'

The threat worked and after Marco had introduced Andre and the others to his replacement, he shook hands with him and boarded the boat, which was anxious to leave for the ship anchored off-shore. Lingering in these waters was dangerous because they were vulnerable to attack both from the air and German U-boats.

Marco left France without a backward glance, his gaze on Sadie, who was nervously holding tight to Pierre. He was fortunately sleeping and when it came to climbing the rope ladder, Marco took the boy and tucked him inside his greatcoat, fastening his belt around himself and the child to keep him secure as he climbed. Once on board, Sadie and the child were taken below and Marco went to speak to the captain, who looked annoyed because his orders hadn't included a woman and child. However, he just grunted that Marco should stay out of the crew's way and barked an order to get underway.

Fortunately, the journey back to England was a fast safe one, unendangered by storms or enemy shipping. Some clouds looked heavy in the skies but served only to help them hide from any lurking hunters and the summer storm held off. On disembarking, Marco thanked the crew and gave one of them a bottle of French brandy for helping Sadie by giving her some food for the child. He took them on to the quayside where he was looking for some form of transport when a man dressed in a dark suit tapped him on the shoulder.

'Your car is waiting, Captain Marco. I've been told to take you straight to headquarters in London.'

'You can drop my wife and child off on the way,' Marco said. He looked at Sadie. 'I'll give you my keys and money. You go to my place and make yourself comfortable until I come. Take a taxi after we drop you off and wait until I return...' He'd explained where he lived and given her the written address. Sadie was a resourceful young woman and he had no doubt she would settle in easily enough by herself, though he would have gone with her had his orders not been otherwise.

The official frowned. 'This is most irregular, sir. I wasn't told about this.'

'What I've been doing for the past two years or more is irregular,' Marco said. 'I had to get my wife out of France, so I brought her back with me.'

The official nodded and led the way to a black car, opening the back door for them to get in.

Marco let Sadie slide in and then gave her Pierre, who was awake and grizzling. When he was in the car and the door shut, he took Pierre and started to tickle him. The grizzling stopped and he started giggling.

'Get some food before you go home,' Marco told Sadie. 'You'll need milk and a few things. I'll get you whatever else you need once we're settled, though you'll miss Marie's food. I'm not sure that you will find as much as you'd like here...'

'I've still got my nursing cards,' Sadie said. 'I think the shops will let me have food once I show them what I was doing before Pierre was born.'

Marco nodded. He'd kept abreast of things while he was in France and though there was no rationing here as yet, he understood that some foods were difficult to buy. The bread was different to what they'd been used to pre-war and pretty awful, he'd been told. On the farm, they'd been self-sufficient and were used to good ham, cheese and milk, as well as Marie's own honey, wine and the preserves she made from fruit grown locally. Sadie was unlikely to find food as good here in the city at present.

Once in London, Marco handed over the keys to his apartment, made sure Sadie had the address and gave her a generous supply of money, before dropping her off. She was carrying a rucksack with a few of her own and Pierre's things. Marco would need to buy her new clothes and the boy, too, as soon as he'd been briefed and allowed to return to his home. He just wished he knew what was so urgent!

* * *

'We brought you back because we were informed your cover had been breached,' Marco's liaison officer told him half an hour later. 'We needed to get you out fast for the sake of the group – and the people at the farm.'

'If they know about me, they will know that Marie and her mother have been helping me...' Marco frowned. 'Why didn't you tell me so that I could warn them?'

'You would have tried to get them away and we needed them to stay until you were safely away,' Major Bryant told him. 'Andre will get them out and the group will reform elsewhere.'

Marco glared at him. 'I should've been told.' His thoughts were dark. If the enemy arrived at the farm to find him gone, their anger would fall on the defenceless women. 'You had no right to risk their lives.'

'They know the risks and Andre is still there. After he picked you up, his men would have moved the family to safety.'

'They will lose their home and their living!'

'That's war,' the major said. 'Someone out there betrayed them – and you. You're lucky we got wind of it and moved you out.' He frowned. 'Look here, Pershing is demanding upwards of three million men to prosecute this war. Think of all the lives that will be at risk and then you'll understand that one family couldn't be allowed to get in the way of things. You know too much to let the enemy take you alive. Don't say you wouldn't break under torture – most do.'

Marco bit his tongue. There was a lot he could say, but what was the use? Either Andre had got the family away or he hadn't; Marco could do nothing. He felt like telling Bryant to go to Hell, but that would get him nowhere.

'What do you want from me now?'

'We feel you've done enough for now,' Major Bryant said and

stared at him hard. 'If we have a job for you, we'll know where you are.'

'And where is that?' Marco was puzzled.

'At Harpers store, I imagine. You may be asked to work with Ben Harper in the future and it is far better that you return to your old job until we decide what to do with you.'

'I would prefer to be sent to a fighting unit,' Marco protested.

'Unfortunately, your preferences are not of paramount importance,' Major Bryant said and glared at him. 'You risked your life once too often, Captain, and we wanted you back here. To be frank, you could have been a liability with all your contacts. However, you have been useful in the past and we may need you again. So, you will damn well stay here until we decide if we can use you elsewhere. Oh, by the way, you're being given a distinguished medal, though I'm damned if I know why.'

Marco was seething inside. For two pins he would have launched himself at the sneering major, but he held the anger inside, aware that he was being provoked. They wanted to see if his tour of duty had changed him, made him less reliable – if he'd lost his nerve. He said nothing and saw a smile of satisfaction on the major's face.

Finding himself dismissed, Marco left the office and caught a taxi. He went to Harpers and asked to see either Ben or Sally Harper. Sally was in the office and she gave a scream of delight as she saw him.

'Marco! You're back! Thank God.'

'Is Ben anywhere around?'

'He's away, but he rang this morning and said he'll be home tonight.' She smiled at him. 'You look tired – are you all right?'

'I had a wound in my side, but I'm fine now.' He returned her smile. 'I need to buy some food and clothes for my family. They don't have much...'

'Your family?' Sally looked startled but quickly got to her feet. 'What do you need? Take anything you want from any of the departments.'

'I can pay – or I can when I get to the bank,' Marco said. 'My wife and child will need everything because we couldn't bring much with us. I've been stood down by the War Office, Mrs Harper, and told to work here until I'm needed again.'

'Yes – well, that's good news for us. We've missed you,' Sally said. 'I insist that you take whatever you need today and it is a gift. You deserve that.'

'You always were too clever for us to keep secrets from you,' Marco said, nodding. 'I do need your help because I have a wife and a small child to clothe and equip and I haven't a clue what they need.'

'Harpers' girls will,' she smiled. Sally Harper took the news of his marriage in her stride, though she was well aware of Marco's previous love life. 'Tell my heads of departments what you're looking for and they will give you whatever you need.'

'You're a lovely person, Sally Harper,' Marco said. 'Thank you and I accept. Pierre is just over a year old and Sadie is a size 36 hip, I believe. We couldn't bring much with us – and Sadie is British born, but Pierre was born in France.'

Sally placed a finger to her lips. 'You don't need to tell me a thing – but do bring them in to meet me and we'll find a few nice things for them both. There isn't as much good-quality stock as there was, but we still have rails more than half full.'

'Well done,' Marco replied with a smile. 'Please tell Ben I'd like to see him when he gets back.'

'Of course. I'll come with you and inform the heads of department of my wishes,' Sally said. 'So, when will you be starting work for us again?'

'Next Monday,' he replied. 'I'll need a few days at home to get things settled, make sure Sadie is comfortable, and then I'll be here as usual.'

'Everyone will be so glad to have you back, even if it is temporary,' Sally told him. 'I still can't believe you're here...'

Marco couldn't either. It felt unreal to be here in this fashionable London store instead of on a farm in France planning how best to attack the enemy patrols. He wondered whether Marie and Maman had got away safely and prayed they had. Perhaps one day, when this wretched war was over, he could go back and visit them...

11

Maggie was feeling so much better that morning when she went out into the rose garden. It was late July now and the sun was shining warmly, making her feel good to be alive. The nightmare of France, with the constant booming of the guns in the distance and the stench from the latrines and the overpowering stuffiness of tents packed with sick and dying men, seemed almost a dream now in this peaceful haven.

When she saw the man sitting in the rose garden in his wheel-chair, she almost turned back because he'd glared at her on each occasion that they'd passed each other in the gardens.

'You don't have to leave. I don't bite...' the harsh voice said as she hesitated. 'You can come and sit on the bench, Maggie Gibbs. I know you want to...'

Maggie walked to the bench and sat looking at him. In her hand she carried the novel she'd intended to read.

'I didn't want to intrude. I know you like to be alone.'

'You know nothing about me, young woman. Don't imagine you do, just because you were a nurse in France and they're giving you a medal for outstanding service to the cause.' He spoke as if he were old, but it was only in spirit; his young body was broken and damaged, robbing him of the vitality he should have felt at his age.

'Who told you that?' she asked but knew it would be Nurse Veronica.

'Don't you know all the men here are in love with you?' he said, a sneer on a face that would be handsome without it. Despite his obvious wounds to his legs and the arm that gave him pain, which often showed despite his attempts to hide it, his face was still untouched. 'All of them except me...' he added bitterly.

'I think you like to mock me,' Maggie said and gave him a long searching look. In France, the men had all declared they were in love with all the nurses. It was just gratitude, combined with a rough humour, and the nurses either ignored it or smiled and went along with the joke. 'I didn't ask to be brought here, you know – nor did I want to steal your annexe.'

'It's only on loan,' he told her brusquely. 'You'll leave and go home. I'll still be here and I'll get it back...'

'Surely, you will go home one day,' Maggie objected. She knew, because Veronica had told her, that he was healed as much as he could be. He'd lost the use of his legs, because his spine had been damaged and might never heal, and his arm would probably always give him some pain, but his heart was strong and he should be able to go home and lead his own life – yet she also knew from her experience nursing the men in France that his mind had raw wounds that might never go away.

'My old friends can't bear to look me in the eye, my fiancée stood me up and my father doesn't understand that I can't go back there. He says he can get a nurse to live in and that if I try, I can live almost a normal life... Normal! Stuck in this damned thing?' His face twisted with pain and anger. 'How the hell can I go home and live when I can't ride the land like I used to and I need someone to help me get to the bloody toilet?'

'A nurse would do that,' Maggie told him patiently. 'In time, if you exercise, you may be able to use a pulley to lift you into bed and things like that, perhaps even walk with crutches...' She wasn't sure about that, but damaged nerves did heal eventually, and she'd seen some miraculous recoveries in her two years of nursing.

'Oh, thanks,' he retorted sarcastically. 'That is something to look forward to...what about all the rest of it? Marriage, love and sex... That's made you blush, hasn't it?' He laughed unpleasantly, clearly pleased by his power to distress her. 'Are you still a virgin then? You must be the only one to have nursed over there and come back untouched. What are you, a saint?'

Why was he so angry with her? Maggie didn't understand. Surely, this wasn't all about the annexe?

She looked him straight in the eyes. 'The man I loved was shot down over the sea. He died in the freezing water serving King and country...' Maggie said, staring him down. 'I had friends, but no one I loved after that.'

She wondered for a moment what had happened to Mick O'Sullivan, the Irish tunneller who had been so kind to her, but she hadn't heard from him for ages. She'd really liked him, but she hadn't had a chance to discover if it might become more. Before she'd truly recovered from Tim's death, Mick had been sent somewhere else with his band of tunnellers and she knew their lives were precarious. His letters had come for a few months and then stopped – her mind closed then, because she didn't want to think of him dead.

She looked at Captain Morgan without flinching. 'I'm not a saint, but I haven't found anyone else to love.'

He surprised her by relaxing into a softer mood, his tone

sympathetic now. 'I shouldn't have said that, Maggie – and I'm sorry you lost your lover.'

'So am I,' she said and opened her book, but the words blurred on the page and she was aware that she was crying. She hadn't done that for ages. 'Sorry, I suppose I'm still weak from my illness...'

'My fault...' he said and stuck his hand out. 'I'm Colin Morgan and I'm an ass and rude with it.'

'Yes, you are,' Maggie said, but the look on his face made her laugh and she took his hand. His fingers closed about hers, holding her firmly but without intent to harm. 'It doesn't matter – it was quite a while ago.'

'You don't get over your first love,' Colin replied, his mouth hard. 'Mine was called Charlotte and she rejected me when she discovered I couldn't ever walk again or have kids. She said she wanted a man not a cabbage.'

'That was cruel of her,' Maggie said. 'You're not a cabbage. Your mind is sharp, you're just stuck in a wheelchair for the present. Besides, sex isn't everything. You could adopt a child if you wanted; there are lots of them needing homes...'

'Yeah – a home with a cripple. Some future to look forward to...' he said, the bitterness back in his voice.

'You know your trouble, you've let her win,' Maggie said, understanding that it was his girl's rejection more than his injuries that had soured him. 'Stop feeling sorry for yourself and fight. You don't know how much you can do until you try. Get strong again and perhaps you'll have a better life than you imagine, you might even learn to walk again. Some men who were badly wounded have done it...' She got to her feet to walk away, but he caught her wrist as she attempted to pass him.

'Please don't go, Maggie. You're the only one I want to talk to –

the only one who understands, because you've lost someone too...'

Maggie nodded. She'd mourned Tim hard, pushing herself to the limit and refusing to take leave, almost willing herself to the point of death in her grief. So, she understood his pain, far more than he could know. She placed her book on his lap and took hold of the handles of his chair. 'Come on, it's a lovely day, let's walk down to the lake.'

'You can't push me all that way.'

'Who says I can't?' Maggie demanded. 'I want to visit it and you know the way – so I'll have a damned good try.'

* * *

Later that afternoon, Maggie sat reading the book she'd neglected until lunchtime. It had tired her to push Captain Morgan to the lake, but, seeing that, he'd wheeled himself most of the way back. Before that, he'd asked her if she would let him sit with her in the annexe on rainy days and she'd agreed he could.

'Sister Foster will give me an ear-bashing if she catches us,' he said with a grin, 'but I like you, Maggie. I'll be seeing you...'

She'd smiled back. His smile was charming when he chose and although he was prone to moods, Colin Morgan was a man you could not help liking. She had learned that day that he had a sense of humour and was thoughtful in many ways. Before the war he'd been planning a career in cricket, at which he had once been very good, so Nurse Veronica had told her.

'His father is wealthy – they have a big house and land. He was intended to spend a few years playing cricket and then take over the running of the estate from his father. As far as Sir Edmund Morgan is concerned, his son will still take over the estate in time. He sees no reason why he cannot employ someone to drive him around the estate in a pony and trap.'

'Perhaps he will in time, but he needs space to heal in his mind as well as his body,' Maggie said then. 'Some men can't wait to get back to their old lives, others just want vengeance on the enemy – and others give up.'

'We thought Captain Morgan was one of those for a while,' Nurse Veronica had told her as she tidied Maggie's room. 'However, Sister says she's seen an improvement in his attitude recently.'

'As I said, it needs time,' Maggie had replied. Yet that day was the first she'd seen him smile properly at her. It was after they'd witnessed the heron rising from the lake and watched a family of ducks squabbling as the swans drifted majestically by.

'This was a good idea of yours,' he'd told her then and smiled in a completely natural way.

Now, she looked up as her door was abruptly swung open and Colin Morgan entered scowling up at her from his chair for all he was worth.

He gave her a belligerent look as she laid down her book. 'You said I could come...' he said ungraciously.

Maggie might have pointed out that the arrangement had been he could use her sitting room when it was raining and the sun was still shining, but she didn't. Captain Morgan was clearly angry and she wondered whether she should ask what had caused his mood but decided against it.

'It's him...' he burst out. 'I was feeling better – happier after our walk to the lake – but then he came. I've told him I don't want to see him, but he won't leave me alone.'

'Your father?' Maggie knew she'd guessed right when he looked directly at her.

'He wants me to go home and have a live-in nurse who can

wheel me about. There's a male nurse who could lift me into the trap and drive me around the estate... as if I was a lump of wood with no feelings and no brain.'

'Wouldn't you rather go home than stay here for years on end?' Maggie felt sympathy for his plight as she saw the conflicting emotions in his face. 'I'll be glad to leave when they let me go home... even though it is beautiful here. I didn't know places like this existed.'

'You can walk and do whatever you want – get married, have a family. I can't do any of those things.' His voice was acrid with bitterness and Maggie winced.

'I'm not sure I want to,' she said. 'I think losing people you love hurts too much.'

'And you ask me why I don't want to go back there?'

'Would the memories be too much there?' Maggie asked and saw the answer in his face. 'Then tell your father – explain that you need time to grieve and get over your loss. Tell him you want to live somewhere else.'

'How could I do that? Where?' he shot the questions at her fiercely.

'Wherever you want,' she said. 'Perhaps a service flat some-where and a nurse or housekeeper to look after you. It doesn't have to be a man. You could employ a woman if you wished, I'm sure.'

Colin Morgan looked at her oddly. 'Yes, I could. I have a legacy from my great-aunt. She left me her house and money. It's in South London...'

'There you are then,' Maggie said. 'You don't have to ask permission, just do what you want.'

He laughed and for a moment she saw the carefree young man he must have been before he went to war. 'You make things seem so easy, Maggie Gibbs.'

'I didn't say it would be easy, just that you could do it if you really wished.'

He nodded, a thoughtful look in his eyes. 'What were you reading when I arrived? Is it a romance?'

Maggie smiled and showed him. 'It's the story of Tristan and Iseult. My father bought it for me when I was fourteen. I've read it many times.'

'It is a tragic love story,' he said and smiled. 'But it's better than a lot of the silly stuff that was written last century. At least it isn't a Gothic novel – that's what most girls read, if they read at all.'

'Not the girls I know,' Maggie said with a challenging look. 'They usually go for romance or family stories.'

'May I borrow this?' Captain Morgan asked, picking up her book. 'I promise I'll return it.'

'Yes – but it means a lot to me so don't lose it,' Maggie said.

'Thanks.' He grinned at her and glanced at his pocket watch. 'I'll take it and get out of your way before tea. I'll return this as I found it.'

Maggie allowed him to take her book. She wouldn't have loaned it to everyone, but she believed that he would return it without damage. He was a strange, moody man but she understood that he had yet to come to terms with what his life would be now, and who could blame him? He'd had a wonderful future mapped out and it had all been taken from him. Maggie had lost everything too. She'd been content at Harpers and in love, but then she'd done what she felt was right and proper by volunteering and the war had robbed her of Tim's love and the promise of marriage.

She had a lot in common with Colin, but she hadn't let her loss make her bitter and that was the difference. It would be good if she could help him to recover from his terrible regret.

12

Marion had been delighted to see Mr Marco back at Harpers before she left for her holiday with Reggie. She knew that he would be in charge of the windows for the foreseeable future and that meant she could go away and not feel she was leaving her employers in the lurch.

'It's a good thing he's back,' Reggie agreed when she told him, 'but that job of yours is only for as long as you need it, Marion love. Once the war is over and I'm home, you can give up work altogether and stay home to look after our family.'

Reggie was clearly thinking that they would have children soon and Marion wanted that too. She'd always had to go to work and had never thought much about when she would stay at home. Most men wanted their wives to stop going out to work once they married and she supposed she should have expected it, but she was a little bit sad to think she would need to say goodbye to Harpers. She'd got on well with everyone and loved serving customers with beautiful hats, particularly brides-to-be, but it was natural that Reggie should want his wife at home, particularly when their children were small. Of course, she might never fall for a baby, and if she didn't, Reggie might change his mind.

Marion dismissed the faint niggle at the back of her mind. Some of the women she knew at Harpers were married, but they didn't have small children – except for Mrs Harper. However, Mrs Harper was different to most women and had a responsible job that no one seemed to think she ought to give up because she'd had a baby.

* * *

Her first visit to a seaside hotel in Yarmouth took all Marion's thoughts concerning Harpers clean away and she relaxed, enjoying lovely long walks along the promenade and on the pier with Reggie. The war, which the newspapers told them was now costing more than seven million pounds a day – an unbelievable sum to someone who earned just a few pounds a week – seemed far away.

It was warm and fun and the days seemed to fly by as they spent their time in a haze of love and excitement. For a young couple parted so soon after their wedding by the war, this was a time of wonder and getting to know each other. As they ate bags of chips flavoured with lots of salt and vinegar or toffee apples on the beach, they explored each other's thoughts and Marion discovered that Reggie was looking beyond his job on the docks.

'I want my own business,' he told her and looked eager. 'I know it won't be easy for a start – but I'd like to do the carpentry for houses. In fact, I'd like to build houses. I've been thinking I might team up with Ron and start up a joint project.'

His elder brother Ron was a bricklayer and together they would have many of the skills they needed to go into the house-building business themselves. They both knew men skilled in plumbing and a couple who could do both plumbing and electrical work; they could offer their friends work with them, but their father, Mr Jackson, could turn his hand to anything in the building trade and was ready to help if they needed him. Ron had talked about it non-stop when he was home.

'It might mean we'd have to wait for a home of our own for a while,' Reggie said, looking at her to see her reaction.

'I could go on working for a while to help,' she suggested and he looked thoughtful.

'We'll see,' he said. 'It depends. I'd like you home, Marion love. You could do the book work for me and Ron – you're good with stuff like that I know.'

'Yes, I think I could manage that if you wanted me to,' she agreed and smiled. 'I don't mind waiting for our own home if it helps you get what you want, Reggie.'

'My father should've done it years ago,' Reggie said. 'He's a carpenter and a plumber by trade. Mostly did plumbing, but he says he's a jack of all trades with a lifetime of experience. I want to get on, Marion. One day we'll have a lovely house we own and we'll have a holiday every year – and maybe a little car!'

Marion allowed herself to dream. After the way she'd been brought up and the hardships her family had endured because of her father's temper and his drinking, she couldn't quite believe it would happen. Reggie wasn't like her father, she knew that, but was it too much to hope that she would actually have the things he talked about so eagerly?

As the days of their holiday passed in a haze of sunshine and pleasure, Harpers seemed a world away and Marion felt a pang of regret as the time came for them to go home and her to return to work.

Reggie didn't try to stop her going in on the first morning back, even though he held her for a long passionate kiss before allowing her to rise. He knew that she needed her job until things were more settled. When he was recalled to the war, which could be at any time, his life would be at risk again and that meant Marion might be a widow before any of his plans could happen.

'I'll see you this evening, love,' he told her. 'I'm going to do a few jobs in the house until I have to go back to camp. It could do with a bit of decorating, amongst other things.'

Marion smiled. Reggie had already done several small jobs that had been neglected for years, because money was tight. He would make things better for all of them and it would save him fretting because she was back at work.

Catching the bus in the early morning seemed hard after two weeks of being spoiled and strolling about in the sunshine or lazing in a deckchair on a sandy beach. They'd both braved the water a few times up amongst the sand dunes and enjoyed watching children riding on the donkeys on the weekends. Once the children were out of school there would be more families at the sea, but they'd often had long stretches of the beach to themselves.

Reggie had said how much his dog would have enjoyed running on the beach, looking pensive. They hadn't brought it, because dogs weren't allowed in the hotel, and Milly had adopted it, thinking of it as her pet now Reggie was in the Army.

'London is where the money for building will be,' he'd told her. 'But I wouldn't mind living at the sea, would you?'

Marion had just smiled. It was fun on the beach for a holiday, but she was a London girl and not sure she'd want to live here.

Back at work, she soon fell into a routine and happily told Shirley how lovely it had all been. She'd bought some small gifts of sweets home and gave them to the girls in her department and Mrs Bailey, who thanked her but said she shouldn't have done it.

Mr Marco came up to the department in the middle of the

morning and told her about some ideas he had for the future. He wanted to discuss them with her and she felt pleased that he actually seemed interested in her opinions.

Reggie was waiting for her when she left work that evening and they caught the bus home together. He'd distempered the kitchen for her that morning in a nice cream and it looked lovely when they got home. Sarah had made some bright cushions for the old sofa and Marion thought how different things looked to what they'd been like in her father's time, when it had all been dingy and worn.

Her father, Sam Kaye, had been in her thoughts more of late and she wondered why. He hadn't been near them since he'd caused her mother's death, which they were all pleased about. Marion hoped he would never return and Kathy still hated him.

'Ron got home this afternoon,' Reggie said as they approached their home. 'He's on a twenty-four-hour pass and I told him I'd go to the pub with him this evening so we could talk – you don't mind?'

'No, of course not,' she said and smiled at him. 'It is ages since you went to the pub with your mates. I've got plenty to do here – washing and ironing from the holiday.'

'Don't work too hard, love.'

'I'm used to it,' she said and kissed him. 'Eat your supper and then get off with your brother.'

Reggie did as she suggested and Marion got started on the piles of washing she'd brought back from her holiday. Staying in a hotel was nice, but if she'd been in a cottage, she could have done some of it while she was there and she knew there were plenty to let down there. Another time she might suggest that kind of holiday to Reggie.

It was as she was mangling the last of Reggie's things in the scullery that she heard a shout of alarm from Sarah. Rushing into the kitchen, Marion stared in disbelief at the father she'd never expected to see again. He looked as if he might be drunk and he'd made a grab at Sarah, who had picked up her sewing shears and looked as if she might defend herself if he came nearer.

'Stay away from her, Pa,' Marion commanded. 'You're not welcome in this house after what you did to Ma...'

'And isn't that a nice welcome for your old father,' he said and her worst fears were realised. He'd clearly had a skinful and was hardly aware of what he was doing. 'Here I am, bringing you money...' He pushed his hand in his pocket and came out with a few pennies that he threw on the kitchen table. If he'd ever had money to give his family, he'd done what he always did and spent it on drink. 'Where's my supper?'

'You'll get no supper here,' Marion told him and his eyes narrowed as he looked at her.

'Filthy slut,' he muttered. 'They told me you'd got another man here – I'll teach you to cheat on me...'

'I'm not your wife,' Marion said, alarmed, as he lunged at her and she only just managed to jump back out of his way. 'I'm Marion.'

'Filthy little slut,' he repeated and stood swaying on his feet.

Sarah moved towards Marion purposefully, her shears at the ready, but before anything more was said or done, the back door opened and both Reggie and Ron entered.

'Stay away from them,' Reggie warned and moved swiftly to prevent his father-in-law getting near to his wife and sister-in-law. 'Lay one finger on either of them and you'll be sorry.'

'Now then, Mr Kaye,' Ron said in an even tone. 'You don't want to cause more trouble for yourself. The police know you're here. You were seen loitering in the lane and someone in the pub warned us – and the coppers are on their way. They still want to know what happened to Mrs Kaye...'

Marion saw her father's eyes swivel and then he blinked. 'I never meant no 'arm,' he muttered. He glanced balefully at Marion. 'Bitch!' he spat and then slunk toward the door. As Ron opened it for him, he threw a punch at him, but the Army had taught Ron a thing or two on his way to becoming a sergeant and he caught Mr Kaye's arm, twisted it and hustled him out of the door.

'I'll take care of this,' he said to his brother. 'I think we'll pay a little visit to the nick.'

Even as Ron spoke, Marion's father kicked him in his groin area, causing him to shout with pain and let go. He swore as the older man suddenly took off. Reggie would have gone after him, but Marion held his arm.

'Let him go,' she said. 'Ron put the wind up him. We may have seen the last of him.'

'I'm not so sure,' Reggie said and looked anxious. 'He's dangerous, Marion. You should keep that door locked when I'm not around...'

'I usually do,' she said and frowned. 'I didn't think he would dare to come back here.'

'The question is, why did he?'

Marion shook her head. She had no idea why her father would visit them like that; she'd thought he'd gone for good and she'd hoped she would never have to deal with him again. Now it looked as if he thought he could just move in when he chose. Fortunately, Reggie and his brother had been there, but next time it might be just her and Sarah with the younger children...

13

Sally did a tour of the various floors, checking that everything was running smoothly. She didn't often bother as all her heads of department were trustworthy people: Mr Brown in men's clothing, Miss Pearson on the glass and china, Miss Philips in the female dress department and Mrs Roberts in the shoe department. Mr Stockbridge had taken it upon himself to look over the chocolate, cake, flower and toy departments as well as being the manager. Yet they were missing so many of their young men, salesmen, porters, office workers, all gone to the war and so many might never return.

'You cannot do it all yourself, Mrs Harper,' Mr Stockbridge had told her when he handed her a list of what was needed in the departments. 'Now that I have my own very efficient secretary, I have time to watch over those departments for you and to make sure they have what stock is available. You could, if you wished, close the top floor for the duration as very few toys are being manufactured at the moment.'

'I've had an idea about that,' Sally had told him and invited him for coffee in her office. After she'd explained her idea, he'd looked astounded and then delighted.

'You really do work miracles, Mrs Harper!' he'd exclaimed. 'How did you manage that?'

'Well, it started by a chance meeting with one of my friends,' Sally had told him. 'Marlene was carrying a large wooden fire engine painted red. She was taking it to a friend whose little boy had a birthday and I happened to ask her where she'd bought it...' She'd paused. 'It turned out that a small group of wounded soldiers had got together to make them out of reclaimed wood.'

'Reclaimed wood?' Mr Stockbridge had questioned. 'I'm not quite certain what you mean?'

'The toys are made out of old wood that has been taken from derelict buildings that were condemned to be pulled down. There are three of these young men, all of them disabled in some way, but all able to work at a bench for short periods. The wood that would otherwise be thrown away or used for firewood is delivered to them at their workshop in the shed at the bottom of one their gardens and they clean it up, smooth all the rough edges and make it look almost like new wood – or at least, matured wood – and then they make the toys and paint them.'

Marlene, the friend who ran Mick O'Sullivan's pub for him, had told her the story and given her contact telephone numbers and an address. In the event, Sally had gone round to the house, looked in the workshop and been enchanted by what she'd found. She'd asked to buy whatever surplus they had over and above what they made for family and friends and was told they would think about it.

Marlene told her that the lads had just started it for a bit of fun and pocket money and were not sure they could do it as a commercial venture. However, after a week, they came back to her and said they could produce about a dozen items each week for Harpers and if some more of their friends joined in, they might up their productivity. A price was agreed, which was about what they'd been charging friends and neighbours. Sally didn't try to beat them down, instead she told them to be sure to factor in at least a third of the price as profit.

'I don't want you to work for nothing,' she'd told their spokesman, Joe Silverman. 'Your toys are individual and beautifully made – and people struggle to buy toys at the moment.'

So, a price was agreed, but Sally's ingenuity hadn't stopped there. They were using reclaimed wood so she wondered about buying old toys and improving them, making them like new again. Joe Silverman said they could probably do it, if she found the old toys. Sally had started haunting the little junk shops and found several bits and pieces that had been mouldering on back shelves because they were damaged. She'd bought them for next to nothing and the little group of wounded soldiers had enjoyed the challenge.

When she had returned to one junk shop to look for more, the owner had asked why she wanted them. 'I'm going to renovate them and put them on sale,' she'd told him and he'd nodded.

'I had an elderly woman in here yesterday,' he'd told her. 'She says she has a lot of old toys in the attic and wants to sell them. She is selling her house and retiring to a small cottage in the country and can't take them with her.'

'Wouldn't you like to buy them?' Sally had asked and the man shook his head.

'I had those things you bought on my shelf for years. I'm more a furniture man, but I'll give you the address.'

When Sally had visited the elderly lady, she hadn't been able to believe the treasure trove that awaited her in the large attic. There were three rocking horses, all needing repairs, a broken scooter, two Victorian dolls' prams and a beautiful dolls' high chair, two old-fashioned swing cots and a huge collection of dolls, trains, lead soldiers and painted animals, also viewers and boxes of slides with pictures of exotic animals, and a kaleidoscope that still worked perfectly. There was also a beautiful automaton of a group of animals dressed up in the clothes of a bygone era, and they appeared to play music, though the music box was broken. Everything had been in need of repair, but with Fred Burrows' helper, Joshua, and a hired van, she'd managed to clear the attic for the lady, who was thrilled to be paid a few pounds when she learned what Sally intended to do with them.

'You're giving work to those brave young men and helping me at the same time,' she'd said, looking pleased. 'You're very welcome to them, Mrs Harper.'

'I think a lot of children will like these things,' Sally had replied with a smile. 'We'll have a section especially for them so people know what they're buying and it should create some interest.'

The soldiers had been intrigued with it, and one of them who had been an engineer couldn't wait to get started. 'I love these things,' he'd told Sally. 'Thank you for bringing them to us. It gives us that much more incentive to get up in the mornings.'

Sally had been thrilled that her little venture was working out so well. She was finding stock for Harpers, but she had also given these men some of their pride back as they pushed themselves to repair the intriguing items she'd found.

Mr Stockbridge took a great interest and a few days later, he too found some old toys that could be used if cleaned, repaired and repainted.

Sally also found a collection of pretty fans from what she thought might have been the Regency era at the old lady's house. She bought those too and Mr Marco made a display of them in the window. Originally, her intention had been to just use them as display items, but people asked to buy them and so most of them were eventually sold at a small profit. It wasn't something she could continue to do, but it helped to fill the shelves for a while and gave Sally something to keep her busy.

She'd been feeling a bit under the weather, not enough to take time off or stay at home, but vaguely unwell. Perhaps some of it was that she continually felt that she was being watched or followed, but mostly when she looked round no one was there. It was an uncomfortable feeling and she wished that Ben was home so she could talk to him about her fears that someone might be following her in order to snatch her darling daughter, but Ben was away again, Beth was distracted by the approaching birth of her second child and Sally didn't feel that she could tell Rachel, who seemed wrapped up in her own affairs.

* * *

Rachel worried about William. He was so seldom at home these days and she felt that their marriage had gone badly wrong. She wasn't sure what she had done to make him withdraw from her like this – his excuse that he had to work or was meeting someone important had begun to sound hollow and she could barely contain her distress. It was only that she felt it would be wrong of her to nag him that kept her from demanding to know what was going on.

Rachel would have liked to talk with her friends, perhaps tell them what was happening, but Sally Harper was always so busy. She had so much to do with the store, trying to keep Harpers stocked was a full-time job and she had her daughter to look after. Rachel had noticed that she looked a little pale recently. In the past, she would have asked if anything was wrong, but she'd felt unable to do so, because, after all, Sally Harper was married to her employer and the old days of sharing a flat together had long gone. Rachel missed those days sometimes, when Beth, Sally, Maggie and Rachel had shared a small flat, sharing each other's joys and problems. They'd had fun and they'd been a family, but now Maggie was far away – too far for Rachel to be able to visit on her day off – Beth had a child and another on the way, and Sally was always so busy...

Rachel was thoughtful as she walked home that evening. Had she been foolish to marry William? She hadn't known him for very long after all – and the war had taken him away almost immediately. Now he was home but so seldom spoke to her that she might as well have stayed single.

He was in the living room of their flat as she entered that evening, but her heart sank as she realised that he must be going out again.

'I thought you might stay home this evening,' she said to him as he smiled and greeted her. 'I'll put a casserole in the oven, it only needs reheating...'

'I'm sorry, Rachel—' William hesitated, then, '—look, I know I haven't been around much lately. I'm sorry – but I'm trying to get things done and these evening meetings are important.'

'I thought *we* were important, William,' she said, looking at him sadly. 'But go if you must.'

'I can't tell you,' he said mysteriously and for a moment she saw emotion in his face. 'Soon perhaps – but for now you will just have to trust me, Rachel. I do love you.' He gave her a hurried peck on the cheek. 'I'm sorry. I must go – but we'll talk soon. I must leave now or I'll be late...'

Rachel nodded. She wouldn't beg, but his abrupt departure left her feeling bruised and lonely.

She switched on the oven. The thought of eating alone again did not appeal, but the food would be hot and nourishing and she must eat. At Harpers she had friends and work she loved, but when she came home at night and William wasn't here, she sometimes felt so unbearably alone.

Pushing thoughts of her own distress from her mind, she wondered about Marion Jackson. She'd been looking a little pale of late. Rachel thought something must have happened because she'd been glowing only a day or so before.

14

Marion did her best to put the incident with her father out of her mind, but at first, she felt as if a shadow was hanging over her. Reggie was convinced that Sam Kaye had been scared and that it would be a long while before he showed up again. He said he would ask his father and the two brothers that were still working on the docks to look out for her. Her husband said she should forget it and after a few days she decided he was right. She knew Reggie had spoken to the local police, so perhaps Pa had heard they were looking for him and scarpered.

Back at work, she was drawn into the busy life of Harpers and now that Mr Marco was back in charge of the windows, she found it exciting to work on them. He seemed to be as full of ideas as ever and they began to sparkle again with that magic something that had been missing.

No one knew why Mr Marco had returned to the store when the war was still raging. He was wearing a wedding ring and that caused some speculation, but Marion didn't like to ask questions. All sorts of rumours were going about and Shirley actually asked

Marion if she thought he was a deserter. She got quite cross with her.

'I've no idea why he isn't still serving overseas,' she told her, 'but Mrs Harper said it might be temporary, so perhaps he's just been stood down for a rest.'

Shirley flushed and went back to her counter. Marion reflected that the younger girl hadn't been at Harpers before the war and didn't know Mr Marco well enough to know he couldn't be a coward or a deserter.

She knew, because Reggie had told her, that deserters were often shot after a trial by a summary court as an example to others. Most men were eager to get back to the front line after being patched up following a stay in hospital, though some were terribly wounded. Mr Marco had been wounded; you could see sometimes when he put a hand to his chest and asked her to reach for something that he was in pain and had done his bit. If he chose to return to Harpers while resting, then that was all right with her.

However, no one else questioned his return in Marion's hearing. He was popular and most accepted he was probably considered unfit for Army service, which happened to quite a few men injured in the service of their country.

* * *

When, at the end of his leave, Reggie left for his new camp, Marion felt a bit weepy, but she knew she'd been lucky to have him home that long. For a few weeks he might not get leave, but after that he expected to get home some weekends. He and Ron had agreed on a plan for the future and his letters home were full of his excitement at what they'd decided. They were going into business for themselves and Reggie couldn't wait for the war to end.

When it began, I wanted to do my duty and fight the enemy,

he wrote in one of his letters.

Now, I'm bored with being stuck down here with the new recruits. An older man could do this, Marion, and I'd rather have a gun in my hand and shoot the so and so's, but they want me to train others because I'm a good shot...

Marion didn't much like the idea of Reggie lying in a ditch shooting at the enemy and being shot at and was much happier that he was on English soil and training others, but she knew it made him restless. She sighed over the letter. Like Reggie, she longed for the war to be over so that he could come back to her. She'd read in the newspapers about the uprisings in Russia that year, but thankfully the Russians were still fighting the common enemy. They knew the war was not yet won, just as she and Reggie did. Much as she longed for peace, she knew they just had to carry on as best they could in the meantime. At least she was getting his letters regularly now.

However, she enjoyed being at work and found herself looking forward to the time spent window dressing more and more. Mr Marco was lovely to work with and she was curious about his wife and son. He didn't often speak of them and of course she couldn't ask, though she would have loved to know more about them. However, his wife had been into the shop to buy some clothes once and she'd met her briefly so she knew she was pretty and kind – and, of course, she thought the world of Mr Marco.

* * *

'Why don't you go down and visit Maggie Gibbs?' Marco asked Sadie when he got home that evening at the end of July. 'Your mother would be glad to have Pierre for a while and I'll fetch him home in the evening. Stay down there overnight on Saturday and come back Sunday. You can visit her more than once then. I know you miss her and I'm sure she's lonely. Mrs Harper was saying she just hasn't had time to visit her and Mrs Burrows isn't up to making the journey. She has her second child in a few weeks – September, I think Fred said...'

Sadie looked at him gratefully. 'You really wouldn't mind?' she asked. 'It seems a bit unfair leaving you to cope with everything, Marco. I already owe you so much.'

'You owe me nothing,' he told her with his gentle smile. 'I enjoy having you both around, Sadie. The boy is a delight and you're a good friend. It will cheer Maggie up to see you.'

'Yes, her last letter sounded as if she could do with it,' Sadie replied. 'She says they won't let her go back to what she was doing and she's not sure what to do.'

'Fred told me she has a home with them if she wants it.'

'But that would bring back all the memories of how much she has lost,' Sadie said. 'When she was there staying with them, she was engaged to Tim and had everything to look forward to one day. Now she has nothing.' Sadie smiled at him. 'I'd be in the same boat if it were not for you, Marco. I can't tell you how grateful I am for all you've done. My parents think you're wonderful and you've given me hope for the future. Maggie has nothing...'

'She has friends,' he said, 'but sometimes that doesn't seem enough.' He frowned as fleeting memories of Julien went through his mind. 'I know she must be lonely, Sadie. That's why I think you should visit.'

Sadie nodded. 'Yes, I shall, thank you. Mrs Harper told me how much everyone likes you when I visited the store to buy a few bits and pieces. She saw you give me some money and came to tell me that I was entitled to a staff discount on everything as your wife. She is nice, Marco, but she likes you – everyone does...'

'I'm lucky in my friends. Ben and I go back a long way.'

'It isn't just the Harpers, though – the staff. One of the girls – Marion Jackson – she told me she loves working with you on the windows. She said Harpers was lucky to have you – and I'm lucky to be your wife, Marco.'

'You're happy then?' He looked at her a little oddly. 'I wondered if you would be...'

'Yes, I'm happy,' Sadie said and held the sigh inside. She was happier than she'd expected or had any right to expect.

15

Maggie looked at the picture in her newspaper. The war was still raging in France and Ypres was under constant bombardment from British planes, despite heavy losses. Although it was summer, rain had been falling constantly and, combined with damage done by the British bombs, the dykes and riverbanks had given way, turning the field of battle into a sea of terrible sucking mud that could pull unwary men under its suffocating stickiness if they slipped from the duckboards. It was the third large battle of Ypres, which had started at the end of July, and the heavy rain was making things so much worse for the embattled soldiers. Maggie could imagine the discomfort and hardship they were enduring far more clearly than anyone who had never been out there.

She wondered why they kept fighting over the same ground, day in and day out, when nothing ever seemed to change and no victory was ever seen. Yet she knew that for the men out there it was just a question of orders. Hang on for another day and wait for your turn to be sent back down the line to a period of relatively safety and rest. The papers could write articles about

General Haig trying to prevent the enemy bringing up fresh troops and the way the war was going well, but for the Allies it was just sheer, relentless slog every hour of the day and night.

Sighing, she put down the newspaper, which seemed not to have a shred of good news and looked at the window. Perhaps she would go out for a walk instead of sitting here wishing she was back at the Front to help in the fight for the wounded. Just as she was about to get up and go, her door opened and she looked in surprise at the woman who had entered.

'Sadie! How did you get here?' Maggie jumped up with a little cry of pleasure as her friend entered the annexe carrying a bunch of flowers and various little packages. 'I didn't know you were back in England...'

'I wanted to tell you my news face to face,' Sadie said and laid her parcels down before hugging her. 'How are you, Maggie love? You do look better than the last time I saw you!'

'I suppose I must be much better than I was then,' Maggie replied with a smile. 'I hardly knew you were there at the end – though I vaguely remember you and Marie visiting me in the hospital.'

'We thought we should lose you for a time,' Sadie said, 'but you are made of stronger stuff. All you needed was a good rest.'

'Yes,' Maggie agreed. 'It had become very hard the last few months or so – but I'd like to go back...'

'I doubt they will let you,' Sadie responded with a frown. 'Once you've had a fever like that it weakens your resistance and next time you probably wouldn't be able to fight it. I've seen some of the men who have had recurring bouts of trench fever get so weak they either die or get sent home as being of no further use on the fighting line.'

'Yes, I know but—' Maggie laughed as she saw Sadie's expression. 'I know they may try to deny me, but I'm going to see if I can wangle it.'

'Well, let's not talk about that – I wanted to tell you... I'm married...' Sadie hesitated. 'I've been married for a couple of months... well nearly. I would've come before, but I was busy settling in.'

'Oh, Sadie, that's wonderful news,' Maggie cried. 'I'm so pleased – where did you meet him and, is he French?'

'No, not French, though he has some French blood... You know him.' She looked at Maggie uncertainly. 'Marcel – or Marco as you know him...'

'You married Mr Marco – the window dresser for Harpers?' Maggie was unsure what to say. 'But I thought—' She stopped, afraid to say something she shouldn't. 'Congratulations! He's a lovely person.'

'Yes, he is,' Sadie said and smiled. 'He has been wonderful to me, Maggie – and yes, I do know that he is different sexually...'

'He told you?' Maggie looked at her. 'At Harpers there was some talk when a friend of his committed suicide... after a bitter argument with his father because he was living with Marco...'

'Marco told me about Julien,' Sadie said. 'I know what he was doing in France – all of it. Our marriage isn't all that unusual, Maggie. Marco told me that a lot of his friends who have the same private preferences marry for various reasons. Sometimes it is for their family or career, to cover up their true feelings, because people are prejudiced, but for others it is because they get on well with a female friend and can be comfortable looking after her, while continuing their other lives in private. Marco felt he owed me because of what happened to Pierre – and he loves my son...'

'Yes, I imagine he would.' Maggie nodded. 'I've always

thought him gentle, honest and a good companion and friend. I think he will make a wonderful father and a good husband.'

'That is exactly what he is to me and little Pierre,' Sadie told her. 'It means that once my son is a little older, I can return to nursing. It's what I want to do and we've agreed that if either of us ever wants our freedom, we'll have a civilised divorce.'

'And are you happy with that?' Maggie asked her and Sadie smiled.

'Yes, I am, very happy. I know you may think I am missing something, but I can assure you I'm not. When I met Pierre, I lost my head and we became lovers, but I really wanted to be a nurse – not just in war, Maggie, but as a vocation. Now, I have my son to remind me of his father and I can hold up my head and my family still welcome me. Had I not married I would have been an outcast, now I'm respectable. Marco has made it possible for me to do that and I shall do all I can to make his life comfortable. We are not in love and yet we enjoy being together. I am very fond of him, even love him in a way – can you understand that?'

'Yes, I can,' Maggie replied, nodding. 'I've met someone here, Sadie. He is a very angry young man and probably stuck in a wheelchair for the rest of his life – but sometimes when we're together, I see the person inside and I like him. He could be a good friend and companion if he chose...'

'You're not in love with him?' Sadie asked, her eyes probing Maggie's.

'No, I'm not,' Maggie said and sighed. 'I'm not sure if I'm still getting over Tim or...' She shook her head. 'Whatever, I know that I'm happy to sit with Colin, but I'm not sure I could spend my life with him.'

'That isn't the same thing,' Sadie told her.

'No, but I might be asked,' Maggie replied seriously. 'Colin's father was here yesterday. He wants to take his son home and thinks if he had a wife who could also help nurse him, he might agree to go. Colin is refusing to have a regular nurse; it is a matter of pride. His father looked at me so pointedly that I knew what he meant, but I didn't answer. I don't believe Colin would want to go home even if I agreed.'

'Surely you'll return to Harpers?' Sadie looked at her in surprise. 'I mean, I know you feel you should go back to nursing over there, but you also know they won't let you. Mrs Harper told Marco that she is going to visit soon and will suggest there is a job for you.'

'I always expected I might go back for a while after the war – until I married and had children anyway...'

'And that's what you should do,' Sadie said. 'Honestly, Maggie. You're feeling better now, love, but nursing is hard work and that fever did things to your lungs. You need a nice, slower pace of life from now on.'

'I feel fine now, but I do know that I might not be as lucky next time...'

* * *

After Sadie had gone, Maggie reflected on what her friend had told her. She seemed perfectly happy to be a wife in name only, but perhaps that was because she believed she would never love anyone the way she'd loved Pierre and didn't want to be a true wife to any other. If one day she met someone she truly loved, she might feel differently and then... Maggie sighed. Sadie had gone into the marriage with her eyes open. Divorce wasn't something Maggie could have contemplated lightly, but perhaps Sadie didn't care that it carried the shadow of social stigma – though she had cared about returning home as an unmarried mother. Maggie hoped the marriage would suit both of her friends, for she counted Mr Marco a friend and would like to think he was happy.

As she picked up the book Sadie had brought for her, the door opened again and Colin Morgan wheeled himself in. His expression was gloomy and she knew something had upset him.

'Did you enjoy your visit?' he asked and the tone of his voice told her what was causing his scowl. 'I damned well didn't enjoy mine!'

'Your father came again today?'

'I've told him not to bother but he's a stubborn old goat.' Colin's face creased with something between anxiety and anger. 'He claims to be suffering from a problem with his heart. Damn it, Maggie! He says he hasn't got more than a couple of years to live and he begged me to go home and let him show me the ropes.'

Tears stood in his eyes and Maggie wanted to put her arms around him, but she knew that he hated any physical contact. He'd brushed her hand away once when she'd tried to touch his face to comfort him.

'Are you sure it isn't just emotional blackmail?' From what she'd seen of his father, Maggie wouldn't put anything past him.

'I thought of that, but he showed me letters from his doctors warning him not to overdo things.'

'I'm sorry,' she said, understanding immediately that this altered things for him. As his father's only son, he would inherit the land and estate, though not the title, which was not heredi-tary. His sister would expect him to look after things for the sake of the family, even though she was married and no longer lived on the estate. In families like theirs, it was expected that the eldest son would do his duty. For Colin it was like a nightmare. He was being forced to return to a place that he had hoped never to see again. 'What will you do?'

'Kick and scream like hell and then give in,' he told her. 'I don't have a choice...'

'You could tell him to sell the place and invest the money for you and your sister.'

'That land has been in our family hundreds of years.' His face wore a tortured look. 'Once upon a time I wanted nothing more than to take it over in the future – but I didn't expect to be tied to this damned chair.'

'I'm sure you can find ways to get around the land,' she said. 'You know how to drive a trap and with a little help you could easily manage it. Besides, it's your home and you may find you feel better there than here...'

'Everywhere I go, she will be there, looking at me and they will all whisper and pity me.' His eyes were dark with the pain of rejection.

'Oh, for goodness' sake, stop pitying yourself,' Maggie said sharply. 'You're alive and you have a family and a home to go to – find a new life and fall in love with someone else. You're not the only one to lose the person you love.'

He looked at her oddly, 'Come with me, Maggie – as my wife. It might not be a proper marriage, because I'll never be able to lie in your bed or give you children – but I'll give you all you want – clothes, pretty things...'

Maggie gasped. She hardly knew him. 'Don't be foolish. You'll find someone,' she said. 'Just because one girl rejected you, others won't if they love you.'

'I don't want them to,' he said sullenly. 'I don't want to be pitied or fussed over... you wouldn't do that...' He turned his piercing gaze on her. 'I'll go back home if you'll come and be my wife, or nurse, whatever you choose... I can't face it without you!'

* * *

As she stood looking out at the moon that evening, Maggie wondered what had made her tell Colin that she would think about his proposal. Was it pity or what Sadie had told her about her marriage that had made her waver? She'd known him a few weeks and had started to like him – but that wasn't a reason for marriage.

At first, she had firmly denied his request, telling him that it was just foolishness, that he would fall in love again, but he'd looked so miserable and when he'd told her he'd rather die than go home to that empty house without her, she'd said she would think about it. His face had brightened immediately.

'I knew you would,' he'd said and grabbed her hand, kissing the back of it. 'You know it makes sense, Maggie, for both of us. You don't have anyone else and you can't return to nursing the wounded – I shan't ask much of you. You just have to look pretty and pretend you're in love with me in company.'

'I do care about you,' Maggie had said. 'I like you, Captain Morgan, but I don't see what you would get out of the arrangement.'

Yet she did see quite clearly what he wanted and needed from her. He'd been rejected and humiliated by a girl he'd loved more than life and he could only go home – to a place he actually loved deep down – if he could rescue his pride. He needed to be able to show the girl who had hurt him so badly that he didn't care and somehow that touched Maggie's heart.

So, she'd found herself saying she was thinking about it and he'd taken that as a yes and gone off to send a message to his father, telling him he was getting married and to prepare the west wing for him and his bride.

Maggie looked up at the moon and sighed. 'I can't have you, my love,' she said, picturing Tim, the man she'd loved and lost to the war. 'So why not make someone else happy?' Sometimes she could hardly remember what Tim looked like, but tonight his image was bright in her mind.

'*Maggie, be happy...*' She seemed to hear the whisper in her ear and shivered. Tim had gone. He couldn't hold her or kiss her and perhaps life with Colin would be interesting and wake her up from this dead sleep she'd fallen into before and during her illness. For the moment she couldn't feel any emotion other than sympathy for a man in need. Perhaps her emotions had taken such a battering in France that she was no longer capable of feeling love or real happiness... perhaps it didn't matter what she did any more...

16

Sally looked at the new window Marco had just dressed and smiled. The summer seemed to be racing ahead, the days merging one into the other during the month of August. It was a scene of harvesting and homecoming, a kitchen table laden with platters and made to look as if supper was about to be served. Outside a cottage window, sheaves of golden corn could be seen in the backdrop. It was a celebration of the end of summer and of the hope of peace again, when the men would return and life would be back to normal. She could almost smell the new bread and meat roasting over an open fire.

'It's perfect,' she told Marco with a smile. 'It holds the promise of plenty and of peace in the midst of war, of friends and family and the kind of happiness we all took for granted before the conflict.' The touch of an old pair of Army boots and a man's combat jacket slung over a chair was a nod to the war, still raging in France, particularly in Ypres, where the town was taking a battering from the artillery fire and the fighting was fierce, as well as in other countries, but it also seemed to say, 'Don't worry, we're winning and we'll all be home soon.'

'I'm glad you like it,' he said. 'I met a family in France who ran a farm and it looked a little like this.'

'Yes,' Sally nodded, understanding in her heart and eyes as she looked at him. Something was eating at Marco but she had no idea what it might be. 'We're all so glad to have you back.'

'I'm glad to be here,' he assured her. 'I've felt a bit guilty at leaving you in the lurch, but I think Marion has some good ideas.'

'Yes, she does, and I know she tries hard, but she isn't quite as good as you at giving them that extra zing.' Sally glanced at her watch. 'I have an appointment, so I must go – but I hope everything is all right...' She hesitated, 'With your family?'

'What? Oh yes, everything is fine.' He nodded, seeming as if she'd dragged him from somewhere else. 'Sadie went to visit Maggie Gibbs one weekend – nearly a month ago now. I think she managed to visit twice before she had to get the train home. It was a long journey there and back and she was tired when she got home, but she enjoyed the visit. She wondered if I'd cope with our son alone, but I enjoyed it; we missed her, of course, but we managed fine. Pierre is a delight to look after.'

Sally nodded her understanding. 'I want to visit Maggie when I can. It isn't as easy to get to visit where she is now, but I must make time. It's just that I've had such a lot on...'

'She should ask to be transferred to London, then you could all visit her easily.'

'That would be ideal...'

Sally left him to the contemplation of his window. It was his afternoon off and she wondered how he would spend it. Would he go straight home to be with his family? Perhaps she was imagining things when she thought he seemed a little reserved, as if his thoughts were elsewhere rather than with Harpers or his family? Perhaps he was just thinking about his next new display, but she thought he seemed sadder than he had before he left for France last time.

Going up to her office, Sally ordered coffee to be brought in when her appointment arrived. It was with one of the best new firms she'd discovered recently. Ben had complimented her on the new ranges, and she was very pleased with the variety of bags and good-quality ladies' leather shoes their salesman had sold her on his previous visit. She hoped he would have some new stock to show her and that she would be able to order a substantial number of bags from him. Rachel's department was doing very well despite the war.

* * *

Sally smiled and rose to her feet as her secretary showed the young salesman into her office. Henry Jefferies had been born with a club foot and was unfit for war service, though he'd joined a civil defence team and took his turn on fire watch in the evenings, as he'd proudly told her. 'We never know when the enemy might try to sabotage our factories, Mrs Harper. I belong to a team of volunteers and I patrol various important sites at night. I may not be able to march or negotiate ditches, but I can shoot straight and I shall if the need arises.'

Yes, she liked Henry Jefferies and she would continue to increase her order with his firm even when the war was over and things were back to normal – if that ever happened. Ben had told her that they were definitely winning the war with the help of their Allies, despite the setbacks and the failures, but sometimes she thought he just said it to cheer her.

Ben had asked her what was wrong the last time he was home and she hadn't felt able to tell him. Sally wasn't sure why she had this sensation of unease, but it might have something to do with her shadow. Everywhere she went she was followed. Sometimes, she saw the woman, sometimes it was just a sense she was there, but Sally had begun to feel haunted and she'd tried to confront the woman but she always hurried away. It wasn't so much her own safety Sally worried about but Jenny's – supposing the woman was watching her so that she could snatch her baby away. Her thoughts had drifted to her problem, the problem she hadn't been able to share with Ben, though she didn't know why. She wasn't feeling quite herself – a bit under the weather, though she wasn't sure what was wrong.

'Is something troubling you, Mrs Harper?' the salesman asked and she made herself smile as she hastily brought her thoughts back to her meeting.

'Nothing at all,' she assured him. 'I like everything you've shown me – now how much of these lines can your firm supply?'

'Not as many as we'd like,' he said regretfully. 'But we'll do our best for you – you're our most important customer now.'

* * *

After Henry Jefferies had gone, Sally did some paperwork and then left the office. She stopped to speak to Ruth for a few minutes, telling her secretary that she would not return that afternoon.

'I'm going to take my daughter out in the sunshine for a couple of hours. Summer will soon start to fade and it will be September,' she told Ruth. 'I'll ring you at four after I get home and if anyone needs me urgently, I'll contact them then.'

'Yes, of course, Mrs Harper,' Ruth said. 'It will do you good to get out for a while – you've been looking a bit peaky lately...'

Sally nodded but didn't answer. She didn't feel her usual bouncy self and put it down to this feeling of unease hanging over her. As soon as Ben came home again, she made up her mind she would tell him about her shadow. He'd rung her a few times but hadn't been able to get home and she hadn't wanted to worry him.

This mystery woman following her might be dangerous, but Sally feared it was her daughter the woman wanted. She'd decided she must be a childless woman and desperate to have a child, which made Sally fear for her little girl in case she was snatched. Both Pearl and Mrs Hill had been warned that if they took Jenny out, they must be careful, but Sally's sister-in-law thought she was being paranoid.

'If she'd wanted to snatch her, she would have done it before now,' Jenni had said. 'Honestly, Sally, she sounds as if she is fascinated with you but afraid to approach you to me. Why don't you just ask to talk to her?'

'I did try,' Sally had said but she'd been sharp, she knew. Was it possible that Jenni was right? Was the woman just lonely, looking for a friendly face to talk to?

Collecting Jenny from her helper, on impulse Sally asked if Pearl would accompany them on their walk in Victoria Park. It was beautiful there with its bandstand and the beautifully kept gardens, and just a short bus ride from where Ben and Sally lived in the nicer area of Hackney. Sometimes, she'd walked it on her own on a good day, but today they took a bus to the park.

Feeling safer with Jenny between them, Sally keeping a firm hold on the leading reins she'd bought to anchor the little girl to her, she relaxed and enjoyed the sunshine. They passed the beautiful Victorian drinking fountain and found a bench to sit on. Sally took the rein from its harness and released her daughter, who was impatient to run and play with her ball. For a time, Jenny was content to run after the ball and throw it in their direction, leaving either Sally or Pearl to toss it back. Then she wanted to explore further and ran off giggling, with Pearl chasing after her. Sally rose to follow and then sat down with a bump as her head spun and she closed her eyes.

She sensed rather than heard the presence next to her and her eyes opened with a start. The woman who had been following her was sitting on the bench, right at the far end, leaving a space between them. She looked at Sally and then said, 'You're ill.'

'Who are you?' Sally asked, not bothering to deny that she didn't feel right. 'Why are you following me?'

The woman hesitated, then, 'I've been wanting to speak to you,' she said. 'Your name is Sally Harper now, but what did the nuns tell you it was when you were little?'

Sally took a deep breath. She was trembling all over and felt close to fainting yet for some reason she couldn't help herself replying, 'Sally Ross – why?'

The woman smiled and despite her age and the clear signs of suffering in her face something made Sally's heart race. That smile was familiar and even before she asked the question, she half knew the answer. Suddenly, it all made sense as it came to her in a blinding flash.

'You're my mother – aren't you?'

'Yes. My name is Sheila Ross and I don't blame you if you hate me. I left you with the nuns because I had no hope of giving you a decent life and it was meant to be just until I was able to look after you – but, when I went to fetch you, they'd sent you to another home and wouldn't tell me where you were.'

Sally felt a rush of anger against the nuns for what they'd done. 'They wouldn't tell me anything about you until I left them – and then one of the nuns, a little kinder than the others – gave me a silver cross and said you were dead.' Sally's head was pounding, and she could hardly see the face of the woman on the bench. 'Are you really my...' She rose to her feet, swayed and then slumped back to the bench. The question died on her lips as the dizziness swept over her and she leaned forward and was suddenly very sick. In the distance, she could hear voices, some she knew and some she didn't.

'What happened to Mrs Harper?' That was Pearl's voice, accompanied by a wail from Jenny.

Another voice, male this time, joined in, 'May I be of assistance? I was with her earlier and I thought she looked a little unwell... I am Mr Marco, we work together at Harpers. I came to the park for a walk on my way home. I had even hoped I might find Mrs Harper here – but not like this!'

'I'm Jenny's nanny,' Pearl said. 'I need to get her into a taxi and take her home.'

Marco nodded. 'She looks as if she needs a doctor. You should take the little girl home and let me take her to the hospital.'

Sally's feverish mind sought another voice but did not hear it. She tried to ask for her mother – for Sheila Ross – but she couldn't form the words. Her mouth tasted awful and her head was still swimming as she opened her eyes and tried to focus.

'What happened? Where is my mother?'

'Your mother?' Pearl looked puzzled as she coped with a struggling child who wanted to reach her mother. 'There was a woman, but she shouted to me to come and then went off...'

Sally's brain wouldn't let her understand. She tried to stand but swayed again and found herself supported by a pair of strong arms and smelled a familiar masculine scent as he bent and lifted her. She let him do it, glad of his help, glad he was there when she needed him, but surely, she could walk?

'I can manage...' she protested faintly.

'What would Ben say to me if I let you try and you fell and hurt yourself?' Marco chided. 'It's a good thing Ruth told me where you were headed and I came looking for you. I was going to ask you for help, but now I'm here to help *you*...'

'You're worried about something,' she murmured hazily. 'I sensed it earlier...' Sally tried to focus, but her head kept going round and round. She wasn't sure if she was talking sense or rubbish.

'I'll come to the hospital with you,' Pearl raised her voice to be heard above Jenny's wails.

'No...' Sally managed. 'I know Marco well – take Jenny home. I'll be all right.'

Pearl agreed then and Sally was vaguely aware of her rescuer hailing a taxi and of being helped inside. However, her head was now spinning wildly again and by the time they reached the hospital, she didn't know much as she was hurriedly taken inside and wheeled into a small room. Because her illness was sudden and unknown, she would be isolated until the doctors knew what was wrong with her. She had some kind of fever, but all she was aware of was feeling wretched all over.

17

'Thank goodness,' Beth cried emotionally as the man entered the hospital room late that evening. 'I came as soon as Pearl rang me and I've been sitting here with Sally for three hours, but she hasn't stirred. I'm sorry I had to call you, Ben. Sally gave me a number to ring if ever something terrible happened – and I thought this warranted using it...'

'Yes, of course it does, though I only got the message when I arrived home. I was already on my way here when they tried to contact me... Pearl was distraught and told me that there was an incident in the park just before Sally was taken ill. Pearl wasn't sure, but she thought some scruffy old woman had attacked her...'

'I know she's been a bit anxious because she thought she was being followed,' Beth told him and placed a hand to her back. 'I'm sorry, but I have to go home, Ben. I'm too close to my time to sit here any longer.' She gave a self-conscious laugh. 'I'm sure the nurses thought I might give birth at any moment and I may!'

'You were good to come,' Ben said, glancing anxiously at Sally, who was lying with her eyes closed. 'Have they given you any idea of what is wrong with her?'

'The nurse I spoke to said she thinks it is some sort of fever or perhaps blood poisoning. To be honest, I don't think they really know yet.' She sighed. 'I hate to leave, although if it is something catching, I shouldn't be here in my condition. I had to come, Ben, no matter what. You know I love her like a sister. You will let me know if there's any change?'

'Yes, I promise,' he said and took Beth's place by the bedside.

Sally looked flushed, certainly as if she had some kind of fever, which made Ben fear for her life. Fevers were unpredictable and could be anything. Leaning over, he placed a hand to her forehead. She was burning up!

He turned as the door opened and a doctor entered. He looked at Ben, who was still in the uniform of a British Army Captain.

'You managed to get here then,' he said gruffly. 'I'm Doctor Rusk and I've been caring for your wife since she was brought in; it's just as well you're here, because we may have a decision to make later...'

'What kind of decision?' Ben's heart caught with fear.

'We're not sure yet if this is typhoid or another contagious fever,' the doctor said. 'We warned the young woman who was here earlier not to get too close. Your wife seems very ill and I may have to move her to an isolation hospital – but I'm concerned about the other condition.'

'What other condition?' Ben's heart stood still. What hadn't his wife told him? Did she have some illness she'd concealed from him?

'The child,' the doctor said and frowned. 'Didn't you know? Your wife must be nearly two months pregnant and we're not sure yet if she has a contagious disease or whether it is something to do with the pregnancy.'

Sally gave a little moan and her arm moved restlessly.

'I didn't know – but would that make her so ill?'

'There are cases of a kind of poisoning in pregnancy. It may be that her body is rejecting the baby or it might simply be another more common fever. We need to monitor her for a while, but she could suffer a miscarriage because of the illness... or we might have to give her medicines that would cause her to lose the baby...'

Ben's eyes closed for an instant. Why hadn't Sally told him about the baby? He remembered the fainting fits she'd had during her first pregnancy but that hadn't happened until later in her pregnancy, and it certainly hadn't made her ill like this – if that's what it was? She'd fallen so easily the first time and he'd hoped they would have another child while Jenny was still small, but there had been no sign until this – and now Sally was ill. He couldn't lose her. He didn't care if they never had another child. Jenny was enough, but he needed Sally.

He looked the doctor in the eyes. 'Can you save her?'

'Possibly... but there is a distinct likelihood that she could lose the child if the fever worsens.'

'That would be sad for us both, but Sally is more important,' Ben said firmly. 'I can't lose my wife, doctor.'

'I completely agree with your decision,' the doctor told him with a brief smile. 'While we'll do all we can to keep both of them alive, we can only do so much and I wanted to prepare you for the worst.'

Ben looked at his wife's face. She had been flushed, but now she looked pale and he felt a flicker of fear. 'Is she going to die anyway?'

'That is always a possibility with a fever. They are unpredictable, but we shall be watching over her and she won't die if I can prevent it.' His gaze narrowed. 'I realise you have other commitments, Captain Harper, and you cannot be here all the time – but how long do you have free?'

'I was expecting to be at home a couple of weeks,' Ben said and frowned. 'But I need to be here for Sally, so I'll take compassionate leave.'

'Good.' Doctor Rusk nodded his approval. 'She will need friends about her when she wakes and her recovery may be slow,'

Ben indicated his understanding. He thought it was good fortune that Jenni was in London, for the store would miss Sally's guiding hand and he could not give it his attention while his wife was so ill. Once she recovered – if she did! – he might be forced to return to his Army work; although he was not British and not obliged by law to give his services, he'd done so willingly, because London was his home now. When America had entered the war, he'd considered enlisting in the Armed forces, but it would have meant starting all over again and he was comfortable in the position he already held here in Britain. Besides, he might have been sent a long way off and his feeling now was that he didn't want to be far away from his darling wife. If he should lose her – but he wouldn't let himself think like that!

'I will arrange for a cup of tea to be brought to you,' the doctor said after he had finished his examination of Sally. 'Not much change, I'm afraid, but don't despair, she is young and strong. It's your child I fear we may lose...'

Ben shook his head impatiently. An unborn child was nothing to him compared to his wife.

Sitting by the bed, Ben reached for Sally's hand, holding it firmly in his own and bending his head to kiss it. 'Please don't leave me, my love,' he said fiercely. 'I can't lose you. I won't. You have to fight – fight for me and Jenny. Live for us, my darling. I beg you, live for us...' He watched her closely in the hope of seeing a flicker of recognition, but there was none. Wherever Sally had gone, he couldn't reach her.

'Ben – why are you crying?'

The question made him aware of the fact and he flicked away the tears he hadn't realised he'd shed from his cheek. 'Jenni! I'm glad you came. I think we may lose her—'

'Nonsense,' Jenni said. 'Sally isn't going to just give in to a fever.' Jenni bent over the bed and placed a hand on Sally's forehead. 'She's very hot. Why isn't someone bathing her forehead to cool her?'

She rang the bell impatiently, gave instructions to a nurse, who came, accepted Jenni's instructions and left.

Jenni then put a comforting arm about her brother. 'Cheer up, sweetheart. We'll soon have her out of this morbid place. She'll do better at home with a private nurse to care for her.'

When the young nurse returned with a bowl, cloth and tepid water, Jenni soaked the cloth, rung it out and began to soothe it over Sally's face and arms. Ben watched, feeling helpless and wondering whether his sister knew what she was doing, but after about half an hour, he noticed that Sally had stopped sweating so much and seemed easier. She was no longer moaning and her colour looked better.

'Is that because of what you've done?' Ben asked, looking at her in awe. 'How did you know?'

'My mother had fevers sometimes. Her doctors said she was prone to them and that's what they told me to do – but Sally needs constant nursing and she may not get it in a busy hospital.'

'You think we should take her home?'

'Yes, I do,' Jenni told him. 'Mrs Hill and I will look after Jenny and Pearl can nurse Sally. She told me that as soon as the doctors say it is all right to move her, she will nurse her day and night.'

'You don't need to be anywhere else?' he asked. 'What about your own life?'

'That can wait,' Jenni replied. 'Andrew is very patient. He has to be to wait for me to make up my mind and then try for the divorce I need – but all of that can wait until Sally is on the mend. I shan't desert her or you while you need me.'

'I knew you'd have it organised,' Ben said and smiled. 'Thank goodness you're here, Jenni.'

'Sally needs to be at home, but first of all we need a proper diagnosis, which is why I've asked Doctor Symonds to come and see her – he is a specialist in treating pregnant women.'

'So, you knew Sally was expecting? She didn't tell me.'

'I doubt she knew,' Jenni said, 'so don't go feeling shut out, Ben. I wondered a few times. I heard her vomiting one morning but I think she was afraid to hope.'

'Doctor Rusk says she may lose the baby...'

'Rubbish!' Jenni said in a brisk tone. 'Wait until Doctor Symonds sees her.' Her calm manner was helping to allay Ben's fears and he smiled at her. Jenni was right. He was letting his terror of losing her rule his head and that was stupid. Sally needed him to be strong and hold things together until she was well again.

18

Rachel visited Sally in hospital the next evening. Ben had returned to the flat to wash and shave, after sitting with his wife all night and day, leaving his sister to sit by the bed. When Jenni saw Rachel, she greeted her warmly and stood up.

'I'm glad you've come. I need to stretch my legs and get a drink of coffee. They brought me tea, but it was undrinkable. The sooner we get Sally home, the better.'

'Is she able to come home?' Rachel asked, looking anxiously at Sally's pale face. 'Has the fever gone?'

'It is abating a little,' Jenni replied. 'They are keeping her cool by bathing her now. Pearl came in today and she gave her a bed bath; it brought her temperature down considerably and the doctor instructed that the nurses continue the treatment.'

'Have they said what is wrong?' Rachel asked. 'I've been thinking of her all day and everyone at Harpers is worried about her.'

'Yes, I know,' Jenni replied. 'The doctors have done tests and one of the nurses told me she thinks it may be some sort of blood poisoning, caused by her pregnancy, but they don't seem to know much about it... toxic something she called it.'

Rachel nodded thoughtfully. 'I've heard about something like that in the past – a woman I knew when I was first married.' Her eyes darkened with distress. 'She died, they couldn't save her—'

'Don't say it!' Jenni begged her. 'Ben couldn't bear that and I should miss her terribly.'

'All her friends would,' Rachel said and Jenni looked as if she would burst into tears. She left the room hurriedly and Rachel took her place by the bed. She reached forward and took Sally's hand in hers, holding it gently.

Sally murmured something and Rachel bent nearer to hear her words. It sounded like mother.

'Are you asking for your mother?'

'Told me...' Sally's words were slurred, but Rachel held her hand and soothed her brow with the cold compress Jenni had been using. 'Her name... my mother...'

'You met your mother?' Rachel was astounded because she knew Sally believed her mother to be dead. She looked round, wishing Jenni was still in the room and wondering whether she should call the doctor, but Sally was trying to talk to her so she leaned nearer. She stroked Sally's damp hair back. 'I love you as dearly as anyone, Sally, my love, but I think your mother is dead...'

'No... she came to me... in the park...' Sally's eyes opened and she was staring straight at Rachel. For a moment she seemed to have regained her senses. 'She wanted to tell me before, but she was afraid...'

The effort was too much for her. Sally's eyes closed and she fell back on the pillows but a tear slid down her cheek, followed by another.

The door opened and a doctor entered, his gaze going to her at once.

'Crying? That's something. We've had nothing from her these past two days.' He bent over to check her pulse. 'She seems a little stronger.'

'She spoke to me about her mother...' Rachel faltered. 'I thought her mother was dead, but she was telling me she'd seen her. Perhaps it was just the fever...'

'Or something on her mind as the fever started to break.' The doctor beamed at her. 'You will be glad to know that the fever *has* broken. She feels much cooler. I think we've been lucky or her friends' prayers have saved her, because I didn't expect her to live when I saw her first. These kinds of fevers often result in swift deaths, because we just don't have anything to combat poisoning in the blood – but either we got it wrong or you've just witnessed a small miracle.'

'Thank God,' Rachel said and her own eyes filled with tears. 'We all love Sally and I don't know what Harpers would do without her.'

'Well, you will have to manage for a while, because this young woman needs rest. Whatever this illness was – and I admit we're still not sure, except that we believe it was a kind of poisoning, probably caused by the pregnancy – she has been, and is still, very unwell and will need a prolonged period of rest.'

'Yes, I agree with you, and fortunately, she has a loving family and friends to take care of her,' Rachel said and looked up as Jenni entered the room. 'She spoke to me, Jenni – and the doctor says her fever has broken.'

'Well, thank God for that,' Jenni said, suddenly practical again. 'In that case, how soon can we take her home?'

* * *

Rachel was feeling much lighter of spirit as she left the small room that was separated from the general ward and walked down to the hospital's main entrance. It was as she was about to leave the hospital that she saw her husband step out of one of the consulting rooms. He stopped as he saw her and for a moment confusion and guilt were in his eyes and then he frowned.

'Did you follow me here, Rachel?' he asked.

'No, I came to visit Sally Harper,' she replied. 'I told you what I was going to do, William. At breakfast this morning...'

He glanced away. 'Sorry, my dear. I'd forgotten, but you did mention it...'

'Why are you here, William?' Rachel looked at him oddly. He'd been acting so strangely lately and she'd thought he regretted their marriage, but now she wondered if there was some other reason, he'd been silent and withdrawn. 'Are you ill?'

'I should have told you...' he admitted and looked resigned. 'I was trying to save you pain, my dear. I wasn't certain of the results of all the tests and examinations...'

'But now you are?'

'Let's get out of this place...' Her husband took her arm and steered her from the hospital into the busy street. 'We'll go to the pub across the road. I could do with a stiff drink...'

Rachel went with him, saving her questions until they were seated in a corner of a comfortable pub just down the road. She watched as he bought drinks at the bar, whisky for himself and a sherry for her, but then she could hold the questions inside no longer.

'Are you ill, William? Please tell me the truth.'

He took a gulp of his whisky and then looked her in the eyes. 'I'm sorry, Rachel, but the short answer is yes. I wanted to keep it from you to save you pain, but I know you sensed something.'

'I thought you were regretting our marriage,' Rachel told him, her throat catching with the tears that she struggled to hold back. 'What is wrong, William? Please tell me.'

He gulped down the rest of his whisky and then reached for her hand. 'I thought at first it was the same illness that took my father young... it's hereditary and shows itself as chest pains, leading to shortness of breath and then a heart problem.' He took a deep breath. 'I went for tests and they've just told me that I have tuberculosis and they want to send me to an isolation hospital on the coast. I shall probably be there for some months...'

'William!' Rachel's tears spilled silently. 'What do they say – how bad is it?'

'I'm not sure,' he said, looking uncomfortable. 'I've been told I must go soon, and in the meantime, I shouldn't have intimate relations with my family, lest I pass it on. I think they want to test you, too. I'm so sorry, Rachel. I shouldn't have married you. You suffered enough with the illness and death of your first husband.'

'Of course, you should have married me,' she said. 'I've been happy with you – and I'll come with you so that I can visit...'

His hand tightened over hers as he shook his head. 'No, my love. That can't happen. I shall be isolated, I'm not sure they will even let me write to you – or you to me...'

'No...' Rachel's wail reflected in his eyes and she saw the pain her grief was causing him. She'd been wrong to think he didn't love her. He'd kept his secret torture from her to save her pain. 'I love you, William. I don't want to lose you.'

'I shall fight,' William promised her. 'I know how much I have to live for and I shall come home to you, my love – if God wills it...'

Rachel fought her tears. The last thing he needed to take with him was a picture of her sorrowful face. She made herself smile, closing her hands around his. 'I know you will, and I'm sorry I doubted you for a moment.'

'That was my fault. I'd hoped for better news and that it would simply be a slow degeneration of a heart condition, but now...' He shook his head. 'We shall get through this, Rachel. You must stay here with your friends and continue to do your job. I thank God that you did not leave Harpers, my dearest, for if the worst should happen...'

'It won't,' Rachel said strongly, even though inside she was fearful that she might never see him again once he left for the hospital. 'You will get better, my love, and as soon as you can return home, I shall take time off to nurse you while you regain your strength.'

He nodded and smiled, but there was a faraway look in his eyes that worried her. She had the feeling that he was already preparing himself to leave this life and it broke her heart. Rachel had known of the hereditary heart problem in his family, but he'd seemed to be clear of it – but now he had an equally distressing illness that might take him from her.

'We'll go home and spend the rest of the day together,' he said, smiling at her. 'In the morning I must leave.'

Rachel nodded and reached for his arm. They left the public house and walked to the nearest cab stand together. Reflecting that troubles never came singly, Rachel thought about her best friend lying in hospital. Sally would have hugged her and told her to keep her chin up had she been well and Rachel missed her. She had other friends, of course, but Sally was the one she needed now and she prayed that she would soon be well again. It would be unbearable if she were to lose either of her dearest friends, for it was William's friendship, his humour and his gentle kindness that Rachel would miss more than anything while he was away.

19

When Marion had been wretchedly sick for the fourth morning in a row, she acknowledged to herself what she had known in the back of her mind for a week or two now. Perhaps if everyone at Harpers hadn't been so worried for Mrs Harper, she would have taken more notice of the signs before now, but all Marion had been able to think about as she got ready for work each day had been what would happen to the store if they lost their chief buyer. They all knew who the driving force behind the store's success was and although Miss Jenni – as Jenni Harper preferred to be known now that she had left her husband – was liked, Sally Harper was generally loved by her staff. She'd been in their shoes and knew what it was like to work on the shop floor and she never forgot that when she spoke to her staff, greeting them all in her open, friendly way. Yet discipline was not forgotten either and even the cheeky young ones, straight out of school, soon learned to respect the way things were run.

Wiping her mouth after rinsing with cold water, Marion looked at herself in the mirror. She looked a bit pale and, now she thought about it, her breasts were a little tender. That didn't prove anything, of course, but there was something that told her she was carrying her first child. She would wait a few days to see if her period came, though counting back she realised that she was more than three weeks overdue, perhaps longer. How could she not have noticed that sooner? It could only be that she'd had too much on her mind.

Everyone had thought that Mrs Harper would die from her mystery illness. Fevers could start so suddenly and the doctors sometimes had no idea what started them and they could kill as swiftly as they came. Fortunately, Mrs Harper's fever had broken and after a two-week stay in hospital, her family was finally being allowed to bring her home. Miss Jenni had found a special doctor for her and she was being nursed by her friend and employee Pearl, who also looked after the Harpers' daughter. The staff at Harpers understood that their employer's wife was still weak and would need bed rest, but she was recovering and everyone had felt a sense of relief.

Marion hadn't yet begun to think about her own future. Reggie would, she knew, be over the moon when she told him that they were having a baby. He wanted a big family and his business plans for after the war showed that he would provide well for his wife and children. He wouldn't be like Marion's father had been, always drinking his wages away and then beating his wife. She smiled as she thought of Reggie's pleasure in the coming birth. His face would light up like a candle when she told him.

Marion had seen both her mother and Sarah give birth. There would be pain, she understood that, but it would be a small price to pay to hold a child of her own. Her one regret was that in the later stages of her pregnancy she would have to leave Harpers and she did not expect to return. Once they had a family, Reggie would expect her to stay at home and look after the house, her child and him. If she wanted extra work, there would be his book-keeping and he was fair enough to see that she had money of her own in return – but she would miss the magic of being at Harpers

Shaking her head, she put her foolish regrets from her mind. Reggie was a loving husband and she loved him. Working in that lovely place, serving customers with beautiful hats was a real pleasure and Marion felt a pang of regret that it would end soon. She'd loved being a part of the window display team, but she must forget that and look to the future and the start of her family. She would love her child and she could always visit Harpers as a customer and see her old friends now and then. The future was exciting.

When she went down to the kitchen, Kathy and Sarah were talking. They both looked at her and then Sarah asked, 'Are you all right, Marion love? We thought you might be feeling a little unwell...'

'I was sick,' Marion said and smiled because they were so obviously curious. 'I'm not sure, but I might be pregnant.'

'That's wonderful,' Sarah said and rushed to hug her. 'I'm so pleased for you, Marion. Once the baby is born, we'll be able to do so much more together.'

'Yes, we shall,' she said and suddenly happiness flooded through her. She was lucky. Many women had to struggle to do menial work like scrubbing floors to survive, even though they had children at home. It was a hard life for so many and she had a caring husband who would make sure she had all he could provide. That meant far more than a career in window dressing.

* * *

Mrs Bailey seemed very serious that morning when Marion arrived just a minute before time. She'd lingered on the ground floor looking at things she might need once the baby was born and had nearly been late. For a moment she considered telling Mrs Bailey her wonderful news but held back because she suddenly realised how sad her supervisor's eyes were. She hadn't noticed it before and a chill touched her nape. Something must be upsetting her.

'Is Mrs Harper any worse?' she asked and then flushed as her supervisor turned a frowning look on her.

'Mrs Harper? No, not as far as I've been told – why do you ask?'

'You looked sad...' Marion said and then bit her lip. 'I'm sorry, I had no right to say.'

'Thank you for your concern, Mrs Jackson,' Mrs Bailey replied. 'Please get to your counter. We shall soon have customers.'

Marion went quickly to remove the flimsy covers they draped over the hats to keep off the dust. There was definitely something wrong with Mrs Bailey, but she dared not push things further as even her gentle questioning had upset her supervisor. She wondered what it could be but did not know who to speak to about it. If Mrs Harper had been at work, she might have noticed, but she wasn't and the only other person at Harpers who knew Mrs Bailey well enough to ask what was wrong was Mrs Burrows. She was at home expecting the birth of her second child any day now and Marion didn't know her well enough to visit her house.

Giving herself a mental shake, she smiled as a customer approached. Marion couldn't ask Mrs Bailey what was worrying her and she certainly couldn't tell her her own news at the moment. She felt unable to confide in Mr Stockbridge, and even Mr Marco had been unusually quiet of late, so for the moment she would simply have to keep her condition to herself.

* * *

Rachel kept busy at work, checking stock whenever there were no customers to occupy her mind. She felt as if her heart would break and there was no one she could talk to about her husband's illness. Marion Jackson was a thoughtful girl, but the bonds Rachel had forged with Sally, Beth and Maggie just weren't there with any of the younger girls she supervised now. Somehow, there had been a special feeling amongst the original Harpers' girls when they first started to work on the shop floor and, of course, she'd lived with them. They had all shared their hopes and dreams and Rachel was missing them terribly now.

Beth hadn't been in for a week. She was very close to giving birth and she spent what time she could spare sitting by Sally Harper's side, encouraging her to get well. Obviously, she had more than enough to occupy her time and thoughts.

Rachel didn't feel she could visit her employers' home without an invitation. She'd visited Sally at the hospital a couple of times before she was taken home, but Miss Jenni was in charge, because Captain Harper had been called away again. He'd stayed by his wife's side until she was over the dangerous period and then given into repeated requests for his presence elsewhere. Miss Jenni didn't see Rachel in the same light as Sally always had. To her, she was just an employee, respected and valued, but not a friend. Whenever Rachel enquired about Sally's health, she was met with polite but brief information that made her feel left out – and she certainly couldn't go and unburden her troubles on Sally and Beth. Sally was still too ill and Beth was feeling under the weather as the birth of her second child approached; it must surely be any day now as September neared its close. Rachel had visited her at home, managing to catch her before she left for Sally's one Sunday morning, but Beth was clearly too wrapped up in her family to have time for her friend's worries. Maggie, of course, was still away in hospital and she'd heard nothing from her for some weeks.

Minnie was always busy with her work for Harpers and being a wife to Mr Stockbridge, and, despite their long-standing friendship, Rachel didn't like to intrude into their weekends together. When Minnie had been so lonely after her sister's death, Rachel had been there for her, but now Minnie was happily married. So, there was no one she could turn to, but Hazel, her first husband's mother, and she'd never been the most sympathetic listener. She was full of complaints, looking to Rachel to solve her problems for her. Normally, Rachel was happy to do anything she wanted, but now, she needed a shoulder to cry on herself.

Wrenching her thoughts back to the present as a customer asked to see silver jewellery, Rachel knew she must stand on her own feet. However, she missed Sally so much and wished that she was back at Harpers so that they could sit and have coffee together. She would not have needed to tell Sally something was wrong, she would have sensed it and asked straight out in her no-nonsense way.

Rachel prayed that Sally would soon be well enough to return to work. The department heads were coping as well as they could, but there was no denying that some of the new stock was not quite up to Sally Harper's standards and, the longer she was away, the more it would show.

20

Sally sat up in bed and looked at the doctor. He was an elderly man with a gentle bedside manner, but he'd proved himself to be strict with his instructions to stay in bed and not move a muscle. She was not at home to start work; she was home to convalesce from a serious illness, being cared for and looked after by her family and friends, and there she must stop until he gave her the all-clear. Yet the news was good despite all, because she'd been told that she was to have another child.

'How much longer, Doctor Symonds?' she asked as he looked at the thermometer. 'I don't have a fever now, do I?' Impatience had crept into her tone, because she was tired of being in bed with nothing to do.

'You were very lucky young woman,' Doctor Symonds informed her with a shake of his head. 'You had a toxic inflammation of your organs and you could quite easily have died. Fortunately, you have a strong constitution and you have fought the poisoning and are now recovering. However, your condition was almost certainly caused by your pregnancy and that means you will need to rest more than you did the last time.' He shook his head at her. 'If you push yourself too hard too soon, it could cause untold harm.'

'Yes, but surely I can get up – and talk to people on the telephone?' Sally reasoned. Why couldn't he understand that lying here fretting was doing her more harm than if she was allowed to get up and sit by the window?

'Not if those people are to do with Harpers and might cause your blood pressure to rise. Let me be clear, Mrs Harper. It is possible that if your body becomes overstressed, the condition may return and you could lose the child and die yourself.'

Sally sighed and lay back against her pillows. She couldn't risk losing her second child, but she felt restless. 'It's boring just lying here...'

'Now, that's not kind, is it? I know that you have lots of visitors to sit with you.'

'Yes, and I love them for it,' Sally said, 'but I've always worked, doctor. I miss it!'

'You have your own health and your unborn child to think of. You may return to work when I think you are strong enough. For the moment, I do not believe you are.' He felt her pulse. 'Do not distress yourself. You may start to get up in the afternoons, providing you sit quietly or just play with your daughter for a while.'

Sally nodded. For all his gentle manners, he was a martinet and both Jenni and Beth had forbidden her to disobey his orders, as had Ben, before he reluctantly left her to travel to the South Coast.

'I'll ring every day and I'll be back as soon as I can,' he'd told her as he kissed her goodbye. 'Promise me you'll do as the doctor and nurses say, Sally. I thought I was going to lose you and I couldn't bear that so please don't make yourself ill again.'

'Yes, I promise,' Sally had said, swayed by his obvious

emotion. However, lying in bed day after day, her frustration grew. She and Jenny were being well cared for – but what of Harpers? Jenni would do her best, she knew that, but many of her suppliers only came up with extras for Sally because they had known her for ages and liked her. She knew she pulled in favours and made sure of rewarding them.

Yet, it wasn't Harpers that was playing on her mind the most – it was her mother, or the woman who had claimed to be Sheila Ross, and claimed to have left Sally with one set of nuns, who had then sent her mother away to another convent, making it impossible for her to find her. And then they'd lied to Sally, telling her that her mother had died. Such unnecessary cruelty!

However, the fact that her mother had said she had asked where she was implied that she had wanted to find her, perhaps to reclaim her once she was on her feet. Sally knew that things like that happened – children were taken from their mothers, women deemed unfit to have the care of them, even though they tried to get them back once they were able, often with no hope of ever seeing the child again. It was unfair and Sally felt angry that she'd been denied her mother for the whole of her life. But why had it taken her so long to come forward? Sally wanted to know more.

She'd spoken to both Jenni and Beth about it, but they shook their heads, looking as if they disbelieved her. She understood they thought she'd imagined the incident in the park, but she *knew* it was real. She remembered clearly the woman following her for a while and rushing up to help when Jenny was frightened by a big dog – and then, when, the woman had finally plucked up courage to speak to Sally, she'd fallen into that awful fever and been carted off to hospital by Mr Marco. She couldn't quite remember, but she thought he'd sought her out in the park to either tell or ask her something.

Sighing, she picked up a magazine Jenni had bought for her, flicked through it and threw it down again. The doctor had gone and neither Jenni nor Beth was there, so it ought to be safe.

Getting up cautiously, she stood up for the first time in ages, her feet planted on the soft Persian rug beside the bed. For a moment the room swayed and she felt she might fall, but then her head cleared and she took a step towards the telephone, which had been placed out of reach to stop her using it.

She smiled as she negotiated the short distance and sat on her dressing table stool, catching her breath. The doctor was right; she wasn't ready to return to work just yet, but she knew someone who would bring work to her.

* * *

Rachel saw Ruth, Sally's secretary, coming towards her in the department and smiled. 'What can I do for you?' she asked, not sure of the reason for the visit.

'Mrs Harper wants you to visit,' Ruth said. 'The doctor has forbidden her to work, but she wants the latest accounts from this department and as many others as I have ready for her. You'll have to smuggle them in, because Miss Jenni and the nurse will take them away if they see you carrying them.'

'Should she have them?' Rachel asked doubtfully. 'I don't want to do anything that might make her ill again.'

'Perhaps she ought not,' Ruth replied, 'but you know she won't be kept in bed for long and she said if I didn't ask you to bring them, she would get up and come in.' She pulled a wry face. 'I think she means it.'

'That sounds as if she is on the mend,' Rachel said and smiled. 'Give me the accounts for my department and the ladies clothing. That should be enough to keep her busy for a while and it will give you time to copy up others she needs to see.'

'Yes, that's what I thought,' Ruth said. 'I haven't visited, because the hospital wouldn't let me and I don't like to go to her home...'

'I told the hospital I was Sally's sister,' Rachel admitted. 'When I rang them, they said only close family, so I'm afraid I told a small lie.'

'Good for you...' Ruth frowned. 'She didn't know you then, did she?'

'For a moment now and then she seemed a little better but slipped back again,' Rachel replied thoughtfully. 'She certainly wasn't truly with us for several days and then she was very tired – but she sounds restless now!'

'Oh yes, I can confirm she is restless,' Ruth said with a grin. 'I'll leave you to get on then, Mrs Bailey.'

Rachel nodded and smiled. Sally was never going to be an easy patient, but she wouldn't mind betting she would escape her well-meaning jailors quite soon.

* * *

Rachel went armed with flowers, fruit, fashion magazines and, hidden between them, the lists Sally had asked for. When she first saw how tired and pale her friend looked, she wondered if she ought to give them to her, but Sally leaned forward with a smile.

'I knew you wouldn't let me down, Rachel,' she said. 'That's why I asked Ruth to give the lists to you. I just can't lie here twiddling my thumbs any longer.' She relaxed back against her pillows as Rachel handed the magazines over and told her the lists were tucked inside. 'Wonderful! I'll go through them later and ring Ruth again tomorrow.'

'Don't overdo things,' Rachel advised. 'I know you must be bored – but we need you back. We all miss you...'

Sally nodded, her eyes on Rachel's face. 'What is wrong? I can see something is upsetting you. Have they given you dire news about me?'

'No—' Rachel gulped back the tears that were too close. 'No. They tell me you're getting better, thank goodness...' She paused. 'I shouldn't tell you, because I know how ill *you've* been, but... William has TB and he's gone to an isolation hospital on the coast. He wouldn't tell me exactly where because I can't visit until they let him out into the gardens, by which time he should be over the worst... if he survives...'

'Oh, Rachel dearest!' Sally exclaimed and leaned forward to catch her hand. 'I'm so sorry. That is terribly unfair. You've been through so much – and William doesn't deserve this either.'

'Yes, I thought that too,' Rachel said, 'but I know lots of people get worse troubles – and so many men have died in this war. I shouldn't feel sorry for myself, Sally.'

'Of course, you do,' Sally exclaimed. 'You had a bad time when your first husband died and now William is ill. It is horrid for you, love. I wish there was something I could do to help – to make the pain and worry you must be feeling a little easier. Promise you will tell me if there is?'

Rachel took her hand gratefully. She'd been nursing the pain of William's news inside and fretting, but Sally's care and sincerity had eased her already. It didn't change anything but just having a friend she could talk to made it seem easier. 'I feel better now I've been able to talk to you.'

'I am so glad and I meant it – anything at all I can do to help.'

'Just talking – being able to tell someone helps.'

'Yes, I know...' Sally hesitated, then, 'Can I share something with you?'

'Yes, of course. We can always talk, Sally.'

'We talked about everything when we lived together,' Sally agreed. 'I told you about my mother – and how I always thought something was wrong – that the nuns were lying to me. Now, I'm sure they were. She is alive and they deliberately hid it from me.'

'You spoke of your mother in your delirium,' Rachel said, frowning. 'Have you truly seen her, Sally?'

'Yes, in the park, just before I passed out.' Sally smiled at her triumphantly. 'She had been trying to pluck up the courage to see me, Rachel. We were talking and then it all went hazy, and I passed out...' Hesitating once more, she said, 'Could you do me a favour? I need someone to trace her for me – Sheila Ross. I doubt if she married. She must have been in trouble when she gave me up because she tried to get me back, but the nuns had sent me to another orphanage, and they wouldn't tell her anything; they didn't think she was a proper person to bring up a child.'

'How wicked of them!' Rachel exclaimed in indignation. 'They had no right to keep you apart if she was ready to take you back.'

'I don't know her story,' Sally said. 'One of the nuns gave me a little silver cross she said was my mother's – and I gave it to Jenny once to protect her. I need to find my mother, Rachel. I know Beth and Jenni think I dreamed it all, but I promise you I didn't!'

'Do you want me to employ a private detective?' Rachel suggested.

'Yes please. It's what Ben would do if he were here and I asked him to find her – but Jenni thinks I imagined it all, I know she does.'

Rachel gave her an intent look. 'Supposing it does turn out to be imagination or hallucination?'

'Then tell me the truth and I'll accept it – but I know I'm right.'

'Then I'll do everything to find her,' Rachel promised.

Sally smiled, nodded and then asked her if she was happy with things at Harpers.

Rachel told her truthfully that Marion hadn't liked some of the latest hats. 'Miss Jenni bought them from a new supplier. They are cheaper but not as well made, but perhaps it is wrong of me to tell you?'

'No, it's what I expected,' Sally grimaced as she tried to sit forward. 'I'm still so weak, but I'm getting better. I'll give it another week and then I shall take over the ordering again, at least for your department and the ladies' clothes.'

'Don't overdo it or I shall be banned from visiting you,' Rachel said with a smile.

'Pearl is on my side. She encourages me to do what I can and she brings Jenny to me three times a day. If it was left to Jenni and the doctor, I wouldn't see anyone.'

'They are determined to look after you, but perhaps it is best to rest as much as you can bear until you feel less tired. You must think of yourself and the baby, Sally love.'

'Yes, it probably is best to rest,' Sally agreed and lay back against her pillows. 'Before you came, I was thinking of our first days at Harpers. We were all so young and so excited to have been given our jobs. This war makes it all feel so long ago. It's like a long dark tunnel with no glimmer of light at the other end...'

Rachel nodded. The papers were filled with dire news most days. In America, the Government had threatened to execute anyone who tried to avoid conscription, while in London the authorities had withdrawn passports from people wishing to attend the peace conference in Stockholm. In France, the Allied forces were driving the Germans back at Ypres but at terrible cost.

It was felt that the movement towards peace was not helpful at this time and too many concessions were being made by those trying to broker it, so the British Government was refusing to listen. Rachel didn't know who was right and who was wrong; she just knew she wished it would stop.

'Yes, it is,' Rachel agreed and held back her sigh. 'But you know what makes it bearable? It's having friends like you, Beth and Maggie. How is Beth at the moment? I haven't seen her for a couple of weeks.'

'She will be here soon.' Sally glanced at her watch. 'At least she said she would. I wonder...'

'I know,' Rachel agreed. 'She was very close to the birth and later than she'd expected when I last saw her. She thought she would give birth at the end of September but she must have miscalculated or she is very late, because we're in October now. I wouldn't mind betting we shall be told she has had her second child any minute!'

Sally smiled. 'She was so fed up with looking like a beached whale and complaining all the time of backache. I think you might be right, Rachel. I do hope so because she will be happier when it is all over.'

Rachel nodded and said that she thought so too. Sally looked a bit tired then, so she left and went out to speak to Mrs Hills and Pearl, who was indulging Jenny by playing with her and some brightly coloured bricks, which the child enjoyed building up so she could knock them down.

Rachel was thoughtful as she caught her bus home. Sally was lucky to have such devoted friends and carers. Both Beth and Sally were fortunate in having their children earlier in their marriage, even though the doctors suspected that this pregnancy had caused Sally's fever and might not be as easy as her first. Rachel herself had never carried a child full term, though she'd had a miscarriage early in her first marriage. After that, her husband had become ill and there were no further hopes of a family. For a moment, the ache of longing and loneliness swept over her, making her catch her breath and hold back a sob.

She'd hoped she might perhaps fall for a child when she married William, but it hadn't happened, and now, she'd given up all hope. If her husband survived his ordeal in the isolation hospital, she doubted they could have a child – but perhaps the fault lay with her. She could only resign herself to a life without children to brighten it...

As she got off her bus, Rachel saw children playing hopscotch in the lane near where she lived and she stopped to watch and listen to their happy laughter. Smothering a sigh of self-pity, she turned to leave and then caught sight of the little girl sitting on the pavement, her knees hunched and her face stained with tears. Something in Rachel reached out to the forlorn child and she went up to her.

'Hello,' she said. 'I'm Mrs Bailey – who are you?'

'I'm Lizzie...' the little girl sniffed. 'I'm five and my mummy went to Heaven this morning and my granny says she can't look after me...' She wiped her nose on a sleeve that was none too clean. 'She sent me off 'cos she didn't want me under her feet...'

'Oh, you poor darling! Are you hungry?' Rachel asked, her heart feeling as if it was being tugged from her chest. She pointed to her apartment building across the road. 'I live up there – would you like some bread and butter with strawberry jam and a piece of cake?'

'Yes, please,' Lizzie's face lit up. 'I know you – Mummy said you were the lady from Harpers and rich.'

Rachel laughed and shook her head. 'I'm not rich, but I have a good job. Shall we tell your granny you're coming to tea with me?'

Lizzie nodded and pulled at Rachel's hand. 'She's there at the gate.'

The child pointed to one of the terraced houses just across the road from her apartment block.

Taking Lizzie by the hand, Rachel approached the stone-faced woman, who looked at the little girl with obvious dislike.

'Excuse me, are you Lizzie's granny?' she asked politely. 'I'm sorry I don't know your name?'

'Vi Robinson, not that it's your business,' the woman said, looking sour.

'I wanted to know if you minded if I took Lizzie for tea with me?' Rachel said politely. 'I understand her mother has just died...'

'Good riddance to her – the slut deserved it,' Mrs Robinson snarled bitterly. 'Why my son married her and then saddled me with her and her brat while he went off to war, I'll never know. It was because of that bitch he went off, to do his duty, he said – and when he's killed, I'll have no one to support me in my old age. How am I supposed to look after a kid, go scrubbing floors and feed us both – that's what I'd like to know?'

'It must be very hard for you.' Rachel made her voice sympathetic while keeping hold of Lizzie's hand, which was trembling in hers. 'You don't know me, but I would be happy to help you care for Lizzie. She can spend some time with me when I'm home... if you wish...'

'Please, Granny...' Lizzie's held on tightly to Rachel's hand.

'I do know yer,' Mrs Robinson muttered. 'More money than sense I shouldn't wonder – and no kids. Have the brat whenever yer like. Yer can get her some clothes because I can't.'

'Yes, I can do that,' Rachel agreed, 'and I can give you a little money to help with feeding her.'

Seeing the gleam of avarice in the woman's eyes, Rachel knew she would take all she could get but Lizzie was unlikely to benefit. It didn't matter. William insisted she kept all her own money, which she used for whatever she liked. He had also put money and property into her name in case he should die in the war and so she knew she was financially secure. She wouldn't allow Lizzie's granny to fleece her, but she would give her a few shillings, even if she spent it on herself rather than the child. It would be worth it to be allowed the pleasure of looking after the little girl.

'I'll bring her back to you later,' Rachel promised and the woman nodded, retreating into her home, where the curtains were grey rather than the sparkling white as many other houses had them, even in these run-down terraced houses. The women who lived there were proud and kept their homes spotless, Rachel knew, despite them being constantly short of money. Vi Robinson was the exception.

Rachel looked down at the child as she took her inside the apartment building and into the lift. 'Don't be scared, Lizzie, it's fun,' she said and showed her how it worked. 'It is a strange sensation, but it takes us up several flights of stairs.'

Lizzie nodded and held on to Rachel's skirt tightly. However, once it started to rise, her eyes widened and then she laughed. Once inside the flat, she stared in wonder at the comfortable furniture, the flowers and the ornaments.

'You have pretty things,' she said and touched the shiny surface of an antique table with tentative fingers.

'Yes, I'm lucky,' Rachel said. William had furnished the apartment for her with satinwood and walnut furniture from the previous century and it shone with the polishing of ages. She'd told him she preferred old things to the more modern furniture that was being made just before the war, though some of the best pieces could be lovely. She did have one or two new things in their bedroom, but everything else had the gracious look of the Regency period. 'Come along, Lizzie, help me with the tea.'

Taking the child into the kitchen, Rachel unloaded fresh bread and cake from her basket. She caught sight of Lizzie's filthy hands and took her to the sink to wash them and then let her put out the plates, cups and saucers as she cut thin slices of bread, spreading them generously with fresh butter and a thick dollop of home-made strawberry jam.

After the bread and jam, they had coconut madeleines she'd bought in Harpers' delicatessen department. It had started out with just chocolate and chocolate cakes, but Sally had added anything she thought worthy of being on her shelves to help fill them and the madeleines were made by a small bakery that had needed a bigger outlet. Rachel loved them and bought them every week. Now she was glad she'd been greedy and bought two – one each for her and Lizzie.

After Lizzie had eaten her fill and drunk a glass of milk, Rachel took her all round the flat and then gave her a little bead necklace from her trinket box. The child's face lit up and she thanked her politely. When Rachel told her that it was time to go home, her eyes filled with tears, but she didn't refuse to leave, though her hand trembled as they neared her home.

Rachel could hardly bear to hand her over to her sullen granny, but she knew she had to. 'I'll fetch you again tomorrow,' she told her and she handed Mrs Robinson five shillings. Seeing the greed in her eyes as she stuffed it into her apron pocket, Rachel knew the visits would be permitted to continue – at least for the moment.

Leaving Lizzie with the woman tore at her insides, but she knew she had to be careful. Mrs Robinson might not want the child, but she wouldn't simply give her away just because Rachel asked.

Her apartment seemed empty without Lizzie. Sighing, Rachel sat down to write a letter to William. She wrote one every evening, even though she had nowhere to send them, because he was not allowed to receive letters until he was over the worst of his illness. Rachel felt that was too cruel, but she'd been told it was part of the rules. So, she didn't send them, but she wrote them religiously anyway. It made her feel closer to him, and at this moment, fearing she might never have the children she longed for, the future did indeed seem bleak.

21

Marion read the letter from Maggie Gibbs, feeling puzzled. Who was this Captain Morgan and how long had Maggie known him? Her last letter hadn't mentioned a new boyfriend, only that she'd made friends with a nurse and some of the injured men. Everyone had believed that she was still grieving for Tim. Now, she was saying that she thought she might be married soon and would visit Harpers to buy a few things before she did and see her old friends.

> I'm not sure when I'll get up to London, but I want to try in the next couple of weeks. I'll be living in the country and I doubt if I'll be able to visit for a long time after my marriage so I thought I would come and see you all now...

Folding the letter and putting it into her pocket, Marion shook her head. Maggie talked about the nurses and how glad she would be when they finally said she could go home, but nothing was said about her husband-to-be. It wasn't the letter of a girl who had fallen in love, surely? When Maggie had been courting before she'd talked about Tim all the time. So, what was going on? It seemed to Marion that something had to be wrong. Yet who could she talk to about Maggie? Mrs Burrows never came in now and Becky Stockbridge hardly spoke to her these days. Perhaps she blamed Marion because she'd been moved to another department, though it had nothing to do with her. The heads of department had arranged it.

Maggie's odd letter played on her mind as she arrived at work that morning. Should she speak to Mrs Bailey? She'd seemed a little happier these past few days, though always busy.

Almost at once, Marion had several customers at her counter and it was only when Mrs Bailey announced that she was going to take her break that she thought of the letter.

'Mrs Bailey – would you read this for me please? I'm a little worried...'

Glancing at the envelope, her supervisor frowned. 'Is this from Maggie Gibbs?'

'Yes, it is – and I'm a little concerned for her. I wasn't sure who to tell...'

Mrs Bailey nodded and accepted the letter. 'I shall read it, Mrs Jackson. Please take charge of the department during my break.'

Marion thanked her and smiled. Mrs Bailey always chose the period when they were less busy to take her own break, giving all the other girls their opportunity first and she did not anticipate being rushed off her feet. Her mind felt relieved now that she'd given Mrs Bailey the letter. She knew that Maggie had shared a flat with Mrs Bailey and Mrs Harper, Mrs Burrows too, but she hadn't seen Mrs Burrows in days.

Her absence was explained a little later in the day when Fred Burrows came up from the basement, where he worked tirelessly to see all the new stock got to the right departments, to tell them the news.

'My daughter-in-law went to hospital two days ago, because they were a bit worried and thought they might have to induce the birth or something,' he said. 'My friend Vera has been looking after young Jack so I could come to work. However, we're all delighted that Mrs Burrows gave birth naturally to a lovely little boy last night at almost midnight and they are both doing well...'

'Oh, that's lovely,' Marion said and her hand moved unconsciously to her stomach, as if reassuring her own baby that he or she was equally welcome. 'Is she pleased?' Mrs Burrows had mentioned hoping she might have a girl this time. Marion didn't care whether she had a boy or a girl, just so long as everything went as it ought and the child was all right.

'Yes, she's delighted,' Fred assured her. 'I know Jack will be pleased – and she's going to call him Tim. It was too soon when the first was born, but now we feel able to give him his uncle's name.'

Marion nodded, feeling sad, because Fred's happy smile had dimmed a little. He must still feel grief at the loss of his younger son, but at least he now had two grandchildren to love and fuss over. Children brought their own love and would take nothing from his memories of his Tim when nursing his new grandson on his knees.

'I think that's nice,' Marion told him. 'When will she be home? I'd love to see her. Perhaps I could pop round once she gets back?'

'The hospital is keeping her for a couple of weeks,' Fred said. 'They seem to think she needs the rest. As I said, I've got a friend of mine looking after the little lad. Vera has brought up four of her own, so he's no trouble to her.'

Marion promised that she would call over if Fred let her know when his daughter-in-law was home and he agreed. Beth

Burrows had long ago told Marion to call her Beth rather than the formal Mrs Burrows.

'I'm not working at Harpers now,' she'd told Marion. 'So, we can talk to each other as friends.'

Marion reflected now that Beth had looked a little wistful when she'd said that she no longer worked for Harpers and she understood that her former supervisor missed coming in to work every day, despite the love she had for her child.

Would Marion miss Harpers when she had to give it up? Once upon a time, work had just been a job to Marion, but there was something special about being a Harpers' girl – a kind of belonging, as if they were all one big family.

Mr Marco had recently told her that she would make the grade as a window dresser with a little training from him. Marion didn't feel she would ever be as clever at making people gasp with surprise and delight as Mr Marco was, but she did enjoy it – and yet the thought of having her own child tugged at her heartstrings. She might be torn and one day she might wish to return to work here again, but she decided her family came first. She was lucky to have a wonderful husband who loved her and to be expecting her first child, though, as yet, she hadn't told anyone at Harpers about her condition.

* * *

Beth sat up in bed as Rachel and Fred came into the ward, feeling a surge of pleasure. Rachel bent to kiss her cheek and tell her how thrilled she was to hear the news, and Fred gave her a bag of grapes and a kiss on the cheek.

'How are you – and the baby?'

'Both doing well,' Beth assured her. 'He's gorgeous, Rachel. Just wait until you see him.'

'I bought a little present for him.' Rachel gave her a small parcel. 'I expect you will be given lots of things.'

'I was loaded up when I left this evening,' Fred told her with a cheerful grin. 'I haven't looked at anything. You'll find them all in your room when you get home.'

'Thank you, Dad,' Beth said with a small sigh. 'No word from Jack I suppose?'

'No, love, not yet,' her father-in-law said with a slight frown. 'He expected to be home by now, but there's a war on and he can't always keep his word.'

'I know.' Beth smiled at him. 'He couldn't have done much if he had been here, anyway. I got through it easily once it started, and I feel fine. I just wish they would let me get up and come home. It's boring just sitting here...'

'That's Sally's complaint. I've brought you some ladies' magazines,' Rachel told her with a smile. 'They will give you something to do for a while – and there's some wool so you can knit if you want, Beth.'

'Yes, I should like to do something useful,' Beth replied. 'How is Sally now? Is she getting better?'

'Yes, thank goodness,' Rachel assured her. 'She gets out of bed each afternoon and walks about for a while to build up her strength. They tried to keep her in bed, but you know our Sally Harper – and the nurse looking after her says it will do her good. She doesn't approve of making a patient rest once they feel able to get up and move about, as long as she doesn't overdo it.'

'Oh good,' Beth said and smiled. 'Please tell her I love her when you see her, Rachel. I shall visit just as soon as I can.'

'I'm sure that will please her,' Rachel said. 'I know she will be delighted with your news, Beth.'

Beth nodded, then, 'I was wondering. Have you heard from Maggie recently?'

'No, I haven't,' Rachel said, feeling a return of her anxiety. 'But Marion Jackson had a letter, which she gave me to read – and Maggie says she's getting married. She expects to be allowed to visit us all next week and will come to Harpers. She hasn't written to you about it then?'

'No... I wonder why,' Beth mused, wrinkling her brow. 'Do you think she feels it might upset me because of Tim? I suppose it isn't that long since he died.' She glanced at Fred, but he was watching one of the women who had got out of bed and seemed to be unsteady on her feet. He moved to stop her falling and Beth looked at Rachel. 'I wonder why she didn't tell us rather than Marion?'

'I don't think she's in love with this Captain Morgan,' Rachel said. 'I think she is getting married for other reasons, but I don't know what they are. Perhaps she feels vulnerable and she can't face returning to Harpers...'

'Oh, the silly girl,' Beth cried. 'Doesn't she know we all love her and will help her all we can?'

'I know she was desperately unhappy when I wrote to her a few weeks back. Perhaps she feels she will never find happiness again and she's willing to settle for a comfortable home in the country.'

'That doesn't sound like our Maggie,' Beth declared and felt a surge of frustration that she was stuck in a hospital bed. She hadn't been down to see Maggie once they'd moved her, because it was just too tiring and then Sally had been ill. Did their friend feel as if she'd been deserted by those who should have been there for her?

Beth determined to write to her the first chance she got – but perhaps she would be in London before she got the letter. It might be best to wait and hear Maggie's reasons in person and maybe then they could persuade her not to jump into something before being certain it was what she wanted.

'Make sure she comes to visit me, either here or at home,' she told Rachel. 'I feel guilty, as though I haven't given her the attention that she needed, but I assumed she would come home to us the minute they allowed her to leave the hospital.'

'I am sure she will be here as soon as she can,' Rachel said. 'If she has doubts, we can help her – but if she's happy then I shan't seek to dissuade her.'

'No...' Beth looked unsure. 'As long as she *is* happy...'

* * *

On her way home that evening, Rachel reflected that she hadn't told Beth her own news, either about William – or Lizzie. Her feelings for the child were becoming stronger all the time. The little girl was endearing and her smiles and delight in the simple pleasures of some good food or a glass of warm milk with a little honey made Rachel ache with love.

She had taken her on her lap the previous evening and read her stories from a picture book. Lizzie's amazement and delight and her questions showed an intelligent mind that only needed encouragement to blossom. Given love, attention and good food, the child would grow into a lovely girl and it saddened Rachel that Lizzie's grandmother was interested only in the money she demanded for allowing the friendship to continue.

If only Lizzie was hers to keep and cherish, she thought as she got off the bus and walked the short distance to her home. As she approached the front door, she heard whimpering and knew instinctively that Lizzie was nearby.

'What is wrong, darling?' Rachel asked as she saw the tiny girl crouched in the dark near her door.

Lizzie gave a cry of anguish and hurled herself at Rachel.

She took her in her arms, holding her, stroking her and reassuring her until she had her inside the warm entrance hall and, kicking the door shut behind her, carried the frightened child into the sitting room and nursed her until the storm of tears was over.

Gradually, she quietened and, as the tears dried, the story came out. Lizzie's grandmother had thrown her out because she'd got into trouble with other children in the lane and her dress had been torn.

'She says I'se a dirty horrible kid and she don't want me hangin' around no more. She says I belongs to you now...'

'Did she?' Rachel held the trembling child closer and closed her eyes.

If only it were true. Rachel dared to think about how she might make that dream come true. Would Lizzie's grandmother sell her to her? What would she accept? Her mind reasoned that the grasping woman would keep demanding more and more unless she could find a way of persuading her into accepting a sum to be rid of the nuisance, she considered Lizzie to be.

'I'm going to put you to bed, darling,' she told Lizzie in a soft loving tone that made the little girl respond and hug her. She smiled and took Lizzie through to the bathroom, where she bathed her and then popped her into the spare bedroom. Everything was a revelation to the excited little girl, from a proper bath to a bedroom of her own. She chattered excitedly, eventually wearing herself out with emotion. Staying with Lizzie until she slept, Rachel sat down on her settee and planned her campaign.

If she asked to buy Lizzie, the woman would plead love for her granddaughter. If she tried to berate her for ill treatment, she would forbid Rachel to see Lizzie again. No, she had to try something different, something more subtle, but as yet, she wasn't quite sure what would work best. For the moment, she would simply keep Lizzie with her and see what happened.

The problem was what to do while she was at work. She needed a kind capable woman who was able to care for the child during the day, but where could she find someone who had all the time in the world? A smile touched her lips as the solution came in a sudden flash.

Hazel was forever complaining of being lonely. She'd asked Rachel to move in with her several times. 'William is away and you're on your own, Rachel. It makes sense.'

Rachel had been reluctant to give up her comfortable flat and move into Hazel's house, but for Lizzie's sake she would do it for the time being. Lizzie's grandmother would have no idea where to find her granddaughter and Rachel could take her time over sorting out this problem.

It did cross her mind that she could be accused of stealing Lizzie, but she wasn't prepared to let the child be pushed out into the cold night by an uncaring grandmother. So, she would take her to her former mother-in-law's comfortable home and they would care for her between them. It was a short-term answer to Rachel's problems and in time she would be able to decide what to do.

22

Sally's health improved with each day that passed, but she was not officially allowed to leave her bedroom until the second week of October, and she was still forbidden to work, though Rachel smuggled in accounts and catalogues whenever she could. Once released by the hospital, Beth brought her new baby to see her and some of the staff of Harpers were allowed to visit. Ruth, Minnie Stockbridge, Mr Marco and Marion were the four that had asked particularly and were amongst her first visitors. Maggie had written to tell her she was coming as soon as she was allowed.

I stupidly caught a chill and that set everything back for at least two weeks. I keep telling them I'm fine and it's just a late summer cold, but I've been ordered back to bed until I'm better. I'm longing to see you, Sally, and send you my very best wishes for your recovery. Rachel visited during her week's holiday and told me how ill you had been. I'm so sorry I wasn't there to help look after you...

Maggie's letter had said nothing about her planned marriage or her husband-to-be and Sally wondered if Marion had made a mistake in thinking she planned to wed soon but was assured by Rachel that she'd read it herself and there was no mistake.

'I can't understand why she isn't telling us,' Sally said when Beth came to visit.

Beth was glowing. Jack had got home at last, when she'd begun to think he might have been killed at sea. He hadn't told her much, but she'd gathered that his ship had been badly damaged and he'd had to wait for a new one to bring him home.

'It sounds as if he and his crew are lucky to be alive,' Beth said. 'I don't ask him much, but he told me he's been given a rest for six weeks – so I know it was bad.'

'It's probably for the best that you don't know,' Sally agreed.

The news elsewhere was not good. Over a hundred people had died in a German bombardment on the Isle of Sheppey and Thanet earlier that year. Also Allied hospitals had been bombed overseas, something that had the ordinary folk on the street up in arms, because hospitals should not be targets. War was war, but to bomb sick people seemed outrageous. And at Passchendaele, the fighting went on relentlessly, all through August and September and now October. It seemed endless.

Sally knew that Ben was working tirelessly to source and supply the Armed Forces with munitions and other equipment they so desperately needed. It was a constant battle and Ben had told her that it felt as if he were fighting his own private war.

'I might not be firing a gun at the enemy but I feel as if I'm under fire,' he'd told her once as he sat drinking the last of his rare old brandy. He had been hoarding it like a miser, allowing himself just a tiny drop when he felt the need. 'I know you must feel much the same when you're being told your regular firms cannot supply what you ordered, but, of course, Jenni is dealing with that side of it for the moment.'

Sally had smiled and agreed with her husband. Neither he nor Jenni knew of all the arm twisting she did on the telephone to secure their fair share of whatever was available.

* * *

At the end of that week, Sally had a visit from a friend she had not seen for months.

When Pearl announced her visitor, Sally sat up eagerly as Michael O'Sullivan entered the room bearing flowers, books and chocolates. 'Oh, Mick how lovely of you,' she cried as he sat on the sofa and looked at her quizzically. 'Yes, I know. It isn't like me to sit around like this...'

'If the doctor advised it, you should take notice,' Mick said and grinned at her. 'I've just been sent back to London for a rest myself. I was injured and stuck in hospital for some weeks. I didn't know what had happened to Maggie until I asked Matron Mayhew – and then when I went to Harpers to ask you a few questions they told me you've been very ill...'

'I was for a while,' Sally agreed. 'I feel fine now, but they won't let me go back to work. I've got to rest for another few weeks, according to my doctor.'

'Well, if he is a good doctor, he probably knows what he is talking about,' Mick said. 'I must say you look fine to me, Sally – as beautiful as ever.'

'That's your Irish charm talking,' Sally accused, but her smile lit up the room and she felt better than she had in ages. 'Maggie is supposed to be coming up to London soon, but she had a bit of a chill, so they kept her another couple of weeks.'

'Is she returning to Harpers?' Mick enquired with an innocent look.

'We're not sure. We think she might be getting married—' Sally stopped abruptly as she saw the smile drain from his eyes and a terrible sadness fill them. 'I think that can't be right, though, because she hasn't told Beth or me – and she doesn't talk about her fiancé. I'm certain she isn't in love with this man...'

'You can't know that for sure if she hasn't told you anything?'

'But Maggie usually tells us everything. That's what makes this a little odd... perhaps she feels as if she has no choice. Because she was placed so far away, none of us have got down to Devon much, so she may feel we've deserted her. I wonder if you have time to visit her and tell her there is a home with Beth and Fred and her job is waiting for her at Harpers...'

Mick fixed her with a stare. 'And why would you be askin' me to do that, Sally Harper?'

'Because...' Sally looked at her old friend consideringly. 'It isn't my business, Mick – but if you care for Maggie, you should go straight there and discover what is going on. I think she may have been tricked into something... because this reticence isn't like Maggie.'

'What makes you think I might care?' he asked.

'You do – don't you?' Mick wouldn't have come asking where she was if he didn't care.

'You always did know how to get to the heart of a man, Sally,' Mick said with a half-smile. 'I fell for Maggie Gibbs after I told her about what happened to Tim Burrows. She was so sad but so brave – and she carried on looking after the men despite her heartache.' He paused, then, 'The last time we were together, I thought she might feel something for me – but then I was moved to a new area and I got injured. I couldn't let Maggie know or write to her for ages...' He shrugged. 'I wasn't sure I would walk again – and I'm too old for her. If she has found someone more suitable, it would be better for her.'

'You don't know that,' Sally said, looking at him directly. 'Tell Maggie how you feel, Mick. You will soon discover whether she feels the same. It's better than not knowing and perhaps leaving it too late.'

Mick looked uncertain and then nodded. 'You're a good friend, Sally Harper. I shall visit Maggie. I'll give her your message and I will tell her that I care for her. If she has found happiness, I shall be glad for her.' His smile was back, though she could sense the heaviness of spirit and understood that Mick had fallen hard for the pretty young woman who had endured so much in France to serve the wounded.

Mick then talked lightly of other things and by the time he left, Sally was feeling so much better that she made up her mind. She didn't feel ill any more and she would go into Harpers the next day, just to see people and have a break. She wouldn't attempt to return to work yet, but she did want to talk to Rachel and see if she'd managed to find a private investigator to discover the truth about her mother...

* * *

'Yes, I have found someone at last,' Rachel said when Sally asked her the vital question in her office the next day. 'Two others I spoke to didn't want to take it on, but Harry Stevens says he'll be glad to. He wants ten pounds down and another ten when he finds her.'

'Did you engage him?'

'Yes. I was going to call this evening and let you know,' Rachel gave her an odd look. 'I'm sorry I haven't been to visit you for a while, but I've had something on my mind...'

'Is it a problem I can help with?' Sally asked and smiled as Ruth brought coffee and biscuits in.

Rachel paused and then shook her head. 'It's a problem I have to work out for myself, Sally. I will tell you another day – but you have all you can manage getting well enough.'

Sally nodded, because it was true and if Rachel needed help, she would say. 'All right – but I must owe you ten pounds,' Sally took two crisp white five-pound notes from her bag and handed them over. Rachel thanked her. It was a lot of money to her, but perhaps not so much to Sally now that she was married to Ben Harper and the chief buyer. 'I'm glad you found someone for me. I am anxious to find my mother and talk to her.'

'What does Ben say?' Rachel asked, looking at her interestedly.

'Like Jenni, he half thinks that I imagined it all. He did offer to make enquiries, but he is so busy that I simply told him it was all in hand – and thanks to you, it is. Are you certain I can't do anything for you in return? Do you need time off to visit William? Have you heard how he is?'

'Nothing except a brief postcard to say his treatment is progressing well – but not written by him.'

'If you did need to go down there, just tell me and I'll do whatever I can to help.'

'You've always been my friend and one day I may need your help. When I do, I'll ask for it, Sally. I know your advice is good – but I've done something rather drastic and I'm not sure yet how it will turn out...'

'Well, I'm a good listener,' Sally offered, but Rachel shook her head. It was obvious that whatever was playing on her mind she wasn't ready to divulge it. They chatted for a while longer and then Rachel returned to her department.

Sally's own thoughts and problems flooded back. When Jenni

arrived and caught her sneaking a peek at some department accounts, she scolded her and insisted on taking her straight home in a taxi.

Since Sally was beginning to feel a little tired, she didn't argue. Jenni was her family and she loved her, even though she could be a little too bossy at times. She knew that she had to be patient for a while and carry on resting at home, with occasional calls to the firms she dealt with the most, and the reports Ruth and Rachel smuggled to her. When she felt stronger, she would return to her desk, though perhaps only for an hour or two in the mornings. Jenny loved having her mother at home and Sally was enjoying having more time to play with her daughter. When her little girl started to go to nursery school, Sally should be over the birth of her second child. She mentally crossed her fingers, because she knew how close she'd come to losing her own life as well as that of her unborn child. God willing, she would recover and be her old self again. Pearl might consider coming in full-time when there were two little ones to care for – and if she considered she was no longer needed at the hospital. Once the war was over... if only that could happen soon.

The British Government had completely rejected a peace plan created by the Pope as being totally out of the question. It seemed that the Allies had made up their minds to fight to the bitter end. Yet surely the tide was slowly turning and one day in the future the conflict and deaths would be over.

23

Mick stood in the shadow of the rose arch and watched as Maggie read her book in the late October sunshine; it was still warm as it is some years, a brief renaissance of the summer warmth. She seemed intent on it, but then she looked up and he saw both sadness and uncertainty in her face. He would swear that she was not happy.

'Colin – is that you?' she called and looked towards where Mick was standing, hidden by the trailing roses.

He took a deep breath and moved forward so that she could see him. She gave a start of surprise, because it was so long since she'd heard anything of him.

'Hello, Maggie. How are you? They told me you nearly died – I'm glad you didn't. The world would be an empty place without Maggie Gibbs, so it would.'

'Mick...' she gasped and all the colour was stripped from her face.

For a moment he feared she would faint and he instinctively moved towards her, ready to catch her. She seemed to sway towards him and he put out his hands to take hers and hold them. He thought she would let him draw her closer but when her face lifted, he saw a look of such uncertainty that his heart caught.

'You didn't write. I thought you must have been killed...'

'They tried their hardest, but I'm a difficult man to kill – and I wanted to come back to you, Maggie love. You're so special to me...'

'Oh Mick...' Her words were a sob on her lips. He'd been so kind to her in France after Tim's death and she'd liked him a lot. If he'd spoken then she might have loved him, but he'd moved away with his unit without a word of his feelings and that had made her so sad. 'No, you mustn't...' She jerked back sharply as though she'd been stung. 'I can't – I've given my word... you didn't write for months and there was nothing else for me...' She choked back her tears. 'I'm going to marry someone else – a man who needs me...'

Mick took a step towards her, all the love in his heart on show as he said, 'Oh, Maggie love. I was too ill to write or ask anyone else to do it for me, but I never stopped loving you.'

She shook her head. 'I wasn't over Tim when we last spoke, not completely, and then you were gone and I didn't know if I truly felt anything for you, but I knew I longed to see you and it hurt that you didn't write...' She caught back her tears. 'It is too late, Mick.' Lifting her head, she met his intent gaze. 'I've given my word to marry someone else and I can't break it – it would destroy him. He is a decent man and I won't do that to him!'

'Do you love him?' Mick asked tensely.

Maggie raised her head and looked him in the eyes, her expression sad, 'No, I don't love him – I feel sympathy for him and I like him, quite a lot, actually,' she answered honestly. 'He wants me to marry him, but I'll really be his nurse and companion. It's the only way he can go home... and he wants that so much. I was lost, Mick, and lonely and Colin gave me a purpose...'

'You're very honest, Maggie. Does he know why you're marrying him?'

'Yes, I'm sure he does,' she said. 'He needs a boost to his pride, Mick – and I had nothing else.' Tears sparkled in her lovely eyes, tearing at his heart. Mick knew that he should have got someone to write for him while he lay ill, even if it was just one line. Had he told her of his love, perhaps she would not be about to throw her life away on a loveless marriage. Even if she could not bring herself to love him, and he'd always feared that he was too old for her, he didn't want her to ruin her life. She was beautiful, young and brave and she deserved more.

'Don't throw your life away, Maggie love,' Mick pleaded, moving closer, his hand out in supplication. 'I know I'm not much of a catch, but I love you so much. I could make you happy. I know I could...'

'You would have made me happy,' Maggie said and the tears brimmed over. She stepped towards him impulsively. 'I could have loved you, Mick. Perhaps I do a little – but I won't break my promise to Colin. If I did, I think he might do something stupid. I won't be responsible for a man taking his own life...'

Mick looked at her helplessly. She was so lovely, so brave, but so misguided – giving up a chance of real happiness for a foolish promise that should never have been asked of her. 'I shan't give up on you, Maggie,' he vowed and reached out, sweeping her into his arms and kissing her before she could snatch herself away. He felt the response of her lips and her body as she melted into him and knew a moment of sheer joy before she broke the spell, wrenched free of him and ran off through the gardens towards

the hospital. He moaned with frustration and regret. He couldn't
lose her this way!

Hearing a rustling sound behind him, Mick spun round to see
a young man in a wheelchair and from the stricken look in his
eyes he knew it was Colin – the man to whom Maggie had given
her promise. Mick did something then he would afterwards
regret.

'You've no right to hold her,' he said, any pity he might have
felt for the other man's plight wiped out because of Maggie's
promise to him. 'You heard what she said – she doesn't love you.
Don't be a selfish brute! You aren't even offering her a proper
marriage, just a position as your nurse and companion. What sort
of a life is that for a girl like her...?' He choked back much more
he might have said. 'I love her and you don't – It isn't fair...'

'Life is seldom fair.' The bitterness in Colin's eyes showed how
deeply Mick's barb had struck. 'But she gave her word.' Colin's
face took on a savage look. 'I don't know who you are or what
rights you think you have – but Maggie belongs to me.'

'Let her go. It is the decent thing to do...' Mick pleaded. His
heart was torn and bleeding, but it was for Maggie's sake he wres-
tled with Colin's conscience. 'I beg you, for her sake, don't ruin
her life. She's given so much for men like you – let her have a
chance of happiness. I beg you—'

'Go to hell!' Colin turned and wheeled himself off in another
direction to the one Maggie had taken.

Mick stood watching him leave. It was wrong, so wrong, but
he knew that Colin was right – Maggie wouldn't break a promise
she had given. It was a part of what made her the girl he loved so
much.

Turning, he strode away by the path he'd taken. He could do
little more here for the moment. Maggie knew what was in his
heart now. He just wished he'd spoken sooner and not held back

from asking her to wed him in France. Now, it was too late. He had lost her.

* * *

Maggie wept for some minutes in the privacy of her room. She could scarcely believe what had just happened. Her time in France had been so busy and so charged with emotion – the kind of gut-wrenching, churning emotion that drained one of all feeling. Seeing the horrific injuries of the men brought back down the line had been shocking and painful, but she'd grown used to it and the numbing drudgery of working in terrible conditions. She had used it to kill the pain of losing her darling Tim. Their love had been sweet and passionate but so brief that sometimes she could hardly recall what his face looked like.

Gradually, the smiling face of Mick and his kindness to her, his unfailing charm and his quiet steadiness had stolen into her heart, but she hadn't really known it. When his letters had stopped coming, Maggie had sealed herself off from all feeling. She had simply been unable to bear any more grief and so she'd refused to let it into her heart and mind. Now it all came flooding out of her and she knew she was crying for Tim, for all those wounded and lost men in France and for *her* lost chance of happiness.

If Mick hadn't been sent away, injured and unable to write to her, if he had only spoken of his love when they were together... she would not have given Colin Morgan her promise. Yes, she liked him and she felt sympathy for his plight, and she wouldn't break her promise, because that would break him. Yet if Mick had come sooner or written, it might not have been given. He could have written before this, when he had recovered, though in her heart she understood why he had not – it was the kind of thing that needed to be said face to face.

He was several years older, of course – but Maggie felt older than her years. Her service in France had taken the last remnants of her innocence and she was a woman mature beyond her years. Mick's kindness and his gentle charm would have brought her happiness, she knew that – and his kiss had awakened feelings she had forgotten deep inside her. Yes, she might have been happy as his wife, although her love for him was not the love she'd felt for Tim. It was softer, gentler and wiser.

But that older, wiser woman understood that she could never sacrifice someone else's chance of a life for her own. Colin needed her and, in a way, she needed to do this for him. Maggie didn't care that Colin's family was well off or that marriage gave her a home or security. She'd wondered for a while if that was her motive, but she knew now that it wasn't – no, it was a need to serve. Illness had taken her from what she'd considered the reason for her life after Tim died, and now, she had another opportunity to look after someone who needed her. But today knowing that Mick was alive, she felt torn. Maggie had hurt Mick and she would never have wanted to do that... Oh, why did life have to be so difficult?

She shook her head. Mick had come too late. She was committed to Colin and she would make the most of what she'd chosen. Maggie would do all she could to make the young man, who had lost so much, happy and in doing so, she was sure she would find her own way – her own kind of contentment.

Wiping her tears from her face, she washed it and put a little powder on her cheeks to take away the redness and then she went in search of Colin. Maggie would never let him think that she had doubts or regretted her promise in any way. She would make a good life for them both. Of Mick's disappointment and pain, she would not allow herself one thought because if she did, she might run to him and forget her promise to a man who needed her so much. Mick was whole and able to make a life for himself – to find a new love – and Colin was not. He needed her and Maggie needed that – it was her reason for being alive when so many were dead.

24

'Jack asked me what I thought we should do when the war is over,' Beth told Sally that October afternoon as they sat together drinking tea and nibbling home-made biscuits. 'I asked him what he meant and he wanted to know if I'd like to move to a house of our own, but I said no – not unless Fred gets himself a wife...'

Sally's interest was immediately caught. She looked at Beth, a smile on her lips. 'Is he thinking about it then?'

'Perhaps, if Vera can persuade him into it! Fred is set in his ways,' Beth said and gave an affectionate laugh. 'You know how fond I am of him, Sally, and grateful for all he has done for me. I don't want to leave him on his own. If he decided to wed Vera, I wouldn't mind moving nearer you, which is what Jack suggested. He thinks if he goes into business with Ben after the war, it will be nice if we live closer to each other.'

'We are considering a move to a house with a garden when things settle down,' Sally told her with a nod. 'I shouldn't move until you see where we decide upon once Ben can set his mind to peacetime again...'

'Jack thinks it can't be long now – a few months or a year at most,' Beth told her. 'He says we are winning the conflict with the help of all the Allies, particularly the Americans, who are making their weight count now. Even though the newspapers are still full of dire news and despite the Germans making a breakthrough on the Italian front. It is a gradual thing, but he's noticed the difference of late. The enemy U-boats aren't sinking so many ships and they're getting a pasting themselves in some waters.'

'Good!' Sally set her face in a determined look. 'I hope they give them a good hiding for all the upset and misery they've caused.'

'Let's not talk about that, it makes me sad,' Beth said. 'How are you getting on, love? I think you look better than you did – is baby doing well?'

Sally placed her hands on her stomach and nodded. 'The doctors tell me so...' She smiled. 'I've told Jenny she will have a baby brother or sister to play with. I'm not quite sure whether she was pleased or not – I think she might prefer a dog!'

Beth laughed. 'Little Jack wasn't at all interested in his brother at first, but I know once he grows up a bit, they will be good friends. However, children would almost always prefer a dog to a new sibling.'

Sally nodded and then stretched to ease her back.

'Getting backache?' Her friend sympathised.

'A little, but I feel much better,' Sally said. 'Now, tell me, how was Maggie when you saw her? I know she paid a flying visit to the store, spoke to Rachel and Marion, Mr Marco and some of the others, but she didn't come here.'

'She spent an hour with Fred in his lunch break and they talked about Tim,' Beth replied with a sigh. 'Fred was touched and she is meeting him on Sunday to have tea and visit Tim's grave together – and then she goes back to the country the following day.'

'Did she mention her marriage?'

'She told Fred everything,' Beth said. 'She explained to him that she wasn't in love with Colin Morgan, but he has been terribly injured and she feels she can make his life bearable. He wants her to marry him and that is the reason she is giving – that she cannot nurse the men at the Front now, but she wants to nurse this man as his wife...'

'That sounds a bit mixed-up to me,' Sally said, shaking her head. 'I wish I hadn't been ill so long. Perhaps if I'd been able to go down more, she would have discussed it with me...'

'I felt the same way,' Beth said, 'but Fred says she seems quietly content, if not happy, and knows what she wants to do with her life. He brought her back for supper last night and she hugged me and asked me to forgive her for not writing more. She said she had been in a dark place and exhausted by the work and the conditions out there...' Beth looked thoughtful. 'I told her I loved her and whatever she wanted to do was all right with me and she asked me if I would go down for her wedding. I'd like to if I can get away – and Vera says she will look after Jackie. I can take Timmy with me, of course. I thought she might have asked you too, Sally?'

'No, she hasn't visited and she hasn't telephoned,' Sally said, frowning. 'I think she is afraid I might try to talk her out of this marriage.'

'It may not be ideal, but I think the family are well off and it is a good one. She will have a decent home and enough money to live on – it is more than many young women can say.'

The war had taken the best and the bravest of the men and it would be a long time before they would be replaced by young blood; women who had lost loved ones to the conflict were unlikely to find new lovers or husbands. It would take a generation or more before there were enough men to go round again, so until then, many women would live sterile lives without love or hope of a partner in life.

'We're lucky,' Sally said sadly. 'You married the love of your life and so did I – and we've held on to them... fingers crossed. Yet Maggie and so many other young women will have lost everything. What seems a less than perfect marriage to us may be all she needs I suppose... though I thought...' She shook her head, because Mick had confided in her and would not expect his feelings to be revealed to others. Sally would respect his trust. She believed he had gone down to see Maggie but didn't know for certain. Mick had not come to see her again and she'd had no further news of him. 'I wish she would come and see me, though.' Maggie had been through so much in her young life. Her father had had a terrible accident that led to a long illness and too much suffering. Her mother had abandoned them both and Maggie's father had used laudanum to end his pain, leaving her alone. Her first love affair had ended in tears and then Tim, whom she'd loved so much, had died in the sea after his plane was shot down. Instead of drifting into melancholy, as some might, Maggie had devoted herself to the sick and dying in the field hospitals in France. 'I just think she deserves to be happy.'

'Perhaps she will be,' Beth said in a gentle tone.

Sally nodded and they turned the conversation to work. Beth had agreed to come in two mornings a week to help Sally do her office work. It was the way Sally had persuaded Jenni that she could start work on a gentle scale and it kept Beth in touch with Harpers. She was one of the original Harpers' girls and she had jumped at the chance to work and visit more with Sally. Her father-in-law's friend Vera was more than willing to look after Beth's children whenever she chose and that meant as they got older, she might be able to actually work in the store part-time again.

'I love my sons,' Beth said, 'and I enjoy looking after them and the house – but Harpers is special and I'd like to be a part of it if I can.'

'Of course,' Sally said, 'and we would love to have you back, even for a few hours once you can manage it. I don't intend to give up... even after this one is born.' She patted her stomach affectionately. 'He nearly killed me, but I shall love him just as much.'

Beth laughed. 'Of course you will, but how can you be sure it is a boy?'

'I thought I was having a boy last time,' Sally said with a fond smile at her daughter who was playing with her doll and crooning to herself as she sat on the carpet near them. 'I was wrong then, but I'm sure I'm right this time...'

'We'll see,' Beth said with a warm smile. 'I do love you, Sally. Nothing ever keeps you down for long, does it?'

'I think I have too much to be thankful for,' Sally told her happily. 'I'm glad you've got your two now, Beth. They are both healthy and happy – is that it as far as you're concerned, is your family complete?'

'I shan't try to control it,' Beth replied, 'but I'm content with two. I'm not sure what Jack and Fred think about a bigger family...'

'They don't have to have them,' Sally said, eyes gleaming with mischief. 'Two is enough for me and I shall try to make sure this is the last – that's why I'm set on having a boy.'

'Well, I hope you get what you want,' Beth told her, amused. 'Knowing you, Sally Harper, you probably will...'

* * *

Sally's wish that she might see Maggie came true the next day. She was looking through some paperwork Jenni had reluctantly brought home for her when the bell rang and then Mrs Hills brought Maggie in. She was carrying a posy of violets, which smelled lovely, and she looked beautiful – older and slimmer than Sally remembered from her time at Harpers, but well again. Her smile lit her face as Sally stood to embrace her.

'I am so glad to see you looking much better, dearest Maggie,' she said and felt her friend relax. 'We were all worried about you when they sent you home. I would have visited more had I not been ill...'

'That's what Beth said.' Maggie looked at her. 'I didn't know you were ill until I got a letter from Marion and then I decided I would see you rather than write to you. I did feel a bit as if I'd been deserted for a while – because none of you came to the convalescent home and, before that, when I was in France, it felt as if Harpers was a dream and the only reality was sickness and death...' She shuddered. 'It was a long dark tunnel, Sally, and I couldn't find my way out. All I could think about was getting up, going to work, and then collapsing into bed – and when they brought me back to England, I just went blank for a while. It was lovely when you and Beth came to see me that once, but after that you didn't come.'

'They moved you and it was more difficult to get there,' Sally tried to explain. 'We all wanted to visit and thought about you all the time, but Beth was too advanced in her pregnancy to make the extended journey and I fell ill... I know I should have come prior to my illness, but I think I was feeling a bit under the weather before it struck me down...'

'Yes, I understand that now,' Maggie replied with a smile. 'But I didn't then... and things happened. I expect Beth has told you. I explained it to Fred because he is entitled to know. Tim is always in my heart and always will be – but Colin doesn't mind that... it's why I can marry him.'

'It won't be a proper marriage,' Sally told her gently. 'Why don't you just nurse him until he feels better?'

'That isn't what he needs,' Maggie said. 'I can't tell you how he feels, Sally. That is private – but I can tell you that I am content with what I've done. I wasn't sure at first but now I am. Please don't try to talk me out of it...'

Sally hesitated, then, 'It's your life, Maggie. If you're sure, I shan't interfere – but I know you had an alternative. Mick cares for you very much...'

'Yes, I knew you must have told Mick where to find me,' Maggie said sadly. 'I'm sorry I've hurt him, Sally. Had he spoken to me sooner perhaps I might have had something to cling to... but he didn't and now it is too late.'

Sally wanted to tell her it was never too late to take a chance on happiness, but she kept silent. She had promised not to attempt to make Maggie change her mind and she would stick to that – even though she felt her friend was making a terrible mistake.

'Am I invited to the wedding?' she asked after a pause.

'Yes, of course, if you want to come. I've invited Beth and Jack and Rachel. William can't come because he is in the isolation hospital – but Rachel will. Becky says she'll come if she can... and Marion says she'll send me a present, but she can't manage it.' Maggie smiled oddly. 'I'll bet she hasn't told you she's expecting her first baby. I think she is nervous of telling Rachel in case she gives her the sack...'

'Of course, we wouldn't do such a thing,' Sally replied, surprised but pleased for Marion. 'She can work until she feels it is the right time to stop. I did!'

'You're the boss's wife,' Maggie said with an odd look. 'It is different for you...'

'Marion should've told me. I would have put her mind at rest.'

'I'm seeing her this evening and I'll tell her what you said,' Maggie laughed. 'She doesn't know you like we do, Sally. Marion didn't join Harpers until after you were married.'

'No, she must see me differently, but I hope I'm not different, Maggie?'

'Not with me – but perhaps you are unconsciously with others,' Maggie said, looking thoughtful. 'You're bound to be – the responsibility for the store falls mainly on your shoulders.'

'Jenni Harper and Ben share it.'

'Yes, but we all know who drives it forward,' Maggie said and sighed. 'Coming back and seeing it again made me realise how much I'll miss it all, Sally – but I may get up sometimes and I'll only be in Sussex. I can catch a train and visit every now and then.'

'As long as Colin understands you need that freedom...'

'Oh, he will. He knows he doesn't own me,' Maggie said and smiled. 'Don't look so worried, Sally Harper. I haven't lost my mind. I know what I'm doing and I have my reasons. I didn't say yes because I was desperate – though it did help me make up my mind when I felt so alone...'

* * *

After Maggie had gone, Sally was very thoughtful. She'd wondered why Mick hadn't been to see her after his visit to Maggie and now she understood. Whatever had passed between them, he'd realised that there was no changing Maggie from the course she'd set herself. She had told Sally she knew what she was doing, but Sally felt that despite her words, Maggie was making a mistake. She felt something for Mick, of that Sally was certain, but she was blocking it out, not allowing herself to feel or think of it – just as she had after Tim died. Perhaps it was the only way she could deal with yet another blow from a cruel fate.

What could Sally do to change things? Did she even have the right to try?

She knew that Ben would say she should let her friend sort out her own life, but she felt the tug at her heartstrings. If there was any way she could prevent Maggie making a terrible mistake and losing perhaps the best chance of happiness she would ever have, surely it was right to at least try? Sally needed no convincing – but she wasn't sure yet what she could do. It would come to her, though, and when it did – she would do her best to rescue Maggie from her own stubbornness.

25

Marion opened the letter and gasped. She hadn't recognised the handwriting, but a warm glow came over her as she saw what Sally Harper had written. It was exactly what she'd thought she might say if she'd been able to talk to her, but she hadn't dared to approach her.

I am delighted to hear that you are expecting your first child and I want to tell you not to worry, Marion. If you should wish to return to us, even part-time, there will always be a job waiting. Indeed, we hope very much that you will find the time to continue as part of the window-dressing team...

Marion beamed as she tucked the letter into her handbag. It had been delivered just as she was leaving for work and she'd been reading it as she sat on the bus taking her into Oxford Street. During the summer, on fine days, she walked in, but it was quite a way and lately she'd started to catch the bus in the mornings; it saved a little time and was easier on her feet and legs. Besides, it was early November now and beginning to get cold at night, and first thing in the morning it could be very chilly. Marion's job involved standing all day and that was as much exercise as she wanted right now. Her pregnancy hadn't started to show yet, but it soon would and Marion knew it was time she told Mrs Bailey. Obviously, Maggie Gibbs had passed the message on to Mrs Harper and Marion couldn't have looked for a better reception of her news.

When she spoke to her supervisor, Mrs Bailey seemed genuinely pleased. 'Naturally, we'll miss you in the department,' she told her, 'but it is wonderful news. Your husband must be so pleased.'

'I told him last weekend. He had a twenty-four-hour pass and he was delighted,' Marion confirmed with a smile. 'I'm happy about the baby, of course – but I shall miss being at Harpers.'

'Yes, it is a good place to work,' Rachel agreed. 'Family is more important, though, so you will soon settle down at home.'

'Mrs Harper wrote to me,' Marion told her. 'Maggie Gibbs must have mentioned it to her – and she says I could come back part-time if I wish...'

'Well, that is nice of her,' Rachel said and nodded. 'I imagine they would like to keep you on the window-dressing team for as long as they can. You might consider working with them for longer than you do on the shop floor, Mrs Jackson. Here, in the department, it will give you backache to stand for long hours, but window dressing isn't so hard on the feet.'

'No, it is the standing for hours that makes your feet and legs tired after a long day,' Marion agreed. 'I never used to notice it, but I've started to feel it just lately – though I'm only a couple of months or so into my childbearing...'

'Yes, I suppose it is the baby taking your strength. I was never able to carry a child, though I had at least one miscarriage...' The sadness flickered in Mrs Bailey's eyes and then was gone.

'Not that it matters now.' She smiled and seemed to light up inside.

Marion wondered what had caused the change. Clearly, Mrs Bailey had wanted children and it must make her sad to know that she might be unable to have her own. With her husband so ill, too. Marion hadn't been told directly that Captain Bailey was ill, but the grapevine at Harpers had got it from somewhere and everyone knew he was staying on the East Coast in an isolation hospital. The air was very bracing there and that was considered good for patients with consumption. It was the reason Rachel had seemed so sad for a time, but these past few weeks she had been distinctly happier and smiled much more than she had for a long time. Marion was curious what had made her smile that way – as if a dream had come true for her – but, of course, she did not dare to ask. It would be impertinent and Mrs Bailey would frown and reprimand her for asking personal questions when she was here to work.

Hearing her name, Marion turned and smiled as Mr Marco walked towards her. 'Good morning, Mrs Jackson,' he said in his easy, charming manner. 'I have just come to ask for your help – if you could visit my office in your lunch break, I can provide a sandwich and a cup of tea. Perhaps if we ask her nicely, Mrs Bailey might let you off a few minutes early?'

Mrs Bailey was standing near enough to hear what he was saying. She glanced at the little silver watch she had pinned to her dress and nodded at him.

'We are not particularly busy this morning, Mr Marco. It wants a quarter of an hour to Marion's break – she could come with you if she wishes.'

'Thank you – if you're sure?' Marion caught the flash of annoyance on Becky Stockbridge's face and it popped into her mind that the younger girl was jealous of her position in the firm.

Becky had been moved to the dress department earlier in the year, but she was helping Mrs Bailey this week as their junior was on annual leave. Seeing the look in Becky's eyes, made Marion think about Becky's distance with her recently and now she realised that she must resent the time Marion spent with the window-dressing team. Instead of understanding that she worked hard for her place there and on the shop floor, she thought Marion was being favoured by their supervisor and Mrs Harper – who had always taken time to speak to Marion when she came in.

'Is that all right with you, Miss Stockbridge?' Marion asked. 'If you wish to go first?'

'It makes no difference to me,' Becky said but flushed as Mrs Bailey gave her a sharp look.

'Then I'll come with you, sir.' Marion smiled at the gentle, pleasant man who was so talented as a window dresser for Harpers. She enjoyed working with Mr Marco and looked forward to seeing his ideas become reality as they worked as a team. It was this part of her work she would miss most, Marion realised. She only spent a couple of hours once or twice a week helping, but she loved it because it was exciting and creative. Sally Harper's invitation to return to Harpers if only as a part of their team was lovely and it had made Marion wonder if that might be possible. She couldn't return to working behind a counter all day, but perhaps a couple of mornings a week helping with the displays could be managed...

* * *

Rachel Bailey watched Becky Stockbridge for most of the day, noticing the faint hostility towards Marion Jackson when she returned from helping with the windows. She was fine with Shirley Jones and Rachel, but less than friendly towards Marion and that was strange, because surely they'd been friends – unless she was jealous of the older girl. That must be it, of course, Rachel realised. Becky felt that Marion was receiving preferential treatment, because she was allowed longer lunch breaks – but Marion was working, doing two jobs and had received only a small rise for the extra work she did. Becky ought to understand that, but she obviously didn't, and that was causing a little atmosphere within the department.

What could she do about it? Rachel wondered. She felt unable to reprimand the girl because she had done so for lateness on three occasions this past month and Becky had made an effort to pull her socks up. Speaking to the manager about his own daughter might be awkward and wasn't something Rachel felt able to do unless strictly necessary. She smiled as the answer came to her. She would visit Minnie Stockbridge, Becky's step-mother, on Sunday, and take Lizzie with her. A note to Minnie – her dear friend – would result in an invitation to tea and it would be good to talk to her again. Rachel could ask for her help in solving the problem of Lizzie's future and just mention that Becky seemed a little unhappy at work as they drank tea...

Becky put aside for the moment, Rachel let her thoughts drift back to her secret delight. Away from the scolding tongue of her grandmother, Lizzie was thriving. She was learning to read and her table manners were now excellent. Lizzie's mother had taught her things, but since her mother's untimely death, Lizzie had suffered neglect and abuse at the hands of her unkind grand-mother and had been pushed out of her home.

Rachel sometimes worried that Lizzie's grandmother would discover where she'd taken Lizzie, though she knew the woman would be glad to be rid of her. However, she'd hoped to wangle more money from Rachel and there might be a reckoning if she did ever discover that she'd spirited the little girl away.

Her first husband's mother, Hazel, was delighted with her new visitor. Rachel had feared she might object and say the child was too much trouble, but she'd taken to her the second she saw her and spent most of the day spoiling her with home-made cakes and biscuits. Hazel was in fact happier than she had been since Rachel had known her and had confessed that she'd always wanted a little girl but had been unable to have another child after her son was born.

'I loved my son,' she'd told Rachel. 'When he married you, I thought you were not good enough – but you were such a loving wife to him, nursing him devotedly through his illness, and you've been a kind daughter to me. Of course, I'll care for Lizzie while you're at work – it is a pleasure.'

Rachel had hugged her, feeling closer to Hazel than ever before. She'd always done what she could to help her after her husband's death, because it was her duty as Hazel's daughter-in-law, but now she genuinely felt that they were friends and it had given her a warm glow. Their new closeness had made Rachel feel less lonely for William and they had something to share – their love for the vulnerable little girl who had been so neglected and their very proper indignation at the way she had been treated.

'Don't you worry about that woman,' Hazel had said stoutly. 'If she comes near us, I'll send her packing.'

There was a new determination and a new fierceness about Hazel that surprised Rachel. She'd always thought her incapable of doing much for herself, but now she was a lioness in defence of their Lizzie. It made Rachel want to laugh but it also made her heart sing. She'd tried all ways to make Hazel find a new life, suggesting voluntary war work and joining clubs for widows, but she'd shown no interest in any of it, complaining if Rachel didn't visit often enough – now she was suddenly younger, brighter and filled with a new energy.

Rachel understood the change because she'd felt a surge of new life herself. Watching Lizzie run and play in the garden, washing and dressing her in pretty things, giving her good food and toys she'd found in second-hand shops, because there weren't many new toys about, so many of them had been imported from Germany before the war, all these things made her heart soar and she knew Hazel felt the same. Lizzie had become theirs; they shared her and enjoyed her pleasure in all the love and gifts she received. It was a good life. Instead of living alone and fretting over William's health, Rachel was able to cook, knit and sew with Hazel in the evenings after Lizzie was tucked up in bed. During the day she had her work and she was finding that her friendship with Sally Harper grew deeper as she helped her by bringing her work – and most recently a report from the private investigator they had hired. Her thoughts flicked to their meeting for a moment, as she continued to watch over her department.

'He has found people who know her,' Rachel had given Sally his first report two days previously. 'However, they don't know where she is now – she was working in a factory making uniforms for soldiers until a month ago. Apparently, she left there without giving notice and she hasn't been seen at her lodgings since then – though it seems some of her clothes were left there and her rent has been paid so perhaps she intends to return when she can.'

Sally had nodded. 'That must have been soon after I was taken ill by the sound of it. Do you think she gave up after she'd spoken to me and went off somewhere different?'

'It might be that... though why go on paying rent, why not just give in her notice?' Rachel had said thoughtfully. 'Perhaps she was offered a better job, though it seems unlikely. They thought a lot of her where she was and she was about to be made a supervisor on the factory floor – so why would she just walk off?'

'Do you think she had an accident or was taken ill?' Sally had then asked anxiously. 'It's so frustrating that I haven't been able to get out for months. She was always there watching me – and she must wonder what has happened to me, too.'

'I'm sure Mr Harry Stevens will find her,' Rachel had replied firmly. 'You mustn't start worrying, Sally. You're doing all you can to find her and I'm sure it will come right in the end.'

'Yes, I hope so,' Sally had said, a wistful look in her eyes. 'Though I was told she was dead, there was a little bit of me that secretly hoped she wasn't and that she would come looking for me one day...'

'You don't resent what she did then?'

'She had no choice,' Sally had inclined her head. 'An unmarried mother with very little money – what else could she do?'

'You don't know that for sure...'

'I'm sure she wasn't wed,' Sally had been convinced of it. 'If she'd had a family, they would surely have helped her keep her child.'

'A respectable family might well have disowned her,' Rachel had reminded her. 'It is often the case – and by the sound of her, she was a decent, well-brought-up girl. That's what Mr Stevens' report says. She was managerial material, Sally. It doesn't sound as if she was uneducated to me – and look how clever you are!'

Sally nodded then. 'Yes, perhaps it was her family who forced her to abandon me. I never thought of that... but why did she let them...? I have so many questions! I want to know everything. I can't lose her now, Rachel! Not without knowing her story. I was so close to discovering the truth before I collapsed...'

'We'll find her, dearest,' Rachel had reassured her.

Sally had lifted her head, a look of determination in her eyes.

'I shan't give up looking,' she'd said. 'She is my mother and I don't mind who or what she has been – I just want to get to know her.'

Rachel brought her thoughts back to the present hurriedly as she saw a little queue forming at Becky's counter. After a brief spell in the dress department, Becky had asked to return to hats, scarves and bags and Rachel was only too happy to have her. She went over to assist her, smiling at her encouragingly. 'You are busier than any of us, Miss Stockbridge. May I assist you?'

'Thank you, Mrs Bailey,' Becky Stockbridge replied. 'We miss Mrs Jackson when she isn't on the floor – Miss Jones had to take over her counter for a while and that meant she couldn't help me. People seem to be buying more gloves and scarves at the moment...'

Rachel nodded and agreed. Becky's counter was usually busy, but with winter approaching, people were stocking up in case there was a shortage during the coming months. Personally, Rachel felt that stock was improving of late, because their suppliers were working flat out to produce as much as they could. Life in Britain had become slightly easier now that many more merchant ships were managing to get through.

Two hundred thousand women were now working on the land and many thousands more in the factories. Gradually, the workforce was making up for the loss of its men and more and more women had joined the ranks of the working class, even refined young women who would never have expected to work had taken up some form of employment. Harpers had seen a steady flow from the beginning, but as the war had bit ever deeper many who would not consider a job as a shop girl had actually found employment somewhere – often on the land as that was seen as patriotic and, therefore, not common.

Rachel read the papers avidly these days and she knew that they were experiencing great difficulties in Germany now, too.

Boys as young as fifteen were being asked to volunteer for armed service, which seemed wicked to her. Change was happening all over the world. Entertainers were giving impromptu shows on the front line and even in Russia a new surge for independence resulting in a Bolshevik revolution and the emergence of a harsh regime had seen the Czar and his family moved to Siberia.

From what Rachel had read recently, it seemed that the Allies were likely to win the war, even though fierce struggles were still going on in France and many other areas of conflict, but the tone was more optimistic now. As yet, she had not dared to think what the future held. An end to hostilities might bring peace and perhaps a slow return to prosperity, but it would not bring William back from his isolation hospital and it would not solve her problem about what to do over Lizzie's grandmother.

Rachel tried not to think too far ahead. She was happier than she had expected to be during William's absence, but the fear of losing him and her unofficially adopted daughter – whom she had rescued from ill treatment – lingered at the back of her mind. Instead, she thought about Becky and was determined to discover what had turned her against Marion Jackson.

* * *

'That doesn't sound like our Becky...' Minnie Stockbridge said when Rachel explained that Becky seemed out of sorts, particularly with a girl she'd been happy working with until a few months back. 'I wonder... you say Marion Jackson recently got married and is expecting a child?'

'Yes – are you thinking that might be the reason? I thought she might be jealous because Marion had been picked out to help with the windows.'

'Well, perhaps that added salt to the wound' Minnie sighed.

'She's had a disappointment in love, Rachel. There was a young doctor – a military man, I understand – and she met him at those first-aid classes she went to with Marion before she was married...' She shook her head. 'He brought her home and then came to tea a few times – and then he was posted abroad and she hasn't heard a word from him since. I think it broke her heart.'

'And she thinks Marion has everything she wants...' Rachel nodded as the little mystery became clearer. Becky had met the man she'd loved when Marion was with her. Now she had lost him, while Marion was married, doing well at work and having a child. No wonder she envied Marion. It wasn't a rational jealousy but entirely understandable. 'I shall have to see what I can do to help her,' Rachel said. 'I can't do anything about her boyfriend – but perhaps if she was promoted to the office, where I know she wants to work, it would help her.'

'Oh, that is easy to arrange,' Minnie said confidently. 'The only reason Mr Stockbridge hasn't done it already was because he thought it might look like favouritism!'

'Well, you tell him his daughter is wasted as a shop girl. She should be doing something more deserving of her talents.'

'I shall – and I'll tell Becky you said it, too,' Minnie said and beamed at her. 'And now, my dearest friend, tell me more about your darling little Lizzie...'

Both women glanced towards Lizzie, who was playing with Minnie's cat on the rug and smiled. Their friendship had never changed, from the time when Minnie was a frightened spinster living with her sister to now, when she was a much-loved wife and stepmother.

26

Sally emerged from her bedroom dressed for work and met Jenni in the hallway. Her sister-in-law had clearly just arrived to visit and was carrying flowers, a newspaper and a box from Harpers' cake and chocolate department.

'Where do you think you're going?' she asked, frowning. 'You don't need to go into work yet, Sally. If you're bored, I could bring you some of the stock lists.'

Sally smiled at her. 'Jenni, I love you, and I thank you for your care of me – but I do need to return to work. My doctor says I'm fine now and carrying the baby well – and I have an appointment in an hour's time.'

'I could...' Jenni began and then closed her mouth as she saw Sally's stubborn look. 'All right, I give in, love. I have to admit you do look wonderful, much, much better – and I'm in a bit of a rush. I'm off to spend the weekend with Andrew. I think he has something important to say to me...'

There was a gleam of excitement in Jenni's face and Sally gave a laugh of pleasure. 'You don't mean he's going to ask you to move in with him at last?'

'He might be,' Jenni admitted. 'I was going to say I couldn't leave London – but I could, couldn't I? You could manage now, Sally – if you're careful, and I would visit every other week or so. You don't really need me now you're well again.'

'Do whatever makes you happy, darling Jenni,' Sally replied and hugged her. 'I want you to find the kind of happiness with Andrew that I have with Ben and I think you love Andrew. You had a miserable time in your marriage and I know you'll never go back to the General; I should think you a fool if you did. I know in the opinion of many you'll be a fallen woman, but the way I see it, you are entitled to be happy – and we'll never criticise or think shame on you. You know both Ben and I love you very much.'

'Ben was lucky when he found you,' Jenni said and lit up like a candle. 'Andrew says I should face all the old biddies down. He's going to write to Henry and ask him to divorce me – but I think my husband would rather sue him for enticement than let me find happiness. Andrew says he can do his worst and he'll spit in his face, but I'm not sure...'

'Andrew knows he can prove that you had already left the marriage by the time you met him, so it wouldn't stand up in court – and, somehow, I can't see your husband wanting to wash his dirty linen in public. Perhaps if Andrew appeals to him man to man, he will give you a quiet divorce.'

'I pray you're right,' Jenni said. 'But I shan't let it bother me, Sally. Our friends will still be our friends – and I'm not the first woman to live with the man I love without the ties of marriage.'

There had been a few cases of the wives of the aristocracy leaving their husbands and living with lovers in the past and it was becoming more accepted in a certain class of what was often termed the 'artistic community', but divorce was still considered scandalous and generally frowned on. Of course, with Jenni being American, it might well be dismissed as something 'those dreadful Americans' might do, but Sally didn't say as much. If Jenni went to live in the north with her lover, much of the gossip might be avoided here in London.

'I don't mind what you do, love – as long as you're happy!'

'I would have moved in with him months ago. He wanted to avoid scandal for my sake, but now he says he can't put up with being without me when he wakes in the morning.' She hesitated, then, 'But I don't want to desert you if you need me. Of course, I'm on the end of a phone and a lot nearer than I was when I lived in America...'

'I can manage, Jenni, honestly,' Sally nodded. She wouldn't have stood in Jenni's way even if she'd felt it would be hard, but, if truth be told, she preferred being left to get on with it.

'I could come to London once a month – and I could keep in touch with our suppliers in the north and if you let me know what you need from them, I'll work on the discounts,' Jenni offered.

'Of course, you must go to him, dearest. I can talk to you on the phone and you can visit whenever you have time.' Sally smothered a sigh. 'I love it when Ben rings me in the evenings. He can't always...'

'You must miss Ben dreadfully,' Jenni said. 'I can't think why he does so much. After all, he needn't have done anything – at least until America entered the war.'

'He wanted to – being thought a coward made him unhappy,' Sally said. 'He'll always be able to look back and think he did his bit, Jenni – and I'm sure that was what he needed.'

'After the war, I think I shall go back to America for a buying trip,' Jenni said. 'Europe and Britain will be exhausted and it will take time for the factories to change back to peacetime needs. I'll need to make new contacts if we're to continue buying some of our stock from the USA – and I think that will be our best route.'

'Do you think it is really necessary?' Sally asked thoughtfully. 'We've had to rely on British-made goods for months now. Yes, I want to stock certain things from overseas – Italy, France and other European countries – but it is such a long way to send things and your home is here now.'

'This shop is owned by Americans and it needs to stock American merchandise,' Jenni said, looking annoyed. 'It's what it was founded on – and I think you need it, Sally, whether you realise or not.'

Understanding that she had inadvertently upset her sister-in-law, Sally nodded and gave in. 'Of course, if that's what you want – but it is a nuisance for you...'

'I shall only make one trip a year,' Jenni said, 'but it's the market I know – and I miss seeing American brands in the store.'

'Yes, we had some lovely things from there before the war,' Sally agreed. 'I'd almost forgotten, Jenni.' She smiled at her sister-in-law. With Jenni living up north and making buying trips there and in America, things would be as they'd been before the war and the slight irritations of working together would be forgotten – after all, two women in one kitchen never worked. 'Let's hope it is soon safe for you to travel again, love,' Sally said.

The papers were reporting with a more optimistic outlook recently, but it seemed as if the conflict had been going on forever and the talk of peace in the future seemed far away still. The headlines had mentioned that the American president Woodrow Wilson had decided to support Women's Suffrage and Sally hoped it would happen here. Beth had been full of what a wonderful man the American president was when they last met and was hopeful that the British Government would do the same. Sally was sure they would have to come at least partway to meet the women, but she knew that certain sectors of the Government were still set against it.

After Jenni had drunk half a pot of coffee, accompanied by chocolate biscuits, she left and Sally sent for a taxicab to take her into work. Once, she would have considered it a wasteful extravagance and used a bus or walked, but Ben had told her that she and the baby were more important than the price of a cab and she was not to walk in until after the baby was born.

Sally was better now, although she admitted that she still tired more quickly than she had before her illness. However, she enjoyed a little walk and, after her meeting with a very eager salesman, who had been invalided out of the Army and was keen to get his first order for his firm, she decided she would take a bus to the park and sit for a while in the fresh air. Her little girl was well cared for and she had no reason to hurry.

Finding the bench where she'd played with her daughter and spoken to her mother the day she'd been taken ill, she looked round hopefully, as if expecting the woman claiming to be her mother would just appear and they could carry on where they'd left off. It didn't happen and she sighed with disappointment as she caught the next bus home. It had been foolish to expect it and Sally wondered if Jenni had been right all the time and she'd imagined the woman telling her she was her daughter...

No, she was certain it had happened, even though she'd clearly been feverish. Besides, Rachel's investigator had suggested he was close to finding her mother in his last report. Where had she gone? After following Sally for months, it seemed as if she'd just disappeared into thin air... Why would she do that? It was a mystery and one that would not let Sally rest. She needed to find Sheila Ross, because only then would she finally know the truth of her abandonment.

* * *

Rachel read the latest report when she got home that evening. The sealed envelope had been delivered by hand to her at Harpers, but she'd been too busy to read it until after Lizzie was in bed and they'd done the supper dishes. She exclaimed aloud and Hazel looked at her expectantly.

'Something wrong, dear – it isn't from that horrid woman?'

'No – it is good news,' Rachel said and glanced at the clock. 'It's too late to go round to Sally Harper's home now – but I could pop down to the box on the corner and ring her.'

'Just as you like, my dear,' Hazel said and smiled. 'Lizzie is fast asleep and I'm here.'

'It won't take five minutes,' Rachel said and got up to put her coat on.

She reached the phone box on the corner and entered, dialling Sally's home number and then heard the engaged tone. Sally must be talking to someone. Rachel waited for a few minutes and then tried again, but Sally's phone was still engaged, so she left the box. She would get a message to Sally in the morning.

It was dark when she left the box and started to walk back to Hazel's house. She had an odd sensation, as if she was being followed, and glanced over her shoulder, but she couldn't see anyone. The street was full of shadows and places where the lighting was inadequate. If anyone was there in the dark corners, she couldn't see them and she thought perhaps it was just her imagination. However, instead of returning to Hazel's immediately, she went to the nearest bus stop. A bus came a moment or two later and she got on, sitting at the back and turning her head to look out of the window. Seeing a man move forward out of the shadows, she felt a shiver at the back of her neck.

Rachel paid her fare and got off at the next stop. She walked back home by a different route.

Hazel looked at her anxiously as she entered the sitting room. 'I was just beginning to think something had happened.'

'I think I was followed, so I got on a bus,' Rachel said. 'I got off at the next stop and walked home as quickly as I could, but I came through the back alley...'

Hazel's face paled. 'Was it that woman?'

'No, but it might have been someone to do with her – someone she asked to find me...'

'Why would she?' Hazel asked, puzzled. 'She doesn't want Lizzie.'

'No, but she wants money,' Rachel said. 'Perhaps I should make her a one-off offer to buy Lizzie.'

'She will just ask for more, you know she will,' Hazel told her. 'Be careful, Rachel – I think she is an unpleasant woman. We don't want her stealing Lizzie from us...'

'I'm the one that did the stealing,' Rachel admitted. 'I couldn't bear to let her go back there.' She sighed. 'I've been dithering, but I think I shall have to have this out with her. Otherwise, they might try to snatch Lizzie.'

'Leave her with me while you go.'

'Yes, I shall. Don't worry, Hazel. I'll make sure we keep her somehow.'

* * *

At work the next day, Rachel passed her message on to Sally's secretary and left her to phone Sally. She came into the department within the hour and Rachel smiled as she came straight up to her counter. 'Ruth got you then? I tried to ring last night, but you were engaged.'

'That was Ben,' Sally said. 'We were talking for ages, must

have cost him a fortune but he wanted to talk.' She looked at Rachel eagerly. 'You said you have definite news?'

'Yes, the report came yesterday – he has found your mother, Sally. She is living in Cambridgeshire and it seems that she has recently married...'

'Married?' Sally didn't know what she had expected, but it wasn't this! 'I've been imagining her ill or dead but never married...' She gave a gasping laugh. 'That's wonderful – does Mr Stevens know her address?'

'He has gone down there to speak to her and ask her to get in touch with you.'

'I can't believe it!' Sally's face lit with wonder. 'I really do have a mother – she's alive and she just got married...' A tear escaped from the corner of her eye, but she swiped it away impatiently. 'I can't thank you enough, Rachel – if you hadn't found that investigator I would probably have given up and never seen her again.'

'You deserve some good luck,' Rachel said. 'I know how much you've helped the wounded soldiers and other good causes. You've worked hard for Harpers and you're kind and thoughtful to your friends and staff. I was glad to help and I'm delighted that she has been found.'

Sally looked excited. 'Will you come to supper this evening and help me celebrate?'

'I'd love to another time,' Rachel said, 'but tonight I have something important to do...'

'Then make it tomorrow. I want to do something nice for you, Rachel.' Sally's eyes sparkled. 'Besides, only a few more weeks to Christmas and I want to make it a good one for the store. We may not have as much special stock as we used to, but there's nothing to stop us making some treats for the children to visit Father Christmas and something for the staff too. I might just have some jars of mincemeat put by for Christmas Eve.'

'Oh, yes, we could all do with that! I'd love to come tomorrow evening,' Rachel agreed. 'Not that you need to do anything for me, Sally. It was a pleasure to help you.'

* * *

Rachel's nerves tingled as she got off the bus and walked towards Vi Robinson's cottage at the end of the terrace. She was determined to be strong and not to give in to the woman's blackmail, but, somehow, she had to persuade her into letting them keep Lizzie.

There was a light on in the back of the cottage when Rachel walked up the garden path. She took a deep breath and knocked and heard a woman yelling. Then the door was flung open and a young woman holding a crying baby stood looking at her. She glared at Rachel from stormy grey eyes.

'What do yer want? I'm busy.'

'I thought this was Mrs Robinson's house?' Rachel was stunned by the woman's rudeness.

'Well, yer thought wrong,' the woman snapped. 'Vi's gorn and we're the new tenants see...' She looked round at a young man who had come to stand beside her. 'Tell her to clear orf, Bob. She wants bloody Vi'

'She ain't here,' the man said gruffly.

'Do you know where I can find her?'

'Up the bleedin' churchyard,' he muttered sourly. 'She's dead, ain't she? Her son came home, what they thought 'ad died at the Front, turned up alive, didn't he? When he found out what she'd done to his wife and kid he bloody belted her – she died in the hospital... he'll be for the chop when the cops get him, poor bugger. In his shoes I'd have done the bleedin' same.'

Rachel stared as the door was slammed in her face. She felt

numb as she walked away, too stunned to work out what this might mean for her. Lizzie's grandmother was dead – killed by the son she'd believed lost to the war. He'd returned unexpectedly, looked for his wife and child and, when he'd discovered his wife dead and his child missing, he'd taken his anger out on the woman he'd expected to care for them.

Rachel felt a slight niggle of guilt. Had she caused this terrible incident, at least in part? No, she'd done what was right for a frightened child who was being mistreated by her grandmother. If Lizzie's father came looking for her, she would tell him that his daughter was safe with her – at least until he could care for her himself.

Did this make Rachel's situation better or worse? She'd believed Vi Robinson would try for as much money as she could wheedle out of her – but what would Lizzie's father want? What would he do if he discovered where his daughter was? He was clearly a violent man – would he try to take his revenge on the woman who had stolen his only child?

27

Marion heard the shouting as she approached the kitchen door of her home when she returned from work that bitterly cold November evening. Frowning, she pushed open the door and to her astonishment saw that her father was in the kitchen. How dare he come here again, knowing he was wanted for questioning over his wife's death? He'd been shown the door before and knew he wasn't welcome. Marion could hardly believe he would have the cheek to do it.

He had clearly been yelling at Sarah and Kathy, both of whom were armed, Sarah with an iron poker, and Kathy the rolling pin she'd been using, which was still covered in flour.

'What is happening here?' Marion demanded, confronting her father. 'You've been told you're not welcome here, Pa. If anyone sees you, you will be in trouble because my neighbours will go to the law.'

'Here she is the filthy little bitch...' his voice was slurred with drink, his eyes wild as he stared at Marion. 'A man can't turn his back before his wife is at it with some other bastard...'

'I'm not your wife, I'm your daughter,' Marion retorted

angrily. 'And you don't belong in this house any longer...' She looked at her sister. 'Kathy run next door and tell Mrs Jackson.'

Their father glared at her and lurched to bar Kathy's way.

She lifted her rolling pin. 'If you touch me, I'll hit you,' she threatened. 'You killed my mother and I hate you. You're a nasty, bitter old drunk and you should do as Marion says and leave now.'

He lunged at her as if he would hit Kathy, but before he could reach her, Sarah struck his arm hard with her poker. The blow stopped him in his tracks and he cried out in pain. For a moment the fury was in his eyes and he might have attacked Sarah, except that the kitchen door opened and a man walked in.

'Dan!' Sarah screamed her relief and delight. 'Thank God...'

Her husband needed no telling what was going on. He grabbed his father by the arm Sarah had struck with her poker, making him scream again; it had broken and was hanging limply and the shock of seeing his eldest son, combined with the pain, seemed to take his senses and he collapsed to his knees in a daze, too drunk to know what he was doing.

The three women stared at the dirty drunken wretch and all fear fled. He was a pitiful sight – brought there by his own temper and addiction to strong drink, but a sad figure all the same.

'You're coming with me,' Dan muttered and half-lifted him, dragging him by the uninjured arm out of the house. 'I'll be back,' he called over his shoulder. The shouts, screams and pleading from Sam Kaye could be heard clearly through the open door until Sarah slammed it shut after him.

Marion looked at her. 'How long had my father been threatening you?' she asked. 'And, did you know Dan was back?'

'Your father turned up about an hour ago,' Sarah said. 'At first, he just asked for you and I offered him a cup of tea. I thought it might placate him, but he demanded whisky and then, when

Kathy came, he started threatening us because we had no whisky to give him. He kept asking for his wife and when you came, he clearly mistook you for her again...it must all be muddled in his mind. He doesn't remember that she died or why—' She drew a deep breath, shaking her head as if to clear it of the unpleasant scene. '—and no, I didn't know Dan was home. I had a letter to say he was on his way, but I didn't expect him until next week...'

'Where do you think he has taken Father?' Kathy asked, sitting down. She was pale and shaking. 'I wish he was dead – I wish you'd killed him, Sarah!'

'I think I may have broken his arm,' Sarah said, looking upset. 'I had to stop him attacking you, Kathy. I'm not sorry I hurt him, but I didn't intend to break anything. I hope Dan doesn't do anything stupid...' She looked worried.

'Kathy is right. We should all be better off if he was dead,' Marion said. 'Dan hates him, but he won't murder him. He might have done it in anger if he'd caught him attacking one of us, but he won't do it in cold blood. He will take him to the police station and they will arrest him for what he did to Ma...'

'I hope they hang him!' Kathy said bitterly. 'I hate him. I wish I'd had the poker and hit him on the head.'

'Then you would be arrested for attempted murder,' Marion told her with a little shake of her head. 'Pa will go to prison for some years – he's in a lot of trouble. He may not hang for Ma's murder, but he will certainly be locked up for a long time.'

'I hope he rots there and never comes out,' Kathy said. 'We're none of us safe while he's free, Marion.'

'She's right. He will go on causing trouble for as long as he's free,' Sarah said with a frown. 'Men like that are relentless, Marion. He'll want revenge...it's the reason he keeps coming back. He thinks his wife is still alive and betraying him with another man!'

'I thought he looked ill,' Marion said, meeting her worried gaze. 'He must have been living rough since they threw him off the ships. I was told he was too much trouble even for the Merchant Navy and they didn't want him – I don't know how he has been living since the last time we saw him, but he smelled bad and he looked as if he hadn't eaten a proper meal for a while.'

'He took a Victoria sponge I'd baked and ate it all,' Sarah said. 'I said nothing because I hoped he would take it and go – but he just kept asking for your mother.'

'And then thought I was her,' Marion agreed. 'That isn't the behaviour of a man in his right senses. Perhaps in prison they can stop him killing himself with drink. Even the food he'll get there must be better than what he's been living on – and if he dies...' She shook her head. 'Whatever happens, he brought it on himself.'

'Yes, he did,' Sarah said and looked anxiously towards the kitchen door, as if willing Dan to return.

It was, however, more than an hour before he walked in. His gaze went straight to Sarah and she jumped up, running to his arms. Dan held her and kissed her and then looked at Marion.

'He's safely locked up,' he said. 'Are you all unhurt? I worried that he might have attacked you? Sarah's last letter said she thought you might be expecting, Marion?'

'I am...' Marion blushed. 'Pa didn't touch me or Kathy. He was about to go for her, but Sarah hit his arm with the poker.'

'It's broken,' Dan said. 'It serves him right. If I'd come sooner, I might have broken his neck.'

'It would be better if he were dead,' Kathy said, eyes glaring.

'He'll pay for what he did now,' Dan said. 'He will be charged with murder – not Ma's. They don't have enough proof to charge him with her murder, just bodily harm, but I've been told he killed another sailor in a drunken brawl and it was witnessed by a dozen men. He will hang...'

His words fell into sudden silence and Marion saw Kathy's face. She gave a strangled cry and ran out of the room. They heard her feet pounding up the stairs.

'Should I go after her?' Sarah asked.

Marion shook her head. 'Leave her to cry it out. I'll talk to her later. She's too muddled up at the moment to know how she feels.'

Marion was feeling drained herself. Their father was a brute and undoubtedly a murderer, but he was still their father and the thought of him being hung was horrible. Kathy said she wanted him dead, but, surely, she didn't really want her father to hang.

* * *

Marion sat on the bed an hour later and listened to her sister pour out her sorrow and her pain. She'd finally stopped crying and she clung to Marion when she put her arms around her and hugged her.

'I know you can't forgive him or what he did to Ma, nor can I,' she told Kathy. 'He is a bully and a brute and needs to be locked away for a long time. It may well be that he'll hang – not for Ma's murder, which would be more difficult to prove, but for another he was seen to commit by witnesses. If they don't hang him, he will be in prison for the rest of his life.'

'I hope he is,' Kathy said. 'Hanging is terrible. I wouldn't wish that on anyone – but I don't want him to come here ever again.'

'He won't,' Marion reassured her. 'It must have been awful with him here all that time before I got home – and then Dan arrived, thank goodness. I would have sent you to get help somehow, Kathy, and faced him alone if I could. I understand your fear and your grief, dearest, but you have to try to put it behind you and learn to live again...'

Kathy nodded, raising her eyes to Marion's. 'I know,' she said. 'I'm leaving school next term and I've been offered a job helping out with the cooking at school. I think I should like to do that – and I might be involved with the cookery lessons in time, when I've learned enough myself.'

'That's wonderful,' Marion said, genuinely pleased for her sister. 'I had enquired about a job in the canteen at Harpers, but there wasn't anything going so I didn't tell you. I might have found you something in the sales department, but I didn't think you wanted that, love?'

'No, I don't,' Kathy agreed and smiled. She sat up and wiped her eyes. 'I'm sorry I've been so awful for ages...'

'You haven't, of course you haven't,' Marion said and gave her another hug. 'You are still grieving for Ma – we all are, but Dan has Sarah and I have Reggie and it was harder for you.'

Kathy shook her head. 'It was you Pa turned his temper on since Ma died. He took little notice of me. I don't look like her; you do...'

'Perhaps, a bit,' Marion agreed. 'I just want you to be happy, Kathy. If I can do anything for you, let me know.'

'I'll need some money for uniforms when I start work,' Kathy said. 'They're only a few shillings – but I don't have any saved, even though you and the boys have given me some now and then.'

'Of course, I'll pay for them and new shoes,' Marion said and smiled. 'You missed supper, do you want me to make you some toast?'

'I'll cook an egg and chips,' Kathy replied. 'Thank you for always being so patient and listening to me.'

'I know how you feel, love. I really do, but we can't change the past no matter how we wish we could.'

'I know.' Kathy took the handkerchief Marion offered and blew her nose. 'I'm going to cook my supper and if anyone else wants any...'

Marion smiled. 'Sarah and I ate a good supper earlier, but Dickon just came in and he's always hungry. He's been celebrating being given promotion and a rise in wages with his friends. I'm sure he would love some of your chips, Kathy.'

She led the way downstairs. Sarah looked at her and she nodded. Dan was enjoying a cheese sandwich and a mug of strong tea by the fire. He frowned as Kathy entered and began to fry her supper, but when she asked if he wanted anything, he asked for a few chips.

Sarah went upstairs to check on her baby and Marion took a few moments to work on a design she'd discussed with Mr Marco. She and Kathy went to bed at nine, leaving Dan and Sarah alone in the kitchen.

* * *

'He's home for three weeks,' Sarah had told Marion when they were washing some cups in the scullery together that evening after supper. 'Dan wasn't hurt, but their ship suffered some damage and they had to limp into port and wait while it was repaired. He would have sent a message, but they were told not to because it might have given the enemy valuable information. He said they'd hoped to be home a month ago.'

'He looks well,' Marion had said, 'and it was a minor miracle that he walked in when he did. We should have got help somehow, but Dan made it so much easier – and I'm glad he took him to the

police rather than giving him the thrashing he has so often threatened.' She'd grinned at Sarah. 'Mind you, that was a sharp blow
you gave him. I think you'd done half the job when Dan got here.'

'I wasn't going to let him hurt you or Kathy. You're my family!'

'I know – and Pa had it coming for the way he treated all
of us.'

'Dan told me that before we married and had a child, he
would've gladly done him injury. He's wanted to kill his father for
years, but that's all gone now. He says he's seen enough killing.
Strangely, he felt sorry for his father and that's something he
never expected to feel...'

'Yes, I feel a bit that way myself,' Marion had said. 'We shall
never know what made him the way he is, but I know he truly
believed Ma betrayed him with another man, though she always
swore she didn't. We can't know the truth for sure, but whatever,
his jealousy destroyed him and her...' She'd sighed. 'I thought it
might have destroyed Kathy's life too, but fortunately, I believe
she is beginning to get over it. Did she tell you about the job
offer?'

'Yes, she did,' Sarah had said and smiled. 'I'm thrilled for her.
I think she will be happy there cooking – and you have everything you want, Marion, so we're lucky...'

'Yes, we are lucky as a family,' Marion had agreed. Many families had lost loved ones to the war, but thus far all Marion's family
had got through with minor injuries. If the papers were right, and
they were hinting the war might end within a few months, they
could all get on with their lives.

* * *

Maggie's letter arrived just as Marion was leaving for work the
next morning. She put it in her coat pocket and read it during her

tea break later. Maggie had written that she was going down to the country with her fiancé and that the wedding would take place in three weeks' time.

> *I'm sorry you don't think you can get down for the wedding. I'm hoping that Sally and Beth will, though Rachel has already said she doesn't think she can make it.*
>
> *Your news about the baby is wonderful. I doubt if we shall meet much in the future, Marion, but do keep in touch through letters and cards if you can.*

The letter spoke of her wedding outfit, which was just a simple ivory velvet dress that she could wear for normal occasions. Maggie said nothing of being in love or being happy and Marion got the distinct impression that she was far from happy.

She sighed as she put it away. It seemed everyone had their troubles, but Maggie Gibbs had had more than her fair share. She knew how lucky she was and felt sorry for Maggie, who she believed was making a mistake.

Later that day, Mr Marco asked her if something was wrong; they were working together on the latest window display and she told him that she thought Maggie was making a big mistake.

'I know Mrs Bailey and Mrs Harper spoke to her about it when she was in London,' Marion said, 'but I don't think she listened. I like Maggie and I know it isn't my business, but I feel sad for her.'

'Perhaps it is right for her,' Mr Marco said thoughtfully. 'Love doesn't always take the same form, Marion. Sometimes, when you've lost the person you loved very much, a compromise is the best you can do. You have to find a way to go on...'

Marion nodded. 'I think that's just what she is doing,' she

said. 'As I said, I can't interfere, but I hope this marriage doesn't lead to unhappiness for her.'

'Maggie is strong,' he replied, 'and if she has agreed to marry this man, then she has her reasons. Reasons the rest of us can't understand.'

28

Maggie perched on the edge of the bed in the room she'd been given. It was the most beautiful room she had ever seen, furnished in shades of cream and rose with gilded, dainty furniture that belonged to a bygone age. 'The Regency room,' her fiancé's father had told her. 'It connects to my son's apartments and is intended for the heir and his wife. You have a bedroom and a sitting room so that you can be private when you choose, Miss Gibbs.'

'Please, won't you call me Maggie?' she asked and offered a friendly smile. If they were to be related by marriage, she felt they needed to be less formal.

He nodded, inclining his head slightly. 'Of course, Maggie. I wanted to thank you for agreeing to this arrangement. You won't lose by it, I assure you. As my son's wife, you will be given an allowance that will make you financially independent.'

'I didn't agree to marry Colin for money,' Maggie said and looked him straight in the eyes. 'I wanted to make him happy – to give him something to live for...'

'You are a generous girl,' he acknowledged stiffly and she

realised he was finding it all difficult. She'd had a good education and she'd won praise and a medal for her war work, but Maggie knew she wasn't of their background and in normal circumstances Colin's father would probably have opposed their marriage. 'That money wasn't meant as payment. His wife would always have received it on their wedding day.'

'Then thank you,' Maggie said. 'I hope we can be friends, sir. Since we will all live here.'

'Of course. I am grateful to you...' For a brief moment he smiled awkwardly. 'I am not much with words, Maggie, especially since my wife died, but I shall give you all the respect you deserve as Colin's wife.'

'Thank you.' Maggie knew that was as close as he could get to being a real friend to her. He wasn't much warmer to his son and she totally understood why Colin had not wanted to return here alone. His home was beautiful, but cold and impersonal. She thought he'd wanted someone warm-hearted to make a home with and understood that need. This room had more warmth than any of the others she'd seen so far and she imagined it had recently been redecorated, most likely with another woman in mind – the woman Colin had intended to wed before his war wounds had ruined his hopes. 'I shall do my best to deserve your respect, sir.'

Her prospective father-in-law nodded and left her to settle in.

The estate and house were bigger and more impressive than Maggie had expected and for a while her new surroundings overwhelmed her, making her wonder what she'd agreed to – how could she ever be the lady of the manor? The ridiculous idea made her smile and suddenly her mood fled. Nothing had really changed. She'd agreed to this marriage because her life had seemed empty and all her friends at Harpers had moved on without her.

She shook her head. Sitting in this lovely room brooding would not change anything.

She knocked at the door which joined Colin's and then entered through when he invited her to do so. His room was elegant but, decorated in maroon, gold and black, very masculine, and Maggie thought a little depressing.

'My father's wedding gift to me...' he indicated the rich maroon hangings at the windows and the matching quilts on the large double bed. 'God knows it was bad enough before – now it is like a bloody mausoleum.'

'It's a bit too grand for me,' Maggie admitted and laughed softly. 'We can soon mess it up a bit with books and clothes left about if you like... and flowers. They always brighten anything.'

'Yes, I should like that,' he said and grinned at her. 'You make me feel so much better, Maggie. I couldn't have faced this without you.'

'It is a little daunting,' she agreed, 'though you grew up here, so I don't suppose it seems grand to you. I lived in a small terraced house with neighbours each side.'

'You should have been born to a palace,' Colin said, surprising her with a smile of such warmth that it lit up his face, making him the man she'd only glimpsed until now. 'You're a wonderful person, Maggie. Thank you for giving me back my life...'

'I haven't done anything much,' she said, but he reached for her hand and held it.

'You've done more than you could ever imagine,' Colin said in a voice deep with emotion. 'I like you more than you realise, Maggie. I was bad-tempered when we met and I may be again if things upset me – but you've made me feel a king to the way I was feeling.'

Maggie nodded. His smile touched something inside her and she squeezed his hand. 'Why don't we go for a walk in the lovely gardens I glimpsed as we arrived? It is a nice day, cold but bright, and that won't last much longer. It will soon be fogs and ice, so we might as well make the most of it – and I'd love to explore a little.'

Maggie suddenly felt excited. She realised that it was a whole new world and with all the trees in the gardens and surrounding countryside, the changes of scenery would be glorious: winter had the dramatic lines of dark branches devoid of leaves against the strangely blue sky and in spring the trees would suddenly burst into life again, sheltering a carpet of woodland flowers that had lain dormant in the icy weather. She was eager to begin exploring this new home she had come to.

'Yes, let's,' Colin said. 'Put a warm jacket on, Maggie. The wind can be colder than you think. I know I'm supposed to be the invalid here, but you were very ill and I don't want to lose you.'

Maggie smiled and fetched a coat and scarf. She didn't expect to be cold, but it was nice to have someone concerned for her. Ever since she'd told Colin she would marry him, he'd been considerate and thoughtful. He really was rather a pleasant person once he knew you and when he wasn't angry. Maggie realised that his anger had gone, for the moment at least.

They went down in the lift his father had had installed for him. It was similar to the one at Harpers and Maggie found it easy to use. She took his chair out by a side door and wheeled him along the path. Outside, she turned to look back at the house. It had a Georgian façade with many long narrow windows, steps leading up to the front door and a terrace with roses growing up it. A thin wintry sun was shining on old grey stone walls, making them golden and mellow for a fleeting moment before disappearing into the grey clouds, as they crossed the lawn heading for the rose garden. Although only the odd hardy rose still bloomed in sheltered corners, Maggie could imagine what it would look like in summer and the scent of a white rose that still clung to life was gorgeous, wafting in the slight breeze. Amongst the shrubs was a wooden bench, hidden from the windows of the house. She thought she understood why Colin had spent so much time in the rose garden at the hospital. It had reminded him of this – his home.

'This was my mother's favourite place when I was young,' Colin told her. 'She was very beautiful but a cold woman. I dare say she loved me, but she was never able to show it. You know how to love, don't you, Maggie? – I don't mean just romantic love. I mean the kind of love that you give to all those you help or care for.'

'I try to help where I can...' Maggie began and then stopped, realising that what he'd just said was true. She had loved her work at the hospital and cared for her patients, her heart aching for those that died and rejoicing for those who recovered and tried to flirt with her. 'Yes, I suppose I do. I like caring for others, helping people. I enjoy making people happy if I can.'

She'd always had an interest in people. It was why her father had thought she would be a good teacher. Maggie had loved her time at Harpers too, serving customers with pretty things, seeing them smile when they found just what they were looking for – and she thought she could be happy here too.

If there was a slight shadow, an ache in her heart, it was for Mick. Maggie knew that if things had been different, she could have loved him as he wanted – perhaps as she wanted too – but he hadn't been there when she'd needed him and Colin had. Maggie was an honest girl and she knew that the young man whose pain and grief had spoken to her had given her back her reason to live. She'd been feeling drained, lost and unsure – but Colin's desperation and his need had awoken a response in her. It wasn't romantic love, but it was a kind of love and she reached down and kissed him softly on the cheek.

'I'll make you happy if I can,' she promised. 'This is a lovely home, Colin. I don't see why we shouldn't enjoy it.'

'I'm hungry,' he announced, turning his eyes so she was unable to see into them. 'Let's go in and ask Mrs Blake for tea and crumpets in the sitting room. She makes some wonderful black-berry jam this time of the year.'

'Yes, why not?' Maggie said and smiled.

She was about to push him out of the rose arbour when they saw someone approaching. It was a beautiful young woman and Colin stiffened, the colour leaving his face.

'God no!' he muttered and grabbed Maggie's hand. 'Don't leave me whatever you do.'

Maggie held his hand. His was gripping hers so tightly it hurt her, but she didn't try to extricate herself, because she had realised who it must be. This girl with the hair like pale sunlight and eyes as green as a cat's must be the girl who had so nearly destroyed Colin.

'Oh, hello,' the girl said. 'Blake told me you had come to the rose arbour, so I thought I would come and find you.' Her green eyes flashed at Maggie. 'You might introduce me, Colin. I understand this is your nurse?'

'Maggie was a nurse,' Colin said coldly. 'But she also happens to be my fiancée. We shall be getting married as soon as the banns are read.'

'Ah, Maggie, not a name I've often encountered, except in servants, though I have a friend called Margaret.' Her tone seemed to imply that Maggie was a name given to those of the lower classes. 'I am Charlotte,' her tone was unaltered, though her eyes narrowed as she studied Maggie. 'Colin always called me Charlie. We grew up together – best friends. My father is the family lawyer and we have a house near the village. So, I know everything about him...' Was she implying Maggie didn't?

She offered her hand but not her congratulations. Maggie might have taken it, but Colin stubbornly refused to let go of her hand. She smiled politely but offered no comment, since there did not seem much she could say. Colin answered for them both.

'Maggie knows all about you, Charlotte. I told her everything...' His tone was so malicious that for a second she faltered but then made a quick recovery.

'Of course, you did, Colin darling. I wouldn't have expected anything else.' She directed a false smile at Maggie. 'It is a lovely house and garden. I'm sure you will enjoy living here – after what you've been used to, it must seem like Paradise.'

Maggie felt the barb beneath the words and was puzzled. She was being rude and there was no call for it – unless she was jealous? But why was the woman who had jilted Colin jealous of her?

'Maggie has a medal for her war work,' Colin said before she could think of an answer. His eyes glittered with anger. Was it for her sake? Maggie wasn't sure, though she sensed the tension between them. 'All the chaps over there were nuts about her – but I asked her to marry me and she said yes.'

'Indeed?' Charlotte's eyes flashed with anger now. 'Can she speak for herself?'

'Yes, I can,' Maggie said quickly. 'Colin is exaggerating – it is natural for men recovering from terrible wounds to fall for their nurse. Most of the nurses out there had the same – but I didn't nurse Colin. I was sent back to hospital because I was ill and we became friends there – and I realised how much he meant to me, so when he asked me to be his wife, I was happy to say yes.' She lifted Colin's hand and kissed it. 'I think we shall both be happy now Colin is where he belongs – don't you, my love?'

Seeing the wicked smile in his eyes, Maggie knew she'd done the right thing. He gripped her hand even tighter. 'I was happy the minute I saw you,' he told her. 'I thought I'd died and gone to Heaven, my angel.'

Maggie lifted her head and looked into the other woman's eyes. 'We're just about to have tea, crumpets and honey, I'm informed – would you care to join us?'

'No thank you. I don't have time. I'm going out this evening. I just brought a message from my father, that's all.' She bent over Colin and attempted to kiss him, but he set his mouth and turned his head to one side so that her lips slid away from his cheek. 'I'm truly glad to see you looking so much better and happy. Good afternoon, Miss Gibbs.' She turned and walked briskly away.

Maggie stood still for a moment and then started to push Colin's chair back the way they'd come earlier. He was silent as they entered the house, and when they reached the lift, she saw his face was grim and pale. He was clearly affected by the meeting.

'Don't let her hurt you,' Maggie said. 'She isn't worth it.'

'What do you know?' he asked coldly, his eyes cold.

Maggie blinked. He hadn't been rude to her for weeks. Charlotte's visit had truly upset him and that made her feel unsure. She'd thought they could be happy together, but if Colin still loved the girl who had hurt him, perhaps she was wrong...

* * *

Colin apologised when they were in their own apartment and she'd rung for tea. 'I'm sorry, Maggie,' he said suddenly. 'That was out of order. You're right. She is a first-class bitch – I shan't let her get to me again.'

'I know you must have loved her – she is very beautiful...'

'I adored her and broke my heart for her,' he said, his mouth a grim line. 'But I was a fool. She never wanted me – just the money.'

Maggie didn't say anything. She knew she must let him work this out for himself. As for Charlotte, she had definitely been jealous of her. Perhaps she'd reconsidered and regretted what she'd given up, but because she still loved Colin or his father's money?

Maggie didn't know and didn't much want to know. Colin would decide for himself what he truly wanted in his life and she would accept his decision.

'You'll still marry me,' he said, looking anxiously at her face. 'You won't change your mind because of her?'

'She doesn't bother me one way or the other,' Maggie said. 'Yes, I'll be your wife, Colin. She doesn't matter...'

'No, she doesn't,' he agreed and smiled at her. 'Can I have the last crumpet?'

'Of course,' she agreed. 'I've had all I want.'

She watched as he ate the last crumpet and then a slice of fruit cake, seemingly unconcerned. Was he truly over Charlotte or was he just pretending?

29

Sally and Beth had decided to take Pearl and Beth's oldest son as well as Jenny to Maggie's wedding. Pearl would look after the two children while they attended the church. They were all going in a hired car to make the journey easier and had their gifts in the boot of the car. They would stay one night at a hotel on the return to London and Fred's friend, Vera was looking after Beth's baby. It gave them a chance to have a nice long talk on the way. Beth had her son on her lap and Jenny sat between them, Pearl was in the front with the driver.

'When I couldn't feed Timmy myself, I thought it was tragic,' Beth confided. 'But now I realise that it was a blessing in disguise. I should have had to bring him with us, which would have made for a tiring day.'

'Yes, poor little love. He will miss you,' Sally said and placed her hands on the gentle swell of her belly. Her second child was doing well now and she'd come so close to losing this baby that she felt protective. 'Specially with that upset tummy he's had. I remember Jenny when she had upset tummies for a while...'

Beth looked at her then. 'Are you pleased you're having another?'

'Yes, yes, of course I am – at first it was awful, being so ill and then having to stay in bed, but I'm fine now and the doctor assures me Baby is doing well.'

'I wasn't sure you would want to go all the way down to Maggie's wedding.' Beth frowned. 'I've never been to Sussex before – have you?'

'Never,' Sally said and sighed. 'I was brought up in the orphanage on the edge of Harlow and I only really know London. I've been for a few holidays to the sea since then, but never as far as this place. It is not far from Hastings, or so Maggie says. I wanted to see where she is and I'm perfectly fit now.' They looked at each other, both excited to see where Maggie would be living.

'I'll bet Jenni kicked up a fuss when you told her?'

'Not really. She is moving in with Andrew next week and I don't think she has time to think about anything else for the moment.'

'You will miss her at Harpers?'

'Yes and no,' Sally said. 'I love Jenni and she has helped me a lot in the past, but...' she hesitated and Beth laughed.

'You like a free hand and she has interfered too much while you were ill?'

'Oh Beth, did it show that much?' Sally asked ruefully. 'I tried not to let it irritate me and I love Jenni dearly, but I must admit it, sometimes I disliked having her take over. I know she is entitled; she is part owner of the business and she could always have had her say far more than she did, but I'd got used to having things as *I* liked them.' She gave a wry laugh. 'That's awful of me, isn't it?'

'You were left to run it single-handedly for ages, so it is natural,' Beth said. 'But she'll still be around – visiting regularly, won't she?'

'Yes, of course, and some of her ideas are good,' Sally agreed. 'I suppose it's like two women in the same kitchen.'

'Yes, I know what you mean,' Beth replied and looked thoughtful. 'Vera comes round sometimes when I'm not there and rearranges my kitchen pots and pans or cleans the pantry out. It is kind of her, but it also makes me cross when I can't find something.'

An altercation between Beth's son and Sally's daughter started then and it took Pearl a few minutes to calm them. Sally took her daughter on her lap and talked to her for a moment, while Pearl sorted out Jackie, who had been a little sick. Pearl took him on her lap in the front seat and he settled, grizzling for a minute or two before falling asleep.

'Some children can't travel in the back of a car,' she said to Beth reassuringly. It might be a good idea to stop and have something to eat soon.'

They were travelling down by easy stages, stopping for meals and a night in the hotel before the wedding the next day. It meant three days away in all from London and Beth was still anxious about leaving her baby behind.

'I hope Timmy will be all right with Vera,' Beth voiced her concerns for the umpteenth time and Sally smiled at her.

'I'm sure he will,' she reassured her. 'You're lucky to have a friend like that to help out. Two children in the car at one time is enough.'

It was more than enough by the time they'd stopped a dozen times for toilet breaks, drinks and some fresh air as both children were sick and had to be taken out on to a grass verge and be cleaned up.

'Remind me never to travel with Jenny again,' Sally said ruefully. 'I should have left her at home with Pearl.'

'You know you hate leaving her,' Beth said with a laugh. 'You're as bad as I am, Sally.'

Sally admitted she was and smiled. 'They wear you out on a journey, but she will look lovely when she's all dressed up at the wedding and Maggie deserves to have as many of her friends as possible.'

They were the only ones from Harpers: Marion, Becky and Rachel were working, none of them asking for time off to attend the wedding, though all had sent cards and gifts with Sally.

'I'd have liked to see Maggie married,' Rachel had said wistfully. 'But it is too far to go. I don't have the time to spare – and someone has to look after Harpers.'

Becky hadn't given a reason why she preferred to work, but it was clear from her attitude that she had no intention of going down for the wedding. Sally had asked if something was upsetting the young girl and Rachel had frowned.

'She has been a little reserved and not always cooperative,' Rachel had agreed when Sally raised the question of Becky Stockbridge. 'Minnie thinks she has suffered a disappointment in love and even though she has been transferred to the office now, it doesn't seem to have pleased her...' Becky's attitude seemed to be one of reserve now and she had not visited her old department since her move. Either she was very angry about something or heartbroken as Minnie believed.

'Yes, I believe there was a young man – I shall speak to her myself and see if I can help her if she is unhappy.'

* * *

Maggie looked beautiful in her simple white ankle-length dress with a posy of fresh roses the estate gardener had somehow found for her in her hand, and a small coronet of artificial flowers on her head. She had chosen not to wear a veil and looked fresh and charming in her dress. She seemed serene and content as she stood by her husband's chair and took her vows. Sally remembered the young girl she'd first met when they'd both applied for work at Harpers. So much had happened since then and the innocent girl had become a woman. Maggie had suffered more than any young woman should and Sally wished that she had been closer to her these past years.

Watching her take her wedding vows, Sally's throat tightened. She did so hope that Maggie would be happy in this marriage – and yet how could she be? It would hardly be a normal marriage; Maggie was as much his nurse as his wife and Sally felt close to tears. She had chafed at Ben being away so long these past years, but suddenly she realised how lucky she'd been to have so much. A wonderful husband who loved her deeply, a child and another on the way – and Harpers and her friends there. Perhaps now, even her mother, if she could be reached.

What did Maggie have? Oh yes, the house and grounds were wonderful and she would clearly be the wife of a man destined to inherit wealth – but how much would that mean to a girl like Maggie Gibbs?

Sally blinked away her tears as the ceremony ended and then went outside with Beth and the other guests to throw confetti and wish the happy couple well. Sally gave her a lucky horseshoe tied up with blue ribbons and kissed her cheek.

'I want to thank you and Mr Harper for your lovely gift of bone china. It is beautiful – and all the other gifts you and Beth brought, from Rachel and the staff at Harpers. They are all lovely, as are your delightful children; they were so good in church.'

'Amazingly so,' Sally said. 'They were awful on the journey but good as gold today, after their sleep last night.'

'You are both very lucky to have them, Sally.'

'I wish you and Colin great happiness in the future,' Sally said emotionally, because it was unlikely that Maggie would ever have children of her own. 'You really deserve it, Maggie.'

Maggie laughed and Sally was surprised as she said, 'But I am very happy, Sally. Believe me, I have all I want. Please, you mustn't worry for me – tell Rachel and the others I'm fine, too.'

Sally nodded, looking into her eyes and seeing the truth. 'You are, aren't you?'

Maggie inclined her head and smiled. 'Yes, Sally. I know what I want...' She hesitated, then, 'If you see Mick, tell him I'm sorry – but he was too late...'

Sally took her hand. 'Yes, I shall if the time is right,' she agreed. 'Take care of yourself, love, and keep in touch. We'd all hoped you would come back to Harpers after the war.'

'I thought I would,' Maggie said honestly, 'but I think that period of my life has closed a door. I'll never forget any of you – especially you and Beth – but my home and my heart is here now, Sally.'

'Your heart?' Sally questioned and Maggie smiled.

'Yes,' she said. 'I must go to Colin – he is being cornered by someone he doesn't much like and we ought to cut the cake soon. Considering there is a war on, they've done us proud, don't you think?'

Sally looked at the tables laden with cold roast poultry and game from the estate with fresh bread, preserves, little pastries and tarts and a large wedding cake and wondered at the abundance. They couldn't have put on a spread like this in town for Maggie. There were obvious advantages to living in such a house in the country.

Maggie walked away, shoulders straight and head up. Sally watched her and wondered. Was she truly happy or had that all been for pride's sake? Sally might never know, but she did know that Maggie had made her choice freely and nothing would change her mind now. Sad as she would be to leave her here, she doubted she would see Maggie often in the future.

* * *

The wedding reception was over and all the guests had gone. It had been a tiring day for Maggie, keeping her bright smile in place, conscious that everyone was watching her, talking about her – about her motives for marrying a man who might never be a proper husband to her. All they saw was the man tied to a wheelchair, Maggie realised. Most of his relatives and friends would think she'd married for comfort and security and they would continue to watch for signs that she was betraying him in some way or taking advantage.

Well, let them! A smile touched Maggie's lips as she silently vowed to confound them all. She would make Colin happy – make him laugh and enjoy his life. It wouldn't be easy, she knew that, because he suffered with bouts of anger and depression, his moods changing with the wind or an expression of pity in a former friend's eyes.

Maggie knew that her friends felt that she'd thrown her life away. Both Beth and Sally had looked at her sadly, as if they'd come to her funeral rather than her wedding. She'd done her best to convince Sally that she was happy, but she wasn't sure her friend had believed her. It was almost true. Maggie was content with her life, content that she was doing something worthwhile.

If there was a longing for something more, deep down inside her, she would not let it destroy her. She did truly care for her husband, that was no lie. If Colin had been able to be a normal husband, she thought their marriage could have been happy – as happy as most were. Her parents had never truly been happy.

Especially after her father's accident. Yet she knew that both Beth and Sally were very happy, still very much in love.

Why had her parents not been happy? Was it her father's accident that had ruined their marriage or had it happened long before that? Maggie had always been conscious of his unhappiness beneath the surface. Was that why Maggie had given Colin her promise? Was she trying to make up for not being there when her father died?

No, she decided after some thought. It wasn't that... then was this feeling she had for him the first small seed of love? Maggie couldn't be certain. She'd loved before and the pain of loss had killed something inside her – at least that was what she'd believed in France, when she'd worked herself nearly to death to forget.

Yet she'd been aware of something more recently – since Charlotte had paid them a visit. The other woman had aroused anger, distrust, and was it jealousy? Maggie couldn't have said, but she knew whenever that woman came near Colin she wanted to rush and protect him from her – to push her away and say, 'Don't trust her! Whatever she says or does, Colin, please don't believe her. She doesn't love you – she just wants what she could have had as your wife.'

Maggie was startled out of her reverie as the door to Colin's room opened and he wheeled himself in, looking about him. 'I like this room,' he announced. Can I sleep here with you, Maggie? I don't want to be in my room. I'd rather be with you so we can talk... about books and stuff or anything you like.'

Maggie was surprised, but then she smiled. 'Of course, you can,' she told him. 'Where I come from, we don't have separate rooms when we're married. You're my husband, you can sleep in my bed if you choose.'

'Thank you.' His eyes took on a wicked glint. 'I might be in a wheelchair, but I'm still a man, Maggie. Can I watch you get undressed? You have a lovely body. I want to see you... without your clothes...'

Maggie looked at him, nodding in silence as she began to disrobe. They might not be able to have intercourse or children, but perhaps Colin wanted more from her than he'd said at the start. She was pleased that he could still take an interest, that he was interested in her.

She took all her clothes off, slowly, her eyes looking into his, allowing him to savour the moment, she stood naked before him. What would he think – did she compare with Charlotte?

'You're are beautiful,' he said. 'Will you sleep naked beside me so that I can feel you skin next to mine – can I touch you?'

'Yes, you can,' she said and walked to him, kneeling by his side. Maggie had always thought she might feel self-conscious when undressing before her husband, but all such inhibitions had gone in the face of his need. 'Do you want me to help you undress and get into bed?'

'I can do most of it myself,' he told her. 'I just need help putting my legs over – but you know. You've been told by the nurses... you've seen me, helped me into bed.' He couldn't quite keep the bitterness from his voice. 'You've seen other men who have lost the use of their legs.'

'Yes, I have – and I've seen men make remarkable recoveries, too. Your upper body is strong, so there's no reason to think you can't do many things you wish,' Maggie replied gently. 'But we'll talk about that tomorrow. Come to bed, Colin, and let's lie side by side and touch and kiss – it is our wedding night after all.'

She pulled back the bedcovers, helping him to swing himself over from his chair once he'd discarded his clothes, revealing a body that was still fit and strong, apart from his damaged and too thin legs. Then she lay beside him and put her arms around him.

The passion with which he responded and his kisses surprised her and she felt pleased that she could stir him.

At first, he was content to just kiss and touch her, telling her how beautiful her body was, but then she sensed a frustration in him and saw that he was aroused sexually but unable to move his lower half. It was then Maggie made a decision, that would have shocked the girl who had worked in Harpers, but was nothing to the woman who had nursed fatally wounded men and washed every part of them. Maggie had often given them a kiss on the lips when Sister wasn't looking and she thought it would help those who would not live to be kissed by their sweethearts – and so, she made love to Colin, shyly at first and uncertainly, but, with his encouragement and obvious pleasure, managing to give him the joy and release his body craved.

Afterwards, he wept in her arms, his body shaking with his emotion. 'I never believed I would ever feel that again,' he told her huskily when the storm of emotion had passed. 'I wasn't even sure I could – though I knew I felt aroused when you touched me.'

Maggie stroked his hair, her cheeks wet with her own tears as much as his. 'There was no real reason why you shouldn't,' she said. 'I was told that you hadn't been affected there – but you couldn't make love to me because you can't move the lower half of your body...'

Colin looked up at her. 'Yet you married me – and you gave me that gift. You are a wonderful, unselfish woman, Maggie.'

'I care for you, Colin, I really do,' Maggie said softly. 'I didn't marry you for money or a home but because I want to make you happy.'

'I'm not sure I can ever be completely happy again,' he told her. 'But I will try – I promise I'll try. You've given me so much, you deserve more than a moody devil as a husband.'

'I rather like him,' Maggie said with a twinkle in her eye. 'You shocked me out of my apathy with your anger. I had nothing when we met, Colin, and you made me come back to life.'

He looked at her strangely. 'I like you, Maggie,' he said at long last. 'I think I might learn to love you – if I could just give you the kind of pleasure you gave me.'

He sounded so wistful that she laughed. 'I'm sure we can find a way, Colin. I can suggest something right now...'

A gleam came into his eyes and she saw a surge of new life and knew she had found the way to reach the man inside. She would teach him what she liked, what made her feel nice, and she would start a regime of exercise to build up his strength, regain the muscle he'd lost, but she wouldn't tell him yet that his legs had moved when he'd found his release. She couldn't be sure, but she'd noticed his right foot moving a few times before then and she had a plan. Perhaps nothing would come of it, but Sister Mayhew had told her once that sometimes men would believe they couldn't do something when, in reality, they might be able to if they tried.

'Even the worst injuries get better and sometimes movement will come back when a man seems paralysed, but at times their mental attitude stops it happening. Exercise and belief will often do what overworked doctors consider an impossibility. Nurses can do wonders now and then, Maggie.' The nerves in Colin's spine had been crushed and damaged, but, although it would be a long job and would need patience, prayer and love, perhaps they could recover enough for him to have some movement, though walking was perhaps too much to hope for.

Maggie would do whatever she could. Perhaps he would never walk again, but he might recover enough movement to ease himself into bed and to push his body closer to hers. Even a small improvement might give him a reason for hope and – as she'd so often witnessed in France – miracles could happen. Maggie had a lifetime to achieve it and she would devote all her time and energy to making him live again, even if he was still confined to the wheelchair. Before their marriage he'd been breathing but not alive – now she could see that he was beginning to truly live as he ought.

30

Marco stiffened as he saw the man walk into his office at Harpers. He'd almost forgotten his time in France. Settled at Harpers again with his friends and his wife and child at home, Marco had found a kind of happiness. Sadie was a good cook and a good mother to the little boy they both loved. He'd discovered she had a sense of humour that he enjoyed and he liked her open honesty. Life was as good as he could expect and the intrusion of the man who had first recruited him to the body of spies made his spine prickle with cold. The Major had not come here for fun.

Marco felt anger and hostility as he saw that his superior officer wanted something of him – something he no longer felt like giving. He'd had enough of the war and he wanted to stop here at Harpers and to watch his adopted son grow up.

'You're wondering why I'm here,' Major Bryant said. 'I couldn't believe it when I realised those fools at Head Office had stood you down, Marco. Half of them seem to think the war is almost over just because our American friends have joined in, but even when we've beaten the enemy – if we do! – we'll still have need of men like you. You did a good job over there – and now I want you to do something a little more difficult for us.'

For once Marco was in agreement with him. Many people seemed to think the war almost over just because the enemy had been pushed back and there had been victories for the Allies, but Marco was certain they were not beaten yet. If he was needed in France again, it would give him a chance to discover what had happened to Marie and her family after he'd left. Yet a part of him was angry at the way he and his French friends had been treated.

'You want me to go back out there? After people were killed in reprisal for getting me out? Surely you've got plenty of other fools to do your dirty work?'

'Angry at the way you were treated when you got back? I don't blame you – I was furious when I discovered they'd wasted your talents. Surely, you still want to protect your country? I heard that you had a wife and child now – you must want to keep them safe?'

'The war is over for them,' Marco said. 'The Germans aren't strong enough to invade us now. The papers are sure of it and I believe the tide may be turning in our favour, though there is a long way to go still. Germany had a huge advantage in the early stages, but they've fought a hard campaign; they're running out of steam, and in time we shall overcome them, but I *am* willing to go back if I can help shorten the war...'

'Perhaps,' Major Bryant replied, 'but I don't want you to return to France or to Germany. I want you to go to Russia... that is where we expect trouble in the future.'

'What possible use could I have in Russia?' Marco exclaimed, shocked and horrified. 'I don't speak the language. No, I'm sorry. I won't go on a wild goose chase.'

'You speak French well,' Major Bryant said. 'All I'm asking is for a little information on what is going on out there. It is like a powder keg ready to explode since the Czar abdicated and the Russians took a beating back in June. They are a volatile lot and something is going on more than a takeover by the Bolsheviks. Lenin could be a tricky customer. We need to know if we should plan an intervention.'

'What do you imagine they would tell me?' Marco looked at him sardonically. 'No, find someone else, sir. I'm not putting my head in the fire for no good reason.'

'You would disobey an order? I could have you shot for that!'

'Then you'll just have to shoot me. Send me back to France, let me fight on the front line, if you wish, but Russia – no! I could not help you there.'

'You underestimate yourself. As a Frenchman seeking a new life buying Russian works of art and selling wine, you have a perfect alibi. You know plenty about French wine and I dare say you know a bit about art – it doesn't matter if they cheat you. You will learn more if they think they're getting the best of the bargain.'

Marco hesitated for one second, almost tempted, but then he shook his head. 'I was discharged from the service, sir. I'm sorry. I can't help you.'

'Lost your balls out there, did you? Not that you ever had much to lose...' The sneer in the officer's voice nearly made Marco lose his temper. A year ago, he would probably have responded to the man's goading and said he would go, but he'd had enough of bloodshed and subterfuge – and the innocent casualties of these games of chance.

'I'm sorry, I can't help you,' Marco said resolutely. 'I'm still a soldier – and you can send me to fight if you choose. I shan't refuse to go, but I won't play your games.'

Major Bryant nodded, his sneer intensifying. 'I always

wondered if you really had the guts for it. You're a disgrace to the service...' With that he turned and walked out of the office, leaving Marco breathing deeply to calm his anger.

The man was a pig, no better than the men who had tortured the German soldier, Kurt Shultz in France, when it was discovered that he'd passed information to Marco. You found them in all nationalities. Marco was glad he'd had the strength to refuse, despite the goading and the insults. Let the man believe he was a coward if he chose. Marco would pick up a gun and fight if given the opportunity, but he no longer wished to run the risk of being a spy. Spies needed safe houses and contacts and those people were vulnerable; they were often the ones who died, left behind to the mercy of suspicious men and tortured or killed for the information they could give. Let Major Bryant do his worst. If they wanted to court-martial him, they could. He had no intention of entering Russia as a spy; to Major Bryant he was expendable, but Sadie relied on him to help her bring up little Pierre and Sally Harper swore he was invaluable to her. Marco had joined up to fight as a soldier and he was perfectly willing to fight on the front line. Secret missions were always a matter of choice. No soldier could be forced to undertake such a mission if he did not wish it.

He smiled as he decided that he would take Sadie some flowers that evening and a box of chocolates. It would show her that he appreciated her, that he was glad they had married. Theirs might not be a conventional marriage, but that was not always necessary for happiness.

Sadie had told him that Maggie Gibbs had married a soldier confined to a wheelchair. She'd had a letter and now believed that her friend was happy in her marriage. Marco hoped that Sadie was too. He had found contentment in the arrangement and that evening he would ask her if she was content in her life with him. He would not ask if she was happy. Marco knew that Sadie still loved Pierre; she always would, just as he would never forget Julien, the lover he had lost so tragically – but life was not over. He had a wife who looked after him and a son and the perfect job. One day he might meet someone who made him want more but for the moment he was satisfied.

* * *

Sadie had been shopping. She enjoyed shopping and Marco always gave her sufficient money for the housekeeping and her own needs, as well as Pierre's. He was a generous man and her life was comfortable, if a bit boring at times.

Sadie had been home to her parents, by herself, and with Marco and Pierre. Her parents had welcomed her and believed that Pierre was her husband's son. She hadn't told them any different and she knew they thought she'd done well for herself – and of course, she had. She knew that if Marco hadn't offered her marriage, she would have had to take menial jobs scrubbing or perhaps washing up all day long to make ends meet. As it was, she had nice clothes, a family who was always pleased to see her – and the prospect of a return to nursing once Pierre was at school. They had agreed she would wait until then, to give her son a good start in life. Marco thought he needed his mother at home until he could spend most of his day at school. Sadie didn't mind; she loved Pierre and wanted to look after him and Marco had made it easy for her – but she did sometimes get a little bored with the long days when Marco was at work and her household tasks were done.

'It is an interesting window...' the voice from just behind her made Sadie turn in surprise. A young man in the uniform of an Army corporal was standing just behind her looking at the

Harpers' window. She'd come to see it because Marco had told her she would like it and she did – it was a scene of nurses and soldiers enjoying a break in a barn after the grape harvesting was done and the wine barrels were stacked. The models were meant to be enjoying a drink with the French farmers and it came with the words: *A toast to our French friends!*

'It's very like...' the soldier went on with a smile. 'It makes you feel you are back out there with them – a friendly bunch where I was stationed for six months.'

Sadie knew she ought to say something about the window having been dressed and designed by her husband, but she kept that fact to herself. 'Have you been home long?' she asked.

'A few weeks. I caught one in my leg. They say it will be a good barometer when the weather changes,' he said ruefully. 'I shall probably always walk with a limp, but I'm still alive – a lot of the poor devils aren't...'

'I know,' she replied. 'I did some nursing with the VADs – more than a year before I had my son.'

The soldier glanced at Pierre. 'He's a fine lad. His father must be proud of him.'

Without thinking, Sadie said, 'His father was killed out there. He was a French partisan.'

As soon as she said the words, she regretted them. Marco was Pierre's father and her husband. She'd made it sound as if she were a widow and free and she'd seen the flash of renewed interest in the soldier's eyes.

'Shame...' he said and glanced at the wristwatch he wore, something that had become popular during the war. Soldiers didn't have time to take out a pocket watch, though many still carried them, because they'd been known to stop a bullet. 'Would you care to have a cup of tea somewhere – just to talk?'

She was tempted, so tempted to say yes because he was attractive and it would have been nice, but Marco had been good to her and she cared enough about their marriage to know she must not betray him, even in thought. 'I have to go in here now – excuse me.'

Pushing open the door, she took Pierre's hand and walked inside the expensive store. Sadie could never have dreamed of buying very much from a store like this before she was married to Marco. The very fact that she could actually buy something here if she wished was because he was so generous – and Mrs Harper had given her a card so that she could use her husband's staff discount.

She spent half an hour looking round and saw a pen set that she eventually purchased for Marco. He had a birthday coming before Christmas and she thought he might like it, because it was a Waterman's black and gold and as elegant a pen as she'd seen.

When she left, the soldier had gone and Sadie gave a sigh of relief. She had come close to going for a cup of tea with him. In itself that was nothing, but it could lead to much more, if not this time, then the next she gave in to her weakness. She'd vowed to herself when she'd married Marco that she would not let him down and she knew she had a good life. Had Pierre lived it would have been a very different life as his wife, but she'd made her choice and she would stick to it despite the temptation. That soldier had not been the first to speak to her and it was likely that he would not be the last – but he was the one who had tempted her most. And she didn't even know his name...

* * *

When Marco gave her flowers and chocolates that evening, Sadie's eyes watered a little. She was so glad she hadn't given into the temptation of a little flirtation. Harmless or not, it would still have been a betrayal of this good man who was her husband.

'What have I done to deserve this?' she asked and smiled, giving him a swift peck on the cheek.

'Just being you,' Marco said and gave her a look that was warm and appreciative. 'You never complain and we haven't been anywhere much. With me so often working later in the evenings, you must get bored. I was thinking we might arrange some babysitting so I can take you to the theatre or dinner sometimes. You deserve that, Sadie – and if you wanted a nurse for Pierre so that you could do a shift in the hospital some mornings, I'd be glad to pay for it.'

'You spoil me,' Sadie told him, relief that she hadn't given in to that brief temptation flooding through her. 'You are a lovely man, Marco. I shall enjoy a few trips to the theatre or to dine out. As for working, I think there is a woman who lives near here who would look after Pierre for a few hours now and then – she is a widow and very friendly, and I imagine she might like to earn a little money.'

'No doubt,' he agreed, then frowned. 'There are a lot of widows who must be lonely – you should make friends with people if you can.'

Sadie nodded. 'I came to Harpers today and had a look round. A lot of people were admiring that window you told me of – I loved it, Marco. It reminded me of Marie's barn.'

'Good,' he said. 'I've been thinking of her and Maman and wondering how they fared after we left...'

'Oh, I should have told you,' Sadie said and smiled. 'I had a letter from Marie when I got home from visiting Maggie. She told me that they are staying with friends in the South of France, well away from the front line and had helped with their wine harvest. The group got them away in time, though she knows that they despoiled her house and her outbuildings. She says that after the war, she will return and rebuild her life there – and she asked after you, said she hoped we were both happy and well and wants us to take Pierre for a visit when this is all over.'

'That is wonderful news and a relief,' Marco told her honestly. 'I have been anxious for them and I know you've thought of them a lot.' His eyes were warm as they rested on her. 'After the war, we'll take Pierre and visit, Sadie. It is right he knows his true father's heritage.'

Sadie was silent for a moment, then, 'You are Pierre's father, Marco. He adores you and you are so good with him. He loves it when we go to the park and you push him on the swings.'

'I love him as much as I would my own flesh and blood,' Marco told her. 'I didn't expect to have a family or a child – and that is a wonderful gift, Sadie, but I do worry about you.' His smile faded. 'I know you gave up a lot when you wed me. Even if I tried to be a conventional husband, it would probably leave you wanting more. I'm sorry I can't give you that kind of love – though I do love you as a friend and as Pierre's mother...'

Sadie turned her face aside as the tears stung. 'It doesn't matter,' she said. 'I don't need that.'

'Not yet perhaps,' Marco said gently, 'but one day you will.' He hesitated then, 'One day there may be a man you want to make love to you. If you wanted it too, I wouldn't blame you.'

'I couldn't just walk out on you! You are Pierre's daddy and it would break his heart.'

Marco turned her gently to look at him. 'You wouldn't have to, dearest Sadie, nor would I wish it. What I am saying is that if you wish for a discreet affair, then I should not deny you nor blame you.'

'Oh, Marco,' she choked. 'Why...' She left the rest unsaid. Marco was as he was and she'd known it when they married. If she sometimes wished that he could give her more, that was her own fault. She had been prepared for this, or thought she was, but he'd made her love him, slowly bit by bit, and that made her want too much. Sadie knew the reason she'd avoided temptation was because in her heart she truly loved Marco. His kindness and care for her had brought her back to life after Pierre's death and now she wanted too much – she wanted what she could never have. What he could never give her. And, being Marco, he had just given her his blessing to have an intimate affair with another man if she wished – but it wasn't what Sadie wanted! She lifted her head and smiled at him through the tears. 'I'm not that fussed over sex,' she told him. 'Besides, I'm not over Pierre yet.'

It was a lie, but to tell him the truth would be cruel and make him feel guilty. Marco had tried to help her. He hadn't intended her to fall in love with him...

Colin was in the library with a huge fire roaring and a pile of the estate books on the desk in front of him. He smiled at Maggie as she entered the room, warmly dressed in coat, hat a woollen scarf and mittens.

'Off for a walk?' he asked.

'I wondered if you would like to come with me?' she said. 'But I can see you're busy, Colin. You don't mind if I walk to the village to post my letters? I thought I might buy a few bits and pieces in the shops. I'd like to make some gifts to send to London…'

'For Christmas I suppose?' He nodded thoughtfully. 'Do whatever you like, Maggie. We usually send to a London store for whatever we need. They could deliver gift-wrapped if you wish?'

'I've already made things myself,' Maggie told him. 'Marion has a baby coming so I've knitted a coat for her and I'll make some bonnets and bootees for her. I've made scarves and a blouse for Sally. But there are a few more things I need to buy…'

Since coming to the estate, Maggie had rediscovered a love for sewing and embroidery that she'd put aside when she left school and started work, but now she needed something to fill the winter afternoons if Colin was wrapped up in his work. She could help with the books, but his visits to various farms and workshops were not for her.

Colin had bent over his books again and she left him to his task of getting the accounts in better order so he could begin to see what kind of shape the estate was in. She had no need to ask the servants to make sure his fire was kept made up or that coffee and biscuits were taken in to him. His devoted household catered for his every need and he had only to ask to have whatever he needed provided.

So, feeling satisfied that he would be fine, Maggie turned to head out for the village. The village was not big, but it had three shops, which flourished. Mrs Carter ran a haberdashery, which was amply stocked with everything a woman could need for her needlework, shelves filled with materials, ribbons, cottons and needles, also wool for knitting, a pastime Maggie particularly enjoyed when sitting watching Colin at work by a cosy fire. She liked doing lacy patterns that were intricate and required patience and skill.

Her days were usually filled, because she had taken an interest in the house and gardens and enjoyed making small improvements to their part of the house. Colin liked the way she'd made things cosier and more homely. Maggie didn't venture into his father's domain, other than at dinner when they sometimes gathered in the formal dining room. Guests came once or twice a week to dine and that meant Maggie was gradually making acquaintances, if not yet friends. Her real friends were still from her Harpers' days, but she'd met two young women she'd liked, so in time their acquaintance might become friendship.

She had made various members of the household her friends and she knew most of those who worked on the estate. There was only one prominent member of Colin's father's people she actually felt uneasy with and that was their agent, Farringdon, who ran the practical day-to-day stuff and ordered whatever was needed for both the house and the land. He interviewed new workers and put the best forward to be approved or rejected and oversaw so much that he was probably indispensable to the family. However, there was something about him that made her skin creep – something in the way he looked at her. He had deliberately stopped her several times to ask if she needed anything.

'I am always at your service, Mrs Morgan. We want you to be happy here and it must be lonely for a woman like you – used to so much more life in London and what you did in France. We all admire you for that, Mrs Morgan...'

His words were welcoming and polite, but something beneath them, something in his eyes when he looked at her, made her uneasy. She could not have said why, but she avoided him as much as she could.

Farringdon was nowhere to be seen as she left the house by the kitchen door and took the short cut the servants used across fields wet with the result of a frost melting. Her boots were stout and her ankle-length grey skirt, worn beneath a three quarter-length coat of red tweed, kept her dry as she walked at a good pace towards the village. Despite the chill of the day, the wintry sun made it pleasant enough and she was used to hard conditions at the Front and the English countryside held none of the terrors she'd witnessed these past years.

She smiled and began to sing to herself as she walked, thinking of the purchases she would make. It was good to keep in touch with her old friends and their letters brought her the news from Harpers and their own lives, which always made her feel that she was still a part of their world.

* * *

Maggie spent just over an hour looking at the wonderful selection in Mrs Carter's shop. She had bales of pretty material and Maggie purchased some fine linen to make herself some nightgowns and a shirt for Colin. She knew he purchased fine things from London, but sometimes it was nice to wear a more comfortable shirt of a warm material and she would make one and see if he liked it.

'I'll send your purchases with my lad this afternoon, Mrs Morgan,' the friendly shopkeeper said, looking pleased as Maggie paid her bill. 'No need for you to struggle with packages – and you could pay me once a month if you chose?'

'No, I shall pay when I buy,' Maggie said. 'Why should you wait for your money?'

She smiled and took her leave, returning the way she'd come with a smile on her face. Her thoughts were with her purchases and the gifts she intended to make and she took no notice of the sound of horse's hooves other than to move to the verge so as not to impede whoever was coming.

Farringdon's voice startled her and she turned her head to look as he brought the pony and trap to a halt beside her.

'Good morning, Mrs Morgan,' he said and his voice made her spine chill. There was a slight slur to his words and she had a feeling that he'd been drinking at the village inn. 'Get in and I'll take you home – save you a long walk...'

'Thank you, but I enjoy walking. Pray go on, sir. I am sure you have work to do.'

Maggie hoped that her remark would remind him of his position, but instead it seemed to annoy him. To her alarm, he threw his reins over the pony's head and dismounted, blocking her path. The pony stood obediently, and between the trap and the man, Maggie was trapped and could not walk on.

'Pray stand aside and let me pass, sir,' she requested politely.

'Quite the lady of the manor, aren't we?' he said sarcastically and deliberately leaned towards her so that she could smell the whisky on his breath. 'Think it will make me keener if you play hard to get, Maggie? You don't need to do that – I'll enjoy showing you what a real man can do in bed. That half a man you married can't be enough for you after being with all those men over there...'

'Sir, you are impertinent!' Maggie said, alarmed. 'Please do not insult me further. I am a respectable married woman and I've given you no cause to speak to me like that – in fact, I will not have it...'

'Filthy little slut,' Farringdon slurred, clearly the worse for the drink he'd taken. 'I know what women like you want – all you nurses are the same. Stands to reason. No decent woman would wash and dress naked soldiers – only sluts do things like that.'

'You insult women who have given their lives to bring hope to the injured, none of whom deserve your disgusting remarks!'

Farringdon continued to leer at her. Something had made him reckless and he suddenly made a grab for her.

Startled, Maggie screamed and stepped back.

'How dare you?' she demanded. 'Farringdon, remember you place. I am your employer's wife!'

'Bitch, I'll show you...' he muttered and made another grab for her.

This time, Maggie was ready for him and she kicked his shins as hard as she could and then pushed her way past him, uncaring of the bramble bush that tore at her skirt and scratched her face. Once she was free, she lifted her skirt and ran. For a moment she thought he would follow her, but one of the estate workers was walking towards them and Farringdon contented himself with a passing insult.

'You'll be begging for it by the time you've been here six months and then I'll make you beg on your knees, bitch...'

Maggie did not bother to reply but ran for all she was worth. By the time she reached the house, she was out of breath, her cheeks red from the wind and her chest heaving. As she burst into the kitchen, Tilly looked at her in concern.

'What happened, Mrs Morgan?' she asked. 'You look as if you've been attacked?'

Maggie put her hand to her cheek and felt the sting of the scratches and the dried blood. 'I was insulted and a man tried to molest me...' she gasped. 'I...'

'On our own estate?' Colin's voice sounded from behind her and she whirled round to see him in his chair. He must just have entered the kitchen, something he often did. 'Tell me who it was – I'll sack him, whoever he is.' Colin's expression was furious. 'How dare anyone insult you?'

Maggie hesitated, then, 'I think I must tell you, for if I do not, he may try again... It was Farringdon and he made filthy insinuations and tried to grab me. I had seen him look at me before but took no notice. However, I believe he had been drinking...'

Colin's mouth hardened. 'Did he harm you? If he did, I'll have him arrested. If I had the use of my legs, I would thrash the bastard.'

'I kicked him and ran,' Maggie said. 'I scratched myself getting past him. The only way through was a huge bramble bush – but you need him, Colin.'

'You leave Farringdon to me,' her husband said. 'Look after her...' he shot at his cook and went out of the door Maggie had entered earlier. 'I'll be back, Maggie...'

'Colin, please,' she cried, but he wasn't listening.

'Mr Colin can handle that scum,' Tilly said soothingly. 'He was brought up to be the master and Farringdon is rubbish – the rest of us have always thought it, but it wasn't our place to say.' She took Maggie's arm gently. 'Now you just sit down here and drink this brandy, Mrs Morgan – and I'll bathe your cheek with a little warm water.'

'But Colin is in that chair...' Maggie stood uncertainly as if she would go after him.

'He needs no protection,' Tilly said. 'Mr Colin knows how to handle bullies, don't you worry; that's why he was such a good officer. We're all proud of what he did in the war. He hasn't said a word, but we all know he got a medal for bravery on the field.'

'Yes, he did.' Maggie smiled. Tilly was right. Colin would not need her protection. Yet Farringdon was needed on the estate and had he not overheard her first breathless words she might never have told him. 'Thank you, Tilly.' She sipped the brandy and allowed the kindly woman to bathe her cheek, which stung now she was not running for her life.

'There, that will heal soon enough,' Tilly said as she rubbed in a little balm. 'It won't show once the scratches have healed.'

Maggie thanked her again and went upstairs to change into a clean skirt and blouse with a little fitted jacket. She was just restoring some order to her hair when the door opened and Colin entered. He had a gleam of satisfaction in his eyes and she guessed he'd gained it from whatever had passed between Farringdon and himself.

'Are you all right, Maggie?' he asked her anxiously. 'I was afraid he might have hurt you.'

'No, I kicked him and escaped,' she said. 'No real harm was done except to my dignity.'

'Harm enough,' Colin replied. 'He'd been drinking at the

village inn. He won't come near you again, Maggie. I've dismissed him and told him I'll have him shot if he's seen here again.'

'Colin, you wouldn't!' Maggie stared at him incredulously.

'For two pins I'd have shot him myself,' he replied angrily.

'He isn't worth it, Colin. He is less than nothing. I've met his sort before, which was why I refused to ride home with him. Usually, they slink off when you look at them in disgust, but he had been drinking rather a lot in the middle of the day when he was supposed to be working for you.'

'I would have dismissed him for that,' Colin said, 'but he deserved a thrashing...'

'Oh, I think you dealt with him well enough,' Maggie replied and smiled. 'Or shall we have him boiled in oil and served up to the pigs?'

Her teasing remark made him look at her and then he grinned. 'Young Marks came with me – he works on one of the farms. He knocked him down and kicked him in the ribs a few times until I told him to stop. Yes, I think we've seen the last of Farringdon, Maggie. Any of my men would willingly shoot him through the leg and Marks would thrash him if I lifted a finger. I have some loyal men. He didn't belong here and my father should never have given him so much freedom.' Marks was a man in his forties, Colin's head groom, an old soldier with strong shoulders and fists like hammers. He never spoke to Maggie but grunted and nodded each time they met and Tilly had told her his young nephew had been one of her patients. 'And Marks is devoted to you, Maggie, so I pity Farringdon if he dares to show his face here again.' Colin looked very satisfied at his own thoughts.

'Since he has been thoroughly punished, perhaps we should go down to lunch before we upset your father?' Maggie kept a straight face though her eyes smiled.

Colin laughed. 'No wonder you've got the rest of them wound

round your finger, Maggie. Yes, come on. Father will be upset enough that I've dismissed his agent without making him wait for his lunch.'

'How is he?' she asked. 'Do you think his health is deteriorating – or was it a ruse to get you home?'

'He won't let us see it, but his health is not good,' Colin told her. 'I asked his doctor and he told me he doubts he'll make old bones.'

'I am very sorry,' Maggie said. 'Is there anything I can do to help?'

'He wouldn't let you, but I am grateful for the offer, Maggie. Now we must go because I need to explain why I dismissed his agent.'

'Will he be angry?'

'I don't mind either way. Farringdon could not remain here after he distressed you. What good would I be as a husband if I just let it slide?'

'Lead on, Sir Knight,' Maggie teased and he grinned once more as she held the door for him to manoeuvre his chair through the open space. It was nice to think she was liked and respected and it made her feel that she had a place here. Her friends were not just those she'd worked with at Harpers, she had friends here, too. Yet Sally, Beth and Rachel would always bring fond memories...

32

Sally glanced up as her visitor was announced and smiled. She invited him to sit and asked Ruth to bring coffee and biscuits.

'I'm so glad you came, Mick,' she said. 'I'd heard you were back in France for a few weeks and wondered how you were.' It was now just over a week until Christmas and the war still went on. America had declared hostilities with Austria-Hungary early in the month and Britain had taken Jerusalem back from the enemy.

It was two months since Sally had been down for Maggie's wedding. She had thought about Mick a great deal during that time. Knowing him, she did not believe he would throw his life away, even though she knew he'd been very upset after speaking to Maggie in the summer. He'd asked the young woman to marry him, but she'd turned him down and Sally was afraid it had broken his heart, but he was smiling now.

'I injured my shoulder again and the powers that be decided I was no longer fit for active service,' Mick told her with something resembling his old cheerful grin. 'So, they've sent me back and given me a position, training others to do my job – and I now spend a lot of time sitting at a desk.'

'Where are you situated – or shouldn't I ask?'

'You can ask what you like, Sally Harper,' Mick said, and she saw the mischief in his eyes, 'But I might decline to answer. It isn't in London but near enough to get back now and then – and that's why I'm here, to take you to lunch. I want to know if you think my latest menus are up to scratch...' Sally smiled, pleased to discover that Mick was still taking an interest in his restaurants despite his heartbreak over Maggie.

'That would be delightful,' she said, feeling relieved that Mick wasn't allowing his pain to destroy him, though she did not doubt he was still suffering. 'When?'

'No time like today. I leave this evening...'

Sally jumped up immediately. 'Then we'll forget the coffee and go now. I'd like to hear what you're doing, Mick – and ask your opinion about the store.'

'I thought it looked as good as I would expect in wartime,' Mick told her and helped her on with her coat. It wasn't just Harpers that suffered from the shortages. Most of the big stores were struggling to find the right stock. 'Where is Ben now – or aren't you sure?'

'He said it was on the South Coast, but I think he moves around a lot,' Sally said and smiled apologetically at her secretary as she entered with the tray. 'We're off to lunch, Ruth. You have the coffee and biscuits yourself – and we'll go through those sales figures when I come back.'

'Yes, Mrs Harper.' Ruth looked at her doubtfully. 'I thought you were only working until lunch?'

'Don't you fuss,' Sally said. 'I get enough of that at home. I shall only do an hour or so – and I'm skiving off now, so it's all right.'

Mick looked at her in concern. 'You look blooming, Sally. Are they still worried you might get ill again?'

'Oh, my family and friends never stop telling me to rest,' Sally told him, laughing. 'I have some news. Did you know I'd found my mother? We haven't met yet because she is married and lives some distance away – but she has written to me and she is coming up to see us with her new husband when she can...' the excitement was in her eyes with a hint of apprehension too.

'Well, that is something to look forward to,' Mick said and for a moment his gaze looked bleak. 'We all need something...'

Sally glanced at him as they left the store and he summoned a cab to take them to the restaurant he owned that he knew she really enjoyed. She glimpsed the pain he was holding inside, her voice was gentle as she asked, 'What of you, Mick? How are you these days?'

'Bloody awful if you want the truth,' he said. 'I know I'm a fool, Sally. I was always too old for her – but, in France, I thought I might stand a chance – stupid of course.'

'I don't think it was stupid. Maggie liked you a lot and you helped her through a bad time. Perhaps if you hadn't been sent to another area you might have spoken to her of your feelings and, if she had committed to you, that would have been it,' Sally spoke gently. 'Maggie told me she felt empty after you went away and she just spent all her time working and that led to her illness. She knows now that you were wounded and too ill to write during that time, but she felt alone and abandoned – and I feel guilty about that, Mick. I couldn't visit as I'd wanted because I was ill too. Maggie needed someone and Colin came along...' She hesitated, then, 'From her latest letter, I believe she really cares for him and she's happy.'

'That's good,' Mick said and smiled sadly. 'All I ever wanted was to see her smile.'

'I think she smiles a lot. She told me that she has been helping Colin with his exercises and he is getting some small movement in his legs now. He isn't walking or anything like that, but he can stand better now and he can manage to get from the chair to the bed easier...' She caught her breath as she saw the flash of hurt in his eyes, but then it was gone. 'To my surprise, it seems they have quite a good marriage.'

Mick looked at her long and hard. 'And I know why you told me that, Sally Harper. You're a good friend and you're right. Maggie is wed to another and I've lost her – but if he ever hurts her, I'll break his damned neck.'

She touched his hand as the cab came to a halt. 'I can't tell you that you will forget her,' she said gently, 'but in time it may get easier.'

'Ah, why didn't I marry you, Sally darlin'?' he said in his old easy way as he helped her from the cab. 'I should never have let that Ben Harper steal you from under my nose.'

'I wouldn't have suited you, Mick,' she said gently. 'And I know you'll come through this, my friend. You are strong and healthy and clever and you've lots to live for. Just give yourself time.'

'I've a good friend in you,' he said and he was smiling in his old way. 'And I like Ben – even if he did steal you from me, but Maggie touched my heart like no other. I can't explain. I wanted to wrap her in silk and keep her safe from all harm.' He paused, then, 'I loved her and I still do, Sally. I suppose I always shall – but if she is happy that is all I want.'

'It was an emotional time out there,' Sally said and smiled as they were shown to their favourite table. 'You are one of the friends I trust most, Mick, and if I knew how, I'd make you happy.'

'I'm surviving and I shall go on,' he told her. 'Forget my woes,

Sally Harper, and concentrate, I brought you here to work. Tell me what you think of everything and don't hold back. I need your wise words.'

Mick had instructed her to forget his woes and so she dropped the subject, but she knew that he would not forget the woman he loved. His uncertainty had kept him from asking her to wed him in France and now it was too late. He might regret that for the rest of his life, but he would make a future for himself somehow.

Blocking her emotion, she offered him her assessment of the menu and the food they tried, all of which was good but not as perfect as before the war. There was probably little he could do to improve things at the moment, but she gave him the truth, as he'd asked. The truth often hurt but holding back just made things worse. Neither the food nor the service was quite as excellent as it had been and would need to be improved. Now Mick was back in the country he might be able to keep a closer eye on things. At least he was getting on with his life as best he could – and that was something they all had to do.

She felt a sudden and intense longing for Ben. He'd been away nearly a month this time and she prayed he would get back for Christmas. She wanted him to see the magical windows that Mr Marco had dressed. The main one had a Christmas tree with lights and lots of parcels beneath. There was a backdrop of a roaring fire and children playing with toys and a puppy. A soldier's coat was slung over a chair, his kitbag near the painted door, toys spilling it out of it. They were running a special offer in the toy department. All soldiers, airmen and sailors' wives were entitled to ten per cent off any toy they chose. It was proving very popular and the sales of those special wooden toys made by soldiers was booming. In fact, Harpers was doing very well this

Christmas. She'd bought a small tree for Jenny and they'd dressed it together, but until Ben was home it wouldn't feel like Christmas.

Sally knew she was lucky to have all she had, but there were times when she couldn't help wishing her husband would come home for good.

* * *

As if answering her prayers, Ben arrived home that evening. His arm was in a sling and she knew a moment of fear that he'd been involved in some dangerous mission she'd not been told of until he explained that he'd trodden on a patch of ice and fallen, breaking his shoulder.

'They had a very cold night up there,' he told her, explaining that he'd been on a tour of various manufacturers and institutions in Scotland. 'I was in hurry, didn't realise there was ice about and went crashing down. They took me to the hospital and put this thing on, but not much else they can do for me. I have to wait for it to heal and the pain to go.'

Her first fear had faded, but she could see he was hurting. 'Come and sit down, Ben. How did you get home?'

'I was driven in a staff car,' he told her. 'Driving is out for me for a while.' He gave her a wry smile. 'It looks like you'll have me home for Christmas and perhaps for a while after that...'

'Oh, Ben,' Sally exclaimed. 'I'm so sorry you've hurt your shoulder and that you are in pain – but I can't be sorry it will make you stay home. I've been missing you so very much, my darling.'

'I miss you all the time,' Ben said and he walked to her steadily but carefully and put his right arm around her. He kissed her softly on the lips, but the effort cost him and his face went white. 'I think I need to rest, Sally. I'll sit in a chair, but with my feet up on a stool.'

'You'd rather be up than in bed?'

Sally could see the answer in his face, so she fetched pillows and a blanket and tucked him up with his feet on a stool. He closed his eyes and she sat in a chair for a little while and watched him, her heart full. Then Jenny woke and started crying so she fetched the little girl and let her come through with them. Jenny struggled to get to her daddy, but Sally made sure she couldn't fling herself at him and jolt his shoulder, and when Ben opened his eyes, he smiled.

'Sit her on my right knee,' he said and so she did, watching anxiously for any sign that she would claw at him and scramble all over him, but she seemed to sense something and patted his face with her little hands.

'Daddy not well?' She amazed them both by putting the words together. Normally it was 'Daddy come' or 'Mummy play 'or 'Jenny wants', but she was looking at him seriously with eyes as big as saucers and the same colour as Ben's. Her eyes had been bluer, but they'd gradually become more grey than blue and she looked very like her father just then, making Sally swallow hard.

'Daddy has a bad shoulder,' he told her. 'It hurts him to move. You get down now and let Mummy get you a drink of milk and honey.'

Jenny looked at him a moment longer and then slid to the ground and scampered over to her mother. She looked up at Sally. 'Daddy bad shoulder...' she repeated like a little parrot.

'Our little girl is growing up,' Ben said and smiled at his wife. 'Perhaps it is just as well with the little one on the way.' His eyes were full of love and concern as he looked at her. 'How are you,

Sally? I know you say you're well and I know you work a few hours each week, but how are you really?'

'I'm fairly well,' Sally said honestly. 'I keep my hours short because I know I need to be careful and I never do too much – but I've been down in the dumps. I haven't heard from my mother recently, even though I wrote to her and asked her to come and see me and she said she would bring her husband to visit me. But then I've heard nothing more to say when exactly, and Mick is going through a pretty rotten time and I felt sad for him. It made me realise how lucky we are to have each other, Ben – and that made me lonely for you.' She drew a shaky breath as her emotion overcame her.

'Darling, Sally,' he said. 'Put little trouble to bed and give her that hot milk – and then we'll talk.' His smile lit up Sally's heart and she felt happy as she took her little girl into the kitchen, gave her some warmed milk with a little honey and put her to bed.

Jenny soon settled and Sally returned to the sitting room, where Ben was fast asleep in his chair. She sat in the chair opposite and watched him, feeling a deep contentment that he was back with her for a few weeks at least. She was so lucky! So many husbands were fighting at the Front or had already fought and been killed and hers was sitting here with her. Sally's heart ached for all those who had lost loved ones, because she just couldn't imagine what it would be like to go through such pain. She decided that her next charitable campaign would be for war widows and bereaved mothers – the women who stayed at home, prayed, wept and went on living when the worst happened, even though it seemed there was nothing to live for.

Ben woke a little later. She offered tea and he asked for brandy so she got it and he sat nursing the glass in his hand, sipping a little now and then, looking at her as if he never wanted to take his eyes off her.

'You're such a lovely person, Sally,' he said. 'It's not just that your face is pretty – it comes from inside. I've been told about all your campaigns and work for the wounded. I haven't been much help to you, darling. I've left you alone to manage everything while I did what I considered my duty – and it was unfair to you.'

'No, Ben. I was proud of you and I like doing what I do,' Sally replied with a shake of her head. 'I'm lucky. You could have been fighting and been badly injured or killed. I often feel lonely for you – but I do know how lucky we've been compared to others.'

'I think they won't need me much more,' Ben said and then sighed. 'Who am I kidding? Even when they lay down the guns, there will be the problem of getting the men home and supplying their needs before they return and when they get back. They are going to need a lot of help settling down when it is over. Men who have been to hell and back can't be expected to just pick up their lives as if nothing has happened.'

'No, they can't,' Sally said and knelt down at his side, lifting her face to kiss him softly on the lips. She could taste the brandy. It was a part of him and she felt so grateful that he was here and with her. Now she could really get into the spirit of Christmas. 'I'm not sure what the government will do, Ben, but we can campaign to help the wounded heroes – just as I intend to help the widows and mothers.'

'Yes, my darling,' Ben agreed. 'Someone needs to do that – and we may not have been making much money these past years, but we can do something – we can make people aware. I've been thinking about it and I'm going to devote some of my time to it when the Government no longer needs my services.' He looked rueful. 'There will come a time when I can help with Harpers a bit, but it looks like you'll still be in charge for the future – and you'll have a second child to cope with too...'

'But I have Pearl and Mrs Hill. Pearl says she will come full-time when the baby is born. She says she isn't particularly happy at the hospital – the matron has it in for her for some reason – and she would prefer to work for me full-time. She feels she has done her duty as a nurse and likes being a part of the Harpers family.'

'Well, at least it means you have reliable help,' Ben said and smiled at her sleepily. 'I think I might go to bed for a while now...'

It was almost morning and Sally smiled at the oddness of it, but that was life when people were ill or injured. Life was often turned upside down and this war had twizzled them all this way and that, wrenching families apart and destroying lives. She knew that Ben thought the tide had turned at Passchendaele and that the Allies were at last getting the measure of the great force that the enemy had brought to bear. America's weight had helped to turn the flood that had threatened to overwhelm France and Europe, and perhaps the German people were as worn down by the conflict as the British people and secretly longed for peace. Maybe at last, in the next few months, the enemy would be beaten and life could return to normal.

Sally only knew for certain that it would soon be Christmas. She had given the store a festive air to make up for any lack of choice in the stock, though she had been keeping a few things in reserve for months and would now instruct Fred to bring the various items out of store and distribute them to the departments so that it gave people something new to look at and buy for Christmas. Also, she would buy in some sweet sherry if she could get some and ask her friends to help her make some tarts and little cakes and on Christmas Eve, the customers and staff could have a small glass of wine and a home-made treat if they wished.

In homes all up and down Britain – and in Europe too – people would celebrate Christmas as best they could. Family members would be missing – some never to return – and the food would not have the richness or variety of other years, but that wouldn't stop folk celebrating. They would make the best of what they had and cherish those that were absent as much as ever.

As she returned to her sitting room when Ben had settled in bed, propped up against pillows to make him comfortable, Sally started to make a list of all she needed to do for Christmas and the future. She had been given so much and she would do all she could to help others less fortunate. Sally decided that she needed to have a word with Becky Stockbridge as soon as she could.

* * *

'Please come and sit down, Becky.' Sally said one morning later that week when the young woman was shown into her office. 'Don't look frightened. You're not in any trouble. I just want to talk to you. Tell me - are you happy in your work here at Harpers?'

'Yes, Mrs Harper...' Becky flushed. 'Has someone complained of my work?'

'No, not at all,' Sally replied. 'It was just noticed that you seemed a little – shall we say out of sorts?'

Becky looked uncomfortable. 'If I've been rude, I apologise...'

'No need for that, Becky. You're not here to be reprimanded, just for a friendly chat, to make sure that nothing is upsetting you.'

'I am upset,' Becky replied haltingly. 'I know I was a bit sharp with...with someone but...' she shook her head. 'I can't tell you anything – but it won't happen again.'

Sally hesitated, then, 'I am sorry you don't feel able to tell me why you're so unhappy, Becky. I would help you if I could...'

'I know...' Becky wiped a tear from her cheek. 'May I go back to work – we're very busy in the office.'

'Of course you may, Becky – and if ever you do need my help, remember I am here...'

Sally sighed as the door closed behind the girl. Was it a broken heart Becky was suffering from or something else? She wished Becky had opened up to her but sometimes things were too difficult. Well, she could do nothing until Becky decided to ask for her help...

* * *

Becky's head was down as she hurried away from Mrs Harper's office. How could she tell her – how could she tell anyone what a fool she'd been? They would all think she was shameful...just because she'd done something that hadn't seemed wicked at all at the time.

No, no, it was impossible. If she dared to talk to anyone it would be Sally Harper but she was too ashamed. Minnie would be terribly hurt and her father would be so angry and all because she'd fallen in love with a man who swore he loved her and would marry her. He'd said he would speak to her father about an engagement and she'd been carried away and now...now she was so afraid of what everyone would think when they found out that she was a bad girl, and it was bound to come out, unless she could find a way to hide her shame...

Blinking back her tears, Becky struggled to compose herself before she entered the office. Her father was often in and out and if he saw her upset, he would demand to know why and she couldn't tell him – she just couldn't.

Oh, why hadn't he written as he promised? He'd seemed so sincere and she did love him so...but now she didn't know what to do. If she told Sally Harper, *she* would be sure to tell Becky's father and she would lose her job.

What was she going to do? It wasn't fair! Marion was married and happy and so was Maggie – why did this have to happen to her? It had only been once that she'd strayed and now she was in terrible trouble, with no one to turn to.

33

'Colin, may I talk to you please?' Maggie asked from the doorway. Her husband looked up from the paperwork before him, frowned and then pushed the papers away with a sigh.

'Thank God you came,' he said. 'These books are in one heck of a muddle and it was giving me a headache trying to sort them. I half thought my father was lying when he said things were getting too much for him. He had let that scoundrel Farringdon take over too much and from what I can see so far, he's been cheating us left, right and centre. Instead of sacking him, I should have had him arrested for fraud and theft.'

'Is it very bad?' Maggie asked, bringing a chair to sit beside him at the huge mahogany partners' desk. 'I thought he was sly when I first saw him, but I didn't suspect he was cheating you.'

'If Farringdon hadn't attacked you, I might not have sent him packing,' Colin told her. 'That was his big mistake, Maggie – and I can only say good riddance to rubbish.'

Maggie inclined her head. 'Yes, he was,' she agreed. 'I noticed his odd looks the first time I saw him, just after we arrived – but I ignored him. If he hadn't tried to touch me...'

'He would still be working here and I wouldn't have discovered this fraud,' Colin told her. 'It is a few hundred pounds so far, but had I not come home he could have ruined father in time.'

'It was good that you did,' Maggie said and smiled at him. She felt a warm glow inside as he looked at her. No miracles had occurred. Colin's legs still refused to take him more than a couple of steps but he could stand now and move his feet a little in the chair and with the minimum of help could move from his chair to his bed much more easily. His exercises had made him so much stronger.

'That is all down to you...' Colin replied. 'You gave me the courage to come back here, Maggie. I couldn't have done it without you. You've cured me.' He grinned as she couldn't resist a glance at his legs. 'No, I haven't learned to walk overnight, but I am getting some feeling back in the right leg – but I meant you've cured my soul. I was bitter and angry and I saw no point in life, but now I do. I've realised that life is worth living, even in this chair.'

'Good,' Maggie leaned forward and kissed him. 'I might help more with the books if you let me, Colin. I'm good with figures.'

'You're good with everything,' he replied and looked at her in a way that made Maggie laugh. 'But I'm damned if I'm going to spend all day working – do you realise it is our anniversary?' He grinned as he saw the expression in her eyes. 'We've now been married more than two months – and I think we should celebrate with a walk and then a bottle of wine with our meal.'

'I agree,' she said. 'Let's put our coats on and go for a walk.'

'Well, you'll walk and I'll ride in the chair.' He smiled. 'We could get someone to drive us into town this afternoon and I'll buy you a present... what would you like?'

'I don't know – a box of bon bons?'

'A real present,' Colin insisted. 'What do you like, Maggie – diamonds, pearls or rubies?'

'I like pearls,' she replied honestly, 'but there is something I should like more than a pearl necklace...'

'What?' He frowned slightly. 'Tell me...'

'There is a family in the village,' Maggie said. 'Three sons went away to war and only one has returned and he is injured. He needs a better wheelchair than the one the hospital gave him... could we buy him one like yours? It is lighter than the hospital's chair, it can be pushed easily and you can wheel yours yourself.'

Colin looked at her, eyes glinting dangerously. 'What is this soldier to you?'

'Nothing. I've never seen him – but his mother came to ask my advice. She thought the hospital might get her a better chair, but they said they can't afford it and she wanted to know how to get a chair like yours, but when I told her how much they were she cried, because she doesn't have forty pounds.'

'It's a hell of a lot of money to give away,' Colin said, 'but the poor devil deserves it and if it's what you want – go ahead and buy one for him. I'll see you have the money.'

'Thank you – it's so kind of you to indulge me.'

Colin gave a short barking laugh. 'Indulge you...' He shook his head. 'We'd better go down to the village and take a look at this wounded soldier to make sure we get him the right size of chair. Some of these farm fellows are twice the size of me.'

'Yes, that's a good idea,' she said and kissed him. 'What a lovely husband you are – you spoil me with your presents, Colin, but it is nice to help others.'

'Yes,' he agreed and smiled at her. 'It is – and trust you to think of it, Maggie. It must be the reason I love you so much.'

Maggie's heart caught. He had spoken lightly, but he had never said he loved her before. Was he feeling the way she did about him inside? They had married because it suited them both, but Maggie knew she was happy and Colin certainly seemed to be too.

'We'll tackle the books this afternoon after our walk,' she told him as they fetched their coats from the hall stand, wrapping up before they went out into the cold December air.

The estate had strung some lights in ancient fir trees in the grounds giving it a festive air and she knew the tradition was to give the staff a big Christmas party on Boxing Day. The family would have a party for friends on Christmas Eve, which was just a few days away now, and spend the day alone, enjoying the fat goose Cook had hanging in her larder, along with pheasant and cockerels in preparation for the party.

The air was crisp and cold, but the rain had held off for a while and it made the footing solid and easy for Colin's chair to move safely on the paths that criss-crossed the gardens and grounds as they set off for the village. The news for that anxious mother was perhaps the best Christmas gift she would receive that year and they were both eager to deliver it.

* * *

It was on the return from a pleasant visit with Mabel Blake and her son James, both of whom Colin remembered from his childhood, that they met Charlotte. Colin had spent a good hour discussing the sturdiness and the merits of a good chair with James, while Maggie ate home-made jam tarts and sipped a little gooseberry wine. She had enjoyed her wine and the sweet tart and been promised the recipe for the wine before they left to walk home. It was quite a long way and she had pushed his chair for most of the time when they saw Charlotte approaching.

'I bring a Christmas invitation,' she cried brightly. 'Let me push Colin's chair, Maggie. You look exhausted and I want to ask him a question, just walk on ahead for a little...'

Maggie hesitated. Charlotte tended to think she could just take over whenever she chose to appear. 'I can manage—' she began, but Colin cut her off.

'Let Charlie push me for a while. Go on ahead, Maggie. I'd like to talk to Charlie in private for a moment.'

The look on Charlotte's face reminded Maggie of a cat that had knocked over a cream jug and scoffed the lot. Colin had been cold to her for a start, but she'd persisted with her invitations and little gifts for both him and Maggie. Maggie now saw that he was smiling; he looked as if he was enjoying Charlotte's attention as she bent over his chair to whisper in his ear.

Maggie stuck her head in the air and walked on ahead. Earlier, she'd thought Colin might have begun to truly love her – as she'd long since realised she loved him, but now she thought he was just grateful.

Walking on ahead, she went into the house and ordered tea for three and was not in the least surprised when Charlotte continued to flirt with Colin throughout the meal. Colin's father came in later and she sent for more tea, crumpets and cake and still Charlotte kept talking and laughing. Colin's father talked and smiled, clearly content and not aware of any tension, and then went off to see one of his staff.

In the end, Maggie excused herself and made a strategic retreat to talk to Cook, who liked to be visited before dinner so that she could explain her menu for the evening and be complimented. In truth, Maggie had never tasted such delicious food, which was a revelation. Many country houses suffered from dreadful cooks and did so in silence because they were lucky if anyone stayed – but Colin's father's cook was wonderful.

A middle-aged woman, who had started out as a kitchen

maid and risen to a place of importance in the house, Tilly, as Colin called her, doted on him and did her best to provide all his favourites. The shortages of food suffered in the big cities and towns, because of the war, were not felt so much here and they always had a ready supply of produce from the walled gardens and the local farms who leased the family's land. They were largely self-sufficient and Maggie enjoyed the fresh fruit and vegetables, though much of the fruit had been bottled in the kitchens in the autumn. She could imagine what it would be like to have fresh strawberries, raspberries and gooseberries every day in season. For the moment there were apples from the barn loft, plenty of root vegetables and fresh greens, brought to the house each day, along with flowers like chrysanthemums and the occasional rose that still lingered in sheltered spots. Maggie had been astonished at finding they still had a few clinging on in December, though the roses would be pruned on a mild day to allow for a healthy growth the next year. Meat and poultry came from the local farms and also game, like hare, rabbit and pheasant, was often served in the evenings.

'I thought we'd have a nice beef pie with mushrooms,' Cook told her. 'I'll make a sticky toffee pudding afterwards. It's one of Master Colin's favourites.'

Maggie chatted to her for a little longer, suggesting that they might have salads and cold meats in the middle of the day. 'With him being in the chair all day we don't want him to put on too much weight,' she explained. 'You play an important part in keeping him as well as he can be, Cook.'

'Well, I'm glad you told me, Mrs Morgan. I want to do right by him – and you. We all wondered what you'd be like afore you came – but anyone can see that you think the world of him.' She frowned and shook her head. 'Them as said you'd got your hooks

into our Mr Colin are wrong... and so I shall tell her next time!'
Cook's voice rose in indignation.

Maggie had no need to ask who had said such things to the
staff. She already knew Charlotte intended to make life uncomfortable for her. 'Yes, I do think the world of him,' Maggie said.
'Why don't you and the others call me Maggie? I'd like that.'

'I'll call you Mrs Maggie if you like,' Cook offered. 'I'm Tilly to
you, just like I've always been to our Mr Colin.'

Maggie thanked her and made her way back to the library.
She hoped that their visitor would have gone, but, as she
approached, she heard Charlotte's raised voice.

'Why can't you see what she is, Colin?' Charlotte was
demanding. 'Don't be fooled by the demure air of hers. She is just
after your money.'

'That is your opinion,' Colin answered. 'I know you hate
anyone taking something you think of as yours – but you threw
me over. You made it quite clear you didn't want to be tied to a
man who couldn't take you dancing or off to London whenever
you felt like a visit to the theatre!'

'I've apologised for that,' Charlotte said, a wheedling note in
her voice. 'You know what I am, Col. I say things off the top of my
head and then regret them. I love you. I want us to be together – I
want to be your wife...'

'I have a wife,' Colin said. 'I'm afraid you left your apology a
little late.'

'But you know you adore me,' Charlotte replied. 'You couldn't
leave me alone last time you were home. You've been running
after me for as long as I can remember. You can't want that
common little money-grabber... you know you still want me. I've
seen it in your eyes.'

Maggie's eyes stung with tears, but she lifted her head

proudly and entered the room before Colin could say anything else

'For your information, this common little money-grabber isn't interested in money,' she said, looking at Colin and not Charlotte. 'Nor would I hold you to something that didn't suit you, Colin. If you wanted to be free, I would give you your freedom...'

'Maggie! Don't—' Colin said, but she turned away.

She would go up to her room and leave them to sort it out. If Colin decided he would rather have Charlotte, then he must be free to follow his heart. Maggie knew little about divorce, but she was sure his family would have a good lawyer.

'Come back...' Colin called, but Maggie went out, along the hall and up the stairs.

* * *

Downstairs, the sound of angry voices could be heard faintly in the kitchen. Maggie might have heard them in her room too, had she not been so lost in her distress, though everyone in the house must have heard the angry slam of a door as someone left a few minutes later.

Maggie was weeping on the bed, her back turned to the door when it opened and someone came in. For a moment there was silence and then Colin's voice said, 'Why are you crying, Maggie? Don't cry. I hate to hear a woman crying – especially you...'

Maggie raised her head, wiping away her tears. 'Sorry. You weren't meant to witness my silly tears. I thought you were with Charlotte...'

'Do you think I'm a glutton for punishment, Maggie?' Colin asked in a strange voice. 'I'd have to be stupid to throw away what I have with you for a cold bitch like that!'

Maggie heard the annoyance in his voice and a reluctant

smile came to her lips. 'Men are stupid over women sometimes,' she said. 'I thought...'

'I know what you thought,' he snapped irritably. 'It's obvious you thought I was still so besotted with her I wouldn't know what she was after. Her father had already told me that he's in trouble for losing a rich client's money in a risky investment – and she was let down by a man she thought wanted to wed her. Someone with more money and a rich lifestyle apparently. I know Charlie too well so I played her along so that I could teach her once and for all. You should have waited a few more minutes, Maggie, and heard me tell her what I thought of her. She thought she would settle for second best – a man in a wheelchair she could cheat on as often as she pleased, who would give her a decent home and all she wanted in a material sense. She could have got her kicks elsewhere... just as I suspect she always did...'

Maggie wiped the tears from her cheeks as she sat forward. 'I know it's true, but I wouldn't have put it that strongly. Perhaps she cared for you once...'

'Charlie only ever cared for herself, but I didn't mind that. I wanted her and she used that to keep me dangling... but that was before she threw me over.'

'I thought you still wanted her – in your heart...' Maggie stared at him as his eyes suddenly lit with fire.

'As I said earlier, I'm not that much of a fool.' His gaze was intent on her face. 'What I can't make out is why *you* care so much?'

'Of course, I care—' Maggie faltered and flushed. 'I know you didn't want a proper marriage, Colin. If you hate it that I love you, I could leave...'

'Do you mean it?' he asked hoarsely, ignoring her last statement. 'I thought at first you were just being kind giving me pleasure, but then...'

'I love you, Colin,' Maggie said quietly. 'I love you in a way that I thought I never could again.'

'Thank God for that,' he said and she saw his rueful smile. 'I was afraid to tell you how much I adore you, my beautiful Maggie. I never want you to leave me. I know it isn't fair to you – I can't give you all you need in some ways, but I do love and need you.'

'Then I have all I want,' she said, 'and I think your condition will get better in time. We can see a specialist, Colin. I'm just a nurse, but we've both seen signs of movement in your right leg and your toes twitch. It may be that the feeling is beginning to return. That doesn't mean you will walk again, but it may mean things are a little easier for you.'

'Yes, I've noticed other things too...' He grinned. 'Maybe in time I will be the husband you deserve, Maggie darling.'

'You already are.' Colin nodded as she reached for his hand. 'We're happy, aren't we?'

'I am and it should only get better - now Charlie knows that I love you and I'm not in the least interested in her.' Colin kissed her hand. 'I'm sorry if you thought I was encouraging her, but I had to make her understand and until she made her play, I couldn't. I didn't mean to hurt you, Maggie, I just wanted to let her put her head in the noose.'

'Oh, Colin,' Maggie's tears spilled over. 'I wasn't sure how you felt...'

'I truly love you, Maggie. If I could make love to you the way I want, I should be the luckiest man alive,' he said, 'but even if I never have more than we do already, I'm happier than I ever expected to be.' His fingers tightened around hers. 'Promise you won't ever leave me, Maggie. I should want to die if you did...'

'I'm not thinking of leaving you,' she replied and bent down to kiss him. 'I consider myself lucky to have you.'

'He wants you,' Colin said, a flash of jealousy in his eyes. 'The man you kissed in the rose garden at the hospital. He told me I should let you go... that I was selfish to hold you. I am selfish, Maggie, I know that, but I refused.'

'Mick had no right to say that,' Maggie said. 'He was kind to me and helped me when Tim died, but it never came to anything and when I needed someone to bring me back to life he wasn't there and you were.'

'I did nothing,' Colin stared at her.

'You argued with me, made me angry, made me laugh... made me realise that life was still good,' Maggie said and smiled. 'It was all I needed and became more than I could ever have expected, my dearest one.'

'Then I'm glad,' he said and gripped her hand. 'I've been afraid you might wish you'd gone with him...'

'No, I haven't wished that,' Maggie told him. 'Perhaps if he'd spoken in France, it might have been different but he didn't – and then I was so ill and you came into my life and made me feel again.'

'Do you think you should write to him... tell him?' Colin looked at her anxiously. 'He does love you. Even I could see that...'

'I don't think a letter would help. If he is hurting, I might make it worse.'

'Wise as well as beautiful,' Colin said. He made a wry face as he heard the dinner gong. 'We'll be late and Father will not like to keep his meal waiting.'

'Then let us go down as we are,' Maggie said. 'If he's cross, we'll say I was busy helping you and I forgot the time.'

'He will forgive you,' Colin told her. 'He wasn't at all sure about you when I first told him, but he likes you – they all like you, Maggie. All our people. The Blakes think you're wonderful and they're right.'

She smiled. 'I know your father likes me. I think he would rather die than admit it, but he does approve of me.'

Colin went into a peal of laughter. 'You know him too well. We shall all be putty in your hands before long, shan't we?' His eyes smiled into hers. 'Let's go down then, my darling, and face a scolding together.'

34

'You should stop work after Christmas,' Reggie Jackson said, looking at his wife with love. 'I don't want you to go on working until the last minute, love. I know you would and you wouldn't complain – but that's not what I want for my wife.'

Marion nodded. Her back ached in the afternoons now and she knew Reggie was right. Mrs Harper had told her she could stop whenever she chose and she didn't need to give notice, because they wanted her back one day. She'd worked long enough and it would give her time to help Sarah with her new project. Sarah's skill with delicate embroidery had become known and she had been approached by several local women to make pretty garments for them. Her success had led to an idea for her own work project and she'd made contact with a small local shop. The man that owned it had been interested in stocking the range of clothes and baby things she'd shown him.

'In shops like Harpers, these blouses and this underwear would be made of silk and very expensive – too much for local women to afford. These are made with cheaper materials, but in a stylish way with some pretty embroidery, so that they are affordable,' Sarah had explained.

Mr Baxter, the owner of the shop, had agreed and asked her to produce a range of things. He said he needed a few examples before he could stock them, so Sarah was busy embroidering the inexpensive blouses she made, as well as baby gowns and shawls. Both Kathy and Marion helped her by making up the plain garments in the evenings, but they both worked and therefore had little time. Marion could help her sister-in-law prepare a batch of garments if she stopped going into Harpers after Christmas, which was now only a few days away.

Mr Harper had been seen about the store more since his injury and there had been an air of excitement, even though he was still wearing a sling and looked a bit strained. He was encouraging his staff to create displays on their counters for Christmas and offering a small prize to the three that were done best.

One of the windows was dressed with snow scenes, a sleigh and intriguing parcels and the staff been promised a bonus at the end of the sales drive. Mr Marco's touch was to have a man dress up as Santa and sit in the sleigh without moving for several minutes at a time and then he would get up and start rearranging his parcels before sitting down again. It had brought crowds rushing to see and speculation as to whether he was a real man or some kind of clever automaton and many of them came into the store to ask and then stayed to buy gifts.

Marion had been running between the department she loved and the window-dressing consultations. However, the Christmas windows were done now and she felt she would be better off at home and decided to take the holiday still due to her. She would not return after Christmas, though she hoped she might one day. Everyone had been sorry she was leaving, telling her that she would be sorely missed. She'd thought Mr Marco looked at her a little strangely, but he'd been quiet the previous few days and she sensed there was something wrong. However, he was senior staff and Marion would not dare to ask what might be thought personal questions.

On her last day before she left, Mr Marco gave her a small parcel. 'For the baby,' he told her. 'If I don't see you again, I hope you have an easy confinement and a lovely life.'

'Oh, I'll pop in from time to time,' Marion told him. 'Even if just to look. I would love to do more window dressing if I could...'

'I'm sure Mrs Harper would give you a job here,' Mr Marco said. 'When the baby is old enough for you to leave in someone's care...'

Marion smiled. Sally Harper had already told her she would be welcome to return in a part-time capacity if that made things easier – but it was odd the way Mr Marco had made such a point of it. She was thoughtful as she caught the bus home that evening, Reggie was still on leave. He said his orders were about to be changed after a period of being settled in England as a trainer, but he seemed to think he might be sent back to the fighting and that made her heart sink. She couldn't bear it if anything happened to him now.

* * *

'Why didn't you tell me before?' Sadie asked when Marco told her he was being sent to a fighting unit in a week's time. 'I've made lots of plans for Christmas and the New Year and now you won't be here to enjoy them.'

'I wasn't sure it was correct. I asked to be sent to a fighting unit at the start, but they said I was more use in another capacity, but now they want me at the Front. I questioned it, but it is official.

When I asked why now, I was told they need men for another big push...'

'Can't you get out of it?' Sadie asked him. 'Why don't you plead your wound – the one you got in France? It isn't fair. You risked your life for months and months out there!'

'Nearly two years,' Marco said. 'They killed good friends of mine. I would have liked to avenge them, but I'll probably be sent to somewhere at the heart of the fighting...'

'What makes you think that? Surely they have plenty of others?'

Marco shrugged. 'I was asked to volunteer for a mission and I refused – so I think someone decided I'd had it too easy and pushed for me to be sent to the Front.'

'You didn't tell me...' Sadie frowned. 'Why did you refuse?'

'Because I'd be no good where they wanted me to go...' he paused, smiled, then, 'And because I didn't want to leave you and the boy.' He looked directly at her. 'You've given me more than I ever expected to have, Sadie. I'd given up the thought of a family long ago. Not many men of my persuasion are happy in a marriage, but I have been with you and little Pierre.'

Sadie's eyes brimmed with tears. She moved towards him and embraced him. 'Thank you, Marco. That makes me very happy.' She hesitated, then, 'Do you think we could sleep together one night before you go? Actually, in bed. If nothing happens it doesn't matter, but I'd like you to hold me as we sleep...'

'I've had women lovers in the past,' Marco told her. 'It was never very satisfactory for either partner so I decided not to try with you. I thought it might spoil what we had – but I could hold you and we could talk. If it happens...' He shrugged eloquently and Sadie smiled.

'I don't mind about sex,' she said. 'I just want us to be close until you go. I do love you, Marco – perhaps not as I loved Pierre, but I shall miss you.'

'Yes, I know – and I'll miss both of you,' he said, cursing inwardly at the fate that would tear them apart. Why did it have to happen that when he'd found peace at last, it was being wrecked by this war? He had no doubt who was behind the posting. It was vindictive and stupid, but he'd refused to volunteer for a suicide mission and now he was being punished.

* * *

Marco rose when Sadie was sleeping. He'd given her what she wanted and although their coupling had not given him the intense pleasure of his relationship with Julien, it had felt warm and right somehow. It was as if they were a proper couple now with a child and had the kind of marriage so many had, where intimate relations were perhaps not important, but comfortable. It was the comfort and warmth that mattered and he'd certainly found that with Sadie.

Marco knew it might never happen again. Sadie had been easily satisfied and would not demand much from him, but he was glad he'd done as she asked. She was truly his wife now and had promised she would be waiting for him when he got home. It would give him a reason to fight, to be watchful and look out for his life, because Sadie loved him in her way. Not with the passion she'd given to Pierre, but much as you might love a worn pair of slippers you particularly liked – and if that was all she asked of him, Marco could give her happiness now and then.

He felt tears on his cheeks as he thought of his one true love, Julien, and his terrible, wasteful death would never cease to haunt him. Marco had turned full circle and felt again the sharpness of loss and the hopelessness of knowing there was nothing he could do – but now he had found a certain contentment in a way he'd never expected.

Damn Major Bryant and his petty revenge! Marco's mouth set in a thin line. He would do what was clearly his duty, but he would make damned sure he survived and came back to Sadie, Pierre – and Harpers.

35

'I wanted to say goodbye,' Marco said as he entered the office, where Ben was sitting at the desk contemplating a prettily wrapped gift. 'Sally isn't here?'

'No, she is treating some of the staff to a little tea party in the canteen, I think. She had some gifts to distribute and there is food and a bottle or two of sherry.' He realised what Marco had said and frowned. 'Where are you going? I haven't been told anything? Is it another undercover thing?'

'Not this time. They asked me to volunteer for something in Russia, but I told Bryant I wasn't the right man this time – so I've been ordered to report to a fighting unit.'

'Good God! That's ridiculous. You've done your share and more – with the wound you had, they should have given you a desk job. I thought you might be sent back to France – but not in a fighting unit.'

'I suppose I can shoot as well as the average soldier, even though I'm not a crack shot... Besides, I refused to volunteer or accept a mission to Russia, so I suppose I'm lucky. They could have had me shot for disobeying orders...'

'They could not! I do have some influence and I would have had my lawyers sort it out in five minutes flat... or before it came to a court-martial anyway.'

'Well, I suppose you might...' Marco conceded with a grin.

'Why on earth didn't you come to me sooner?' Ben Harper asked. 'It is ridiculous, Marco. You volunteered at the beginning and you've more than done your duty. If you'd told me sooner, I would have spoken to someone – had the orders rescinded. I could still try—'

'I leave in the morning,' Marco said with a wry smile. 'I did think about asking if you knew someone who might help, but then I realised that if I did that, then I should be the coward Bryant named me.'

'That's the last thing anyone could ever call you,' Ben said, looking at him anxiously. 'Are you sure you're fit enough – your wound?'

'Is well and truly healed.' Marco smiled. 'I'm as fit as the next man and I do know how to fight, Ben. Perhaps not as well as some Frenchmen I know but good enough to kill a few of the enemy. I'm sorry to leave you in the lurch, but Sally has ideas for windows and my team isn't too bad at the practical stuff. It's a pity that young Marion Jackson had to leave just at this time. I would advise you to get her back after the baby is born, even if she only comes in a couple of mornings...'

'The war will soon be over in my opinion, maybe a few months,' Ben replied with a frown. 'Keep your head down and know that we need you back – on a personal as well as a business level.'

'I know and I'll do my best to get home,' Marco said with a wry smile. 'But if I shouldn't – make sure Sadie is all right please. I've left her money, but she will need more than that – support from friends...'

'Yes, of course I will,' Ben assured him and gripped his shoulder with his good hand, his shoulder still too sore to do much. 'There was a time when I would have envied you your posting, Marco, but I've had enough of this damned war. I'll do my duty to the end – and if I can help with some of the logistics to get the men home again, I'll do that, but after that I intend to lift some of the burden from Sally's shoulders. She's borne most of it all this time.'

'Sally Harper is made of strong stuff,' Marco replied with a warm smile. 'But she does need looking after. Why don't you see if you can find out what has happened to her mother, Ben? A private detective traced her and I know that your wife wrote to her mother but she hasn't been to see her yet. Sally might not have said much to you about it – perhaps she doesn't want to worry you. I know Jenni didn't approve. She thought the woman an impostor trying to take advantage and Sally may feel you think the same.'

Ben nodded. 'Thank you for telling me, Marco. I appreciate your honesty – and I think you may be right. I'll have a talk to her this evening and if she wants, I'll go down to Cambridgeshire and investigate.'

'You do that,' Marco said. 'Well, I must go. Sadie was preparing a special meal this evening, as it is our last together for the foreseeable future.'

'Good. Enjoy it!' Ben touched his shoulder once more. 'Go with God, my friend, and I shall pray for your safe return.'

Marco smiled and left.

Ben frowned and then reached for the phone. Even if it was too late to stop the orders, he would ensure that Major Bryant got a rap over the knuckles for what he'd done...

* * *

Marco glanced round his office and then turned out the lights. He knew there was a likelihood that he would not see it again and he felt a pang of regret. Perhaps he ought to have asked Ben to pull some strings for him and yet in his heart he knew he would never have done it. It was the way of the coward and he'd always expected to be sent to the fighting – wanted it. At first, he'd hoped he might be killed because his grief for Julien had still been so strong. Now it was just a deep ache that he lived with – and much of the reason for that was Sadie and her son. Yet another parting he must endure. He had found happiness with her – the kind he would never have expected. He had a wife and son and he was content – and they were worth fighting for, worth making sure he stayed alive for.

He left Harpers, stopping to exchange a few words with all those who called out to him, wishing him good luck. He had so many friends here – it was a real community and he hoped to return when the war finally ended.

Ben thought it couldn't be many months, perhaps a year at most. The Americans had certainly helped to turn the tide with their money and their sheer weight of numbers. They were a powerful force and Germany had felt their hammer blows; combined with the other Allies from all over the world, Marco believed they were winning and a part of him wanted to be in at the kill.

He smiled as he hailed a cab. It would get him home sooner. He would have a little time with Pierre and then he would eat dinner with Sadie and afterwards take her to bed. Now that he knew he could make her happy, he would not hold back. She was a lovely, generous woman and she deserved all that he could give her...

* * *

Ben stopped in the doorway of his apartment sitting room, watching Sally as she looked through yet another catalogue. She never stopped working. He knew that she would have played with Jenny before putting her to bed and she would have prepared their supper in readiness for him. It would probably be steak with salad and chips or one of her special casseroles. She seldom cooked chops or pies. On Sundays she would roast a joint, unless he took them all out to a restaurant. Often, they dined at one of Mick's places, because the food was wholesome and well-cooked, but Sally's cooking was fine for the nights they just wanted to stay home. Mrs Hills sometimes cooked for them, but Ben preferred his wife's simple meals.

Sally looked up and smiled at him. 'You spoke to Marco? Was there nothing you could do?'

'I might have if he would let me, but he says it is his duty to go, the damned idiot. Still, I don't think he has a death wish. He will come back if he can, Sally.'

'Yes, I think he really cares for Sadie and the little boy. I've met her a couple of times. She came to the shop a while ago and Marco introduced her... seems a nice young woman. I know it seems strange to think of him married but it appears to work...'

'He wanted a family. I'm not sure how much of a marriage it is – but he asked me to look out for her, so I shall if he doesn't get back.'

'I pray he will,' Sally said. 'He should have asked you for help sooner, Ben – but I suppose it is pride.' She frowned. 'I just hope he comes back to his wife and child and to us.'

'Marco feels that it would be wrong to shirk his duty when so many others have no choice,' Ben told her. 'I understand completely, but he should never have been sent to a fighting unit. He was taken out of basic training when they needed him else-where and now he is being thrown back in at the deep end –

although, perhaps having learned to survive in France as one of the partisans, he will find a way to survive this war.' Ben sighed. 'War is never easy, darling. We all have to make sacrifices and sometimes you just have to do what you think right.'

'Yes, I know.' Sally smiled at him. 'I just feel sorry for his wife. They haven't been married long and I don't think she has many friends.'

'Visit her yourself and see what she needs,' Ben replied. 'I'm sure you can think of something, Sally. You organise everyone else, so Sadie shouldn't be any trouble.' There was a teasing light in his eyes.

'Ben! Are you saying I'm bossy?' Sally demanded with mock indignation.

'Oh very,' he said and laughed. 'But in a good way that we all love you for. Have her to tea or lunch and introduce her to some of your friends and acquaintances.'

'Yes, I shall.' Sally nodded. 'I'll give a little tea party here in the flat after Christmas. She and Beth might get on – or Rachel. I'll ask a couple of nurses from the hospital too, because Sadie has hopes of returning to her job one day.' Sally had made friends with several nurses at the hospital she regularly visited on her mission to help badly wounded men. 'It will be a thank you to them for all their hard work and good company for Sadie... I only wish Maggie could have been present, but I don't think she would come all this way.'

'Why don't you ask her? She can't be short of money now and perhaps she would like a day or two out in the New Year.'

Sally looked at him thoughtfully. 'I could ask. I doubt very much if she will be able to leave her husband, but it doesn't hurt to ask.'

'Good – and now, I want to talk to you about your mother, Sally. I know you wrote to her new address, but she hasn't answered your last letter and it has made you anxious for her. Would you like me to go down and find out why?'

Her eyes lit at the suggestion. 'Oh yes, Ben, I should – but are you sure you feel up to it? You couldn't possibly drive yourself...'

'I can get a car and driver easily enough,' Ben told her but looked at her seriously. 'Are you prepared for whatever she might say? I don't want you to go breaking your heart over her if she isn't what you think...'

'I am sure she is my mother and she does want to see me – why else would she approach me and follow me for so long?'

Ben shook his head. 'I don't know, Sally. I don't understand why she hasn't replied to your last letter – but I intend to find out.'

Sally nodded. 'I'll write to Maggie and invite her up after Christmas – on a Sunday afternoon. That will make it possible for Rachel to attend.'

'Whatever suits you, my darling.'

She frowned. 'Have you spoken to Rachel recently, Ben?'

'No – why do you ask?'

'Because she seems a little distracted, as if she has something on her mind – I've wondered if she is frightened of something... Of course, William is in the hospital and she can't see him, which must cause her terrible grief. I can't imagine how awful that must feel. To have your husband ill and not be able to see him would be agony.'

'Well, there you are then,' Ben said. 'She is probably worried about her husband. There isn't much you can do about that, Sally, because they won't let her visit until he is rid of that terrible disease.'

'No, I know – and yet I feel there is something more... something she won't say. I shall have to make sure I take time to talk to her and discover what is wrong...'

36

It was the Saturday before Christmas, and Rachel was planning what for her could be one of the happiest she'd ever known. Both she and Hazel had been buying little gifts and hiding them away for the big day. Having Lizzie to fuss over and spoil had drawn them closer together and given Rachel's mother-in-law something to fill her empty life. Lizzie called her Nanna and climbed on Hazel's lap to be petted at every opportunity. Rachel might have felt jealous, except that Lizzie's face lit up when she got home and she always ran to her to be picked up and kissed. She had brought such joy to their lives that Rachel did not resent sharing her with the woman she now genuinely felt was a friend and was fond of.

She had received a letter from William recently. Penned for him by a nurse, it reported that he was feeling better and making good progress and now had hopes that he would completely recover.

When I came here, I thought I would die here. However, the doctors and nurses are excellent but strict and I am being well

cared for. There is a marked improvement in my condition,
Rachel dearest. I feared I should leave you a widow too soon
and blamed myself for ruining your life once more – but now I
believe I shall have another chance to make you happy. I know
you love your work at Harpers, my dear love, but perhaps we
could think about retiring to the sea somewhere? We shall talk
when I am well again, for I have no wish to tear you from you
friends if you feel it would upset you...

Rachel wasn't sure how she felt about retiring to the sea. She loved her job and did not want to leave, at least for the moment – but that did not worry her as much as what William might say when he returned and discovered what she had done.

Since the night she'd felt she was being shadowed, nothing untoward had occurred and she had begun to lose her fear of having Lizzie taken away from her, although she could never quite forget that Lizzie had a father out there somewhere and he had taken revenge on Lizzie's grandmother, his violence leading to her death. What would he do to the woman who had stolen his daughter if he ever came after her?

For some weeks after that incident, Rachel had lived in fear of being attacked, but it hadn't happened. Had he been arrested for beating his mother or had he returned to his fighting unit? And what ought she to do for the future? Rachel had taken Lizzie away to protect her on an impulse, but she knew she had acted unlawfully and had no right to keep the little girl without her father's permission. So far no one had questioned it, but what would William say and what if the authorities became interested and decided she wasn't a fit person to have charge of Lizzie?

It was concerning, so along with the happiness of caring for their little girl had come the worry of what the future might bring. Rachel knew she needed to confide in someone and Sally

Harper would be the person she would normally ask for her opinion, but Sally had so much to do and she was carrying her second child. Rachel suspected that her friend did not have as good health as she pretended. She'd seen her looking tired and had begged her not to do too much, but that was like asking the tide not to come in. Sally Harper was Sally Harper and she would carry on even if she felt unwell.

Glancing round her department that morning, Rachel was pleased to see that it was busy and both Shirley and the new salesgirl she'd taken on to replace Marion – Ruby Marlowe – were selling stock easily. Rachel had been busy the whole morning on her own counter and Susie Browne, the new junior, had been helping her by wrapping gifts and handing them to the shoppers. It was mostly men buying gifts for their wives and daughters and the silver jewellery had taken a pounding. An extra order from one of their preferred makers was due in that morning, just in time for the last-minute rush, and Rachel gave a sigh of relief when Fred Burrows came in with two parcels for her.

'Is that my new stock?' she asked and he nodded.

'Yes, just arrived, so I brought it straight up, Mrs Bailey. I knew you would be wanting it.'

'That is so kind of you, Mr Burrows – how is Beth? Are you both ready for Christmas?'

'Well, I am, but Beth is rushing around like a demented ant,' he said with a grin. 'I think those kids are going to be utterly spoiled this year. My friend Vera tells me she's bought them lots of little things and I haven't been behind in buying them treats – still that is what it is all about, isn't it? The children...'

'Yes, it is,' Rachel agreed and smiled as he left the department.

Fred had reminded her about the Christmas she was planning for Lizzie. Of course, he had no idea she'd adopted – how she liked to think of it – a little girl, but she was sure he would approve... Of course, she remembered now: Fred had a friend called Harry who was an ex-policeman. If she took Fred into her confidence, she was certain he would understand *and* he might also be able to give her advice or help her make it right...

Suddenly, Rachel felt the shadow lift a little. She hadn't considered talking to Fred, but now she saw that he was ideal. He would be loyal to her because of Beth and he might have some idea of how she could find out about Lizzie's father and whether she would be allowed to keep Lizzie once the authorities found out what she'd done.

Turning her mind back to work, she left her new assistant at the counter and took the boxes into her office to unpack and price them. If this volume of trade kept up, she knew they would need some of the beautiful silver bracelets, brooches and necklaces inside. They were mostly repeat orders of popular stock, but Sally had told her about a range of new brooches that were silver representations of ballerinas, well-dressed ladies and novelties, like a riding whip and a sword set with tiny diamonds, which was rather expensive but exquisite. For an hour or so, Rachel was lost in the wonder of such lovely things and her amazement at Sally Harper's ability to keep finding such treasures. However, as soon as she was able to take her lunch break, she headed for the basement to talk to Fred before she lost her nerve.

* * *

'You could have knocked me down with a feather and that's the truth,' Fred said to his friend Harry that evening over a pint of beer in his kitchen. 'Mrs Bailey is a most respectable lady and I was shocked when she told me what she'd done – but of course I see why she did it. Given the situation, I might well have done it myself!'

Harry nodded but looked grave. 'She's broken the law, of course – but she's not the first woman to let her heart rule her head when it comes to kids. There is a tradition of it in the East End – we look after our own, don't we, Fred? Well, I reckon the best thing is to find the girl's father and see what he is up to. If he's serving in the Army, he might not be able to care for her – and he'll need someone to look after Lizzie if he does want her. He might see sense and let her stay where she's safe, loved and cared for – and he might sign a paper giving her over into Mrs Bailey's care.'

'Knowing Rachel, it would break her heart if she had to give the child back,' Beth said. 'I wish she'd told us before... I knew something was worrying her last time she came for tea, but I thought it was her husband being away in the hospital.'

'We all thought the same,' Fred agreed. 'I think she was afraid to tell anyone and then this morning something made her realise that she could talk to me.' Fred smiled at his daughter-in-law. 'Mrs Harper has too much to do, though we all know she would try to help – but it's best this way. Harry will help us, won't you?'

Harry grinned and swallowed another mouthful of beer. 'Be glad to, Fred. Life gets a bit dull when you live alone and you've no work. I'll do my best to find this chap – and I'll persuade him to do the right thing if he has any sense of decency.'

'Thanks, Harry,' Fred said, looking at his mate's empty glass. 'Fetch us another beer, Beth. I think this deserves a little celebration, don't you?'

'Yes, I do, and I'll pop into Harpers in the morning and tell Rachel,' Beth said. 'She must bring Lizzie to tea on Sunday and I'll find something nice for her for Christmas.'

Fred chuckled over his beer. Beth was enjoying herself buying and making gifts for everyone and he loved to see her happy. His heart still ached each time he remembered Tim and that was every day, but he hadn't let it destroy him. He knew that life had to go on and his memories were good ones. He just wished that Jack could get home for Christmas. Beth was keeping her fingers crossed, but Fred didn't expect it. Jack had told them he was on the Atlantic run and that took longer and was still dangerous despite the escorts. The U-boats could attack suddenly and unseen and could still sink an unsuspecting ship before they were attacked in retaliation and driven to the bottom of the ocean or destroyed. All Fred prayed for was that it wouldn't be Jack's ship that took a fatal hit next time.

* * *

'I didn't feel I could burden anyone with my worries,' Rachel told Beth when they shared a pot of tea at Betty's Café across the road from Harpers in Rachel's afternoon tea break. 'You have your children and Jack to think about – and I know you're busy getting ready for Christmas.'

'So is everyone,' Beth retorted. 'You know I would have time for you, Rachel. Now, I want you to promise you will bring Lizzie to tea tomorrow – and you must tell Sally. She can come too.'

'Yes, I shall talk to her now – and I can't thank you and Fred enough for understanding.'

'Harry is going to do all he can and I would trust him with my life,' Beth declared a little too forcefully. 'Well, you know what I mean.' She laughed as Rachel looked at her, eyebrow raised. 'He is clever, knowledgeable about all matters of law and he says if he can find Lizzie's father and get him to sign, you can probably keep her – at least until Mr Robinson makes other arrangements.'

'Thank goodness! I thought I might get arrested for stealing her.'

'No, Harry's says not – he says it happens quite a bit in the poorer homes where a mother dies and neighbours take in orphaned children, often splitting the family up amongst several other families. Most of the time no one knows and no one cares – unless a complaint is made. Then the police have to investigate, but otherwise they tend to turn a blind eye. Their problem is with the kids on the street who aren't lucky enough to be taken into neighbours' or relatives' care... Besides, Lizzie's father is wanted for questioning over the beating he gave his mother. We might think she deserved what she got – but if they find him guilty, he is still a murderer – and as such, he would not be allowed access to his daughter from prison.' Beth looked around the café with interest. 'Nothing changes much here, does it? Do you remember when we first came here? It was mostly Sally, Maggie and me then – but afterwards you came too. That all seems so long ago.' She sighed wistfully.

'Do you miss working at Harpers?' Rachel asked her.

'I do and I don't.' Beth said. 'At first I missed it terribly. I hardly knew what to do with myself all day – but now I have two children I have too much to do to think about myself much. I've made more friends locally and Fred's Friend, Vera comes round most days and gives me a hand. She will look after the children if I want to pop into Harpers and see my old friends so I've got used to it – but I'd like to come in part-time when the boys are at school.'

'I'm sure we'd all love to have you back,' Rachel said and looked up as the café owner came over with their Chelsea buns. 'Oh, those do look lovely, Betty. How is trade now?'

'Busier than ever,' Betty said, beaming. 'We get most of your young ladies in here for their break, Mrs Bailey – and your customers come here too to sit and have a cuppa before they catch the bus home. Going to Harpers is such a treat, they don't want the day to end so they linger and talk to their friends about what they've bought.' She waved her hands as Rachel opened her purse. 'No, they are on me, Mrs Bailey. I know you send a lot of customers my way when they ask where they can get a decent cheap meal.'

She went back to her counter to help her husband serve more customers and Rachel smiled. 'Now, wasn't that nice of her – but she's always good to us and I'm glad Harpers is bringing her more trade.'

'By the looks of it, she can hardly keep up with it,' Beth said and gathered her things. 'Now don't forget, Rachel. You bring Lizzie to tea on Sunday and Harry will talk to you – he might even have some news.'

'Oh, that would be a relief,' Rachel said, 'but I don't expect anything too soon. I'll see you this weekend then... Lizzie will like playing with your boys...'

37

It was Sunday, the day before Christmas Eve. Ben looked at the neat semi-detached house and frowned. Somehow, he hadn't expected it to look so spick and span. Jenni had made him think that the woman claiming to be Sally's mother was an imposter or, at best, if she really was Sally's birth mother, a rogue who just wanted to get her hands on some of the Harpers' money.

'Why else would she appear now?' Jenni had demanded when he rang her and told her of his plans to go down and see Sally's mother. It had seemed a reasonable question to ask given that it had taken so many years for Sally's mother to approach her. 'You be careful, Ben. She will get her claws into Sally and you will forever be putting your hand in your pocket.'

'I'm not a fool, Jenni – and neither is Sally...' Ben was slightly annoyed with her. He was fond of Jenni, but sometimes she tended to ride over other people's feelings, perhaps without realising what she was doing. 'I should not let Sally be hurt.'

'Well, I'd leave things as they are.'

Ben ignored her and carried on with his plans. Having

arranged a car, he'd had nothing to do but sit back and read some paperwork. Despite his efforts to get clear of his war work while he needed to rest his shoulder, he was still having to advise on certain matters of purchase and logistics.

He walked up the path and knocked at the door. After a moment or two, it was opened and the woman who stood there wore a dark blue dress with a white collar and she was wearing a pinafore over it, her hands floury as if she had been baking.

'I'm sorry to disturb you, but I'm Ben Harper...'

'I know who you are,' she said. 'I've seen you with my daughter, Mr Harper. That is how I discovered where she was – from a photograph in the newspaper. I'd searched for years and eventually gave up hope until I saw that photo.' She laughed and he saw Sally in her immediately. 'Here's me wittering on and you still on the doorstep. Would you like to come in? I just have a cake to finish and some sausage rolls to go in the oven.'

She led the way into a spacious kitchen, set with pine dressers and a large table on which stood the evidence of her industry. Going to the sink, she washed and then dried her hands and turned to look at him.

'You want to know why I haven't answered my daughter's recent letter, don't you?'

'Yes, please. She is upset by your silence. You told the detective that you would visit her, but she's heard nothing since.'

'Do sit down. I'll make a pot of tea and try to explain...' A smile lit her eyes and any doubts Ben might have had about her being Sally's mother melted like snowflakes. That was Sally's smile. He would know it anywhere.

'Thank you, I shall. I think you have a long and interesting tale to tell – Mrs Ross?'

'Mrs Tarrant now,' she said. 'But you may call me Sheila if you'd like?'

Ben nodded. Already he liked her and he was very curious about what she would have to say – how she would explain what she had done.

* * *

It was past nine that evening when Ben walked into their flat. Sally had started to worry that he might not get home that night and was wondering what was wrong.

'Are you all right, darling?' she asked, looking at him anxiously.

'Sorry it's so late, my love,' Ben said, 'but Sheila had to wait for her husband to get home before she could leave.'

'You mean...?' Sally stared at the woman she'd seen appear in the doorway behind him. She gave a little sob of emotion. 'You – you're my mother? I can't quite recall what you looked like that day.'

'You were very ill, Sally, my love,' Sheila said and moved towards her, arms wide open. 'And I wasn't quite as well-dressed as I am now.'

'Mum...?' Sally said tentatively and was caught up in a warm hug. Tears ran down her cheeks, mingling with those of her mother's. 'I've always wondered about you – if you were alive and why—'

'I left you with the nuns on the understanding that I could have you back once I was on my feet again.' Sheila drew back and looked into her eyes. 'It took a little while and when I finally knew that I could manage to look after you, it was too late. The nuns had moved you on and I couldn't find you.'

'But when you came to me in the park...' Sally hesitated, then, 'You looked different...'

Sheila nodded. 'I didn't earn much and my lodgings in

London were expensive. The way I look now is down to my Trevor. He's a small builder and not short of a few pounds and he insists on spending it on me – before I finally agreed to marry him, I hardly had enough to pay for the room I'd taken in London and food.'

'Come and sit down,' Sally said and drew her into the sitting room. 'Now, take your time and tell me everything – or do you want a cup of tea first?'

Ben said, 'I don't make tea well, but I can make coffee or cocoa?'

'Cocoa please,' both women said and smiled at each other.

'I'm sorry I didn't answer your letter,' Sheila said. 'It came at a bad time. Trevor had just had a nasty accident at work and was taken to hospital. I was up there all the time because it was touch-and-go for a while. They thought he might die or be paralysed – had a bad fall from a roof, see. He was out of his head for a few days and I feared the worst, but then one day he woke up, smiled at me and asked for a cup of tea. The doctors said it was a miracle!'

'I am so sorry he was hurt,' Sally said. 'Is he well now?'

'He had a broken ankle and a lot of bruising to his spine, as well as the bang to his head, but his ankle is healing. He still hurts and he's had a couple of dizzy turns, but since they let him out of hospital he is managing. He insists on going into his office to check on the work schedule each day, though he can't do any physical work yet, of course, and he isn't ready to drive.'

'But he will recover completely?'

'So, the doctors tell me.' Sheila looked at her sadly. 'But how are you, Sally. Ben told me about the baby and you being so ill – are you better now?'

'Yes, much better, thank you – especially now I know you're all right. I worried about you...'

'Oh, Sally, darling.' Tears sparkled in Sheila's eyes. 'I've let you down badly, love. I should never have left you in that place all those years ago, but at the time I thought it for the best.' She looked down, an expression of sadness on her face. 'I was sixteen when I had you, Sally. I got proper taken in by a rogue who left me in the lurch when he knew you were on the way. He took everything we had of value in the house, leaving me with nothing. I was pregnant, homeless and penniless. After you were born, I struggled on for a couple of years, but then I became ill. The nuns took me in and nursed me back to health. They pushed me into giving you up, saying I couldn't look after you properly. I was promised I could have you back when I was on my feet – but when I did look for you, they'd sent you away and wouldn't tell me where...' Sheila paused. Sally was crying and she passed her a clean handkerchief. 'I did try to find you then, but I couldn't. For years I kept writing to places like the one I'd first left you at, but they either didn't answer or said they had no knowledge of you. I'd given up hoping – and then, as I told Ben, I saw a picture of you in the paper.' She smiled. 'I was sure I knew who you were, but I had no proof so I paid an investigator to discover what he could – and I kept running out of money.'

'That photograph must have been taken when I did the big charity drive at the shop. I remember it was in the paper.'

'Yes – just over a year ago,' Sheila confirmed. 'I'd just met Trevor and he told me to get a better private detective to find out if you were who I thought you must be, as the other one never seemed to discover anything but just kept asking for more money... You looked so much like me as a young girl, but I couldn't know for sure.'

Tears were running down Sally's cheeks. 'And he told you my history?'

'You hadn't made any secret of the fact that you were brought up by the nuns and one of your sales girls was very obliging. Your staff all think you're a marvel...' Sheila paused.

'Please go on. I want to know everything. You followed me yourself for a while. Why didn't you approach me?'

'Because I was afraid to. You were successful, married to a rich man and I thought you might think I was trying to get something from you – to ask for money.'

'I would have given it to you if you needed it,' Sally said and wiped her tears. 'I wish you had told me sooner. I always wanted to know who you were...' She gazed at Sheila wonderingly. 'Who my father was – whether I had a brother or sister...'

'No, there was only ever you. I didn't meet anyone else I could trust for years – not until Trevor came along. Your father's name was Mark Gresham, but I never heard from him again after he abandoned us.'

'It wasn't very nice with the nuns. I wondered why anyone would leave me there...'

'If I'd known what they would do, I would never have left you.' Sheila sighed as she looked at her again, tears in her eyes. 'I thought it best for you at the time. Can you ever forgive me? I searched for you for so long and when I approached you and you became ill, I blamed myself...'

'It wasn't your fault,' Sally said and moved towards her impulsively, putting her arms about her again and giving her a gentle hug. 'I was very ill and didn't know it. I do forgive you for everything – even though I wish you had answered my letter.'

'I was going to, but after Trevor's accident, I hesitated again.' Sheila looked at her nervously. 'I'd committed myself to him and I couldn't leave him. He's sitting in the car now waiting and we're going to a hotel your husband has booked for a few days so that I can spend some time with you.'

'Thank you.' Sally looked at her husband gratefully as he brought their cocoa. 'You can spend tomorrow and Christmas Day with us, Boxing Day too. We shall open the store for a few hours in the morning and you must come and visit it and meet everyone, Mum – and Trevor?' She nodded, smiling though her tears. 'You are definitely spending all Christmas with us. We have plenty of everything. I shall enjoy getting to know you both and you have to meet Jenny.'

Sheila was crying now and Sally gave her back her handkerchief. She glanced at Ben. 'Why don't you fetch Mum's husband in and we'll all get to know one another…'

* * *

Later, after tea, sandwiches, cake and something stronger for the men, Ben called a cab and Sally's mother and stepfather were taken to their hotel for the night. They would return on Christmas morning to meet their granddaughter and spend the day with their family. Trevor had never stayed in a smart hotel before and he was pleased and overcome when Ben insisted the treat was on him.

Trevor looked at his wife proudly as he said to Ben, 'A lot of men might think my Sheila was a wrong one because of what happened to her as a young lass, but she hasn't got a bad bone in her body. She had a hard time, but I intend to see she enjoys life in the future. She'll visit with your Sally whenever she can – and you're welcome to come to us if it suits you.'

'You are very kind,' Ben said. 'I'm glad we've all had this chance to get to know one another.'

After they'd left, Sally got up and went to put her arms around Ben very carefully so as not to jog his arm and send pain through his shoulder. 'That was a lovely thing you did, Ben. Thank you so much.'

'You deserve far more after all you've had to put up with, my darling,' he said and kissed her. 'Now, we should get to bed before Jenny decides it is time to get up and ask if it is Christmas Day yet and whether Father Christmas has been!'

Jenny was now very aware of Christmas and what it meant and asked a dozen times a day when Father Christmas would bring her presents. She kept looking at the tree and the glittering lights and tinsel and jumping up and down with excitement, sure that she would be getting her share of whatever the old man with a beard brought.

Because of his shoulder, Ben had reluctantly allowed Fred Burrows to be this year's Father Christmas at the store. It had only been for one Saturday and the few days before Christmas because they couldn't spare Fred in the busy days the week before when the last-minute stock arrived and needed to be delivered to each department.

'Yes, let's go to bed,' Sally said and he pulled her tight against him. 'Be careful of your shoulder, darling. I don't want to hurt you.'

'You never would,' he said valiantly, but he let her go, wincing a little. The broken bones were healing slowly but they still caused an enormous amount of pain and soreness. Once the pain ebbed, he would do exercises to get his movement back, but at the moment it still hurt too much. He followed her through into the bedroom and Sally helped to ease him out of his clothes. 'I'll be glad when this damned shoulder is healed and I can hold you again.' he said huskily.

'Me too,' she said and kissed him softly. 'Come to bed, my darling, and I'll show you how happy you've made me.'

Ben's eyes lit with humour. 'And how are you going to do that?' he demanded. 'With you pregnant and me with a damaged shoulder?'

'Come to bed and you'll see,' she promised and so he did...

38

'Well, Mrs Bailey,' Harry had said as he was introduced to Rachel and Lizzie at Beth's home that Sunday afternoon. 'So, this is the young lady who caused you to break the law.'

'This is Lizzie,' Rachel had replied a little nervously. 'I cared for her too much to leave her in danger.'

'Yes, I'm sure. You need not look so anxious, Mrs Bailey. I am entirely on your side in this. I've seen enough kids mistreated in my time and I've been tempted to give some of the perpetrators a good hiding, I can tell you. However, it needs to be sorted and I'm happy to do what I can.'

'Yes, thank you – it is very kind of you,' Rachel responded. 'I suppose there is no news of her father yet?'

Lizzie's father must be keeping a low profile. Not only was he wanted for questioning, he was also AWOL and could be shot by the Army. Rachel felt sorry for him. What he'd done was wrong, but understandable once he'd heard how his mother had treated his wife and daughter.

'I can tell you he hasn't been arrested,' Henry then said. 'My old colleagues at the nick did look for him, but they gave up when he wasn't to be found – but I've got a few leads.'

'Thank you.' Rachel sighed inwardly. She had hoped he might have constructive news, but that was expecting too much. Lizzie was playing with some of Jackie's bricks and showing Timmy his rattle and enjoying herself. 'I don't think I could bear to part with her now.'

'No reason why you should in my opinion. There are enough homeless orphans on the streets. A child that gets taken in by a good-hearted woman like yourself rather than the orphanage is lucky. Some of my colleagues might not agree, but there is no reason they should find out about it – and her father isn't likely to complain, is he?'

'No.' Rachel smiled at his honest talking. 'I don't suppose there is.'

'We'll sort it out for you, never fear.'

Rachel nodded. She knew he was doing what he could, but if Lizzie's father chose to stay hidden it might never be resolved in the way she hoped – yet all she could do was to wait and hope. It was the same with William. After his one letter, there was no more news and the worry never quite left her – when would he come home again and what would he say to her about Lizzie?

* * *

It was on Christmas Eve, that Monday morning that Marion entered the department. She walked up to Rachel and waited until she had finished serving her customer.

'Good morning, Mrs Bailey. I just popped in to see if I could buy a present for my mother-in-law. I wanted to buy her a really nice gift as she is so kind to all of us. I wondered if I could still have my staff discount?'

'Yes, of course you can,' Rachel told her with a smile. I am quite certain that Mrs Harper wouldn't mind. As far as she is concerned you can return to Harpers whenever you wish.'

'Oh, that's lovely,' Marion said and beamed with pleasure. 'I was a bit afraid to ask but I'm glad I did. I want to buy her one of the best quality leather handbags. She's never had a really good one...'

'What colour do you think she would like?' Rachel asked. 'We have a lovely black one, a red one – and this tan. There are lots of others but they are the best ones at the moment.'

'I love the tan one,' Marion said. 'It has a good zip and it will hold a lot. I'd seen it before but I thought it might have been sold.'

'It almost was this morning but the gentleman settled on a silver bracelet and a brooch instead.'

'Then I was lucky,' Marion said. 'I'll take that one please. I know the price.'

Rachel wrapped the bag, took the money and refunded the staff discount to Marion. 'You're looking very well,' she said as she handed it over. 'Let me know when the baby is born and I'll come and visit.'

'You can visit whenever you like,' Marion said and smiled. 'I'd like to come back to Harpers one day. I know I shall miss seeing all the lovely things and talking to friends.'

'We'll miss you, Marion,' Rachel said. 'I do very much hope you will be able to join us again one day, if only on a part-time basis...'

Marion went off clutching her purchase and Rachel turned to the next customer. It was still very busy in the department. Everyone seemed determined to enjoy Christmas despite the war dragging on.

'Damn the enemy,' one gentleman had told her. 'My wife and

daughter will have a good Christmas, even if we couldn't buy a goose this year – managed to get two cockerels instead, mind, but we've always had a goose before.'

He'd gone off laden with bags and jewellery, still grumbling about the war, but Rachel had just smiled and made no comment. The customer was always right whatever their complaint or manner – unless they abused a junior member of staff. In that case, Rachel stepped in and firmly asked the unruly customer to leave. It didn't happen often at Harpers, but this time of the year a few of the men – and the occasional woman – had been celebrating a little early.

* * *

Marion was delighted with her purchase. She'd been saving for the bag for ages, but hadn't had quite enough put by when she'd left work. However, Reggie had sent her a postal order for extra expenses through the post. Her fear had been that without her discount she might still have to buy a cheaper bag. Now she had the gift she wanted for her mother-in-law and her Christmas shopping was complete.

Reggie had left for an unknown destination several days earlier, but she'd sent him a package to the usual address and Sarah had his gift for Marion for Christmas morning. The postal order had been extra in case she needed something. It was lovely that he'd been so thoughtful, but she would rather have had him at home for Christmas – forever if she told the truth.

You never knew exactly where your husband was being sent, but there was a clearing address and most of the mail sent was delivered most of the time. She knew that Reggie had read most of the letters she'd sent when he'd been posted abroad before this and could only hope that he would receive his gift in time for Christmas.

He'd taken a new warm scarf and good leather gloves with him, because that was what was needed, and the parcel was just a few treats to cheer him up whenever it arrived. She knew he hadn't wanted to leave her now that the birth of their child was approaching fast and would worry that something might happen, but his mother and Sarah would look after her and Marion wasn't frightened of what she knew would be a painful ordeal. She could bear the pain to hold her first child and know that Reggie was thinking of her and what she hoped would be a son for him.

Sitting on the bus home, she was conscious of having a backache and thought how good it would be to sit down with a cup of tea and a slice of her mother-in-law's seed cake. Although she might return to Harpers one day, she was rather glad she wasn't there now.

* * *

Rachel was glad when the day was finished. She had been rushed off her feet the whole time and was feeling tired, but she knew that when she got home, the sight of Lizzie's eager little face would make her feel better. She said goodnight to her staff and walked through the store.

Fred was walking round the ground floor checking everything was all right. He did it every night and would only leave when he was sure it was all secure and safe. Rachel thought Sally Harper had left earlier in the day and Ben Harper had been in for just a short period. Mr Stockbridge, the general manager, was checking the top floor and he and Fred would meet somewhere in the middle and then they would make sure the doors were locked before leaving together.

Glancing back at the windows that seemed to glow with Christmas cheer despite the lack of bright lights, Rachel thought how much Mr Marco would be missed once these windows had to be changed. Marion's ideas had been quite clever too so that left Sally with extra work if they were to keep up their standards. It wasn't easy to find a window dresser as talented as Mr Marco and she wondered what he was doing and how his wife was getting on without him.

There was no sign of her bus and Rachel soon felt chilled waiting at the stop. She stamped her feet, impatient to be home, and then something made her look over her shoulder and she saw him. She was sure it was the same man she'd seen that night outside Hazel's. He was watching her!

Rachel started to walk away very fast. As soon as she saw a bus, she would jump on and get away from him, but she heard the sound of him following and then, suddenly, he grabbed her arm and swung her round to look at him.

'You're the one,' he said gruffly. 'You're the one that took my Lizzie!'

Rachel raised her eyes to his and what she saw shocked her. His face was gaunt, and his eyes looked haunted.

'Yes,' she said carefully in a slow clear voice. 'I took Lizzie because she'd been turned out into a cold night and she was hungry and frightened. She was being ill-treated and I decided to protect her from her grandmother...'

'I hit her... my mother,' he said. 'They told me she died in hospital. I was sorry for that; I didn't mean to kill her.'

'I doubt it was all your fault. She was probably in poor health,' Rachel said. 'You should explain to the police...'

Something flickered in his eyes. 'I'm a deserter from the Army. I had to get home to see what had happened to Lizzie. I knew that bitch would hurt her... she was the same with me when I was a kid.' The desperation in his voice got through to Rachel and suddenly she wasn't afraid of him.

'Would you like to see your daughter?' Rachel asked in a gentle tone. 'I could feed you and you can have a bath too. I might have some clean clothes that would fit you.'

'Someone told me you were all right,' he said. 'I just wanted to know – you will look after my Lizzie? Tell her I love her and one day I'll see her – but I have to get away, because if they catch me, I'm dead.'

'Surely, they would listen to your side of the story?' Rachel said. 'Come home with me, eat and see your Lizzie – and I know someone that might be able to help.'

'It's too late for me,' he said and shoved something at her before backing away from her. 'If I don't disappear, I'm dead. Just look after Lizzie...' And then he was walking away and soon lost in the shadows.

He'd given her a rather grubby piece of paper, but when she opened it, her heart leapt with excitement. It named her as Lizzie's legal guardian and was signed by her father and witnessed by someone, making it legal and likely to stand up in court if necessary. He must have found out what he needed to know about her, decided she was all right and then done this to make Lizzie safe. Tears stung her eyes and she looked back, but he'd disappeared into the shadows.

Rachel walked to the next bus stop deep in thought. She'd felt sympathy for him despite what he had done. Deserters were usually shot. It was the only way they prevented men deserting when faced with an enemy they dreaded. However much they feared enemy fire, to run was considered the lowest thing you could do and most officers would order deserters to be shot on sight, though some were court-martialled and then shot as an example to others who might consider deserting. It was a terrible situation, because some of the deserters were the youngest soldiers – little more than boys who had joined thinking war was fun and then suddenly realised what it meant.

Lizzie's father was guilty of battering his mother, who had died of her injuries – and despite what she'd done to Lizzie – it was wrong that he'd beaten her so hard. Yet Rachel understood his anger and her heart ached for his predicament. Had he not been a deserter, she thought they might have got him a lenient sentence in the circumstances, but he was right; if he was caught by the Army, he would be shot.

He'd risked a lot speaking to her this evening. Had she screamed, he might have been arrested, but he cared about his daughter, he cared about what happened to Lizzie and for that much Rachel respected and pitied him.

Her bus came then and she climbed on board. It was only as she began to feel warmer that she realised she need not be afraid any more. Lizzie's father had signed a paper giving the child into her care and no one was going to demand that she hand her back. Perhaps one day there might be difficulties as to whether it was legal, but with any luck, Lizzie would be grown up by the time someone asked questions she couldn't answer and then she could make up her own mind. After all, there were enough orphans begging on the street. Who was going to bother about one little girl when there was a war going on? Why would anyone question whether she was Rachel's real daughter?

Only William might ask awkward questions when he came home, but if he loved her, he would let her keep Lizzie. She just couldn't give her up now...

As she descended from the bus and walked towards Hazel's house, Rachel's thoughts were on the gifts she'd bought for Lizzie and the sweets she had in her bag. It looked as if they could all relax and enjoy Christmas. Pushing away the niggling worry that she might still lose the child she loved, Rachel smiled as she opened the door and a little bundle of sweet-smelling love flung herself into her arms.

She was home to enjoy Christmas with her daughter and perhaps soon William would come home too. She refused to think beyond that. William loved her, he would surely want to keep the child who had comforted her and made her happy these past weeks. Yes, he would. Rachel suddenly knew for certain that William would not turn against her or the child and the shadows lifted. All was now so much better and when William returned, they could look forward to a wonderful life as a family.

39

It was two days after Christmas and Sally was having a rest before returning to work the next day. Her mother and Trevor had returned home just that morning, promising to keep in touch often. The telephone rang just as she was thinking whether she ought to do some work and she answered it.

'Sally?' Maggie's voice came over the wire and surprised her. Her friend sounded so excited and happy. 'I wanted to thank you for the wonderful gift you sent me – those pearl earrings go well with the necklace Colin got me...'

'I'm so pleased,' Sally replied. 'Did you have a nice Christmas, Maggie?'

'Fantastic! We had carol singers from the village and we invited them into the house. Tilly – that's our cook – made mince pies and tarts and we offered them to the villagers with a glass of hot punch and it was all very jolly. The tree was huge and Colin's father gave me a diamond brooch that had been his mother's. Colin says that is the final seal of approval!'

The sound of Maggie's laughter banished any worries Sally had had for her friend. 'That's good. I was wondering if you could get up for tea one day. I know it is a long way but you could stay over and see everyone at Harpers – they'd all love to see you.'

'We're coming up in a couple of weeks to see a specialist so I'll pop in then and have tea with you after,' Maggie said. 'I'd better go now. Colin wants me to take him for a walk...'

'Look forward to seeing you...'

Sally was thoughtful after she replaced the phone. You never could tell how things would turn out. She'd thought Maggie's life would be nothing but sadness, but it seemed she was enjoying her role. Her thoughts turned to young Becky Stockbridge. Becky had been unresponsive when Sally had asked her if something was wrong, but she'd sensed the girl's inner turmoil. After Christmas, she would speak to her again, but not in the store. Try to find out what was upsetting the girl. She would ask her to tea and...a thought came to her that made her smile. Perhaps she could find a way to get Sadie and Becky together. Marco was out there in France, and Sadie was alone with her child. It might help both of them to form a friendship...and Sally thought she might know how to do it.

Sally's own life was so good; she must not let complacency allow her to ignore signs of distress in others, especially her girls. Harpers' girls were special to Sally. Somehow, she would help Becky...She was sitting lost in thought with Jenny at her feet when the doorbell rang and Mrs Hills opened it to admit Beth and her two children. Sally looked up with a smile as her friend entered.

'Oh, lovely. I was going to ring you shortly. I was too busy over Christmas with Mum and Trevor here – well, Dad, as I'm going to call him.' Sally smiled, her happiness bubbling out of her. 'We had a wonderful Christmas, Beth. Ben got on well with Dad and Mum was so excited playing with Jenny. All those years she spent trying to find me – and now she has a granddaughter, a son-in-law and another baby on the way... She told me so many times how happy she was.'

'And you too,' Beth said with a smile. 'You must feel that your family is complete?'

'Yes, I do. I was very happy with Ben, Jenny – and his sister, but this makes life even better, Beth.'

Beth nodded and made a grab for Jackie as he tried to take Jenny's new doll away from her and for a moment indignant yells from both sides made it impossible to talk. Mrs Hills saved the day by bringing in milk and buns for the children and they settled down, the dispute over the doll forgotten.

'I was going to ask you to tea – say Saturday week,' Sally said. 'I want to invite Sadie – that's Mr Marco's wife. She doesn't have many friends, yet so I want to make sure she isn't lonely. If I can arrange for Rachel to bring Lizzie too, it will help Sadie make friends...'

'Yes, of course I'll come and bring the children.'

'I might invite Maggie too, though it is a long way for her to come, but she could stay with you for a night or two if she wanted, couldn't she?'

Beth's face lit up. 'If only she would...' she said. 'I'd love to see her – and I think Becky and Marion might too. I could invite them both to my house for tea on the Sunday.'

'Well, yes, if you think they would come they could come here...'

'You're the boss's wife – they might be more comfortable at mine,' Beth said with a smile. 'No disrespect, Sally love. Besides, I think Maggie might get to the bottom of Becky Stockbridge's trouble... you know she has been difficult at work?'

'Rachel thinks she has had a disappointment in love...'

'I think it might be partly that,' Beth said nodding. 'I'll telephone Maggie and ask her to come – and I'll talk to Becky too. See if I can discover what is upsetting her.'

'Yes, thank you. We all thought she would be happier in the office, but I'm not sure she is.'

'I think it may just be that she hasn't heard from that officer, Captain something or other.' Beth smiled. 'Young love...'

'Well talk to her,' Sally suggested. 'If there is anything I can do to help...'

'Don't worry,' Beth said. 'Between us, we'll sort her out, you'll see.' She laughed and picked up Jackie as he was about to pull coal from the fire bucket. 'No, mischief, you may not eat coal!'

Sally laughed. 'Jenny tried that for a while.' She glanced at Timmy, who seemed to sleep through anything. 'This one is no trouble.'

'Not yet.' Beth held the struggling Jackie on her knee. 'No doubt he will get there as he grows,' She laughed and gave her little son a kiss. 'Now get down and play nicely with Jenny.'

'Was Christmas good for you?' Sally asked. 'Was Jack able to send you anything?'

'He left a beautiful card and a lovely necklace for me last time he was home,' Beth said. 'Fred bought me a cardigan from Harpers and you gave me that wonderful gold bracelet.' She looked at Sally fondly. 'So how does it feel now that you've met your mum at last – truly, deep down?'

'It feels good,' Sally said. 'There was so much I wanted to know and now – it's like a missing piece has slotted into place.'

'Good. I'm so glad for you.' Beth smiled. 'The war is still being fought, Sally, but there seems to be more optimism about now – don't you think so?'

'Yes. The Allies have had some victories in France and we're fighting in Italy too now. Ben feels we're winning – but says we have a way to go yet.'

'Perhaps next Christmas it will be over,' Beth said. 'We haven't seen a Zeppelin raid since October, when all those people were killed – and in America women have won the right to vote in New York. Surely it will come here soon, too?'

'Shall we drink to that?' Sally agreed. 'Tea, coffee – or a drop of sherry?'

'Tea please,' Beth said. 'I think I might try to come into Harpers more this year, Sally. I can help you in the office – and Vera will babysit sometimes. She is round at ours so much now I'm expecting her to move in any time.'

'Do you think Fred will pop the question at last?' Sally asked.

'Perhaps, with a little pushing,' Beth said. 'She will be good for him if we find somewhere bigger to live in time, but that is for the future and we're in no hurry and nor is Fred.' She laughed. 'It will all come right this year, Sally. You'll see. Ben will be home more often; Jack might be soon – and I'll see if Maggie and I can sort out young Becky. Oh, yes, things will be better – and we'll say goodbye to the wartime blues once and for all...'

MORE FROM ROSIE CLARKE

We hope you enjoyed reading *Wartime Blues for the Harpers Girls*. If you did, please leave a review.

If you'd like to gift a copy, this book is also available as an ebook, digital audio download and audiobook CD.

Sign up to Rosie Clarke's mailing list for news, competitions and updates on future books.

http://bit.ly/RosieClarkeNewsletter

If you haven't already, explore the rest of the *Welcome to Harpers Emporium* series now!

ABOUT THE AUTHOR

Rosie Clarke is a #1 bestselling saga writer whose most recent books include *The Mulberry Lane* series. She has written over 100 novels under different pseudonyms and is a RNA Award winner. She lives in Cambridgeshire.

Visit Rosie Clarke's website: http://www.rosieclarke.co.uk

Follow Rosie on social media:

twitter.com/AnneHerries
bookbub.com/authors/rosie-clarke
facebook.com/Rosie-clarke-119457351778432

ABOUT BOLDWOOD BOOKS

Boldwood Books is a fiction publishing company seeking out the best stories from around the world.

Find out more at www.boldwoodbooks.com

Sign up to the Book and Tonic newsletter for news, offers and competitions from Boldwood Books!

http://www.bit.ly/bookandtonic

We'd love to hear from you, follow us on social media:

facebook.com/BookandTonic
twitter.com/BoldwoodBooks
instagram.com/BookandTonic